THE VARIOUS

THE VARIOUS

Steve Augarde

David Fickling Books

OXFORD · NEW YORK

Dedicated to all those who live precariously,
yet remain hopeful.
(And this includes my family, of course –
Gina, Camille and Marcelle).

A DAVID FICKLING BOOK

Published by David Fickling Books
an imprint of Random House Children's Books
a division of Random House, Inc.
New York

Published simultaneously in Canada by Random House of Canada Limited,
Toronto. Originally published in Great Britain by David Fickling Books,
an imprint of Random House Children's Books.

www.randomhouse.com/kids

Library of Congress Cataloging-in-Publication Data is available upon request.

ISBN 0-385-75029-3 (trade)
ISBN 0-385-75037-4 (lib. bdg.)
Printed in the United States of America
January 2004
10 9 8 7 6 5 4 3 2 1
First American Edition

An Introduction

The Various were not as Midge had imagined they would be. They were much taller for a start – well above knee-height – and rather grubby-looking. They gazed up at her in wary silence, their dark eyes full of suspicion, never blinking. Midge felt dizzy, overwhelmed by the sudden reality of it all. She stared back at them, a ragged little group, dressed in black and white for the most part, their weatherbeaten skin and broad features made yet more strange by the mottled sunlight at the edge of the clearing. Spears and arrows they had – not pointing at her directly, but obviously at the ready – and it occurred to her that she might actually be in some danger. She had forgotten what was expected of her. Shouldn't she kneel, or curtsey or something?

Their Queen, she couldn't help thinking, wasn't a bit beautiful. She was dumpy, and her eyebrows met in a deep scowl. Her grey hair was tied back in an untidy bun. She was obviously quite old – and this was more shocking than anything, somehow. Midge had never expected that the little people might grow old, as we do. The Queen sat, carefully posed, and looking ridiculously pompous, in a sort of wickerwork sedan chair – a rickety affair with carrying handles at either end. Her off-white dress had a purplish stain down the front of it (blackberry?) and she held a tatty black fan, half-raised and motionless, as though she were poised to issue a command. Her lips were painted, but badly smudged, and she wore long grey gloves, that looked as though they had been mended a few times. Midge pictured her trying to fly, this tubby little creature in her faded finery, and she began to bite the inside of her cheeks to stop herself from giggling. The silence had become a strain.

Then a tiny spinning movement caught her attention, as a stray sycamore seed – a relic of the previous autumn – twirled gently down from the trees and landed abruptly on the Queen's head, where it remained, a homely decoration, perched just so on her grey bun. And that did it. Midge started to laugh. Her snorts and splutters rang through the sunlit clearing, startling the pigeons in the trees, as the strange assembly stared up at her, outraged.

Chapter One

A week ago she had been bored, bored, bored. The prospect of spending most of the summer holiday in the West Country with her cousins wasn't so bad – although she could barely remember them, not having seen them for years – but for the first fortnight they would still be away with their mother somewhere, and so that meant staying on her own with Uncle Brian until they arrived.

Uncle Brian was her mother's elder brother. He was OK, as far as she could recall, but he was unlikely to be much fun. And anyway, she felt weird about living in some big old half-derelict farmhouse with just Uncle Brian for company.

'Do I *have* to go?' she asked her mum. 'Can't I wait until Katie and George get back? Couldn't I stay here till then?'

'Darling, you know you can't stay here all by yourself,' her mum had said. 'We've been through all this. Please don't make me feel any worse than I do already. You'll be fine, and anyway, Brian's easy enough to get along with. You'll remember him when you see him.'

Well, it was easy for *her* to say, thought Midge. Swanning around with the Philharmonic and having all the fun ('actually it's *not* much fun, darling, it's really quite hard work,') while she, Midge, had to kick about a deserted old farm waiting for her cousins to arrive.

'I still can't see why you don't take me with you,' she grumbled – although this was an old tack, and she knew it would get her nowhere. Worth a last try, though.

She remembered something else. 'Mr Powers takes *his* children.' Mr Powers was second oboe, and lived quite close by. They occasionally bumped into him in Safeway.

'Mr Powers does *not* take his children, Margaret. Mr Powers *sometimes* takes his *wife* and his children. There's a difference. And only then if it's just a week-end concert and not too far away. This is a four week tour, darling. Four weeks! Living in hotels, up late every night, flying around here there and every-where. It's no life for a twelve-year-old.'

'Yeah, it sounds like hell,' said Midge, and knew even as she said it that she'd crossed one of those in-visible lines that her mother drew around their conversations.

'Listen, Margaret. This is my job. It's what I do, and believe me it's not easy. I'm a single parent and a professional musician. The two don't always go together very well. Now Brian has *very* kindly said that he'll look after you for a few weeks, and I think we should both be extremely grateful. I know I am.'

Midge came within an inch of saying, 'Yeah, I bet,' but managed to bite back the words. She felt, as she had always felt, that the 'job' came first as far as her mother was concerned, and that her daughter was often an inconvenience, something to be organized, palmed off, dealt with. And lately things had become worse. Her mum seemed to be perpetually distracted and on edge – hardly there, somehow. The best times were when the orchestra was resting and there was time off from the otherwise constant round of rehearsal and performance. Then they got along pretty well. But as soon as a new tour was scheduled, Midge felt that she was just a nuisance, no longer deserving of much attention.

'Left playing second fiddle,' she often thought, wryly. Second fiddle was what her mother actually *did* play – although she didn't call it a fiddle of course.

And so she arrived at Taunton bus station after a two-and-a-half hour coach journey, collected her bags and magazines together, and tried to look through the dusty windows to see if her Uncle Brian had arrived to meet her. Midge recognized him almost straight away, although he looked a bit older now than when she had last seen him. He was peering up at the windows in the way that people do when they're meeting some-one from a coach or train – smiling already, even though they can't yet see the person they're smiling for. He wore a very red jumper and those awful yellow corduroy trousers you only ever seem to see on people who live in the country. (Midge thought of herself as a 'townie', and a rather sophisticated one at that.) His hair – which Midge had remembered as being black – had gone much greyer, and he had a very definite bald patch, which she could clearly see from her high position in the coach.

'Hallo Midge! You look cheerful!' Uncle Brian stretched his arms out towards her as she got off the coach, and Midge wondered for a moment if he was going to kiss her, or shake her hand, or something embarrassing like that. But he was only reaching for her hold-all and carrier bags. 'Here, let me take those things. Had a good journey?'

'Not bad, thanks. How are you, Uncle Brian?'

'I'm *extremely* well, my dear. Can't grumble at all. Now then, let's see if we can't get you back home before the soup's ruined. Car's parked just round the corner, right opposite the Winchester.'

Midge remembered hearing about the way in which Uncle Brian's sense of geography always seemed to involve the name of a pub, or hotel. Her mum sometimes said that Uncle Brian would probably describe the Pyramids of Egypt as being 'just down the road from the Dog and Sphinx.'

Mum didn't seem to have much time for Uncle Brian – not that it stopped her from using him as a babysitter now that it suited her. 'He's a "nearly" man,' she would say. 'Good at everything – but not quite good *enough* at anything.' She had never forgiven him for inheriting Mill Farm, that was the trouble. Mum and Brian had grown up there as children. Mum had left home, gone to university and music college, then had become a professional musician and something of a success. Her brother Brian had stayed at Mill Farm, got married, fathered two children, separated, looked after his mother, Midge's granny, until she died, and then the farm had been left all to him.

'I got *nothing*,' Midge's mum would say bitterly. 'What a slap in the face that was. Nothing at all. It should have been shared between us. And what does Brian know about farming? Lived there all his life and *still* wouldn't know one end of a hay-rake from the other! Or rather he'd know how to *fix* it, without knowing when to use it. Tried pig-farming. Didn't work. Tried cider-making – planted acres of trees and used up God knows how much capital. Didn't work. Agricultural machinery auctions, bed and breakfast, go-karts – you name it, he's messed it up. He's messed up his life, the farm and his marriage. Brian's a fool. Or rather he's not, and that's the trouble. He's a nearly-man. Nearly good enough. But not quite.'

Yes, she could be pretty scathing, could Mum, when she got on to the subject of Brian. Until she wanted him to do something for her, of course.

But he was being friendly enough now, and actually quite funny in a shy sort of way, as they threw the bags into the back of his battered old estate car and drove out of Taunton.

'Poor old Midge, you must be wondering what you've ever done to deserve this. Stuck on a farm with Mad Brian,' (he rolled his eyes and stuck out his tongue), 'and nearly two weeks till the cavalry arrives.

You must have been a terrible sinner in a previous life. Seriously though, when Christine phoned to ask if you could come and stay, I said *delighted*, of course, but what on earth will the poor girl *do* until Katie and George get down here?' Uncle Brian glanced across at her. 'I gather you're a big reader,' he said.

Yes, thought Midge, that's just the kind of thing her mother *would* have said. 'Don't worry about Margaret, Brian. Just give her a stack of books and you won't see her for a fortnight.'

'Yes,' she said. 'I do like reading. Don't worry, Uncle Brian, I'll be fine.'

'Well listen, I thought perhaps we could try and organize a couple of trips out at least. Perhaps go to the cinema, or maybe ten-pin bowling at that place in Taunton. What's it called – the Hollywood Bowl?'

Poor Uncle Brian, he *was* trying. Midge imagined him in his big old yellow cords, attempting to have a jolly time at the bowling alley. 'It's OK, Uncle Brian,' she said kindly, but half mischievously, 'I'm sure you like skittles better.'

'Well, you know, I *do* like a game of skittles. I won a pig a few summers ago at the local fête. Mind you, I was up to my *ears* in pigs at the time, so I gave it back. But Midge, if there's anything you want to do, or anywhere you want to go to pass the time a bit, then you will speak up, I hope.'

The inside of the car was scruffy, and smelt of dogs and hay. The back seats were folded down and the vehicle was obviously a maid-of-all-work, used for everything and anything. One of the foot control pedals kept making a funny noise – a long protesting squeak – every time Uncle Brian pressed his foot down on it. Midge glanced down into the driver's footwell, and noticed that her uncle was wearing quite a smart pair of polished brown brogues – but no socks. His ankles showed up pale and strange in the shadow of the footwell.

Midge was so surprised that she spoke without thinking; 'Uncle Brian, you've got no socks on!' and immediately felt embarrassed.

Uncle Brian laughed, though, and said, 'Less a case of *not* wearing socks, and more a case of *am* wearing shoes!' This made Midge feel even more confused. Did her uncle usually go barefoot then? But Uncle Brian went on, 'I was padding around the house in bare feet looking for my sandals – it suddenly felt like that kind of weather – then realized that the time was getting on and I needed to be heading for Taunton to pick you up. So I bunged on the first pair of shoes I came across. Happened to be my Sunday best. Don't worry,' he added, 'I may be crazy, but I *can* dress myself.' He saw that the remark had hit home and that Midge may well have had her doubts about him, and he laughed again. 'What *have* they been saying about me?' He was obviously amused and not at all offended.

'Sorry,' said Midge. But it was true that her mum's remarks had led her to expect that her uncle might be a bit weird. *Harmless* probably, but definitely a weirdo. And yet he wasn't really *that* odd, as far as she could tell. He just wasn't much like her mum, that was all.

'Do you mind if I phone Mum?' she said. 'I just remembered I promised.'

'Yes, do,' said Uncle Brian. 'You've got a mobile then?'

'For my birthday,' said Midge. She pulled out her new phone, and took it out of its soft case.

'Coo!' said Uncle Brian, sounding like a schoolboy and obviously impressed, 'it's tiny!'

Midge's mother answered the phone in the slightly breathless manner she always affected – as though she were either just rushing out or just rushing in. Which very often was the case, of course. 'Christine Waaalters!'

'Hi Mum, it's Midge.'

'Margaret! Everything all right, darling? Have you arrived?'

'We're in the car. I'm fine.'

'Uncle Brian found you then?' She sounded as though there may always have been the possibility that he wouldn't.

'Yes, he was there waiting.'

'Now have you *got* everything?' Midge looked out of the window, bored now, and answered her mother's questions automatically. No thought was required. It was a 'yes' or 'no' conversation. Finally, her mum got to the end of the list and said, 'Well have a *lovely* time, darling. Be good and look after yourself.'

'You too, Mum. Bye.'

'Say hello to Brian for me.'

'OK. Bye.' Midge snapped the little popper shut and squeezed the phone back into her pocket. 'Mum says "hi",' she said.

'*Good* old Chris!' said Uncle Brian, with an enthusiasm that took Midge rather by surprise. 'What a gal! Very clever woman, your mum,' he added. 'Always knew she'd go far. Always had that *drive* – you know? That *drive*!'

'Yes,' said Midge. She did know.

And so the journey passed comfortably enough. They crossed Sedge Moor, the Somerset Levels, flat and still partially flooded from the recent summer storms, then rose up higher through narrow leafy lanes, past some dense and ancient-looking acres of woodland – thickly overgrown and untended – and finally wound in through a rickety wooden gateway, once painted white but now peeling and green with tree-sap. The sign on the gate said 'Mill Farm' in whitish letters on a faded blue background. The car swung into a weed-strewn cobbled yard, past a couple of tumbledown farm buildings and came to a halt in front of the main house.

Midge's passenger door window was open, the weather being warm and dry for a change, and she was instantly struck by the peaceful silence as the car engine died. There was no noise other than the sound of the birds, the warm rustle of the leaves in the trees, and the buzz of a passing insect. No traffic, no roaring jets, no people, no city. Just peace. She looked up at the house. Remote, overgrown and neglected, the old Somerset longhouse nevertheless seemed friendly and unthreatening in the bright sunshine. The honey-coloured stone from which the house was built, although weathered and stained, could never look sinister or forbidding.

Midge got out of the car and looked about her. Rust-red barn doors hung uncertainly on their hinges, bits of disused machinery lay everywhere, overgrown with nettles. An ancient milk churn, once used as a plant-holder but now perforated to the point of disintegration, stood by the open farmhouse door. (Uncle Brian had obviously not worried about locking the place up before he left.) A couple of tatty hens scratched around on the doormat, just inside the threshold, and she caught a glimpse of a tiny kitten – far too young to be out by itself – playing in a tipped-up Wellington boot that lay on the front path (where it may well have been lying for weeks, judging by the state of it). The whole place looked derelict, disused – and entirely delightful. Midge just loved it instantly. She had never been here in her life before, to her knowledge, and yet she felt somehow as if she had come home. Home to Mill Farm.

'And of course, my time's pretty well my own,' said Uncle Brian. He had not spoken for half an hour, but was obviously still continuing their earlier conversation. 'So if you *should* want to pop over to Taunton, to the library or whatever, then you just say so. Always best to go in the morning though. Don't do much in the afternoons usually.'

'Don't you have to work then?' said Midge, curious to find herself in the company of an adult who was not forever frantically busy.

'No,' said Uncle Brian, standing in the cobbled yard, hands in his yellow corduroy trouser pockets, and staring up at the rooks in the cedar trees. 'Not any more I don't. Coming into a bit of money, old girl. Or at least I hope to be by the end of the holidays. I've got the land up for sale – some of it anyway. Come and have some soup.'

The soup was homemade leek and potato, and very good it was too.

'Used to be a chef,' said Uncle Brian, 'for a while.'

There were not many things, Midge was beginning to learn, which Uncle Brian had *not* been 'for a while'. He talked, as they ate their soup, of the numerous ideas he'd had for Mill Farm, cheerfully acknowledging his failures and seemingly not embarrassed to confess to his twelve-year-old niece that he was pretty hopeless as a businessman. He was interested in her too, and what life was like for her in London, not asking too many questions about school, and occasionally remembering bits of her past that she had forgotten or hadn't known about – telling her

17

at one point that he had some snaps of her with his own children, Kate and George, taken when they were tiny and on an outing to Bournemouth.

'Or maybe it was Sidmouth. Or Exmouth. I've still got them somewhere. I'll hunt them out later. You loved the sea, I remember. Kate could take it or leave it, George – poor George – was absolutely terrified, wouldn't go anywhere near it. But you were in there like a shot.'

Midge took a tangerine from the bowl of fruit on the table and dug her thumbnail into the soft spongy peel. 'How old were we?' she said. She suddenly felt comfortable. This was family. Uncle Brian's children were her cousins. He was her mum's older brother, and best of all, she realized – she liked him. He was cheerful and easy to talk to. Her mother could be difficult to talk to. She often seemed preoccupied, even in the middle of a conversation, on edge – and snappy. Uncle Brian was more relaxed. He didn't appear to be continually wishing he were somewhere else.

'Happy in his own skin' – it was a phrase she had once heard Mr Powers, the oboist, use. He was talking to her mum about such and such a conductor. The words had struck her as being curious at the time and she had wondered what he meant. But now she thought she knew. Uncle Brian was someone who was happy in his own skin. Was she happy in hers? She looked at her freckled arms and thought about it.

The kitchen where they sat to eat was a large room, and typical of the house generally in that it hadn't been altered or redecorated in years. The doors and all the woodwork, including the great table at the centre and the tall Welsh dresser that held the crockery, were painted cream – or at least they may have originally been white, but cream they now certainly were. The floor was red-brick and worn into dips where the traffic of heavy boots had passed most often – at the threshold of the main door, in front of the Rayburn stove (also cream) and by the massive and badly chipped porcelain sink. The walls, white-washed scores of times – though not very recently – were largely unadorned. There were no tasteful prints, no artful displays of kitchen utensils or gadgetry, no pinboards and no curtains. The single window, iron-framed and thickly coated with (cream) paint, looked out on to the farmyard where the car was parked. On the windowsill stood a fruit-bottling jar with a dish-mop in it, and next to that a container of Fairy Liquid. And that was about it. Above all, it was quiet. She could hear the fast tick of a small travel alarm clock, an old wind-up one, that stood high up on the great Welsh dresser next to a couple of pewter mugs.

A solitary black-and-white photograph, ancient and now yellowing in its heavy black frame, hung on the wall to one side of the Rayburn. It was of a child, a girl in a complicated looking dress and high lace-up boots, sitting very upright on a wickerwork box. Her feet dangled a few inches above the ground, and she held something in her lap – Midge couldn't make out what it was, some sort of strap with bells on it – as she stared out of the picture. The girl had a round and beautiful face, with a curling mass of fair hair and dark faraway eyes. In the background, pale and blurred, a clock face was just visible. Twenty-five past ten. The girl was smiling, but she looked uncomfortable. And who wouldn't be, thought Midge, dressed like that.

'Uncle Brian,' she said, 'Why are you selling the house? Don't you like it here? I do.'

'Do you?' Uncle Brian seemed pleased. 'You haven't really seen it yet. Anyway, I'm not selling the house, just some of the land.' They had come straight into the kitchen from the car, and apart from a glimpse of the dim flagstone hallway where a black spaniel lay (barely acknowledging their arrival with the briefest twitch of her stumpy tail), the rest of the house remained unexplored.

'I love it here,' said Midge. 'It's really cool.'

'Cool enough in the winter,' said Uncle Brian a little grimly. But he hadn't misunderstood her, and went on – 'Yes, I love it too.'

Midge looked around the kitchen and said, 'It's so . . .' she searched for a word, '. . . friendly. And unspoilt.'

Uncle Brian chewed on a piece of crust thoughtfully and regarded her. She looked like a typical city kid, this twelve-year old niece, dumped on him (and his own children) for the summer by her high-flying mother. Her jeans, T-shirt and trainers, as he was sure Katie and George would recognize instantly, had not come from the local supermarket, nor had her blonde hair been cut at the shop on the corner. The total cost of her outward appearance would probably be more than he'd spend on himself in two years. She was neat, sharp, and, if not exactly pretty with her over-abundance of freckles and rather square jaw, she was certainly enough of a city-slicker to turn the heads of any of the lads in *this* backwater. Yet the words she had chosen in order to describe Mill Farm could be equally applied to her – friendly and unspoilt. He had been worried that she might not get on with Katie and George but . . . well, it could work out. The three children hadn't seen each other since they were what, five, six years old? Before he and Pat had separated in any case. And now he was to have charge of the lot of them, right in the middle of everything else that was going on. But there. It looked like he'd be able to muddle along without too much disruption to his routine. Speaking of which . . .

'Had enough to eat? Come on then, I'll show you your room and you can get settled in. Then I must take poor old Phoebe for her walk. I take her out every day for a couple of hours, straight after lunch.'

'Oh, couldn't I take her out sometimes? Mum won't let me have a dog. Wish she would,' said Midge sadly, following Uncle Brian out into the hallway where Phoebe lay. The old spaniel raised her head slowly and gazed at Uncle Brian half expectantly. Midge thought that she hardly looked capable of a daily two-hour hike.

'Well, to be honest,' said Uncle Brian, rather sheepishly, 'I usually stroll over the fields to the Crown at Withney Ham with the old gal. Have a couple of games of crib and head for home around three,

21

half-three. Keeps us both sane. Of course,' he added, a rather alarming thought coming into his head, 'if you're likely to be worried – about being here on your own for a couple of hours I mean – then I can always scrub round it. We only go for the company, don't we, Phoebs?' The dog raised herself into a half sitting position, waiting for a more definite signal than simply the mention of her name.

'I'll be fine,' said Midge, for what seemed like the umpteenth time that morning. 'I feel really safe here. Anyway, I've got my mobile. I could always ring if I needed to.'

Uncle Brian looked relieved, if slightly guilty. 'Well, come and have a look at your room anyway,' he said. He stepped around Phoebe and led the way up the narrow wooden stairs, turning right at the landing when he reached the top.

The room was a revelation. In keeping with the rest of the property, Midge had expected bare walls, bare floorboards and maybe an old iron bed. This room looked as if it belonged in a hotel brochure. There was an en suite shower and loo, matching materials on the quilt and curtains (which were swagged and fastened back to the walls with silk cords), a jug-kettle and teapot on the bedside cabinet – which also had its own little curtains. Everything looked clean, neat and impersonal. Midge was so surprised, she wanted to laugh.

'It looks like a motel or something,' she couldn't help saying.

'Thank you,' said Uncle Brian, taking that as a

compliment. 'I was going into the bed-and-breakfast business at one stage.' He chuckled. 'This room was as far as I got.'

Midge dumped her carrier bags on the divan bed (pink velour headboard and frilly-edged pillows) and decided she liked the room after all. It looked so silly and frivolous, plonked in the middle of the tumble-down chaos which was the rest of Mill Farm – like a wedding hat on a scarecrow – and Uncle Brian was obviously so proud of it, that she made up her mind to love it. 'It makes me feel like I'm really on holiday,' she said.

'Good,' said Uncle Brian. He pulled open the wardrobe door. 'Look. Coat hangers and everything.'

Midge wandered over to the window and looked out over the ravaged farm buildings to the sunny land-scape beyond. To her left, the land climbed steeply up to a ridge, a long hill crested with a dense mass of trees. The hill was separate from the area of woodland they had driven through on their way to Mill Farm. It rose from the surrounding Levels like an island, or the humped back of some great beast, the thick forestation growing like tufted fur along its spine.

Uncle Brian stooped slightly and looked over her shoulder as she gazed at the tangled horizon. 'Ah yes, The Wild Wood,' he said, and glanced at her. 'We river-bankers don't go there very much, you know.'

Midge laughed, recognizing her cue instantly, 'Aren't they very *nice* people there, then?' she said.

'I *thought* you'd have probably read that one,' said Uncle Brian. He looked up at the dark dense trees.

23

'You'll find this hard to believe, but I've never actually been in there. It was impossibly overgrown, even when we were children. The brambles and nettles are so thick around the edge – and all the way in, for all I know – that you'd need a bulldozer to get through it. I remember Chris and I making a pretty determined effort on one particular occasion. Or rather, I was determined and I'd dragged Chris along with me. We . . . well, we managed to get about three yards in, I think. Scratched, stung, ripped to shreds we were. We came home, clothes in tatters, bleeding, Christine crying. Mum took the stick to the pair of us, and that was it. Never tried to get in there again. Don't suppose I ever shall now. The hill's called Howard's Hill. Been in the family for donkey's years – since Noah was a boy, most likely.'

Midge remembered their earlier conversation – still unresolved. 'Why *are* you selling the land?' she asked, and as she spoke she felt a sudden jolt inside somewhere. It was important to her, but she didn't know why.

Uncle Brian seemed not to have heard her at first. He was still looking across at the woods. Then he said, vaguely, 'Oh, money,' and looked at his watch. 'Well, I think perhaps I'll take that walk and leave you to settle in for a bit. Sure you'll be OK?' He was being a grown-up now, and doing that thing that grown-ups do when they don't want to talk any more – changing the subject. 'If you get hungry, just pick at whatever you can find. There's fruit and biscuits and various odds and ends around. It's all in the kitchen. I'll be back sometime around three, half-three at the latest – and

I'll write down the number of the Crown now, and leave it on the kitchen table.'

Midge followed him to the top of the stairs and watched him descend, crablike, sideways, as some people do, one hand on the dark wooden banister, his bald patch bobbing in the dim stairwell. She was reminded of his pale ankles in the car.

'Come on, Phoebs, walkies!' he called out, when he reached the flagstone hallway, and Phoebe, properly summoned at last, struggled to her feet and shook herself free from sleep. She stretched and ambled stiffly out into the sunshine, whilst Uncle Brian glanced at himself in the oval hallway mirror, running one hand through his untidy and thinning hair, as he searched in his pockets with the other for money. 'I'll just go and jot that number down for you,' he said.

Midge walked back along the landing corridor to her room, suddenly happy. She was pretty sure that she could get along with her uncle for a couple of weeks until her cousins arrived, so that made her happy. She loved Mill Farm, so that made her happy. 'And,' she thought, as she entered her room once again to begin unpacking, 'I even love this silly room.' So that made her happy too. She picked up her heavy hold-all and humped it onto the bed next to the carrier bags. On a sudden impulse, she walked over to the window, opened it, and looked out to see if Uncle Brian had disappeared yet. He was halfway across the yard, waiting for Phoebe, who was sniffing at the Wellington boot where the kitten was hiding.

'Uncle Brian!' she called, and he looked up, raising

one hand to shield his eyes as he squinted into the glare of the sun above the farmhouse roof. 'I'm really happy!'

'Good!' he shouted, 'I'm very glad.' The sun was too bright and he couldn't really see her.

'Do you mind if I explore?' she said.

'Not a bit. Watch out for some of the old machinery though. There's all kinds of junk about. Make sure you don't go and cut yourself or anything. Oh, and stay away from Tojo.'

'Tojo?'

'Whacking great tom cat. Black-and-white thing, big as a badger and much worse tempered. I'm not joking, Midge, he can turn very ugly. If you see him, don't you go anywhere near him. He'd take your eyes out, given the chance.' Not wishing to frighten the girl any more than necessary, Uncle Brian added, 'But don't worry, he doesn't come in the house at all. He's a barn cat – and worth his weight in gold when it comes to keeping the place free of rats. He's just not for petting, that's all. Stay away from him, and he'll stay away from you.'

'OK, I will.' Midge dismissed the idea of the fearsome Tojo – she was too happy to worry about some stupid cat. 'Uncle Brian, I *really* like it here. It's like . . . well, I really feel at home.'

Uncle Brian moved into the shadow of a barn and turned again. Now he could see her.

'Well, not so surprising perhaps. You were born here after all.' He smiled at her, then saw her look of bewilderment. 'Didn't you know? Really? Has your mum never told you that? Well, we can talk about it later, if you like. Come *on*, Phoebe! Leave that poor creature alone.' He wandered out of the shadow, continued across the untidy yard, and opened a rusty metal gate leading into a scrubby field, where rabbits fed undisturbed among tufts of thistles. The dog followed him through and he lifted the gate back on to its catch. The metal squeaked and clanged, a clear harsh ring in the peaceful sunshine. Another thought occurred to him, just as he turned to go.

'In fact,' he said, squinting once more at Midge, as she stood stunned, her hand holding tightly on to the window frame, 'now that I come to think of it, you were born in that very room. I remember it extremely well. The telephone had been cut off, and I had to go for the doctor. But that's where you were born, old thing – pretty well where you're standing.'

He strolled away across the field, kicking occasionally at a thistle, while Phoebe walked placidly beside him, ignoring the rabbits she was now too old to chase.

Chapter Two

The sharp edge of the old metal window frame was hurting her hand. She let go and looked at the mottled indentations across her palm as the circulation flowed back. Her knees felt funny, so she walked over to the bed and sat on the corner nearest the window. She was too low down to see Uncle Brian or Phoebe now. Her head was a bit swimmy, and she wasn't sure if she wanted to cry. And yet she wasn't unhappy, she found. She was overwhelmed. So many thoughts began rushing around her head that it was hard to catch hold of any of them.

She tried to remember if her mum had ever said anything to her about where she had been born. Had she ever asked – 'Mum, where was I born?' Certainly she had never been lied to, that she could recall. Her mum had never said, 'You were born in London,' or 'You were born in a hospital.' This thought comforted her a little. But the subject *must* have come up before ... must have done ... and then she *did* remember something. She had come home from school one day, junior school, and her mum was in the kitchen with a friend drinking coffee. Her mum was leaning against the sink, and the woman was sitting on the corner of the kitchen table. They were drinking from the peacock mugs, and they were talking about babies. Midge had walked between them to get something she needed for homework. The woman said, 'It helped that the midwife was a friend of mine. We'd known each other for years. It made that whole hospital environment less impersonal. My next one, Seb, was a home delivery though. I made sure of that.' The name 'Seb' had caught Midge's ear. She'd never heard it before. And Midge's mum had said, 'Margaret was a home birth . . . my God! Is that the time? Sorry, Lou, I'm going to have to kick you out and make a dash for it.'

'A home birth,' was what she'd said. And Midge (*now* she remembered) was walking through the kitchen doorway back through to the sitting room and had briefly thought – 'Where? On the carpet? In the bedroom?' Then, she supposed, she'd more or less forgotten about it, but if someone had asked her where she'd been born she'd have probably said, 'at home, I think.' Meaning at home in the flat. She had never known any other home – had lived in Teck Mansions all her life. Teck Mansions. It was an impressive sounding address, but really it was a bit of a joke – just a rather run down Edwardian building, split up into six flats. Her mum owned the building – something that Midge had only recently discovered. 'It used to be your Grandad's – then it was left to Daddy, then to me. More trouble than it's worth, half the time.'

29

But she had been born here, at Mill Farm, in this very room. Maybe in this very bed. No, it would have been a different bed, of course. She looked around the room and wondered about all the other things she didn't know – who else had been here? The doctor, presumably, and Uncle Brian, somewhere, (but not in the room surely?) Her dad perhaps? Was her dad here? Was he still alive then? Yes, of course. But it was all so confusing. Was her mum still living here at Mill Farm then? Phrases from overheard conversations, phrases that were usually murmured in low voices, ran through her head. Was she 'an accident', as she'd heard some babies were – unwanted, a teenage pregnancy? No! Her mum was married to her dad then. He'd died later, when she was four years old . . .

Oh! it was all so confusing. She got up from the bed. 'This is too weird,' she said out loud, and wandered through the open door and out into the corridor, pausing for a few moments in order to get her bearings once more. She turned right, hesitated at the top of the stairwell and then carried on walking along the corridor, peeping into the rooms as she passed them. The doors were open, and Uncle Brian *had* said that she could explore – nevertheless she still felt as though she were intruding in some way.

The first two doorways opened into bedrooms. The furniture in both of them was dark and heavy – mahogany wardrobes and dressing tables, great high beds with solid wooden headboards – and there was an old smell to them, not unpleasant, just old. A smell of heavy linen, cloth-backed books, linoleum flooring and the (very) faint ghost of furniture polish. The end doorway led into what was obviously Uncle Brian's room, and on the opposite side of the corridor was a bathroom. It was tiled in black and white, and smelled slightly of fly-spray, which made Midge wrinkle up her nose. There was a gold-framed extendable shaving mirror mounted on the wall by the sink. Midge was attracted to it, and as she moved closer to examine it, she caught a reflected glimpse of her eyes – grey-blue, shining and alive – amongst all that was so old and dusty. She paused, and felt that it was a dramatic moment.

'Behold the eyes!' she said out loud. Her voice, bouncing back from the tiled walls, sounded strong and clear. She turned her head sideways, continuing to look at herself in the mirror. 'Behold the eyes of – the Mistress of Mill Farm!' Then she clapped her hand over her mouth and giggled at her audacity. A sudden delicious panic overtook her and she fled back to the top of the stairs. Here she paused again.

'The Mistress of Mill Farm!' she cried, by way of announcing her entrance, and swept as majestically as she could down the dim creaking stairway, narrowly avoiding stepping on the kitten, who had ventured out of her Wellington boot and into the hallway now that Phoebe had departed.

Midge sat on the low balustrade wall in front of the house and looked across the yard, towards the gate that led into the Field of Thistles. As Mistress of Mill Farm she had bestowed formal titles on all and sundry

– even now, the Favoured One sat on the wall beside her, lapping at a ramekin dish of milk, her tiny tongue flicking in and out relentlessly, her skinny tail quivering in nervous ecstasy. It was a good game, lasting well into her third day at Mill Farm, with no signs of growing stale and certainly no shortage of material. The cider barn (where the Favoured One's brothers and sisters eked out a far less favoured existence) had become the Orphanage. Here the Mistress would tend to the poor – with her own hands – and deliver small kindnesses.

Tojo, the huge brute of a barn cat whom she had met one day by accident, and who was indeed as big as a badger, had become the Assassin, and the two of them had reached an agreement. She would give him at least ten yards of clear space in future, and he would refrain from threatening to turn her into a bundle of rags. She was terrified of him. The sly and roguish hens that lurked, forever hopeful, around the front door, had become the Deputation from Rhode Island ('There's a Deputation from Rhode Island, waiting to see you ma'am.' 'Tell them I can't be bothered with them at present.' 'Very good, ma'am.') Her bedroom had, of course, become My Lady's Chamber. The dense wood, which dominated the horizon, was now the Royal Forest, and the Mistress of Mill Farm – whose position in the world seemed to have suddenly risen to that of royalty – was considering whether she might go there to hunt the hart. It didn't seem a very realistic proposition though, what with the brambles and everything. It was also far too hot to be chasing anything.

Part way up the hill to the Royal Forest sat a low farm building, almost white in the bright sunshine, though slightly obscured by the curve of the land. It reminded her of a picture she'd used as part of a homework project on India – something to do with the British Army and how officers' wives had travelled up into the hills during the hot season. Or was it the rainy season? Either way, they had headed for the hills. Midge looked at the little low farm building, high up in the distance, and decided that she would appreciate a short break in a cooler climate herself, and so the building became the Summer Palace.

'Uncle Brian, what's that little barn up on the hill for?' Midge had wandered back into the farmhouse where her uncle was sitting at the kitchen table, dismantling an adaptor plug. 'Oh, I built it for the pigsh,' said Uncle Brian. He had a small metal spring between his lips and so the words were indistinct. 'Ushed to keep pigsh, for a while.'

Midge watched the thick clumsy hands struggling with the delicate internal workings of the adaptor plug, and wished that she could have a go. She was good at things like that. Anything mechanical, she loved. Design and Technology was her absolute favourite subject at school, and she was resentful of the fact that a lot of people saw it as a 'boy' thing. She was better at it than any boy *she* knew. She had even managed to mend the old clock that her grandad had left to her mum – just by taking bits of it apart, seeing how it worked, cleaning it, and putting it back together again. Now it chimed and everything.

'What's in the barn now that the pigs have gone?' she asked.

'Lord knowsh. More junk probably. No, actually, the Fergie'sh in there. Forgot.'

'The Fergie?'

'Little grey Fergie. Fergushon tractor. I think there'sh a shide-rake in there too. Why?'

'I just wondered. Could I have a look?'

'If you like. Blasht! Losht the shpring now – oh no, had it here all the time. Forget my own name some-times.' He gingerly placed the spring somewhere down in the white plastic adaptor plug, held it in place with a stubby fingertip, and looked about in exasper-ation. 'Where've I put the screwdriver?'

'It's by your elbow,' said Midge. 'Your other elbow.'

'I knew that,' said Uncle Brian, good-humouredly. He reached slowly for the screwdriver, and then laughed as the spring suddenly shot across the table and pinged against the side of the fruit bowl. 'Why don't I just buy a new adaptor?' he sighed. 'Anyway, you were saying. Can you look at the pig barn? Yes, you can. Just be careful, as always. I want to be able to give you back to your mother in one piece. Oh, and some-thing else I should have warned you about – stay away from the lagoon.'

'Lagoon?' Midge had a vision of some tropical paradise, some secret aspect of Mill Farm yet to be revealed.

'It's what we call the old slurry pit – where all the animal muck used to go years back. It hasn't been used for ages now, and, to be honest, it may even be safe enough to walk on. But it was deep enough, and we were always warned against it as kids. Also, you have to remember, the land can be pretty boggy around here, especially when it's been raining. Anyway, it's the bit of marshy ground at the back of the old stables – you can't really miss it. I just don't want you finding yourself up to your ears in you-know-what, that's all.'

'Could I take a picnic?'

'To the *lagoon?*'

'No, to the pig-barn.'

'A picnic? In a pig-barn? Well, I don't see why not. Do you mind organizing it yourself though? I think I may be here for some time yet.'

Midge made herself a cheese and pickle sandwich and filled a plastic Coke bottle with orange squash, while her uncle tackled the adaptor again. She remembered that she had an empty carrier bag upstairs and ran up to get it, clearing Phoebe with a leap on the way. The old dog didn't stir.

Now, when she entered her room (My Lady's Chamber) it took a conscious effort to remind herself that she'd been born here. The mystery had been solved, or rather the explanation that Uncle Brian had given suggested that there had been no mystery about it in the first place. Her mum and dad were here on a flying visit, he'd said. Simple as that. They were passing through on their way back from Exeter to London and her mum had gone into labour a few days early. The worst of it had been that there had been no phone, Uncle Brian having omitted to pay the bill.

He'd had to rush off for the doctor who, luckily, was playing darts at the Crown. He in turn had contacted the community midwife and that was it. Job done. Midge's mum and dad had stayed a few days until both mother and baby were fit to travel, and away they went. It was all very straightforward. What wasn't so straightforward, from Midge's point of view, was why, after three days at Mill Farm, she felt more as though she belonged here than in London. Now *that* was a mystery.

When she returned to the kitchen, she found Uncle Brian sweeping the parts of the adaptor from the table and into the palm of his hand. 'It's had its chance,' he said, 'and now it has to pay the price.' He tossed the bits into the pedal bin beside the porcelain sink. 'I'm a hard man, when crossed,' he continued, 'and I won't be trifled with. Especially by a plug. Phoebe! Walkies!'

Midge took an apple from the fruit bowl and put it in her carrier bag. 'Back around the usual time?' she said.

Uncle Brian paused as he reached into the kitchen drawer where he kept Phoebe's lead. 'Midge,' he said, 'believe me when I tell you this; you're going to make someone a wonderful wife someday. If only I'd married a girl like you then ... well, I might still *be* married, that's all.'

Midge wasn't sure how she should take this. She supposed it was a compliment, but it was rather an odd one. Still, that was Uncle Brian, being Uncle Brian. She grunted and put her sandwich and drink into the bag.

It was further to the Summer Palace than Midge had anticipated. By the time she had reached the end of the Field of Thistles, itself on a steeper incline than it had at first appeared, her fringe was sticking to her forehead. There was a sheep-gate in the drystone wall that bordered the field, and here she rested for a moment, wiping the perspiration from her face and looking up at the Royal Forest that crested Howard's Hill. It looked denser than ever, and she was glad that she'd decided not to hunt the hart after all. She set off again, her carrier bag of provisions banging against the side of her leg as she climbed. Once the Summer Palace came into view, a welcome breeze also greeted her, gently blowing onto her face and cooling her brow. She opened her mouth and let it play across her tongue and teeth.

The Summer Palace, now that she drew close to it, looked as though it might benefit from a little care and attention, like every other building about the place. What had appeared to be white from a distance turned out to be a dirty grey close up – a concrete building with a tin roof and a roughly screeded fore-court. There was an outside tap on the end wall of the building. It dripped, and had made a dark rusty stain on the concrete. An ancient muck-heap, now over-grown with grass, stood to one side of the sliding galvanized iron door that seemed to be the only entrance. The door itself looked wonky somehow, not quite square with the building.

As Midge approached, she thought she heard a noise. She stopped to listen, now about half a dozen paces from the building, and listened. Yes, there it was again.

The breeze was both carrying the noise to her, and obscuring it. It was a kind of scuffling sound, beating, flapping. Perhaps it was a piece of tarpaulin or something around the other side of the building, catching in the wind. She moved a little closer, cautious and slightly apprehensive. No, the sound was coming from inside the building. She could see a slight gap between the crooked sliding door and the frame, a dark slit – and the sound was coming from there. She crept closer still. Again the sudden noise, which made her jump back: a beating, flapping, desperate sound. A bird? Something trapped in there? The sound seemed too heavy for a bird, unless it was a very large one. Midge didn't like the thought of that. How big? Like a goose? Geese could be nasty. Well, it wouldn't be able to get out through that little gap, she reasoned, and moved forward again. It wasn't until she was within a foot of the door that it occurred to her that a goose could get its *head* through that gap, if nothing else. It could peck her. Midge took another hesitant step backwards at this thought, the sole of her trainer making a slight scuffing sound on the gritty concrete. The flapping ceased abruptly. There was a long silence, a listening silence, as though her presence had suddenly been recognized. Then she felt the strangest sensation beginning to creep over her – an aura – as of something travelling towards her at great speed, and from a great distance. Her scalp tightened and it really did feel as though her hair had begun to stand on end – for there was a voice.

Spindra? The word was hissed, cautiously. The word made no sense – but it was a word, and the word was somehow . . . in her head. *Spindra? Spindra!* – once more the sounds came bursting like soft explosions, coloured explosions, visible somehow, inside her head.

Midge's hands flew up to her ears, and the carrier bag fell from her fingers with a rustle and a faint thump. The apple rolled across the concrete, bumped against the galvanized door, rebounded on her foot and came gently to rest in the gap between the door and the frame.

At the first rustle from Midge's picnic bag, the voice had immediately ceased. Again there was absolute quiet, and a tension that put a strange taste in her dry mouth. Midge shakily lowered her hands, and stared at the apple. A small piece of skin had been nicked off during its fall. The frozen silence from within the building pressed against her eardrums.

Whoever, whatever was in there, had heard her, and could hear her now. Had seen her, perhaps, and could see her now. Her palms were wet with perspiration. She was frightened. She was frightened of the extraordinary thing that seemed to have just happened to her, but she knew that *she* was also frightening to whoever was in there. She was frightened like two children playing hide-and-seek are frightened – the one of being discovered, the other of discovering. She breathed in at last, and said – to her own surprise, 'I think I'd better go and get my uncle.' The words came

39

out quite loud, but the effort made her shake. She stooped to pick up the apple. It felt like an act of courage.

She picked up the carrier bag too, and put the apple back in, glimpsing her sandwich, now skewed apart, with bits of cheese and pickle showing. 'My uncle will be here shortly,' she said, the words sounding silly and unconvincing. She waited for a few moments, terrified that there might be a reply, yet needing to know that she had not been mistaken, that she was not talking to herself. She moved, as if to go, then—

No! A soft voice, barely a croak, and a renewed flurry of beating. *Stay. Help . . . me . . .*

Again Midge's first instinct was to cover her ears in confusion. The flapping, beating sound came from inside the barn, but not the voice. The voice was definitely inside her head.

Chapter Three

Midge wanted to run. The back of her neck felt cold and tight and prickly, and she wanted to run and run, back down the hill, flying and flying as fast as ever she could. Her legs weren't moving though. She was aching to run, but her legs weren't moving. She was still standing by the gap in the barn door, and she was clutching her carrier bag tightly. The sound of the voice, strange and foreign, had made her whole body lock tight, rigid. Eventually she realized that her neck was hurting and she somehow managed to let her shoulders drop. She moved her head slightly, and shifted her balance. Now she knew that she could run, if she wanted to. Yet she remained, listening at the door. Then another sound came from the warm darkness of the barn – and it *was* from the barn this time. There were no words, just a gasp. A gasp of pain, and despair and utter defeat.

Midge suddenly stopped feeling frightened. Something in that terrible despairing sound drove her fear away, and made her feel that she must do something to help. Whoever was behind that door was in real trouble. She dropped her carrier bag again and caught hold of the metal grab-handle on the door, pulling it to one side in order to slide it across. The door *wouldn't* slide though. It moved backwards and forwards just a little, but she couldn't make it slide open. Something was stopping it. She stepped back and looked up. There was a kind of metal runner on the top of the frame and she could see that the door was supposed to hang on this, rolling backwards or forwards on two small wheels. One of the wheels had come out of the runner, and that was why the door was hanging at a crooked angle. She would have to try and lift one side up and hook the wheel back into its place. The door was big and she didn't see how she could manage this, but she tried. She found that she could barely raise the side of the door that was hanging down; she certainly didn't have the strength to manoeuvre the wheel back into its runner at the same time. It was hopeless. Gasping now, desperate to help, all her fear forgotten, she ran around the outside of the barn, looking for another entrance. There wasn't one. The sliding door was the only way in. Midge was close to tears. Should she run for help after all? She looked around for inspiration.

There was a rusty roll of pig-wire round the back of the barn, and an old tin bath with a little pool of green water in it. Nothing that was of any use to her, as far as she could see. Next to the dripping tap at the side of the building, however, lay half a dozen wooden fencing posts. They had sharp points. The ones at the bottom had rotted from lying on the damp concrete, but the top ones looked OK. Midge picked one up, with no clear notion of what she would do with it, and carried it round to the front of the barn, accidentally banging it against the corner of the building as she did so, and feeling the sharp prick of a splinter going into her thumb as she struggled not to drop the thing. The idea came to her that she might be able to use the post as a lever, or perhaps use it to hook the wheel back into place somehow. She managed to wriggle the pointed end of the post under the door and heave it upwards. The door creaked, and was raised moment-arily, but she still couldn't get the wheel to go back into its runner. After a couple of attempts, however, she found that if she lifted the post and pulled it side-ways she could make the door move sideways a little, too. Bit by bit, and with a lot of heaving and struggling, she managed to lift and jiggle the door across until there was a big enough gap for her to be able to get through. By this time she was out of breath and her hands were sore and scratched, but she was pleased with what she'd done. She stood by the entrance, hesitant once more, and tried to look into the barn without actually crossing the threshold.

Directly in front of her, where the light fell through the doorway, she could see the front of a grey tractor. The radiator grille was all cobwebby and tilted to one side slightly – one of the tyres was flat. Midge slowly put her head in through the doorway to try and see more.

'Where are you?' she said quietly. A rustle and another gasp of pain came from the darkness, making her jump back yet again. The sound had come from the furthest corner of the barn. She looked nervously in once more, but couldn't see a thing. 'Shall I get help?' She was almost whispering now. There was a smell, not pleasant – an animal smell of dung and ammonia. Another sharp gasp of breath from the darkness, then the voice – and once more the words seemed to appear from somewhere inside her. *No!* A pause. *You . . . help . . . me. You!*

Midge stood her ground this time, but again her first reaction was to put her hands up to her ears. The voice frightened her. It was as though someone was talking to her on a strange kind of telephone. A telephone inside her head. She could hear the words, she could see them somehow, like pictures, like colours, and yet there was no sound in the air. The accent was foreign, or unusual at any rate, and the voice seemed distant – not human. It wasn't her own voice, she was sure of that. Was she dreaming?

Her left thumb hurt, but she was too frightened to look at it – too frightened to look away from the darkness inside the barn. Finally she managed to pluck up enough courage to creep slowly forward.

She shuffled to the left, once she was through the doorway, and edged along the wall a little so that she was no longer blocking the light. The tips of her fingers brushed the cool roughness of the concrete behind her. She moved forwards slightly. Now she could see more. In the furthest corner of the building she could make out a piece of farm machinery. It had several large spiky wheels – like spiders' webs or

Catherine wheels – which were overlapping, the spokes slightly bent in a crooked regular pattern. The wheels were pale yellow, or so they seemed in the dimness of the barn, and were mounted on a heavy red frame. Some kind of raking machine? A sudden movement beneath the frame made her jump back against the wall, and again she was ready to run. That's

where it was! Lying beneath the machine! It looked like – a bundle of rags or sheets, whitish, something flapping. Midge glanced back at the doorway, reassuring herself that she could flee at a moment's notice, then edged away from the wall, and crept slowly towards the machine, her heart bumping. More movement! She stopped. She could see – what? A leg? Legs. The pale limbs of some creature, an animal, skinny, like a greyhound or a small deer. Was it a deer? A white deer? The game she had thought of playing suddenly came back to her – hunting the hart in the Royal Forest. Was it a white hart? No. But this was too weird. And what about the voice? She was frightened again, thinking that there must be someone else in the barn besides her and . . . whatever was lying there. She looked around, but could see nothing, nobody else. What *was* it?

Aaach! Another groan and more flapping of the sheet, or whatever the creature was tangled up in. Midge caught the flash of what looked like a tiny hoof, delicate, familiar, but so small . . . well it certainly wasn't a dog at any rate. She could make out a pale belly heaving, slim legs, bits of . . . cloth, maybe, flapping. Hair, long matted hair. But no head. Where was its head? It still made no sense. She crept closer . . .

Spick! Spickitspickitspickit! Midge felt her heart bounce up into her throat, and once more the cold prickly feeling shot up the back of her neck. She knew now that there was nobody else in the barn. There was no doubt that the voice came from . . . whatever that thing was. Whatever it was – and it was certainly an animal – it had a voice. But the *sound* of the voice was in her head.

It was moving again – some other part, something that had been hidden, was moving. The tangled mess of a creature, covered in dung, bloodstained, trapped and exhausted, seemed somehow to unravel itself. Slowly and painfully, it lifted its head. Midge stood, unable to move, eyes wide open in disbelief. It was a horse. It *couldn't* be – and yet it was . . . though like no horse she had ever seen before. Tiny, slenderly built, not much bigger than a baby deer after all, it nevertheless appeared to be full-grown. A small white horse.

46

The head, fine and delicate but streaked with muck and sweat, turned slowly in Midge's direction. Its silvery mane was caked and clagged with blood, and its expression was one of absolute anguish. The dark eyes, deep and glistening with pain, looked directly at Midge as she stood in the middle of the barn floor, her mouth open, transfixed. A long moment passed as they stared at each other.

Then the horse spoke to her, and Midge felt her knees begin to buckle. She almost fell. The voice, dry and croaking, thickly accented, seemed to enter her mind from another world. There was no sound in the still foetid atmosphere of the barn, yet the words were as clear to her as if they had been spoken closely into her ear, as clear as colours on a screen – and strange beyond belief.

Help . . . me . . . maid. Some mercy . . . I beg.

The struggling creature, elegant, beautiful even in its agony, arched its slim neck and attempted to look over its blood-streaked shoulder, indicating to Midge where the trouble lay. Midge stumbled closer, almost against her will, and the back of her hand banged across her open mouth as she did so. Now she could see clearly. At last she realized what had been causing the noise she had first heard, the frantic beating that had drawn her towards this moment. The tiny horse was skewered to the filthy concrete floor by the spiked wheels of the raking machine. The prongs had pierced straight through one of its . . . wings. The other wing flapped in the muck a couple of times, uselessly, and then ceased.

Chapter Four

The drifting sunbeams and dappled shadows gave perfect cover for Glim the archer, as he slowly moved towards his prey, among the high branches of the East Wood. A nice fat throstle – more intent on singing to the heavens above than watching out for enemies below – puffed out its speckled breast and filled the air with its morning song.

Never taking his eye off the bird, Glim felt for the shallow groove in the end of the arrow, and fitted it to the taut waxy bowstring. He drew the bow back till the knuckles of his left hand brushed against his bearded cheek. He would not miss. He was an Ickri – a hunter – and was reckoned by most to be the best archer of that tribe.

It had been a good morning's work. Three finches and now a fine throstle, to swell the leather pecking bag that swung from his waist. The finches would go in the meat-basket to be shared by all, but the throstle he would keep. He would give it to Zelma. She would bake it in clay and it would taste good. It was rare nowadays to find such a bird, such a large bird, in the

East Wood. There were pigeons sometimes, but the rooks and crows, the blackies and throstles, had almost disappeared. They had learned to make their homes elsewhere. Only the visitors, the little finches and swallows that came and went with the seasons, could be found here in any quantity. And with each season that passed it seemed that their numbers, too, had dwindled.

Now the summer had come at last and the times were easier, but the winter – the winter had been hard. He would not forget. The Ickri, hunters and tree-dwellers, had survived. But the tribes that dwelt on the land – the Naiad and the Wisp – had suffered. And as for those below ground, the Tinklers and the Troggles . . . well, he would not think of that this morning. They had starved, and some had died, so 'twas said. But he would not think of that. Summer was here and on this day at least, nobody would starve.

Glim spread his wings and floated down to a lower branch. A grey squirrel, sensing the hunter's approaching shadow, broke cover and scrabbled up the trunk of a nearby ash tree, seeking the safety of the higher foliage. This was an old trick of Glim's. Sometimes it was better to show yourself, to panic your prey into movement. Just a little movement, that was all he needed. Keeping his sharp eyes fixed on the whereabouts of the squirrel, he patiently began to climb once more.

Hunting was in his nature, it was his daily task and required but little conscious thought, so Glim was able to turn his mind to other things as he tracked the

49

squirrel through the branches of his stretch of the wood. He thought about the Naiad horse, Pegs, and the growing rumour that the animal was lost, somewhere on the wetlands, out there in Gorji territory. Two days had passed and the creature had not been seen. Now the talk was that Pegs had gone to seek out fresh pastures – to the Far Woods, if the gossip was to be believed. These were harsh times for the Various tribes, he knew that. Who knew it better? Aye, and they needed food, and fresh hunting grounds. They could never survive another winter like the last. But to send Pegs into Gorji territory . . . it was too dangerous. What if the horse were seen? Or captured? Men would come, the Gorji giants, they would come at last. All the forest – East Wood, North Wood, West and South – all would be overrun. And all the Various tribes – Ickri, Naiad, Wisp, Tinklers, Troggles – all would be finished. The Various would be doomed. The winged horse should never have been allowed to go.

Glim quietly followed the squirrel to the topmost outer branches of the East Wood. He glanced downwards from his high perch to the landscape below – the wetlands, stretching out towards the far hills. Pegs was out there somewhere. He saw the flat open countryside, criss-crossed for miles with rhynes and ditches, still flooded here and there, the rows of pollarded willow trees dipping down towards the shimmering waters. He thought of eels and wondered if any of the Wisp had been out fishing in the night, and whether they had been successful. All this in the merest glance, but then something caught his attention for a second and he stopped concentrating on the squirrel.

On the hillside that sloped away from the edge of the forest, far below, stood a small Gorji dwelling – a cattle-byre perhaps – an ill-repaired thing, ugly with its rot-metal red roof and dirty grey walls. Glim had seen it before, and had turned his back on it before, as he turned his back on all the works and ways of the giants. But some tiny movement had caught his practised eye, and he paused. A pale flicker by the corner of the building had appeared and disappeared. A hand? Ah, he had not been mistaken, for just then a Gorji child – a maid, he would judge – ran around the building and out into the open. She stopped to study an object half hidden among the nettles. A trough or a cauldron. Some Gorji thing. Then she looked quickly about her and ran back the way she had come, disappearing from view once more. The impression of her remained. A worried child. Panicking, frightened. A child who was not at play.

Glim watched and waited for a minute or two, thoughtfully combing his thin brown fingers through his curly beard. He saw nothing more, and could hear nothing but the breeze whispering among the leaves around him. Finally he shrugged. 'Twas no business of his. He hitched his quiver of arrows a little higher onto his leather-clad shoulder and melted back into the deep foliage. The squirrel, of course, had long gone.

Chapter Five

The galvanized door of the pig-barn felt cool to the touch, and Midge leaned her head against it as she gulped at the fresh air outside. She had no recollection of how she had got there. It was as though she had somehow managed to both faint and run, at the same time. Wings! The thing had wings! Like . . . a bat. Like huge bats' wings – not the feathery little wings of fairytale horses – but skin, and bone, velvety, covered in fine downy hair. Whitish, beneath all the blood and dirt. And it spoke! It spoke to her in strange voices, and colours, and oh, but this was too . . . this was . . . She held on tight to the door for support. A semi-circle of young cattle, black and white heifers, had gathered before her. Midge had not noticed them till now. They edged closer, their front legs splayed as though some invisible force were pushing them from behind. There was something comical and reassuring about them, with their dribbly noses and woolly fringes. They were comfortingly real. And wingless.

Midge pushed herself away from the door, and jammed her hands into the back pockets of her dungarees. The sudden movement took the heifers by surprise, and they skittered sideways. Midge ignored them and tried to think. What should she do? She must go and get help, of course. This was too much for her to deal with. She was only twelve. She must go back to Mill Farm, tell Uncle Brian – then he would phone . . . who? The police? The vet? The zoo? Midge wandered around to the side of the barn, thinking. How could this be? Something that Mr McColl, her English teacher, had once said came drifting into her thoughts. 'What's *for* ye, won't go *by* ye.' He was fond of delivering Scots quotations, was Mr McColl, though he didn't really have a Scots accent. He just put it on sometimes. The words didn't seem particularly appropriate. *Was* this for her? Was *she* meant to do whatever needed doing? The creature, the horse, had said '*You* help me. *You* . . .' Help me, maid. You. The words went round and round.

She raised her head and let her gaze travel up the hill towards the overgrown wood, the Royal Forest. She knew then, suddenly and instinctively, that the horse had come from there – belonged there. And she knew that it was up to her, somehow, to get it back there. This *was* for her. She would not let it go by. She would do what she could. Turning around, she found herself confronted once again by the heifers, stupidly shuffling and nudging each other towards her. Now they were a distraction, a nuisance, and they made her angry.

'Yah!' she shouted, waving her arms at them. 'Yah! Yah!' The animals scattered, kicking their back legs into the air. The ground tremored slightly with the weight of them. Midge tucked her hair behind her ears and strode purposefully back inside the pig-barn. She knelt down in the muck beside the poor broken creature that lay there, and bravely put her hand on its slim white neck. It didn't move.

'I'm here,' she whispered. 'I'll do whatever I can.' She felt a slight shiver beneath her hand in the darkness, and – overcome with fear and pity, and the utter strangeness of it all – she began to cry.

High up in the forest, Glim had caught the faint echo of Midge's voice as she shouted at the cattle. 'Yah! Yah!' – a tiny sound drifting in from the outside world. The Gorji child. He paused, but did not turn around. His curiosity had already cost him one squirrel that morning.

There was a bucket, battered and rusty but reasonably sound, and there was some folded blue polythene sheeting, stiff and unyielding. There were a couple of ancient bales of straw, musty and grey. There was a sack, one of the old-fashioned hessian sort, not a paper one, that had served as a cushion on the seat of the tractor. Two feed troughs. A bottle jack, thick with grease and furry grey dust. A worn-down scrubbing brush. A fuel can. A huge wooden rake, riddled with woodworm. And there were sundry stones, bits of wood, and a few broken concrete blocks.

Half-remembered snippets of first aid came into

Midge's mind as she assembled her finds: 'First clear the windpipe of any obstruction. Place the body in the recovery position. Treat as for shock.' None of it seemed likely to help. And besides, her first obstacle was the raking machine – somehow she had to move that. Or get the horse out from under it. She looked doubtfully at the pitiful collection of resources that somehow had to serve as an animal hospital. The scrubbing brush could be useful. And the bucket. Maybe the sack . . .

She turned her attention to the raking machine. The sight of the impossible creature, crushed and motionless beneath it, nearly broke her heart. But she had dried her tears and would cry no more. Being frightened would not help. Crying would not help. A wild idea came into her head that maybe she could use the tractor to remove the raking machine, and she wasted precious minutes sitting on the tractor seat and examining the controls. Stupid. Stupidstupidstupid. How could she drive a tractor? She could barely manage a bumper car.

She clambered down from the tractor and knelt once more beside the horse, holding her nose until she was gradually able to bear the smell. What exactly had happened here? The animal was lying on its side. Two spikes of one of the wheel-rakes had pierced through the uppermost wing. The other wing was twisted awkwardly beneath its body. The spiked wheels, arranged in an overlapping line, were not quite touching the ground. Midge found that she could freely turn the wheels that were not entangling the horse. She examined the way that the crooked spikes had pierced the wing, entering at an angle. Maybe she could withdraw the spikes just by turning the wheel backwards. She tried, very gently, to see if this would work. It didn't. The wheel moved a little, but more spikes just got in the way. Somehow she needed to raise the whole line of wheels, lifting them away from the body beneath them.

She walked around the machine. There were big levers, orangey red, mounted on the frame, close to where it would hitch onto a tractor. What did they do? She tugged at them experimentally. Nothing happened. One of the levers, she noticed, was mounted in a kind of curved slot that had notches in it. Maybe this was to make the wheel-rakes higher or lower. Her eye followed a long thin rod that ran from the lever to the frame, and her heart jumped. She thought she could see how, by pulling on the lever, the wheels were lifted. It all seemed to connect up. She would try it. She grabbed the lever with both hands and attempted to yank it towards her. Nothing moved. Then she realized that the lever was held in one of the notches, the next to last one. She would have to pull it *out* of the low notch, *then* back towards her, and up to a higher notch in order to raise the wheels. OK then. She grabbed the lever again, and heaved it sideways with all her might. The lever came out of its notch – and was nearly ripped from her grasp as the weight of the mechanism pulled her forward. The lever hit the end of its travel with a clang, and the spiked wheels were now resting on the floor. Midge gasped and ran round the machine to see what she had done. 'Oh no, no!' She had made matters infinitely worse. The spiked wheels had been lowered completely, and the animal was more securely trapped than ever. In vain she tried to pull the lever back again, tugging and tugging until she was exhausted. She simply wasn't strong enough.

This was impossible – the whole thing was just mad and impossible. She would have to get help. Tears of frustration blurred her vision as she made her way to the door. She couldn't pull the lever back by herself, and she had no way of lifting the machine. It was as heavy as a car. And nobody could lift . . . she suddenly remembered the bottle jack.

Midge knew what it was, and what it was for. She had once earned two pounds just for watching someone use one. The bottle jack, the bottle jack. She stood and looked at it, trying to remember what she had seen.

Her mum had left for rehearsals one morning, and then had run back into the flat two minutes later. 'Damn!' she said, slamming the front door. 'Got a flat tyre.'

'Can't you fix it?' said Midge.

'Got no thingamajig.' said her mum. 'No jack. The idiot who sold me the car forgot to give it to me.'

'Phone the AA then.'

'No time for that. They could take ages – it's hardly an emergency. I'm supposed to be at rehearsal in twenty minutes. Rats! I'm going to have to ask Colin Bond. Aaaaaaghhh!' she screamed.

Colin Bond lived two floors up, and her mum could never get away from him. She reckoned he fancied her. He was a pest. But he could fix things.

'Listen,' she said, 'if I ask Colin to come and change the wheel, then you've *got* to come with me. I'll give you a pound, *two* pounds, to stay with me until it's done.'

'OK,' said Midge, who would have watched anyway. And so Colin had come down, delighted to be needed, and he had brought his bottle jack with him. 'Bottle jack,' he had said to Midge, though she hadn't asked. It was a silvery-blue thing. Mum had hovered around the car, subjected to Colin's dull running commentary, and continually glancing at her watch. Midge had sat on the garden wall watching – and earning herself two pounds for being Mum's chaperone.

The car was a Citroen, small but quite high up off the ground, and Colin had to find a brick to put under the jack so that it would reach. Midge had hung around, dutifully, but vaguely interested nevertheless.

'Screw in this little knob here, see, shove this handle in here, see, and pump it up and down. And . . . *up* she rises – easy peasy.' He had changed the wheel and then said, 'Course, when you're ready, and you want 'er to come back down again, you just *un*screw yer little knob, see, and *down* she blows.' The whole thing sounded quite nautical.

'Thanks, Colin,' her mum had said. 'You're brilliant.' She glanced at Midge and raised her eyebrows slightly. 'My hero.'

So Midge looked at the bottle jack, much bigger

than the one Colin had used, and knew what it was for. But where was the handle? She found it, eventually, under the front axle of the tractor – which was probably where the jack would have been have been last used, the front tyre being flat. She worked out how the handle fitted into the jack, and tested it out. This time she would *think* before acting. No more stupid mistakes. She pumped the handle up and down, noting with satisfaction how the centre of the jack rose up. The freshly exposed metal tube, that slowly appeared as she worked the handle, was shiny and clean – in contrast to the blackened greasy outer casing of the object. It *was* a bit like a bottle, she supposed. She saw that by twisting the little tap-shaped thing on the side of the casing, the central tube could be slowly pushed back down again. And she blessed Colin Bond for that piece of information. She doubted that she would have figured it out for herself. Satisfied, then, that she knew how the thing worked, she dragged the heavy object over to the raking machine, and paused to consider where best to put it.

It wasn't going to be easy – but after walking around the machine a couple of times, she thought that she could see which part of the frame the jack should be placed under in order to rise the spiky wheels. She had to make a platform out of concrete blocks for the jack to stand on, and it was a struggle to then lift the heavy object and manoeuvre it into place – but she got it there somehow in the end, and found that it now just fitted beneath the frame. Good. She stood back, panting a little, and thought for a moment, trying to get it right. OK, then. The half-blocks made a firm base on the concrete floor, and the jack stood squarely on top of them. The centre of the jack was just below the corner of the frame. It all seemed right. Now she was ready. She looked at the poor animal, lying so still beneath the spiked wheels. Later. She would think of that later. 'Well, here goes,' she whispered.

She fitted the jack handle into position and gingerly began to pump it up and down. The centre of the jack wasn't moving. Something was wrong. Then she remembered the little tap thing on the side. She'd forgotten to screw it back up. She tightened it as much as she could, and started pumping again. This time it worked. The centre of the jack rose up smoothly and locked beneath the frame. Midge pumped some more and the frame began to lift. It was like a miracle! The frame creaked with every action of the handle, and Midge kept stopping to check that nothing bad was happening. She left the jack, cautiously, and bent down to look at the spiked wheel that had pierced the horse's wing. It had moved. It had definitely moved. The spikes were no longer so deeply embedded. She pumped the handle again and again, till eventually the whole of the front end of the huge raking machine was well off the ground. She crouched down once more to look at the horse, and saw that the spikes were no longer even touching it. There was a clear space between the machine and the creature beneath it. It had worked! It had really worked! She stepped back, amazed at herself. It was easily, *easily*, the cleverest thing she had ever done.

Now she had to somehow drag the horse from under the raking machine, and out into the open space of the barn floor, where she could look at it properly. She looked at the floor. It was filthy. And in thinking this, she suddenly realized that *she* was filthy too. Her dungarees were black with muck and grease, her hands and arms were ingrained with the same oily mixture. Her watch, new for her birthday, was in a similar state and . . . what? . . . was that really the time? A quarter to four? She couldn't believe it was so late. Uncle Brian would be wondering where she could be. He would come looking for her perhaps and oh, this was terrible! But she couldn't go back to the farm in this state – and anyway, what about the horse? There was so much to do yet! Think. Thinkthinkthink. She had her phone. She could phone the farm and say . . . what *could* she say? . . . that she wanted to stay out a bit longer? No better plan occurred to her, and at least Uncle Brian wouldn't come looking for her then. She wiped her hands on the seat of her dungarees, walked outside the barn, and reached in her pocket for the mobile.

The ringing tone went on for a long time.

'Hullo?' Uncle Brian's voice sounded bleary. He'd probably been asleep, after all.

'Uncle Brian, it's Midge.'

'Midge? Where . . . where are you? Are you OK?'

'I'm up at the Summer . . . the pig-barn.'

'The pig-barn?' He was obviously struggling to comprehend.

61

'Yes. I came here for a picnic, remember?' Some picnic. 'Uncle Brian, I'm having such a lovely time . . . exploring and everything. Do you mind if I stay a bit longer? I'm absolutely fine. It's just that I'm having such a lovely time.' She thought of the winged horse, injured, dying perhaps, and it felt so weird to be talking to Uncle Brian.

'Well, as long as you're safe, I suppose . . . I'll, um, just do a bit of salad and ham or whatever for tea, and, uh, well that'll be OK, then. Er, will it?' Poor old Uncle Brian. It had obviously been a long crib game.

'Thanks, Uncle Brian. Don't worry if I'm a bit late. I'm not very hungry, and I'm absolutely fine. I'm only playing in the barn.'

' 'Kay, then. If you're sure you're all right. See you when I see you. Keep safe.'

'I will. Bye.' Right, then. To work.

Midge took the large wooden rake and raked away as much of the muck from the barn floor as was possible. Then she broke open one of the musty straw-bales, using the jack handle to lever off the binder twine, and spread the straw around on the dirty concrete. She scuffed it and kicked it about with her trainers in an effort to dry the floor off as best she could. Grabbing the wooden rake once more, she scraped the wet dirty straw away. Now the floor looked much better.

All the time she was thinking, thinking. Her first idea had been to drag the horse out on to some clean straw. But then she wondered if she could unfold the blue polythene sheeting and put that on top of a bed of straw instead, making a kind of mattress. It might be easier to tend to the animal's wounds if it was on top of a polythene sheet, rather than half covered in dusty old straw. She was pleased with that idea. So she took armfuls of the grey, frowsty smelling straw and spread it liberally over the concrete floor, the dust making her sneeze. The heavy polythene sheet wasn't so easy to spread out. It had been folded for so long that it really didn't want to be unfolded ever again. After a few minutes of hopeless struggling, Midge hauled it outside, where there was more room to manhandle and coax it into becoming a sheet once more, rather than a solid block of plastic. She trampled the crackling material into submission, finally, and then dragged it back into the barn, where she was able to arrange it over the thick carpet of straw. It was heavily creased and lumpy, but it was a big improvement on what had been there before. At last she was ready. She looked at her watch. Ten to five. She could risk another hour, maybe, before going home. Suddenly she was starving. She'd had nothing to eat since breakfast. Maybe she should have a sandwich. It seemed wrong, somehow, to be eating at such a time – but she could think and plan while she ate, and that might help her to do the right thing.

Her picnic bag was still by the barn door, and she was about to delve into it when she caught sight of her blackened hands once more. The tap. The dripping tap at the side of the building – she could wash her hands there. The water didn't remove much of the oil and grease but it did at least wash the dung off. Her hands were stinging from cuts and splinters, but there was little she could do about that. She grabbed a broken sandwich from the carrier bag and munched at it as she stepped back inside the barn. Her eyes grew accustomed to the dimness once more and she stood by the horse, astonished all over again by what was happening to her and what she had achieved. For the first time today she began to think seriously about what this animal could be, and *how* it could be. Such things simply did not exist. And yet they existed in books – sort of. Flying horses. Angels. Mermaids. Unicorns. Fairies. *Had* they all been real, once? Was this an ancient survivor from another time? Or was it just a freak thing, escaped from some mad zoo or laboratory? Yes, maybe it was an experiment. Maybe it had been bred in a secret lab somewhere, a weird cloning thing. That was possible. That seemed very possible. She finished her sandwich and thought about how she would get the animal on to the polythene mattress.

Moving the poor creature wasn't as difficult as she had imagined it might be. It was so light. She began by carefully folding its wings up into what seemed like their natural position – but oh, how strange they were to her touch. They were velvety and warm, yet bony at the same time. She didn't like it at first – it was just too weird – but her initial repulsion turned to curiosity and then amazement at how delicately constructed they were. They were more bat-like than bird-like, but they also reminded her of paper fans or Chinese lanterns somehow, the way the pattern of quill-like bones could clearly be seen beneath the skin, and the way in which they folded up so neatly. The blood around the gaping holes in the damaged wing had congealed and turned dark. Midge was as gentle as she could be.

Next, she brought the edge of the polythene sheet right up close to the horse and tucked it under both front legs and back. The legs were so slim that she was able to grasp the front pair with one hand and the back pair with the other, as she knelt on the polythene sheet. Then she simply pulled the little animal from under the raking machine and towards her, edged backwards a bit, pulled some more, and so gradually slid it on to the polythene. She hauled the unconscious creature in this fashion to the centre of the mattress, where the straw underneath was thickest. A damp smear of blood and muck had been left as a trail from the edge of the blue sheet to the middle. But at least the poor thing was on a dry and comfortable bed.

Twenty past five. She could allow herself another half-hour or so to try and clean the patient up. But what was she to use? The sacking was going to be a blanket. The scrubbing brush? Too harsh, she thought. She was wearing a T-shirt, but she could hardly turn up at the farmhouse without a top on. Knickers and socks were the only other possibilities. She decided on her socks. But two small white summer socks would hardly do to wash a horse down with – even a miniature horse. Finally, she reasoned that it was only the wounds that were really important. If she could wash the dirt away from them, then the rest could wait.

She ran round to the outside tap, carrying the battered pail, and half filled it with water. Back in the barn she pulled off her shoes and socks, put her shoes straight back on again, and carried the bucket unsteadily to the centre of the mattress where the horse lay. Putting her hand into one of the socks, she dipped it in the cold water. Then, using her free hand to gently extend the damaged wing, she carefully began to bathe the wounds. The sock quickly became stained pink, but Midge kept rinsing it in the bucket and applying clean water to the torn skin until all the muck and grit had gone. The wounds opened up again and fresh blood began to appear, but Midge felt that this was preferable to the filth that had been there before. When it was as clean as she could make it, she used her other sock to dab the area dry and then gently let the wing fold into a natural and, she hoped, comfortable position. When that was done, she ran round to the tap once more, tipped the dirty water away and refilled the bucket. She rinsed the dirty socks under the running tap. There was just time to wash the horse's face, and then she would have to go.

The animal was alive, she knew that. Gently sponging around the closed eyes and blood-spattered mouth, Midge was aware of the fast shallow breathing of the unconscious creature. It was still alive, and she would keep it alive. She would not let it go. She would pour strength and healing from her fingertips, she would wash away the pain. Unblinking, in a trance almost, she dipped her hand into the cool water again and again. Every movement she made was filled with care.

Finally there was no more she could do. It was six o'clock. She had to go. The heavy old potato sack made a perfect horse-blanket, as she had known it would, and she draped it across the fragile and vulnerable creature as a shield against the long night ahead. As a last thought, she drank some of the orange squash from her plastic Coke bottle, tipped the rest away, and re-filled it with clean water from the tap. Kneeling by the horse, she gently tipped a little water from the bottle into its mouth. There was no swallowing reaction, as she had hoped there might be. A slight movement of the tongue, a twitch of the small delicate nostrils perhaps, but nothing more. Midge stayed a few moments longer, stroking the backs of her fingers against the horse's cheek, then said, 'I'll be here in the morning, I promise,' and left.

She could hear the sound of a woodpecker, echoing from high up in the Royal Forest, as she walked quickly back down the hill towards Mill Farm

Outside the farmhouse, Midge paused and listened. The noise of the television came through the open window of the downstairs sitting room. With a bit of luck she might be able to sneak in, and dash upstairs to the shower without Uncle Brian seeing her. She crept in through the front door and walked a little way along the corridor. The sitting room door was slightly ajar.

'Hi, Uncle Brian!' she called, in as cheerful and normal a voice as she could manage.

'Midge! I was just beginning to wonder about you – I'm in the sitting room. Come and look at this.'

'I'm just going to have a shower. Back in a bit!'

'What?'

But Midge had fled upstairs.

She scrubbed and scrubbed, but ordinary shower gel made hard work of the oil and grease on her hands. They still looked pretty black, and the cuts and scratches stung like anything. Washing-up liquid might do the trick she thought, but that would have to wait until she was back downstairs again. She gave her hair a quick blow with the hairdryer, changed straight into her pyjamas, and screwed her dirty clothes into a bundle. So far, so good. Now she had to get her clothes into the washing machine. She crept down the stairs and padded barefoot across the flagstone hall, through the kitchen and into the little washroom. She'd just managed to get the dirty bundle into the machine as Uncle Brian walked into the kitchen.

'You there, Midge?'

'Yes, I'm just washing some clothes.' Midge had used the washing machine before, and now she quickly rotated the programme switch and pulled it towards her. The machine came on with a click and a hum. Uncle Brian stuck his head round the washroom door and looked at her guilty face.

'Aha,' he said. 'I *think* I can guess what's going on here.'

Midge looked horrified.

'Yeeess,' continued Uncle Brian. 'This looks like a girl who has fallen into a ditch, rolled in umpteen cow-pats, sat in a pond, and then thought she could get away with it undetected. I *do* have children of my own you know,' he added. He wasn't really angry, she could tell. 'Anyway, as long as you're not hur . . . Good God, girl! Look at your hands! Let me see them. What *have* you been doing?'

Midge held out her hands in embarrassment. 'I was . . .' – she hesitated – '. . . playing on the tractor. And I fell off.' It sounded bad enough to account for her dirty clothes, and a few scratches, without being *so* bad as to merit a real storm. She had judged her reply nicely, for Uncle Brian said, quite sternly, 'Midge, that could have been dangerous. Now *I* know that there's no way that you could have started the thing, or come to any real grief, but for all *you* knew you could have pressed a button and been roaring across West Sedge Moor by now. Please don't touch machinery that you don't understand, OK? Come and have some supper then and we'll say no more. I've saved you a bit of salad.' He brightened up. 'Bring it in the sitting room. There's this amazing nature programme on. You'd like it, I think. David Attenborough.'

So Midge, after a final and futile attempt to get her hands really clean, sat with her salad on her lap and tried to be interested in what was on the television. It was something about life under the sea, but she couldn't concentrate. So much was going round her head, that she felt dizzy, and a bit sick. The day had been crammed with such impossible events and such astonishing achievements, that she just wanted to be alone in her room to think. She was sure that she would never sleep, although her whole body ached with fatigue. She tried to focus on the television. What was the winged horse doing now? She thought of it lying alone in the little barn on the hillside, with the sun going down and all the long dark night ahead. The television voiceover broke in on her thoughts, '. . . and it is a fact, an absolute fact, that there are creatures on the surface of this earth that have never been observed by man . . .' Midge glanced up. 'There are other worlds – worlds within this world – that we can only begin to imagine. We may think we have seen all that there is to be seen on this tiny planet of ours. We most certainly have not – and perhaps we never shall.'

The words were a comfort. She held them to her, as the credits scrolled up the screen. '. . . *there are other worlds – worlds within this world . . . creatures on this planet that have never been seen by man . . .*'

'Uncle Brian, I think I'll go to bed now. I'm really tired.'

'OK, poppet. You do that. You haven't had much to eat, though. Is everything all right?'

'Yes. I'm just tired.'

'Off you go then and get some rest. Sleep tight.'

' 'Night, Uncle Brian.'

' 'Night, Midge. God bless.' Brian watched the girl leave the room and wondered, not for the first time, whether it had been a good idea to agree to look after her for the holidays. It must be so odd for her, after London and the life she was used to. He wasn't much company for her, but then how many middle-aged men *would* be company for a twelve-year-old? She seemed happy, on the whole – though she had certainly looked absolutely washed out tonight. Well, George and Katie would be here in a few days and perhaps she would have a bit more fun then. Poor old thing, life was pretty dull for her at present.

Midge clambered into bed and took off her watch. She placed it on her bedside cabinet and looked at it from the delicious softness of her pillow. The pale blue strap and outer casing were still stained and grubby from the day's events. Everything that had happened to her, had also happened to her watch. Everything she had seen, the watch had seen. The marks and scratches, the tiny flecks of blood and oil, were a diary of her day. Proof that she had been there. Like the army campaign medals of her grandad, her dad's father, which Mum let her play with sometimes. Her watch was like a medal. How strange it was.

But the strangest thing of all, in some ways, and the last thought in her head as she fell asleep, was the business with the heifers. She was really, really frightened of cows. They terrified her. Or they had done . . . till today.

Chapter Six

Little-Marten took a short run up, flapped hard, and gained the lowest branch of the Rowdy-Dow tree – the dead beech that stood in the south-western corner of Counsel Clearing. He swarmed up the trunk, using the rough footholds that had been hacked into the hard dry wood, and swung himself up onto the Perch – the broken limb that jutted out about twenty feet above the ground. Sitting astride the Perch, he drew the heavy clavensticks from his jerkin and made himself ready, awaiting the signal from Aken, his captain, on the ground below.

Aken stood at the base of the Rowdy-Dow tree, and kept an eye on the Royal Pod, which swung gently, like a great wicker beehive, among the lower limbs of the Royal Oak on the other side of the clearing. The painted oilcloth flap remained drawn across the circular entrance. Maglin had been in there for some time. Aken wondered whether the General was having trouble in persuading the Queen of the urgent need for a meeting. Ba-betts had grown weaker in the brain of late. Her temper was uncertain. Maglin would need much patience if Ba-betts was in one of her black humours – and Maglin was not long on patience. Aken waited apprehensively.

Finally, the gorgeously decorated oilcloth was drawn aside and the Ickri General appeared at the entrance of the wicker pod, briefly glancing down at the four winged guards who stood at the base of the Royal Oak. Maglin turned momentarily, bowed in the entrance-way, then opened his wings and launched himself across the clearing, towards the Rowdy-Dow tree. An unseen hand drew the curtain again behind him. He landed – rather stiffly, Aken thought – and walked the last few paces, scratching his short grey beard, and looking grim.

'Hemmed woman!' he muttered darkly, as he reached Aken. 'She grows madder by the hour. Muster the Various, Aken, all tribes to gather at sun-wane.'

'*All* tribes?' said Aken.

'All tribes.'

'Tinklers and Troggles . . . ?'

'Are you become deaf, Aken? Or does my breath grow faint? Sound the Muster – all tribes!'

Aken stepped back and glanced upwards. Little-Marten was looking down from the high Perch, awaiting his signal. 'Muster the Various!' shouted Aken. 'All tribes, at sun-wane.' Little-Marten hesitated, saw the look on his captain's face, and thought better than to question the command. He took the hard-wood clavensticks and beat two very short tattoos on the trunk of the tree. Then a longer burst, at in-credible speed. A hard, dry sound. He paused for a few seconds, then gave a few short taps in quick succession, biting his lower lip as he concentrated. Five lengthy bursts ended the message. The woods rang with the paradiddle of the Ickri lad's clavensticks – sounding for all the world like a green woodpecker at work. No Gorji ears in the vicinity would have known the difference. Little-Marten took off his cap and waited.

Maglin grunted. 'The chi' beats well. Who is he?'

'Little-Marten,' said Aken. 'Son of Fletcher Marten, and a chi' no more. A youth he is now, though small for his years.'

'Ah yes. Fletcher Marten's son. Well well, the lad will make a Woodpecker. Till sun-wane, Aken. All tribes, mind.' The Ickri General turned and left the clearing, disappearing into the dense trees.

Aken watched the General depart, noting the slight stoop of his shoulders and the greyness of his hair – more marked than ever in the bright afternoon sunlight. He had aged this last season, and 'twas little wonder. These were worrying times. Aken could guess the purpose of the Muster – the disappearance of the Naiad horse was the talk of the forest, though only the tribe leaders were supposed to know the reason Pegs had gone. No doubt the Counsel would be discussing some rescue plan – more foolishness in all likelihood. He wondered if Ba-betts herself would attend. Aken began to walk away, deep in thought – then remembered Little-Marten. He turned and glanced aloft to where the lad sat patiently on the high Perch. 'That'll do,' he said, and added, 'Woodpecker.'

Little-Marten remained on the Perch, *his* Perch now, a while longer – savouring the moment. He clacked the clavensticks softly against the palm of his hand and let his legs swing to and fro in time. He knew he had done well. A long year it had taken him to learn his craft – apprenticed to the hands of Petan, the retiring Woodpecker. It was Fletcher Marten, Little-Marten's father, who had noticed that Petan was struggling to reach the lower branch of the Rowdy-Dow tree, and had noticed also the occasional falter in the old Woodpecker's timing. More than once had a confused message been beaten out on the hollow trunk. And it was Fletcher Marten who had introduced his son to Petan, as a possible apprentice.

'The youth casn't keep still nor more than two winks at a time,' he explained to Petan. ' 'Twould be a mercy to us all if 'e were learning summat useful wi' his jumpsy ways. He don't have the patience to be a fletcher, I knows that.' And so Petan had taken the little fellow on, and found in him a willing and gifted pupil. His small quick hands had grasped the heavy clavensticks eagerly, and his mind was sharp and precise. He learned quickly, practising for long hours away from the clearing, using a rotten log to deaden the sound. From Petan he learned the basic commands; how to summon the Various tribe leaders, how to warn of danger such as the nearby presence of the Gorji, the arrival of a Renard, and the likelihood of attendant red-jackets. He learned how to announce the appearance of the Queen – a rare enough occurrence – how to call the Elder Counsel to meeting, how to inform the Naiad field workers of an approaching storm, how to bring the tribes in at Basket-time. And his hands grew quicker all the while, until at last even Petan said that he was beginning to sound like a Woodpecker, and that today he might climb the Rowdy-Dow tree and take up the Perch. The old Ickri was actually glad to see the back of it. It took too much out of him, that frantic ascent to the first branch – and the clavensticks had seemed of late to grow heavier at each sounding.

So Little-Marten was enjoying his moment, and his new position in the world. A Muster! His first day, and he had been required to beat out a full Muster of the Various! Tinklers and Troggles too! Such a thing was almost unknown. And he had never missed a beat. On the western fringe of Counsel Clearing, far below him, he noticed the figure of Petan standing quietly among the beech saplings. He seemed to be nodding his head approvingly. Probably he had been there all the time. Little-Marten tucked the clavensticks into his jerkin and rolled lazily backwards off his Perch. He turned a half-somersault, spread his wings, and spiralled grace-fully to the ground. It was a trick he'd been planning. Petan, alone among the saplings, frowned slightly and then shrugged his shoulders. He supposed that he too must have been young, once.

At sun-wane, the rattle of the Woodpecker rang out again, drilling through the peace of the early evening. Little-Marten sounded Basket-time, followed by the Muster of the Various – indicating that all were to bring their provender to basket before attending the Muster. The wicker baskets, four or five in number according to the season, were arranged near the base of the Rowdy-Dow tree. Always there would be baskets for meat, fish and vegetables, one for each, and in season there would be a fruit basket and a grain basket. At Basket-time, the hunters, farmers and fishers – Ickri, Naiad and Wisp – would bring a daily harvest to basket. Then each would take according to his family's needs. What remained would be left to the Troggles and Tinklers – who brought nothing to basket, but appeared to live on the charity of the other tribes.

Little-Marten felt sorry for the tribes who dwelt below ground. They were poor, and led a curious existence, troggling for the base metal ore that lay in the caves and fashioning, from the metal they called tinsy, worthless trinkets – strange drinking vessels, and arrowheads that nobody wanted. These they gave in exchange for a little food, but for the most part their efforts were but time wasted. The upper tribes generally preferred to eat and drink from wooden trenchers and bowls, turned by the Naiad carpenters, and the bright tinsy gewgaws and adornments of the Tinklers and the Troggles, so strangely fashioned, were soon grown dull and given to the children as playthings. The arrowheads, though sharp, were con- sidered to be more trouble than was worth the effort of splicing to shaft, and the majority of archers simply hardened their wooden arrow tips in the charcoal pit. The caves were at the far end of the forest and the

Troggles and Tinklers would usually only come out at moonrise, to creep shyly about the forest, grubbing for what they could, and to empty the meagre leftovers from the baskets. Some of the Naiad farmers would complain that their crops had been stolen in the night, but there was never any real evidence to support this. Strange sounds, too, would emanate from the caves at night, when the Troggles did what they called 'singing'. Their voices would rise and fall in unnatural ways, sometimes together, sometimes alone – rather like the sounds the birds made, but with words. This was viewed with great suspicion by the upper tribes, who had better things to do with their time than squawl like throstles. And anyway, singing was noise – and noise of any kind was to be avoided.

But Little-Marten did not share the opinions of most of his kind – for he had a secret. A shameful secret. He had heard the Troggles sing, and he liked it. He had crept down to the hawthorn bushes near the entrance of the caves many times, even through the cold evenings of late winter and early spring, and had stood hidden, listening, enthralled by the curious sounds echoing from deep within – the voices that rose and fell together in patterns, patterns that he instinctively understood, that reminded him somehow of the clavensticks and made him itch to tap his fingers. This was bad enough, but there was worse. He feared that he was in love with a Tinkler maid. He even knew her name – Henty.

The evening when first he had seen her still danced

through his dreams at night, and though he had tried to forget her, he could not. He had grown reckless on his last visit, and, as the light began to fail, at dimpsy dusk, he had emerged from the bushes and edged close to the cave entrance, the better to hear the Troggles at their singing. A single voice chanted softly:

Sweet Celandine, when leaves are turned to amber,
And the wild winter-time would take our breath
* away . . .*

Then, it seemed that a hundred voices joined the single voice, yet still softly, deeply . . .

Into our open hearts, your golden star will shine,
To make our darkness bright again, Sweet Celandine.

Little-Marten was won over heart and soul at this, and was even tentatively trying his own voice – a shocking heresy – to see if it too could perform such magic – when a Tinkler maid suddenly twirled out of the darkness of the cave. Little-Marten had been caught with his eyes half closed, his mouth half open, and his whole being off-balance, as the dark-haired creature came spinning to within a yard of where he stood. Her huge eyes flashed white in the dimness of the evening, her pupils as black as charcoal, as she stared at him, horrified. An Ickri! The singing had ceased.

'I . . . I . . . I was . . . I heard . . .' Little-Marten began to stammer, feeling the hot tingle of blood rushing from his cheeks to his hair roots – but the Tinkler maid was already backing away from him, drawing the thin, loosely woven cloth of her shawl protectively around her neck and shoulders. Her pale round face, with its shocked expression, beautiful, so beautiful, retreated into the murky cave – disappearing like a spirit. A faint orange glow illuminated the corner of a passageway far back inside the cave, but the maid had vanished into some darker side-shoot. Little-Marten heard a muffled voice calling 'Henty?' and thought he heard a murmured reply, but no more. He stood at the mouth of the cave a little longer, till the silence gradually made him feel self-conscious and then he eventually left, walking back across the Great Clearing through the deepening darkness, smitten, moon-struck, hopelessly conquered. And ashamed.

Now, from the high vantage point of his Perch, Little-Marten watched as the Various began to arrive in response to his summons.

The Rowdy-Dow tree stood in a corner of the Royal Clearing, where South Wood and West Wood met, and so the first to arrive were the Ickri, the winged hunters, who patrolled these nearby stretches of the forest. Scurl, captain of the South and West Woods, and some of his younger followers – Benzo, Grissel, Dregg, and Flitch – came gliding down from the trees. They swaggered over to the baskets and nonchalantly emptied their pecking bags, tossing the limp carcasses of birds and squirrels into the wicker receptacle for meat. Tulgi and Snerk, two more of Scurl's crew, arrived soon after and did likewise. The seven Ickri sprawled around the base of the Rowdy-Dow tree, chewing grass stalks, comparing the latest decorative designs which they had painted, tattoo-like, on their wings, and boasting idly of their exploits that day. Occasionally they would punch or kick each other in response to some insult or slighting remark. They were young, apart from Scurl, their captain. Unattached, unruly and unchallenged – they thought highly of themselves. Scurl was cock-of-the-woods in his own estimation, and his followers encouraged him in this belief. He was flattered by their admiration of him, and they in turn were flattered to be chosen as his disciples.

Little-Marten, high above the seven lounging hunters, kept still and hoped that he wouldn't be noticed. No such luck, however, for presently Benzo shaded his eyes against the evening sun and looked upwards.

'Greetings, Petan. How quiet you be. Or do you still catch breath, you old fool? Hullo, though! 'T'ain't Petan at all! 'Tis some young snip! What, is the old 'Pecker finally dead then? Did 'e finally come unsticked from his Perch?'

The others looked up and laughed at this, and Grissel said, 'Now I wonders if young'un here is made o' stickier stuff. I means to find out.' He fitted an arrow to his bow and flicked it lightly upwards at Little-Marten. The arrow glanced harmlessly off the end of the broken limb, but it made Little-Marten jump.

'Grissel, thee shoots like an old hag!' cried Benzo.

He hopped to his feet and said, with exaggerated menace, 'Now then, young Woodpecker! What have 'ee done to our poor old Petan?' He drew his bow back to its full extent, aiming an arrow directly at the little Ickri, who shrank back in fright against the trunk of the Rowdy-Dow tree.

'Don't!' he whispered.

Benzo shifted his stance slightly, and let fly. The arrow whipped past Little-Marten's cowering head, so close that he heard the zing of the feathered flights.

Scurl growled, and kicked out at Benzo from where he lay. 'Leave 'un be, Benzo. 'Tis Fletcher Marten's cub.'

'Is it then? Well, I suppose *'twould* be a sad day for a fletcher to see his cub come home stuffed full o' feathers,' laughed Benzo, sitting down and making himself comfortable once more. ' 'Specially feathers he'd tied hisself.'

In truth, Scurl cared little or nothing for the well-being of Little-Marten, but he had caught sight of Aken and some of the North and East Wood hunters dipping through the branches on the other side of the clearing. Braggart though he was, he didn't quite like to be seen allowing his underlings to fire arrows at an unarmed youth, even if it was only in jest. 'Now then, Aken!' he called, rising to his feet and dusting himself down, 'What sport?' He adopted the bluff brotherly tone he reserved for the captain of the East and North Woods, his equal in rank, but who nevertheless contrived to make him feel inferior.

Aken strolled up to the baskets, flanked by two of

his archers, Uzu and Raim. 'Fair,' said Aken, calmly. 'A few finches. A pigeon,' – he dipped his hand into his pecking bag, and looked directly at Benzo – 'but no Woodpeckers.' Benzo dropped his head, glanced sideways at his friends, and smirked. Aken turned to Scurl. 'If I find anyone at that sport again, Scurl, then they'll answer for't. If not to you, then to I.'

'Garn,' muttered Scurl, ''Twas only chaff.' But Aken had already turned away, having spotted Glim and his wife, Zelma, descending from the East Wood trees. He walked over to meet them.

Feeling safer now that Aken and Glim were on hand, Little-Marten turned his attention to the crowd beginning to arrive from the Great Clearing at the far end of the forest. The Naiad, once a water-tribe, now farmers for the most part, came bearing fruit and vegetables, which they carefully placed in the baskets. Phemra, Spindra, Stickle, and two of their wives, Zophia and Fay, stood in a group and stared up curiously at him. Finally Zophia recognized him. ' 'Tis Little-Marten.'

The others raised their eyebrows. 'What? Be he Woodpecker now?'

Members of the Wisp tribe, Peter, Tod, Will, Isak and Little-Isak, brought strings of eels, their catch from the previous night, and threw them in the fish basket. Two of the Wisp children, Etta and Lori, danced around the Rowdy-Dow tree and tried to catch Little-Marten's attention – but Little-Marten was suddenly oblivious to their cavortings. A hundred Benzos firing a host of arrows could not have distracted him at that moment, for the Troggles and the Tinklers, so rarely seen by day, had appeared at the far end of the Royal Clearing.

They made their way along the narrow pathway between the bushes that separated Royal Clearing from the Great Clearing beyond, a straggly line of hooded creatures, wingless, like the Naiad and the Wisp, but generally smaller and stockier.

The muted chatter of the upper tribes gradually ceased, as all became aware of the approaching cave-dwellers. Even Scurl and his crew rose to their feet and watched in silence as the Troggles and Tinklers made their way to the middle of Royal Clearing. They stood in a huddle by the Whipping Stone, the age-old lichen-covered hamstone post that marked the centre of the clearing. Ghostly they looked. Their skin, what little could be seen of it, was very white. Dressed in drab grey cloaks, their huge eyes peered out from the cowls that they wore to protect themselves from the sunlight. Yet their heads were not bowed, and their bodies were not bent. They stood upright and gazed about them, meeting the stares of the curious onlookers – until it was the onlookers them-selves who dropped their heads and stared uncomfortably at their own boots.

Little-Marten, of course, was on the lookout for Henty, the Tinkler maid, whom he had last seen at the entrance to the caves – but the faces of the hooded figures below him were mostly hidden from his view. One of the hoods was suddenly thrown back, however, and the close-cropped head of Tadgemole, the leader of the Troggles, was revealed. Tadgemole was a stocky figure, broad in the shoulders, as befitted a miner – still strong and upright despite his years, although his face looked gaunt and pale. He left the group and walked over to the provender baskets, drawing something from the folds of his threadbare cloak, a large dead animal which he held, cradled, in his short powerful arms. It was a hotchi-witchi – a hedgehog. The gathered crowd watched him in silence. Tadgemole leaned over the meat basket and put the hotchi-witchi into it – not tossing it in casually, as the Ickri hunters might have done, but placing it carefully on top of the pile as though it was the most precious object he possessed – which may have indeed been the case. Such a thing was unheard of! A soft ripple of sound ran through the crowd, and Little-Marten heard Grissel muttering to Benzo, 'Vurst useful thing 'e's done this day. Or any other.' But Aken, who was standing directly below the Perch, hissed up at Little-Marten. 'Maglin!'

The Ickri General had appeared from the direction of the Counsel Pod, the wicker construction that hung from a low outer branch of the Royal Oak. Little-Marten just had time to beat his arrival on the clavensticks, as the old warrior landed and took command.

'Circle the clearing!' shouted Maglin.

The Tinklers and Troggles moved away from the central Whipping Stone towards the edge of the clearing and joined the circle that the Naiad and the Wisp had already begun to form. The Ickri stayed more or less where they were, spreading themselves out a little until their numbers joined with the first of the Wisp. Soon the outer rim of Counsel Clearing was lined with all members of the five tribes – Ickri, Wisp, Naiad, Tinklers and Troggles.

Maglin strode towards the Whipping Stone, his dark eyes scanning the semicircle. 'Where's Maven-the-Green?' he growled. Silence. Nobody had seen the old hag for a moon or more. Maven was a law unto herself, mad as a pike and almost as dangerous, with her poisonous darts and fearful incantations. She was given a wide berth by all – the youngsters were frankly terrified of her, and even the Ickri hunters were glad to avoid her. If she was missing, then so be it. Nobody would be very inclined to go and seek her out. Maglin decided to let the matter pass. He turned in the direction of the Rowdy-Dow tree and shouted up to Little-Marten, 'Woodpecker! Sound the Counsel!'

The clavensticks drummed on the hollow beech, *drrrr–drrrrrrr–drr*, and the entrance cloth to the Counsel Pod, just visible among the shadows of the Royal Oak, was drawn aside. Out stepped the three ancient Counsellors – Crozer, Ardel and Damsk, eldest members of the Ickri, Naiad and Wisp tribes. They slowly negotiated the little willow ladder that had been placed at the entrance to the pod and made their way unsteadily to the ground, where they stood waiting – three grey and wizened figures, leaning heavily on their hazelwood staffs.

Little-Marten wiped his hands surreptitiously on his

leather jerkin and grasped the clavensticks in readiness once again. He knew what was coming next, and bit his lip as he rapidly ran through the patterns in his head. Queen's Herald. He kept his eye fixed on Maglin, who for some reason was walking over to the edge of the circle where stood the Tinklers and the Troggles. Maglin said something to Tadgemole, the Troggles' leader, and then returned towards the Whipping Stone. Little-Marten's eye was still fixed on Maglin, waiting for his signal, but he was aware of some movement among the Tinklers and Troggles. He glanced at them quickly, and saw that they had all thrown back their hoods, their dark hair and delicate skin exposed to the day. How very pale they were. Their faces were the colour of moonlight. Just like moonlight . . .

Then Maglin shouted up at him, 'Queen's Herald!' and made him jump. For a horrible moment his hands fumbled and one of the clavensticks turned a somersault into the air – but he caught it and beat straight into the pattern of Queen's Herald, the woodpecker rattle sounding clear and true through the evening stillness of the forest. He *was* good, and was conscious of the many faces that had turned their attention from the Royal Pod to look at him instead. His fingertips flew like the wings of a sparrow as he reached the final long crescendo of Queen's Herald. *Drrrrrrrrr–*tappity*–drrrrr–*tappity*–tap–tap–tap*. He stopped abruptly. A pause. Another short rattle. Pause. Three more quick taps. Finish. Perfect.

He glanced over to where his father stood, along

with Petan, and the approval on their faces made him feel very happy. He tried not to look directly at the Tinklers on the far side of the clearing, but couldn't help peeking slyly over to see if Henty was there. He saw her eventually, half hidden behind the shoulder of Tadgemole, and his heart jumped as he recognized her. She was holding the hand of a tiny Tinkler chi' – a brother perhaps? Her hair was tied back and she was looking less wild than when he had first seen her. Fragile she seemed now, and ghostly in the slanting shafts of sunlight. And yet still so beautiful. She was not looking at him.

There was silence as all waited for the Queen to appear. Long moments passed. Benzo yawned, rolled his eyes, and laid his head in mock weariness on the shoulder of Flitch – only to be kicked by Scurl and told to stand aright. The three Elder Counsellors stood bent and motionless, grasping their staffs and staring sadly at the ground. Some of the children started to fidget and scratch themselves as the evening midges began to bite. Little-Marten, high up on the Perch, wondered whether he should begin again, and looked down at Maglin for a sign, but Maglin remained in the centre of the clearing, calmly looking towards the entrance of the Royal Pod. He knew Ba-betts of old. She'd be out when she was ready, and not before – though she was probably watching them all even now, through her little spyhole in the wicker wall of the Royal Pod. Or, more likely, getting Doolie to watch for her and report what was happening.

Finally the painted oilcloth was drawn aside and

Ba-betts, Queen of the Ickri, and therefore of all the Various, appeared. She was dressed in blue – a light blue gown, and a dark blue cape, tipped with squirrel fur. In her right hand she carried the red Touchstone – a sure sign that this was a serious occasion. Doolie, the Queen's maid, helped her mistress over the lip of the circular entranceway and thence to the edge of the little platform which had been added to the Royal Pod once it had become clear that the Queen was no longer capable of using her wings to reach the ground. Here was suspended, by simple ropes and rough wooden pulleys, a wicker chair, once painted sloe-blue but now rather faded, with carrying handles at either end. It was known as the Gondla, though nobody could remember why.

Doolie lent an arm to Ba-betts as she clambered heavily into the Gondla, which swung to and fro rather alarmingly. Once the Queen was safely seated, she was carefully lowered to the ground by two of the Ickri guard, the wickerwork creaking slightly under the strain. Then, with one guard at each end, the Gondla, with its royal occupant, was lifted by its handles and transported to the edge of the clearing. Here the Queen was placed, in full view of her gathered subjects. She raised the Touchstone high, her white mottled arm quivering slightly with the effort. The rays of the evening sun caught the polished surface of the red jasper globe, and for a moment it seemed as though the squat little figure in the wicker chair was holding aloft an orb of fire. Ba-betts lowered the Touchstone once more. She was ready.

Chapter Seven

'Your Queen,' began Ba-betts, in the rather high sing-song voice she adopted when looking for sympathy, 'is not a well Queen.' She turned to look at the three Counsellors, who stood with their heads bowed, and continued. 'Your Queen has been taken *from* her sick-bed, and brought into the *chill* of the evening – which will surely *do* her more evil than good – in order to attend,' and here she reverted to her more usual harsh tone, 'to some trifling matter of runaway goats.'

'Not run away, my Lady,' began Crozer, the Elder Ickri Counsellor, 'and not goats. If you remember . . .'

'*If I remember?*' cried Ba-betts, rising from her seat and brandishing the Touchstone threateningly. '*If I remember?* I'll thank *you*, Crozer, to remember your station. I'll thank *you* to remember that the Queen remembers *everything*! Certainly she remembers *you*, Crozer, for the snivel-snitched little toady you ever were!' She waved the Touchstone in the direction of Damsk, the Elder Wisp, who looked suitably alarmed. 'You!' she cried. 'Remind all those whose wit may be feeble, of the reason we are Mustered on this inclement eve. A full account, mind, that *all* may understand why,' she sank back into her chair once again, 'your Queen appears before you, *in* her suffering.'

Damsk bowed and, steadying himself with his staff, he took a step forward. He had an awkward task ahead of him. The truth was that the Counsel had acted, in the matter of the winged horse, without the Queen's knowledge. Only Maglin and the other tribe leaders had been informed of their decision – and they had been against it. He was now aware that rumours of their action had begun to filter downwards, and it was possible that the Ickri captains also knew, or guessed, what had happened: the Elder Counsel had decided that Pegs, the Naiad horse, should fly to the Far Woods to see if it was possible for the Various to leave their home and start anew. There was no real hope that the distant woodlands would prove to be as protected – by briars and brambles and Gorji neglect – as the Royal Forest, but all possibilities had to be explored, even those that were remote. And the horse had been willing to go. The Queen's approval should certainly have been sought, but that could have taken a full season perhaps, and time grew short. Now he needed her to believe that she *had* been a party to that decision. Her memory was so erratic, that he might just persuade her that her approval had been given.

'As you know, my Lady,' he began, diplomatically addressing Ba-betts first, then gradually turning to face the crowd, 'and as all here know, the last few winters have been hard. The forest is not what it was and game grows short. Neither does the Great Clearing bring forth as once it did. The people have suffered,' here he turned to the Queen, ingratiatingly, 'and my Lady has suffered with them. Aye, and *for* them. Summer is here, and once again the times are more plentiful, but if we, the Various, are to face another such winter as the last, then we've to find new pastures, or new ways to make our woods rich in provender once more.'

Damsk paused, and considered his next words carefully. 'It was decided, as my Lady will recall, that Pegs, the Naiad horse – bred by Spindra of the Naiad, and a strong flyer – would go to search for fresh pastures, to explore the far woodlands at night . . .'

'What foolishness was this?' interrupted the Queen. 'To explore *what* lands, pray? All lands are Gorji lands, but for the Royal Forest. Did you think to move the Various, unnoticed, into the very midst of the giants? I knew *nothing* of this. Why was I not told?'

Damsk sighed inwardly. This was the danger with Ba-betts. One moment she was like a sick chi' with a wandering mind, and the next she was as sharp as an arrow. He knew, as the Counsel had known when they had discussed it, that to send Pegs off to explore other areas of woodland, with the idea of transporting the Various thither, was hopelessness indeed. The Gorji were everywhere nowadays. But the Counsel had needed to find a solution, or to at least act as though they believed that there was a solution to be found. Yet they knew, and Maglin knew, and the other tribe leaders knew, that the Various were facing a slow extinction. Not this year, nor the next perhaps, but eventually it would come. Who would openly say it though? Not he.

'We believed, my Lady, that the horse might return with news of the other woods hereabouts, which we can see from our own treetops, not so very distant, and which . . .' Damsk began to improvize, '. . . which, as you so wisely suggested, could be *visited*, rather than inhabited, and perhaps then harvested under cover of night.'

No such plan had been discussed, either by Queen or Counsel, but it sounded just plausible – a possibility. There was a faint murmur from the crowd. What confusion was this? For the most part they believed that Pegs had simply disappeared. What was this expedition into the Gorji lands?

Ba-betts was confused again, having lost the thread, but thought that she might remember a meeting . . . 'Ah yes,' she said, 'harvesting at night. And what does the horse say? Yay, or nay?' There were some stifled sniggers from the crowd at this, and even old Damsk was struggling to keep a straight face, though nobody knew it save he.

'The horse has not returned, my Lady. Pegs has been two days gone. It is my belief that we should send a party to seek him out.'

Glim snorted with exasperation. This was foolishness upon foolishness. To send Pegs in the first place had been an addle-headed notion – for what possible lands or forests could now be found which were not thick with the Gorji? It was obvious that some ill had befallen Pegs, and for that he was sorry, but to now talk of sending more of their number . . . he caught a warning look from Aken and restrained himself, with some effort, from speaking out.

Crozer, seeing that the wily old Damsk had managed the Queen rather skilfully, felt that he should support his fellow Counsellor. 'I am certain that Damsk is right in this,' he said, quickly searching for some arguments to support this statement, 'for Pegs may still be alive, perhaps captured, and may lead the Gorji to us . . . wittingly or unwittingly. We must discover the fate of the Naiad horse, ere we may sleep easily again.'

Ardel, the Elder Naiad, thought that perhaps he might be able to carry this idea a little further. He addressed the Queen. 'May *I* have permission to speak, my Lady?' Ba-betts nodded, but muttered, 'Though let us not still be here at moon-wane, Ardel. The Queen's patience is short, and your tongue is apt to be long.'

The old Naiad moved falteringly into the circle of the clearing, gripping his staff, his dark brown cloak brushing the ground. He raised his head and stood, twisting the end of his white beard between the tips of his fingers, as he prepared to address the crowd. Ardel, it was true, liked to speak – and opportunities like this were not to be missed.

'There are two paths,' he began, his high steady voice sounding much younger than might have been expected, 'which we may choose from. Where either leads, we cannot foretell, but choose we must. We can choose to *act* this day, or we can choose to do nothing. Let us consider each of these paths.'

The sound of an exaggerated yawn was heard, no doubt from one of Scurl's crew, but Ardel was just climbing into the saddle of his speech and had no intention of dismounting at this point.

'If we do *not* search for Pegs,' continued Ardel, 'then our hopes of gaining knowledge are forfeit. We shall never know whether the Far Woods, which we can see in the distance, are sufficiently untended that we may harvest and take benefit thereof. None but Pegs was strong enough in flight to seek or gain such knowledge. Pegs alone was able to spy out the land and bring us news, and now Pegs has gone. The Ickri may glide' – here a note of disdain crept into Ardel's voice – 'from tree to tree, but only Pegs, of *Naiad* breeding, could truly fly – as a bird may truly fly—'

'Yes, yes,' interrupted Ba-betts, irritably. 'The horse could fly. What is your point, Ardel?'

'My Lady, *without* such knowledge as Pegs may be able to furnish us with, we are . . .' he hesitated, then decided to say it, '. . . doomed. The Royal Forest cannot support us for much longer. The woods grow tired and the soil grows thin. Yet we may thrive, even now, if we can harvest *elsewhere*, and still remain here. Fourseason upon fourseason and through many generations, the five tribes have lived in these forgotten woods, protected by the briars we have long nurtured and by the idleness of the Gorji. We have been fortunate to remain undiscovered for so long. But what Crozer says is true. If the Gorji have found

Pegs, then they will find us. They will come at last. *They will come*. We are in grave danger. We must therefore take the path of action, not of *in*action. We must seek new pastures, aye though it mean treading on Gorji soil, in order to survive; yet we must continue to protect ourselves from discovery. For both of these reasons, we must find Pegs.'

Ardel had expected a noisy reaction to this, but his words were met with a faint murmur and then thoughtful silence. Even Ba-betts seemed, for the moment at least, to be considering the gravity of their situation. Finally, the Queen spoke.

'No doubt you have a plan to suggest?'

'I do, my Lady. If we . . .'

'Then may it keep,' interrupted Ba-betts. ' We have heard enough from the Counsellors. Let us hear from the tribe leaders. Maglin! What words do you have to offer in this matter?'

Maglin spoke from his position at the Whipping Stone. 'My Lady, the Counsellors already know my opinion in this. What is done is done. I can't see that there be any action worth the risk of taking. To venture out into the Gorji lands would be foolishness. If Pegs be dead, then where's the sense in sending a party to search for him? If Pegs be captured then I don't believe he would lead the Gorji to us. He would never speak to 'em – and if he did, I doubt they'd hear or understand. 'Twould be a greater danger to us all to seek him out than to let matters bide.'

'Very well,' said Ba-betts, 'let us hear from the Wisp. Isak – what say you?'

Isak, the small and wiry leader of the Wisp, immediately stepped forward from the line of his tribe, red-faced and obviously itching to speak. There were one or two mutters of 'Goo on, Isak!' and 'You tell 'em, now!' as he swung his arms and strode out towards the Whipping Stone.

'Well, I've ztood and listened to some talk,' began Isak, not even bothering to acknowledge the Queen, ' 'bout the zo-called dangers of venturing on to Gorji land. What do 'ee think *we* do? An' almost every night too! We'm out there, clottin' for eels, settin' our traps an' such, while you'm all still abed. We'm creeping through ditches, hidin' in the withies when the cutters be almost treadin' on our toes as we try to get home of a morning. We knows the Gorji by *name*, half of 'em! I could zay what they had for *breakfast*, by the stink of 'em! I tell 'ee all this – thee who hasn't left this vorest in a hundred fourseasons, if 'ee be lookin' to zend out a party on a *horse*-hunt, then it might as well be *we*. 'Cause we'm out there already!' And Isak huffed his way back to the line of the Wisp, to be met with the approval of his fellows: 'Well said, Isak.' 'That told 'em!'

And it was true. The Wisp, who had lived off the wetlands for as long as could be remembered, continued to work it still – though whereas once it had been their home, they now visited the nearby rhynes and ditches only by night, setting their eel-traps and night lines, and retreating to the safety of the forest by day. The other tribes, by contrast, had set no foot upon Gorji soil for many generations.

97

Ba-betts raised the Touchstone once more, and Maglin gestured with his hand to quiet the rising hubbub.

'And what do the Naiad say – they who have bred this remarkable horse,' said the Queen, 'that is the cause of all our grief?'

Phemra, leader of the Naiad, exchanged a few words with Spindra, from whose stock Pegs had been raised, then stepped forward from the ranks and into the arena, a broad figure in a belted cloth jerkin and leggings which were tied beneath the knee. He removed a wide brimmed hat, woven from coarse grasses, and bowed briefly in the Queen's direction. His round face, normally cheerful, had grown sombre in the last two days, and now looked deeply creased and troubled. His voice shook slightly as he spoke.

'With respect, my Lady,' he said quietly, 'Pegs was hardly the cause of our grief. He did what he were asked to do – or tried to, leastways. 'Twas not his choice, nor ours neither, but he were willing. And now, if he's gone, then we ought to be athinking on what *has* gone, and what we've lost. Pegs was born of Spindra's herd, 'tis true, but Spindra didn't breed 'un. No one can breed a hoss with wings. We don't know where he come from – nobody do. But he were wiser then arn o' we, I do know that. And now we stands here while our friend, thass right, our *friend*, for a right good friend he were to us, lies out there among they giants, or maybe injured in some gurt ditch and we'm just *standing* here? And there's Spindra, sick wi' worry these two days past, and me *knowing* where Pegs has gone but not saying anything, for Counsel says to keep a still tongue. What does that make me? A hemmed fool, thass what – for listening to such clap-trap in the first place, and for allowing Pegs to go. But I'll tell 'ee what – I means to make amends for it. And you may all decide what you hemmed well please, but I be goin' out there arter Pegs, and I bisn't comin' back till I've vound 'un, and wass more . . .' and here the burly farmer thumped his fist into the palm of his hand as he looked directly at the astonished Maglin, 'I'll punch the head of arn o' one who tries to stop I, be 'un carryin' a bow or no!'

The assembled tribes of the Various, who had been simmering uneasily up until this point, now fairly boiled over. Two hundred voices were raised in approval or disapproval of Phemra's speech, and the darkening woods rang with the sound of angry tongues. There was a lot of pushing and shoving as the tribes began to mingle. Ba-betts stood up in her Gondla, shouting and waving the Touchstone around, as the three Elders tried to calm her.

Maglin waded into the crowd, grabbed hold of Isak and pulled him out into the arena towards where Phemra still stood, astonished at the seeming effect of his words. Having collared the two tribe leaders, Maglin faced them both.

'Calm your tribespeople, now!' he said, 'before they get hurt. I shall do the same.' And he strode im-mediately back into the throng where Aken and Scurl were already close to blows.

'Aken!' he shouted. 'Find Tadgemole and help him

to quieten the cave-dwellers. Scurl! Gather your archers and line 'em up. Don't argue. Do it.' Maglin paced around the edge of the clearing, pulling the woodlanders apart, and giving them strict warning to *stay* apart. Gradually the situation was brought under control, and the Ickri General was then able to devote some attention to the Queen, who was now seated in the Gondla once more, with Doolie fanning her face.

'Your permission, my Lady, to address the tribes on your behalf,' said Maglin.

'You have the Queen's permission,' gasped Ba-betts, 'to *roast* the tribes on my behalf for all I care. Doolie! Get me back to the Royal Pod. I'll have no more of this. The Queen is not a well Queen.'

'I believe you should bide a little, Lady,' said Maglin. 'What I have to say'll not take long.' Ba-betts did not reply, and Maglin took up his position at the Whipping Stone once more. He raised his arm until the crowd was once again silent, and then brought his hand slowly down to rest on the top of the ancient stone post, still warm from the heat of the day.

' 'Tis many seasons,' he said grimly, 'since this stone were used for its purpose. Shall this be the day, I wonder, when 'tis brought back into play? I've no qualms in the matter, and none shall find themselves exempt, if I deem it so.' He looked pointedly at Phemra, then at Aken and Scurl. 'None. Are there any here who'd doubt me? So. Let us bring this Muster to an end.' He turned to look at the Counsel Elders. 'We shall vote upon the matter.' The Elders nodded their consent – what else could they do?

100

'Raise hands,' said Maglin, 'all those who reckon on letting matters lie – of trusting that, whatever may've befallen Pegs, no good would come of sending more of our number from the forest.' About a third of the crowd raised their hands.

'Very well,' said Maglin. 'Now raise hands all those who reckon on sending out a party to seek for Pegs.' Well over half the crowd raised their hands at this – a few had refrained from voting either way. '

'So I take it that we be in favour of seeking out the horse,' said Maglin. He signalled for them to bring their arms down. Then he said quietly, 'And now, raise hands all those who be willing to go themselves.'

The crowd had not been expecting this, and whilst there were a few hands that were raised immediately, the majority hesitated. Some hands went up, after a few moments of thought, and were then lowered again, after more thought. Of those that had gone up immediately, some were lowered, only to be raised again. Maglin waited.

A stillness settled on the tribes as Maglin looked from face to face of those with their hands finally and firmly raised. That Scurl and his archers were all seem- ingly willing to go, did not surprise him – though he noted wryly that one or two of them had originally voted *against* sending out a party. Phemra and Spindra he had expected. Little-Marten, the Woodpecker, sat on his Perch with his arm raised, the young fool. Aken, Glim and the rest of the North and East Wood archers had the sense apparently, to keep their hands down. Good. He could ill afford to lose them. Isak,

Will and Tod of the Wisp had indicated that they would go. Several of the Troggles and Tinklers, whose names he did not know, had also raised their arms. That did surprise him. What was Pegs to them? He sighed. He would pick five – one from each tribe. That would be seen to be fair. But should he pick the five most likely to succeed, or the five he could most easily lose? For he had little faith in their return. He would sleep on it, and decide in the morning.

'I shall choose five,' he announced. The clearing was now hushed. 'One from each tribe. And I shall make my choice known at sunrise. 'Tis better we all sleep on this. 'Twould be better still,' he couldn't help adding, 'if we knew whether Pegs were alive or dead this night. But that we cannot tell.'

'*I* can tell.' The voice, harsh but clear, had come from somewhere behind Ba-betts, and there were many in the crowd who thought at first that it was the Queen who had spoken – but Ba-betts had leapt to her feet in fright and spun round. She lost her grip on the Touchstone as she did so, and the heavy ball of red jasper was flung from her hand, landing with a soft thump in the damp grass, a few feet from the Gondla. All eyes followed the direction of the Queen's startled gaze. A strange, humpbacked creature emerged from the dark fringe of trees close to the Royal Oak. The thin face and long straggling hair had been dyed green, to match the patched and tattered green robe that hung in folds from the stooping figure. Trails of ivy were wound about the creature's neck. The ivy rustled slightly as the wild-looking apparition moved

102

slowly towards the Gondla, a skinny painted arm out-stretched. It was Maven-the-Green.

'By Elysse, 'tis the old crone,' muttered Maglin. He left his position at the Whipping Stone and strode quickly across the clearing. The Queen was standing, open-mouthed in fright, as she gripped the side of the wicker chair – hypnotized it seemed by the approaching figure of Maven-the-Green. Maglin beckoned to the four Ickri guards who were positioned at the foot of the Royal Oak. 'Hold, till I speak,' he muttered, as he passed them. He ran the last few paces towards the Gondla, in order to reach the Queen before Maven did.

'Maven!' he called warningly, 'Bide there!' He began to unsling his bow. There was no telling what the fey old creature might do. She was known to carry a little blowpipe within the folds of her sleeve – and the darts she used were said to be tipped with deadly poisons of her own devising. The slightest scratch from one of Maven's darts could supposedly kill a full-grown brock, stone dead in two winks. Maglin had never known her to actually harm any of the tribes-people, despite her frequent threats and curses, but he would take no chances with her. He notched an arrow to his bow, and stood at the ready beside the Gondla.

Maven had stopped. Her thin arm, streaked with paint or dye, still reached out – seemingly in the direction of Ba-betts – but her eye was on the ground. She stooped, as everyone watched in silence, and the green fingers of her outstretched hand reached down

103

and grasped the Touchstone, which lay, half-hidden, in the damp grass. She lifted it gently, and brought it towards her ivy-wreathed body, laying her other hand over the top of the red globe – wet with the evening dew – in a protective, cradling gesture. She wiped the stone dry on the emerald sleeve of her gown.

Ba-betts looked at Maglin and said, indignantly, 'That's mine!'

Maglin couldn't help but smile. The Queen sounded like a chi' who had lost her plaything. He said softly, but quite sternly, 'Bring it to me, Maven.'

'*I* can tell,' said Maven, fixing her wandering gaze on Maglin for a few moments. ' 'Bout the horse. I can tell.'

'What can you tell, Maven?'

'Whether 'ee be dead or no.'

Maglin glanced at the Ickri guards, who were beginning to inch round to the back of Maven-the-Green, out of her line of vision. He pursed his lips and shook his head imperceptibly.

'Just give me the Touchstone, Maven. It belongs to the Queen.'

'Do it?' said Maven. She stuck out her tongue – a startling pink against the surrounding green of her painted face – and looked directly at Ba-betts. She brought one of her hands up to her mouth, extended a twig-like finger and rested it on the tip of her tongue. Taking her hand away from her mouth once more she said, 'The Naiad horse be *dead*,' and drew her moistened finger slowly across the surface of the Touchstone. She regarded the smooth curve of the red stone for a few moments. Raising her dark eyes to stare at Ba-betts as before, she again stuck out her tongue, and dampened her finger with spittle. 'The Naiad horse do *live*,' she said and drew her finger once more across the shiny jasper. She watched the stone for a while and then said, 'Yes. The horse *do* live. But only just. Looksee!'

Extending her arm, she offered the Touchstone to the Queen. Maglin quickly stepped forward, but Ba-betts had automatically reached out and accepted the ball from Maven. The Queen held the Touchstone in both hands and stared at it. Where Maven's finger had been drawn across the surface, there was a faint mottled streak, dark blue it seemed in the failing light. Maglin glanced at the stone, while continuing to keep a wary eye on Maven. He too saw the mottled blue streak, and immediately assumed that it was paint from Maven's fingers, though the colour seemed wrong. But as he watched, the mark faded. Like misty breath on polished metal, it simply melted away.

Maven had leaned forward slightly, and was carefully plucking a hair from her head. She held the grey-green strand up and regarded it as it floated gently in the evening summer breeze.

'The horse lives,' she said, 'though his life do hang by a thread no more thick than this 'un.' She turned and began to make her way back towards the dark mass of trees that fringed the clearing. Her stooping body rocked from side to side as she hobbled along, head down, thoughtfully winding the single strand of hair around one of her fingers. The four Ickri guards who had crept round behind her, now parted to let her go by. As Maven drew level with the guards, she suddenly snaked sideways and screeched like an owl in the face of the nearest one. The poor fellow literally fell over backwards with fright, and Maven shuffled on, chuckling to herself, as the red-faced guard was helped to his feet by his companions.

Maglin looked at Ba-betts, whose expression was vacant, perhaps with shock, and wondered what she had made of this episode, if anything. He wondered what *he* was to make of it. Was it just some trick of Maven's, or did the Touchstone hold some kind of witchi power – some way of telling what was, and what was not? He would have to give it some thought. He was certain of one thing – none but he and the Queen had seen the appearance and disappearance of the bluish mark on the stone. And the whole exchange had been so quiet that he doubted if anyone else could have heard much of it.

'Doolie!' He called across to where the Queen's maid waited, still staring wide-eyed towards the belt of trees where Maven had vanished. 'I think your mistress would wish to return to the Royal Pod.' The Queen sat, looking blankly into space, lost in some thought of her own.

Maglin walked slowly back to the Whipping Stone. He would make no remark. Nothing had happened, save that the Queen had dropped her bauble, and mad Maven had handed it back to her. He looked around at the crowd. 'The Muster is ended,' he announced, firmly. 'I shall summon the five who are to seek for Pegs, tomorrow at sunrise.'

Little-Marten beat out the Muster on the clavensticks, and the five tribes of the Various slowly began to disperse, amidst much talk. But Maglin quickly returned to his quarters, and spoke to nobody.

As the Ickri guards fixed their ropes to the Gondla, and prepared to haul it up into the Royal Oak, Ba-betts peered short-sightedly in the direction of the Rowdy-Dow tree.

'Doolie,' she said, curiously, 'what *is* that thing over there in that blighted tree?'

' 'Tis but the Woodpecker, my Lady,' replied Doolie. The Queen was obviously tired. Her mind was on a wander. The Gondla was raised jerkily to the little platform that projected from the Royal Pod, and Doolie helped her mistress out of the wicker chair and across to the entrance. The Queen's boots were too big for her and caused her to move clumsily. She *would* wear the outlandish objects, though.

Ba-betts turned before entering and once more looked across to the dead beech. 'It's a very *big* woodpecker,' she said. 'I wonder the archers don't shoot it.'

'I believes one or two 'ave tried,' said Doolie, drawing aside the painted oilcloth curtain.

'I feel great sorrow for that farmer,' said Ba-betts, as she lifted her blue gown and stepped carefully over the lip of the entranceway. 'I do hope they find his goat.'

Chapter Eight

It was one of those dreams, just below the surface of consciousness, where you know perfectly well that you're dreaming. She was wearing a white nightie and floating, like a moth, through space. Space was dark, dark blue, and around her were many other moths, all flying in the same direction – towards a bright light, far away. The bodies of the moths were covered in a fine downy fur. A huge red planet loomed out of the darkness – it was like a red shiny ball in space – and from around the far side of the planet, the white horse came flying. It joined the moths, but it flew faster than they did and was soon disappearing towards the bright light. She tried to keep up with it, but she couldn't.

'Come in,' Midge said, hearing the gentle knock on the door. 'I'm awake.' Uncle Brian had brought her some tea. She didn't really like tea, but she hadn't wanted to hurt his feelings the first time he had offered her some, and so she had said yes. Now she was stuck with it rather – although this morning she found that she was thirsty and actually quite glad to see the cup and saucer appearing round the door.

'Gosh,' she said, yawning, 'You look smart.' He did too, in an old-fashioned sort of way. He was wearing a tweed jacket and an open neck shirt, with a mustard-coloured jumper. The familiar yellow cords had been ditched in favour of a pair of brownish moleskin trousers.

'Should have told you about this last night,' said Uncle Brian, putting her cup of tea on the bedside cabinet. He had a scrap of tissue paper stuck to his neck, where he'd cut himself with his razor. Midge could smell aftershave. 'But you were off to bed so quickly that I didn't remember till after you'd gone. I'm going to pop into Taunton. It's market day – don't suppose you'd like to come, would you?'

'Um . . .'

'*Not* terribly interesting for you, I must admit – but you're welcome to join me if you'd like to.'

'Well, maybe not this time . . .'

'OK. Don't blame you. Bunch of old giffers talking about fatstock prices – not much fun, really. Actually I'm meeting an old friend, antiques dealer, for coffee. That's the real reason I'm going. I used to have an interest in antiques, a few years ago – well I still do of course – but I mean I used to *buy* a few bits here and there. Thought I might take it seriously at one stage, and that's how I met Frankie. We haven't seen each other for a while now, and so it seemed like a good idea to have a get together. You'll be OK, then? I'll be back for lunch, probably.' He was obviously itching to be away.

It *was* a bit much, thought Midge – although it

actually suited her purpose very well to be left alone. She thought she might string him along a bit.

'Well . . . I *might* come with you,' she said. 'What's he like?'

'Who?'

'Frankie.'

'Um, well, Frankie's a she actually. She's a woman, I mean. Francesca. Old friend, like I said.'

Hullo, thought Midge, *you're* a dark horse. Thinking this reminded her of the white horse up in the pig barn, and all that she hoped to do this day. She said, teasingly, 'Really, Uncle Brian, what are you *like*? I've a good mind to tag along and cramp your style.' She sipped her tea. It was too sweet. Maybe she would like it better with less sugar. 'But don't worry – I'll stay here. I've got lots to do – try and get my clothes sorted out for a start. Would you bring me back some post-cards? I keep meaning to write to people.'

'Consider it done, old thing,' said Uncle Brian, looking rather sheepish. 'I'll, um, see you later then.'

'OK.' She let him get to the doorway, and then said, 'Uncle Brian?' He turned. She pointed to her neck. 'Tissue paper,' she said.

Under the big old sink in the kitchen she found a plastic bucket and a sponge. There was a torch and various cleaning products, but Midge decided that washing up liquid would be all that she would need, so she put a big squirt of that into the bottom of the bucket. The tap by the side of the barn was useful, but hot water would be better, if she could carry some up there. She boiled a kettleful on the Rayburn, then, seeing how this only filled the bucket up a little way, she put on a second kettleful. She lifted the bucket experimentally. Two kettlefuls would be all that she could realistically carry – and besides, she didn't want to splash it around and perhaps burn herself. She dropped the sponge into the bucket and watched as it slowly sank into the steaming foam. The rest of her supplies were in a carrier bag, and she checked to see that she hadn't forgotten anything – food, a plastic bottle of water, a couple of tea towels, a small aerosol canister of iodine from the first aid box in the bathroom cabinet, some scissors, sticking plasters and a bandage, tightly sealed in its cellophane packaging. She wasn't sure that the plasters and bandage would be much use, but still. She picked up the bag and the bucket of hot water. Time to go.

Outside the pig-barn, she had a worrying premonition that the horse would no longer be there. Maybe it had all been a dream, or just her imagination. A large bird suddenly flew over her head, startling her as it landed on the tin roof of the building, its feet making a clattery scratching sound on the metal. She glanced up at it as she caught her breath – it was a magpie. How big it looked, so close, how white its breast and how bright the flashes of bluey-green on its wings and tail feathers in the morning sunlight. The bird took off again almost immediately, and flapped away in the direction of the Royal Forest. For some reason Midge felt reluctant to enter the barn straight away –

111

she was sure that disappointment, or anti-climax, awaited her – and so she watched the magpie as it flew lazily up to the woods and coasted in to land on one of the high branches. One for sorrow, she thought, automatically. The magpie had barely settled when it gave a sudden squawk, clearly audible even at that distance, and tumbled, fluttering, down through the branches. It disappeared into the darkness of the lower foliage. Midge watched and waited, but nothing more happened. The air was silent. Midge felt creepy around her neck and shoulders and she shuddered slightly. What was *that* all about? It was a relief to pick up her bag and bucket once more, and sidle through the doorway of the barn.

The horse was still there. Midge had been so sure that it wouldn't be, that the sight of the small animal lying, half covered by the potato sack, made her heart pound. Nothing had changed. The hay-raking machine was still jacked up at a crazy angle in the gloom, and in the foreground lay the winged horse, on its square blue mattress, pinpointed by stray shafts of light from the holes in the roof – like something on a theatre stage. All was quiet. Little flecks of dust floated in the beams of light, and the sharp smell of ammonia still lingered, mingled with musty straw and ancient tractor oil. Midge gently put down the bucket of hot water and the carrier bag, which crackled in the warm silence. The horse stirred at the sound, and lifted its head slightly. It turned to look at Midge, the soft dark eyes still haunted, but less agonized than before. For a few moments it gazed at her, as if remembering, then, with a sigh, the head was lowered once more. Midge crept forward.

'It's me,' she whispered. 'I said I'd come back, and I have.' The horse made no sound, but continued to watch her.

Midge bent down and gingerly tested the water in the plastic bucket. It was still hot. Good. She found the metal pail that she had used the previous day, and took it outside to swill it under the tap, leaving a little clean water in the bottom when she had finished. Back inside the barn she added hot water from the plastic bucket to the cold water in the metal one, until it was lukewarm. Then, picking up her soapy sponge, she walked across the makeshift mattress towards the horse, her feet sinking deep into the blue plastic sheeting. She kept one hand on the bucket to steady it, as she gently knelt beside the animal. Its eyes were open and it regarded her every move.

'I'm going to clean you up,' said Midge, quietly. 'If there's anything you don't like, or if you want me to stop, then let me know. I promise I won't do anything to harm you. I promise.'

There was still no sign from the horse, so Midge squeezed out the warm sponge and gently began to wash the caked-on muck and blood from the animal's body.

Its coat was whiter than had first appeared – as white as the magpie's breast, she thought – and the long mane and tail were a silvery blond colour. It was a beautiful creature. Absolutely beautiful. She took special care in washing the fine delicate face, changing the water as often as her limited supply would allow – and all the time the grave dark eyes watched her, gradually relaxing, occasionally half-closing as she continued her task. Finally there was just a little drop of water left. Midge had not yet examined the damaged wing, and she was hesitant to do so as it would mean unfolding the fragile membrane in order to see the wounds. She knelt with her hands on her knees, slowly rubbing her palms dry on the denim of her jeans, and looking into the deep brown eyes of the miraculous creature. A window of colours seemed to open up in her mind, as before, when the horse finally spoke.

My thanks, gentle maid. A kindness . . .

This time she did not put her hands to her ears at the strangeness of the sounds in her head. She accepted that she heard the voice in the same way that she would be able to hear the sound of her mother's voice, if she so wished – now, or at any time she chose. She accepted it in the same way that the sound of the magpie's startled squawk could still be conjured up, in her mind, though nearly an hour had gone by since the magpie had squawked its last.

'What should I do?' she whispered. 'Can I get you some food? Some water?'

A little water. Yes . . .

Midge rose and walked unsteadily across the soft mattress. She had been crouching down for a long time and her knees felt stiff. She took the plastic water bottle from the carrier bag and returned, unscrewing the top. Sitting by the horse, and leaning on one elbow close to the animal's head, she managed, little by little, to dribble water from the bottle into the sore dry mouth. More was spilt than was drunk, but of clean water, at least, there was no shortage.

Enough. I thank you. The horse laid its head down again, with a slight gasp.

The blue plastic sheet was by now quite wet, and Midge wondered how she could turn it over so that the horse was lying on the dry side. Perhaps she could use the potato sack.

'I'm going to see if I can make you more comfortable,' she said. She was able to manoeuvre the horse on to the sack without too much difficulty, and then slide it off the mattress and across to a fairly clean bit of concrete floor. Then she half-folded the plastic sheet, rolled it off the straw and hauled it out of the way. After rearranging the straw bedding and plumping it up a bit, she managed, rather awkwardly, to turn the sheet over and reposition it, dry side up, on top of the straw. Good. Soon she had pulled the sack, with the horse lying on top of it, back to the centre. Now it was clean, and lying on a dry bed.

Midge was still anxious to look at the wounds in the horse's wing. She had the iodine aerosol in her carrier bag, and knew that it would probably be good idea to use this as a guard against germs and infection – but also knew that it was likely to sting. How would she explain? To the horse she said, 'Listen. I have some medicine in my bag. Do you know what medicine is? It's to make you better – to help heal your wounds. And I think it *would* help them to heal, but it'll probably hurt a bit when I put it on. I think we should try it though.'

The horse raised its head with an effort, and tried to look over its shoulder, as if to see the wounds for itself. *I am not able to open my wing.* The horse painfully lowered its head again. *But if you have some physic . . . then I am willing that you use it.*

Midge found the little blue and white aerosol, pulled off the white plastic cap, and knelt by the horse's side once more, shaking the canister. With her free hand she very gently opened out the damaged wing. The horse groaned slightly. Where the velvety membrane had been pierced and torn by the metal spikes, there was angry-looking bruising and quite a lot of congealed blood. Midge wondered whether to try and bandage the wing somehow, but she couldn't really see what good it would do – neither could she see how she would go about such a task. She also wondered about trying to close the wound with sticking plaster – but again decided against it, for fear of doing more harm than good. Her first instinct – of trying to keep the wound from becoming infected, and letting nature do the healing – still seemed the safest way to go.

She shook the canister once more and said, 'I'm going to spray this on to your wing now. Be brave.' She pressed the little button and the horse immediately flinched at the sharp hiss of the aerosol. The wing muscles contracted instinctively, but Midge held on firmly, feeling the strange texture, the ridges of bone beneath the delicate membrane, warm between her fingers. She kept the aerosol button pressed down until the wound was obliterated by the orange colour of the iodine spray. The wing jerked in her grasp and the horse looked at her with panic in its eyes.

'Sh, sh,' said Midge, soothingly. 'That's it. All done.' She gently allowed the wing to fold once more, and leaned back, stroking the horse's neck as the animal gradually relaxed. 'I'm sorry to have frightened you,' she said. 'I know it stings at first, but I think it will help your wing to heal – it's happened to me lots of times.'

And your wings were healed?

'Well, no . . .' Midge began – then realized, with a little jolt of surprise, that the horse had been joking. It wasn't something that she had been prepared for. But then she hadn't been prepared for any of this. She laughed, and continued to stroke the animal's slim neck.

'Who *are* you?' she said. 'And . . . *what* are you? And how did you get here?'

The horse looked at her for a long time. The dark brown eyes – which were weighing her up, she felt – became troubled once again. Eventually, the words came through to her.

I am Pegs. And I am in your debt, maid – to the worth of my life. For I shall live, who would have surely died, were't not for the hands of a Gorji child. As to your other questions, I must hear more of you before I answer. Who are you? And what will you now do? Who of your kind knows of me?

'Nobody knows,' said Midge earnestly. 'I wouldn't tell. And I don't know what to do now – whatever you want me to do, I suppose. I just want to help you. My

117

name is Midge, and I'm staying here for a few weeks, with my uncle – and my cousins, when they arrive.'

Midge. And these others – they are of your tribe?

'Well, I don't know that they would be called a *tribe* exactly. They're part of my . . . family, I suppose. My uncle – that's my mother's brother – he owns this land. And my cousins are his children. But they're not here yet.'

The one who has charge of this land . . . your . . . ?

'Uncle.'

Your kinsman . . . uncle. He knows nothing of this?

'No. Nobody knows.'

It would be better, for me, that they did not. And I would ask you that favour. Tell no one of me. Pegs sighed and half closed his eyes. *Let me rest now, child . . . Midge . . . and let me think. There is much – much – to think on.*

'You live in the Royal Forest, don't you?' Midge blurted out, reluctant to go. The horse's eyes opened again with a startled look in them.

What do you know of the Royal Forest?

'Well, *I* call it the Royal Forest,' said Midge. 'It's just a name. I made it up.' She felt puzzled. 'Do you call it the Royal Forest too?' she said.

Pegs regarded her once more, and Midge thought that he might finally trust her, and tell her what she wanted to know. *You must ask me no more questions. Leave me now, to think.*

Midge got up, rather sadly, and collected together all her things – the bucket and sponge, the canister of iodine, her carrier bag. She stood, feeling aimless now, by the grey tractor near the entrance to the barn.

'Shall I come back later?' she said.

Tomorrow. Tomorrow, maid, we may speak again.

Tomorrow you may be gone, thought Midge, stepping from the dark humid barn and into the bright afternoon sunshine. You may be gone and this will all seem like a dream, and I shall never be able to tell anyone about it. Ever.

Uncle Brian was already back at the farm when Midge wandered in. She had seen his car in the yard, and had half-hidden the bucket and the sponge beside the old milk churn – thinking to avoid any awkward questions about what she had been doing. Her uncle was in the kitchen making a late lunch for himself – some cheese on toast and a pot of tea.

'Hullo, old thing,' he said as Midge dumped her carrier bag, the top casually folded over, onto a kitchen chair. 'What have you been up to? Want something to eat?'

'No, I've got a sandwich here, thanks,' said Midge. 'I made myself a picnic again, but I haven't eaten it yet.' She avoided the question of what she'd been doing by saying, 'How was Taunton? Did you meet your friend?'

'Frankie? Yes, we went to Clarke's for coffee and a bun. Good to see her again and catch up a bit. Doing pretty well for herself, I think. Tea? No? Well, this is about ready – shall we have lunch together?'

They sat at the big old table and Uncle Brian talked a little about the antiques business, and how he'd dabbled in it a few years ago. Midge gathered that

119

his dabblings had not resulted in any lasting success. She found herself gazing at the photograph of the child, which hung on the kitchen wall, and wondered who she was. She was about to ask, when another thought that had been nagging at her suddenly surfaced.

'Uncle Brian,' she said, 'you know you were saying that you were selling some land? Which land is it? I mean which bit?'

'Oh, a couple of fields,' said Uncle Brian. 'As agricultural land it's not worth all that much – I've been letting it out as grass keep for years now to a neighbouring farm. But as *building* land of course, it's worth much more. Especially when you're looking at a whole new housing development – maybe sixty or seventy houses. I've had a very good offer from the building firm. We're just waiting for final planning permission – and then it'll be all systems go. It's the land – can't see it from here – at the far end of the woods up on the hill. The Wild Wood, remember? Plus the wood itself, of course. Most of it anyway.'

'You're selling the Royal – I mean the *wood*?' said Midge, horrified.

'Yes,' said Uncle Brian, catching a piece of melted cheese as it dripped from his toast, 'and then, as they say, our troubles will be over. Good eh?'

Chapter Nine

As the evening sky grew dark above the Royal Forest, Maglin met once again with the five he had chosen to send out into the Gorji lands. He still had deep misgivings about the wisdom of such an action, but could see no way out of it. The vote had been taken before the entire Muster, and at his own instigation. He had gambled that the vote would be against searching for the Naiad horse, and he had lost. The chosen ones had been informed at sunrise, had then been briefed as to what their course of action should be, in his opinion, and given the day in order to make their preparations. Now the five were met, as had been arranged, beneath the Rowdy-Dow tree.

Maglin left his pod, and walked across the dark clearing towards the dead beech. He had spent some sleepless hours the previous night deciding upon who should go from the volunteers. After much reflection, he had decided to pick the best of those who were unwed. From the Ickri, he had chosen Grissel – a good archer, wild perhaps, as all of Scurl's followers were apt be, but steadier than Benzo and the rest. Tod of the Wisp he had chosen as being the only volunteer of that tribe who was without wife or family. Spindra, the Naiad who had bred Pegs would have been hard to gainsay, and, besides, who knew the horse better than he? From the Tinklers he had chosen Pank, largely because the little tinsy-smith was one of the few of that tribe whose name he knew, and from the Troggles, after private consultation with Tadgemole, he had picked Lumst – a miner of reliable character and some intelligence, according to his tribe leader. Grissel, Tod, Spindra, Pank and Lumst. He hoped that their names would not need to be remembered in sorrow.

It was an awkward group who waited beneath the Rowdy-Dow tree, watching Maglin as he approached through the deepening gloom. Grissel stood alone, annoyed that none of his companions had been chosen for this venture. What was he, an Ickri archer, doing in the company of Tinklers and Troggles? He had imagined a bold and daring foray into Gorji lands with his brothers at his side. If he had known that *this* was to be the outcome of his spirited gesture, then he would have kept his hand on his bow, like Aken and his crew of poltroons, and let the horse go hang.

Tod and Spindra stood and conversed softly together. They both felt that neither the Ickri, nor the cave-dwellers should have been chosen for this task. Whilst not friends exactly, they each respected the other's right to be here – Spindra as knowing the horse better than any, and Tod as one who ventured into the Gorji lands almost nightly, albeit close to the safety of the forest. Lumst and Pank, the Troggle and the Tinkler, were long acquainted and therefore stood comfortably with one another – each glad to have a friend for company, but neither used to being at close quarters with members of the upper tribes.

Maglin, with his experienced eye, saw how things were as he approached, and wondered whether his decision to send a member of each tribe had been a wise one. The alternative would have been to pick five of his own Ickri archers, and neither he nor the Various could readily afford to lose such providers. He tackled the problem, as he tackled most problems, instantly and directly.

'Come now,' he said. 'If you would be a company, then a company you must decide to be. 'Tis no good, Grissel, to stand alone and sulk for the want of better fellows. What would 'ee? That I should send five archers that never set foot from the forest? Who understands the Naiad horse better than Spindra? Who more used to being out after moonrise than Lumst and Pank? Who more familiar with the ways of the Gorji than Tod o' the Wisp? You'll find, all of 'ee, that I have chosen fairly, and as well as I know how. Put faith in each other then, and know that you be all here to a purpose. Come, draw close together, and listen to me.' Four out of the five looked at each other, shyly, and shuffled in a little closer, but Grissel still kept slightly aloof.

'We know,' said Maglin, 'that Pegs was bound for the Far Woods on t'other side of this vale. I see no reason why he would have done other than fly there direct – over that Gorji settlement that lies between. If we reckon that he were able to explore that forest and make his return, then he would have flown back direct in that line. Do 'ee agree, Spindra?'

'I do,' said Spindra. ' 'E were a good flyer, but 'e 'ad no more strength than 'e would've needed – none to throw away, thass for certain. I take it 'tis a good long way, there and back, and I don't believe 'e could 'ave done it in one go. If 'e'd reached t'other side, then 'e would stop a bit for sure, in the Gorji forest, before trying journey home – and would surely have flew the shortest line 'e could.'

'Then lost, dead or captured, we can but reckon Pegs to be somewhere along that line,' said Maglin. 'You must follow that line as you seek for him – and that means passing through, and searching, the Gorji settlement – and especially the storehouses, or "barns" as the Gorji do call them. 'Tis a dangerous task, be in no doubt of it. There may be hounds, or any manner of beasts there – and in the Far Woods, should 'ee get so far, there may be brocks and renards. Stay close together, learn what may be learned, and come back alive. Grissel has his bow, but what do the rest carry for arms?'

Lumst and Pank drew forth tinsy daggers from their belts. As implements for teasing walnuts from their shells they would have served admirably – as weapons they looked hopelessly inadequate. Maglin sighed, and Grissel looked contemptuous. Spindra carried a small wooden club, a truncheon of dark seasoned oak. Tod had some large Gorji object, picked up on a night-fishing expedition. It had several prongs and was made of rot-metal. Tod had spliced a new handle to it, thus fashioning for himself a kind of trident. He used it as an eel-spear.

Maglin's heart sank within him at this pitiful display, though what more he could have expected, he didn't know. These were farmers and fishers, not hunter-warriors. He could only encourage them and wish them speed.

'Let us hope that you have no need of these things,' he said – which sounded more ambiguous than he had intended. 'Tod, you will lead the company out through the North Wood and across such ground as may be familiar to you. Pank and Lumst, you will use your eyes to help the company through the darkness. Spindra, you will advise on the likely actions of Pegs. And Grissel – you will act as defender where there may be danger.'

Grissel looked even more sour and discontented than he had done previously. So, he was to have the honour of protecting these hobbledehoys from whatever may come. Well so be it. But, he thought secretly, if they were to be pursued by packs of brocks and renards and Gorji hounds, then it would be look out all and each for himself. Then let them see, Tod and Spindra, how inferior it were to be wingless. Fishers and farmers! What did they know? And as for the others, the Troggle and the Tinkler, he felt ashamed to be in their company, the miserable paupers. Pank and Lumst! Names to hawk up and spit on the earth. He was an Ickri! Where were his brothers?

Maglin led the search party across the now moonlit clearing, to the inner fringe of the North Wood. Many of the Various tribespeople had turned out to watch them go, and there were well-wishers standing around in small groups to offer encouragement and parting advice as the company passed by.

'Don't 'ee worry, Spindra. You'll find 'un.'

'Bring us back a gurt eel, Tod, while you'm about it.'

'What be doing up so late, Pank? 'Tis past thy bedtime!'

And so on. Only Grissel kept his head down, and acknowledged nobody, avoiding the faces of Scurl and his companions lest they be laughing at him.

The Ickri General stopped under the trees of North Wood and wished them all speed. 'Now mind what I say,' he told them. 'Come back alive. There be no life worth risking for that of a horse – no matter what Spindra may think.' Spindra did indeed think differently, but had the sense not to say so.

At the outer edge of North Wood, having made passage through one of the emergency wicker tunnels woven through the thick briars, the five cautiously emerged into the open and surveyed the dark land that stretched out beneath them. The moon shone through a hazy sky, and far below they could see a thick carpet of mist lying upon the silent wetlands. The rows of pollarded willow trees protruded from the bed of fog, like shock-headed creatures rising from a steamy swamp.

Eerie and strange it seemed, to all but Tod who was well acquainted with such sights. A perfect night for fishing, it would be, and no doubt some of his tribe were already preparing to take advantage of it. With wicker eel traps, clotting rods and night lines, the Wisp would be silently making their way down through the East Wood, to where the rhynes and ditches came closest to the outer belt of trees, and looking forward to a good catch under cover of the summer mist. And here was he, fishing not for eels, but for horses. A strange errand indeed.

Moonlight was more natural than sunlight to Pank and Lumst, yet never had they seen such a sight as this. It was their first venture from the confines of the forest and they hung close together, gazing about them in nervous wonder. Spindra was glad at last to be finally searching for Pegs – he was eager to be off, and Tod had to catch him by the sleeve in order to give pause whilst he surveyed the land. Grissel was the most apprehensive. This was all unfamiliar territory to him – the treetops in daylight were his natural habitat, not the open ground by night. He felt vulnerable. Some of his former bravado and disdain began to waver, and for the time being he was glad to let the fisher Wisp take the lead.

Tod waited and watched. Satisfied at last that all was safe and quiet, he cautiously moved off down the hill. Spindra fell in directly behind him. Lumst and Pank walked parallel to each other, a few feet apart and slightly behind Spindra. Grissel brought up the rear and had already unslung his bow. He turned from left to right as he walked, and occasionally glanced behind him. The white scut of a disappearing rabbit caught his attention, and he began to lose some of his nervousness. A coney! These were a rarity indeed inside the forest – most of them having been hunted down long ago – but now that his eyes were growing more used to the darkness, he could see that there were quite a few of them on the hillside. Maybe he could shoot one and pick it up on the way back. That would be one in the eye for Scurl – and Aken for that matter. He looked about him. There was nothing within easy range, and he was loth to become too sidetracked at this early stage. The others had already moved quite a little way ahead. He spread his wings and launched himself gently from the hillside, in order to catch up. He had originally intended to land at the rear of the company and take up his former position, but at the last minute he flapped a couple of times, flew over the heads of the other four, and alighted directly in front of Tod – nearly catching a spear between his shoulder blades for his folly. Tod was furious.

'What bist playing at, Grissel?' he hissed. 'Do 'ee want to get theeself skewered?'

Grissel was unused to such treatment – from a Wisp moreover – but seeing the look on Tod's face he contented himself with a 'Garn with 'ee, fisher. I were only taking a stretch. You'm as jumpsy as a cricket.' He allowed the others to pass him, and resumed his position as rearguard.

'Hemmed fool,' muttered Tod, and pressed on.

On the side of the hill and to their far left, perhaps a hundred yards distant, lay a small outbuilding – whitish in the hazy moonlight. Lumst, who noticed it first, tapped Spindra on the shoulder and pointed. Spindra in turn whispered, 'Tod,' and all five paused to regard the shabby looking concrete barn. Tod spoke quietly to Spindra.

'What say you? Could the horse be there?'

Spindra moved down the slope a little more and peered towards the distant building. He could just make out the dark opening of the doorway. The others joined him.

Spindra shook his head and whispered, 'No. Don't make no sense for him to be in there. See, he could get in and out o' that easy enough. Too close to home for him to stop there, anyways. No, he be further away than that, I reckon.'

The others were inclined to agree. It would be too easy, and too much to hope for, to find Pegs so close to home. They moved on.

Eventually they came to a sheep gate that led into a field of thistles, and here they rested, crouching beside the low drystone wall that separated the field from the long steep slope back towards the forest. Tod climbed cautiously up onto the ancient metal gate to get a better view of the farm buildings in the distance. He could see one dim light shining from an upper window. The rest of the buildings were dark. As he was about to descend from the gate, some movement caught his eye. It was on the other side of the wall, about fifty yards to his right. Tod leaned over the gate and looked along the line of rough stone. Trotting along the edge of the field, keeping close to the wall, was a big fox. Thin wisps of low mist hung by the wall, turning the fox into a ghostly figure as it passed through the swirls of pale vapour. It was heading straight for the sheep-gate.

'Renard!' hissed Tod, scrambling down from the gate, as quickly and quietly as he could. He joined Grissel and Lumst who instantly huddled behind the wall to the right of the gate. On the left side were Pank and Spindra. Tod dropped down on one knee, the only one among them who was in a position to run if need be. The others sat hunched with their knees by their chins, heads down. Grissel was further hampered by his wings, which were pressed uncomfortably into an awkward position against the wall. His bow was in his hand, but he had dropped the arrow he was holding, and his quiver was tucked behind him. He was used to being the hunter, not the hunted, and the situation had caught him unprepared. Listening intently, with pounding hearts, they waited for the renard to come.

They had expected that the great animal would continue along the other side of the wall, and, with luck, would pass by the sheep-gate also – but a slight scrabbling noise, the light tap of claw on stone, told them that the dreaded monster had jumped up on to the wall, not two yards along from where they crouched. They could hear it, high above them, panting slightly as it shifted its stance. Pank, from his position behind Spindra, was able to raise his eyes and see the beast, as it stood on the rough stone wall, seeming to fill the moonlit sky. It was his first sight of such a creature, and the thing was huge – almost as high at the shoulder as he, Pank, was tall. It was as big as one of Spindra's horses. The great vulpine jaws opened in a horrible grinning yawn, silhouetted against the filtered moon, as it turned its head to look up the hill towards the forest. It sniffed the air a few times and then jumped lightly from the wall, its pale shadow passing over their heads. The rest of the wood-landers were then able to see the beast, as it landed on the dewy grass, just a few feet away from them. Sniffing the air once more, the great dog-fox began to amble casually up the slope in the direction of the forest. It paused to snuffle at the ground, half-turned as it picked up another scent – then looked up, and stiffened. It had seen them. Motionless it stood, hypnotic, sinister, and graceful – the very stuff of all their nightmares. Its merciless yellow eyes fixed upon the small cowering figures, its cool gaze assuring them

that their fate was now inescapable, as the dark-tipped ears slowly flattened on the handsome, terrifying, head.

Tod was first to his feet. He grasped his eel spear and advanced a couple of paces – holding the weapon in front of him, threateningly, desperately. The big fox raised its hackles, and the huge jaws drew back in a silent snarl.

'You better get an arrow to that bow smartish, Grissel, for I shan't hold 'un long with this thing!' yelled Tod. But Grissel was still scrabbling to his feet, cursing, his wings catching in the crevices of the wall and his bow tangled round one of his legs.

'Quick!' roared Lumst, and at the same time Spindra shouted, 'What bist doing of Grissel?' and flung his club at the beast, narrowly missing its head. At the sudden loud chorus of apparently human voices, the fox, towering over the strange little creatures as it did, seemed confused. It flinched at the missile hurled by Spindra, and backed away. These were no rabbits or chickens that it had stumbled across. A sharp stone in the ribs, thrown in terror by little Pank, was all the convincing it finally needed. The fox continued to sidle away up the hill, pursued by shouts, curses, and further lumps of loose stone which were lying around and subsequently flung by Pank and Lumst – so that by the time Grissel had finally notched an arrow to his bow it was clear that the dog fox was unlikely to be a further threat to them. It had slunk off into the shadows. There was easier meat to be had.

In the little pig-barn on the hill, Pegs raised his head and listened in the darkness. He had heard distant voices – shouts. Spindra's voice, he was sure, had been among them. Were the Various abroad then? Had they left the forest? He listened again, for a while, but heard no more. Perhaps they were out looking for him. There was nothing he could do – he had not yet the strength to stand. Lowering his head once more, he half-closed his eyes. Then, after another minute or so, he heard a slight panting sound and became aware of a shadow appearing in the narrow frame of the doorway. Pegs looked up. It was a renard – a full-grown dog-fox – and such a beast as might consider a defenceless and wounded animal to be ready prey. The red hunter cautiously sniffed the air inside the barn. Blood. The smell of blood was in this place. It slunk forward a pace or two, crouching slightly as it caught sight of the stricken creature lying there, familiar, yet unfamiliar, injured, and – alone? Yes, alone, unprotected, helpless, exposed. The fox edged forward a little more, its courage now returning, and licked the drool from its jaws.

Good evening, Renard. How now, old friend? The fox jumped back with a shrill yelp, shaking its head as though there were a bee in its ear. It turned and fled through the gap in the doorway. It had had quite enough for one night.

The searchers were quietly jubilant at their success in routing the fox.

'Did 'ee see the size of it?' whispered little Pank, awestruck at his own audacity in throwing a stone at the great red beast of legend. 'I could have walked upright beneath his belly, almost!'

'Ah, but 'twas Tod who had 'un on the go!' said Spindra in admiration. 'Old Renard didn't much like the look of thy gurt fork, Tod – and thass the truth.'

'Well, perhaps so,' said Tod, modestly, 'but I reckon

thy gurt stick whizzing past 'is old lug'oles didn't make 'un feel too bold neither.'

'But what happened to thee, Grissel?' said Spindra. 'Did 'ee get stuck?'

'Caught a wing in that hemmed wall,' muttered Grissel, shamefacedly, 'otherwise I'd have had 'un.'

'Ah, that's right,' said Lumst. 'A couple arrows would've just about finished him off, I believe.'

'Well, I reckon we've survived about the worst that could happen,' said Tod. 'If we can best a renard then I ain't too worried about much else. Only thing that frightens me more'n a renard is a gurt pike – and we shan't be seeing many of they tonight. Let's move on.'

They climbed through the bars of the sheep gate and began to make their way across the misty field, walking in the same formation as before, their confidence and trust in one another grown mightily.

Grissel was feeling rather humbled as he walked at the rear, his bow now at the ready. The bravery of Tod and Spindra had impressed him – and even the cave-dwellers had more than stood their ground. They could have easily scattered in all directions, leaving him, still struggling, to face the renard alone. He was supposed to be their protector, not they his. He resolved to be more alert from now on.

They had reached the gate, at the far end of the thistle field, which led into the cobbled yard of Mill Farm. None of them had ever been so close to a Gorji dwelling before. They crept among the thistles and clumps of camomile that grew around the gateposts, and peeped fearfully through the lower bars of the gate at the silent yard beyond. Directly opposite them loomed the dark bulk of the main building, fronted by a balustrade wall. An ancient rusty plough stood, abandoned and overgrown with nettles and coarse grass, close to the other side of the gate. After some whispered consultations, the five woodlanders crawled beneath the gate and scuttled over the deeply rutted ground, to hide themselves in the tangle of weeds beneath the plough.

'Spick it!' muttered Lumst. 'Hemmed nettles.' He sucked the inside of his wrist. Peering through the rusted spokes of one of the plough's iron wheels, they now had a clear view down the length of the untidy farmyard – the line of rickety outbuildings being to their left, and the old farmhouse rising high above them on their right.

The first of the outbuildings was open-sided, and seemed to be crammed with more derelict machinery. There was no reason to suppose that Pegs might be in there – but what reason was there to suppose that Pegs was anywhere here at all? Spindra, for one, was beginning to have doubts about this whole expedition. He had been eager to come, just to be doing something other than waiting – but now, knowing the horse as he did . . . well, it seemed so unlikely that the animal could be behind one of these doors. It didn't feel right.

Tod didn't hold out any great hope of finding Pegs in this fearful place either, but he felt that Maglin had been right in supposing that the Naiad horse would be *somewhere* along the line between the Royal Forest and the Gorji woods on the other side of the wetland, and if he wasn't here, then so much the better. He would far rather be searching the wetlands and the forests than a Gorji settlement. The quicker they were away from here the happier he would be – but in the meantime there was work to do. Tod looked up at the darkened farmhouse, wondering if they could get in there.

'Bide here, a bit,' he whispered to the others, laying his eel spear aside. 'I'll take a glim.' He crept out from under the plough, waited a few moments, then, crouching low, he scuttled over to the balustrade wall in front of the house. He moved softly along the moonlit shadow of the wall, turned the corner where the front path to the house began, and disappeared from view.

The others watched and waited. Grissel was once again struck by the fearlessness of the little fisher. He himself was feeling far from confident. The knot in his stomach was a sensation he had never known before – for in the Royal Forest there was nothing for an Ickri hunter to fear. He also felt, for the first time, encumbered by his wings. He wasn't built for crouching beneath rot-metal Gorji contraptions, confined and hindered in a place where sudden danger might present itself.

Lumst and Pank were both caught up in the moment, straining their eyes for the reappearance of Tod – nervous, certainly, but alert and excited also. They had believed the fisher when he had said that the fox would probably be the worst thing that could happen to them – his experience of the outside world was far greater than theirs. And hadn't they seen that old devil off?

All had their eyes fixed on the place where Tod had disappeared, and so they didn't notice him as he returned by a different route, slipping between the balustrade pillars and dropping into the shadows. Consequently he was almost upon them before they saw him, and his arrival made them jump.

'Here's a strange business,' Tod said softly, as he squeezed in amongst the others. 'There's two doors in one. See . . .' he looked for words to describe what he had seen '. . . there's a gurt *big* door, big black 'un, made o' wood, as 'd seem about right for a Gorji giant to get through, and then, right at the bottom, there's a *little* door – made o' some other stuff, I dunno what – that don't make no sense at all. A Gorji newborn couldn't hardly get through there – but *we* could. 'Tis most puzzling – almost like it were put there for us. I gave it a push, and it swung open right enough, so I reckon 'tis best I go and have a proper look inside. You bide here – no sense in us all trying to get in – and I'll go back.'

'No, hold,' said Grissel. He was beginning to feel that his role as supposed guardian of the group was looking like a sham. What was he to say to his captain upon his return? 'Tod did all the work, whilst I kept in hiding'? He could picture the sneer on Benzo's face. It was time to show some mettle. 'I'll come with 'ee,' he said. 'Thee doesn't know what might lurk in there.'

137

Tod regarded Grissel doubtfully. 'I ain't so sure thee'd get through the door, wi' those wings,' he said.

'Well, you casn't go alone,' said Spindra. 'What if you didn't come back? How long should us wait? 'Tis safer you have company.'

'Tell 'ee what, then,' said Tod. 'Let's get this over and done. I'll take smallest with me – that's Pank here – and us two'll look round the inside. The rest of 'ee can search these byres, or whatever they be, and we'll meet back here when we've done. How's that?' All were agreed. The sooner they could move on, the better. 'Right then, Pank, you come wi' me,' said Tod, and the two small figures ran softly over to the shadow of the balustrade wall and quickly rounded the corner.

Grissel, Spindra and Lumst looked across at the line of moonlit outbuildings which were to be their responsibility. 'We'd as well start this end and work along 'em,' said Grissel.

'Perhaps I should run along to the furthest one and search there,' said Lumst. 'Then we'd meet in the middle. 'Twould be quicker.'

This seemed a good idea, so it was agreed upon. The three crept cautiously from their hiding place and moved quickly over the weed-strewn yard to the corner of the open-sided barn. From here Lumst ran past the row of stable doors until he reached the last one, a shambling affair, the bottom half of which hung partly open on its sagging hinges. He peered nervously into the dark interior and whispered, 'Pegs?'

In the meantime, Tod was already on the other side of

138

the 'little door' he had found – a redundant cat flap – and was holding it open for Pank to climb through. All was black as pitch in the hallway of the farmhouse, and the two stood listening for a few moments, taking in the strange smell of the Gorji dwelling, and wondering where to begin. A sudden groan, deep and horribly loud, caused them to shrink back in fright against the foot of the heavy oak front door. There was something there, in the darkness, just ahead of them! Motionless, with thumping hearts, they waited for whatever evil was about to befall them. The low breathy sound of some great animal seemed to fill the cavernous space around them. Another deep rattling groan caused the two intruders to press their backs even harder against the door. But gradually their horrified eyes grew a little more accustomed to the dark, and, although the strange noises continued, they could sense that there was no immediate danger of attack. Whatever this monster was, it appeared to be asleep. Creeping forward very slowly, Tod was gradually able to identify the dark shape. It was a Gorji hound, as he might have guessed, lying on its side, lost in dreams at the foot of some steeply rising wooden construction.

Backing away again, Tod leaned towards Pank and whispered, ' 'Tis a gurt black hound. Sleeping.'

Pank was horribly frightened and began to lose heart. 'Let's be gone,' he said, shivering. 'Pegs ain't here.'

But Tod was determined to make sure. 'We'll just have a glim,' he said. ' 'Twon't take us long.' He moved to his left and pushed gently at a large painted door which swung silently open. Here was a great chamber, full of looming shapes and shadows, but helpfully illuminated, in part at least, by the moon which shone through an uncovered window.

They had found their way into the giants' kitchen, and although they had no word for this, or indeed for most of the objects that surrounded them, they were able to make some inward guesses as to purpose. The warmth of the Rayburn, with its unmistakable smell of ash and wood-smoke, spoke of cooking – and the forest of chair and table legs, through which they crept, were presumably things for the giants to sit upon. The vegetable rack seemed self-explanatory, if underemployed, containing as it did but a single potato. It was less easy to fathom the purpose of the waste-bin, however, as this appeared to be filled with a mixture of both the edible and inedible. The only sound to disturb the heavy warmth of the atmosphere was a fast unfamiliar ticking, and they tracked the source of this to a luminous object, perched upon a high shelf. They found its yellowy-green glow curious and attractive, but as to its possible use they were defeated.

Beneath the strange bulk of the chipped porcelain sink, they discovered a small curtain – vaguely reminiscent of the oilcloths used by the Ickri to cover the entranceways of their pods. Tod lifted the hem of this – more out of curiosity than with any conscious notion of searching for Pegs – and lowered his head to see what might be under there. Pank looked on nervously.

* * *

In the farmyard, the other three woodlanders were
making steady, though fruitless, progress. Grissel and
Spindra had clambered over, and peered under, the
piled up machinery in the open sided barn, and were
now stumbling around amongst the broken bales of
musty hay that half filled the first of the stables. The
dust made Grissel sneeze, and Spindra was inclined to
tell the Ickri to wait outside. He was frightened that
Grissel's muffled snorts might wake someone – or
something.

Lumst had poked around in the stable at the
furthest end of the row. It stank of oily liquids – black
and greasy substances – and he was glad enough to
leave. He had then managed to gain entrance to the
next building by crawling under a damaged bottom
section of the bolted door. Here were sacks of reeking
white powders, long abandoned, together with a
variety of coloured metal drums, tangled rolls of
unfathomable tubing, and tarry wooden posts. A
rickety wicker basket, close to collapse, stood in the
middle of the gently sloping stone floor. It contained
a shabby coverlet, thickly coated with animal hair, and
there was a strong, musky smell about it – unfamiliar
and unpleasant. Pegs was not in this place, and never
had been. It was time to move on.

Lumst was used to foraging around in the darkness
– albeit under less trying circumstances. His eyes were
sharp, and he could see well enough for his purpose.
But there was one abroad that night whose eyes, and
ears, were sharper still. As the Troggle crawled back

under the broken door of the stable, thinking to move on to the next, he caught a whiff of the same musky smell that had lingered around the basket. He looked up, and his breath was instantly snatched away from him – chills of terror tightening his scalp. He was face to face with a huge animal, a frightful, shock-haired, unearthly thing, whose ferocious gaze made his insides quake and churn beyond all control. The creature seemed to swell up to an impossible size, blotting out the entire world, its coarse fur standing on end like the spines on a hotchi-witchi.

He was aware of the sinister flexing movement of the great sable paws – and of the deadly claws, curved and vicious, testing their grip on the rough cobbles. He was aware of the tension in the broad shoulder muscles, and of the massive broom of a tail flicking and lashing as the beast gathered itself into a crouch – aware also of the scars on the flat ugly head that sank slowly toward the earth, lower and lower, till the bristling grey muzzle was almost touching the paws. But it was the eyes of the beast that petrified him, that held him to the spot – those deep yellow eyes, malicious and horrifying. He was paralysed completely – fixed in amber. There could be no turning away from that fearful glare. And then from somewhere deep within the belly of the monster, he heard a chilling sound, a low winding moan. Rising up as from a dark pit it came, louder and closer, until at last the great jaws split apart and a terrible shriek burst upon the still night air, harsh and raw and final. There was no escape.

Tojo – the Assassin – the scourge of all living things

that dared cross his path, burned with fury. The brutish and murderous farm cat was returning from a visit to the cider barn where he had thought to call upon his harem of queens. Tonight the doors had been barred, however, and his purpose had been thwarted. His vicious temperament was consequently at its worst. In outrage, he had retreated to his sanctum, only to find that his right of way here was also obstructed – not by a heavy door, against which even he was impotent, but by some crawling creature, a two-legged rat, occupying and defiling his jealously guarded domain.

Lumst had no chance. The great tom-cat was without fear, and wholly aggressive. The cowardly blood of foxes did not run in Tojo's veins – nor did the quality of mercy. He launched himself at the doomed intruder who dared block his way. The noise was dreadful. There was not a living creature for a quarter of a mile that didn't wake in fright at the sound of Tojo, wreaking his vengeance beneath the hazy summer moon – his blood-curdling yowl, and the cries of his victim, causing innocent sleepers, animal and human, to start up, wide-eyed, from the jagged shards of their broken dreams.

Grissel and Spindra, horrified at the ferocious sound of the attack, quickly realized that it was Lumst who was the likely victim. Quaking with terror, they forced themselves to peer around the door of the stable. They were in time to see a monstrous animal, a creature such as they could never have imagined, dragging the lifeless form of its prey towards the end of the row of outbuildings. The thing paused for a moment and turned, instinctively looking in their direction – the pale moon momentarily reflected in its baleful glare. Unspeakable evil seemed held in that brief look. Then a light appeared in the dwelling opposite and the animal vanished.

Tojo had no wish to come under investigation in a confined space. It had happened before when he had caught a bantam cockerel, and had been cornered in his den, taking a blow across the back from a yard-broom as a consequence. There were other places, more secluded, where he could go. He disappeared into the night, still emitting a low siren wail from his heavily burdened jaws.

Grissel, to his credit, and notwithstanding the horror of what he had seen, was prepared to give chase. He hastily began to unsling his bow. At that moment however, the front door of the farmhouse opened and a Gorji giant emerged, waving a beam of light. The light cut through the night in the direction of the fleeing assassin. A hound barked.

Grissel instantly backed towards the stable door, bumping into Spindra who was just behind him. They stumbled in a panic back into the darkness of the stable, quickly burying themselves beneath the hay. Grissel tried to choke back a sneeze.

When the peaceful silence of the kitchen was suddenly rent by Tojo's first vengeful yowl, Pank instinctively grabbed at Tod's shoulder in fright. The two looked frantically about them, for it seemed in that instant that they themselves were under attack. As the terrible noise increased, they blundered through the awkward jumble of chair and table legs in an attempt to gain the hallway once more and escape. However, the caterwauling was so sustained that the sleeping hound had been awakened. It staggered to its feet with a low bark, and walked stiffly over to the front door. It sniffed the cat flap, turned its head to face the staircase, and barked again. The woodlanders' escape route was blocked, and they backed silently into the kitchen once more, trapped and panic stricken. Where could they hide?

Gorji voices could now be heard, and heavy feet began to descend the wooden staircase. A child's voice – 'What is it Uncle Brian? What's happening?' Then the deeper tones of a man, angry and loud – 'I'll tell you what's happening – it's that damn cat, again. Tojo is what's happening – and if he has got hold of another of my bantams, then he may catch a brick behind the ear. Where's the torch? Any idea?' The heavy footsteps had reached the bottom of the stairs.

'Under the sink.'

'Under the *sink*? What the devil's it doing there? All *right*, Phoebe! Shut *up*! See if you can find it, will you, Midge, while I get my wellies on.'

The kitchen was suddenly flooded with light and the sound of bare feet came padding across the red brick floor. Beneath the sink, Tod and Pank crouched fearfully among the strange-smelling containers. The small curtain was lifted and a great pale arm reached in, fumbling around their hiding place. Pank, head low, shivering with fright, flinched as the groping

145

fingers of the Gorji chi' touched his shoulder. He was discovered! The hand brushed the outside of his cloth jerkin – he could feel the slight pressure of knuckles against his ribs.

'Got it!' said the child's voice – and the curtain was lowered once again. The light footsteps crossed the room once more, and the man spoke again from the hallway.

'Well done. Let's see what's going on.'

Grissel and Spindra raised their heads from the musty smelling hay and tried to interpret what was happening outside from the noises they could hear. The booted footsteps of the giant had disappeared at the far end of the buildings. Presently they heard his voice shouting as he returned.

'Well, Tojo's gone. Lord knows where. No point in running around in the dark looking for him, that's for certain. Come on, Phoebe. Phoebe! Come *on*! There's nothing down there for you. *Now* what's she up to? Oh, all right then, let's have a look.'

Phoebe was snuffling her way along the line of stables. The old spaniel may have been going deaf, but her nose was as good as ever – and it was picking up all sorts of strange signals. Grissel and Spindra buried themselves in the hay once more as the click and scratch of the hound's claws on the exposed cobbles drew closer, and the insistent snuffling grew louder. Presently the dog entered the stable where they lay. They could hear it sniffing the floor where they had lately been standing. Grissel's eyes were streaming. He

146

held his nose and fought back the sneeze rising within him. The resonant clump of rubber boots, and the searching beam of light, told the fugitives that the Gorji had now arrived.

'See?' said the loud voice, letting the light play around the mildewed walls. 'Nothing here. It's empty, you daft old thing. Come on then, daftie. Let's go.' His voice boomed in the shadowy confines of the stable.

Phoebe was unconvinced. She had been a half-decent gun dog in her day, and she still knew a thing or two. Raising her head towards the mess of hay piled high at the back of the stable, she approached it, snuffling softly. She paused, moved slightly to her right, then returned to her original position. Another snuffle. Yes, she knew. She pushed her head deep into the hay.

The soft muzzle came thrusting unerringly towards where Grissel lay hidden. The shock was so great that the Ickri let go of his nose in an attempt to defend himself – and instantly sneezed. Phoebe opened her mouth to give a triumphant bark, but then she sneezed as well. And again. And again. She withdrew her head from the dusty hay, sneezed once more, and looked up at Uncle Brian, expectantly. The man laughed.

'You *silly* old sausage,' he said. 'Now look at the state of you. Come on, then. Told you there was nothing there.'

Grissel and Spindra were lucky. There was little of the fox's predatory instinct in Phoebe – and none of Tojo's malevolence. She was simply curious – and she had been right. There *was* something there. The fact that her master had chosen to let it be was of no consequence. She had done her job. She looked towards the pile of hay once more, gave a low woof, and then followed the man contentedly as he clumped back across the yard towards the farmhouse doorway where the girl still waited, framed in the light and shivering slightly in the cool night air.

An hour later, when all seemed quiet and their beating hearts had calmed a little, Grissel and Spindra emerged from their hiding place and crept once more to the stable door. The two were horribly shocked at the fate of poor Lumst, and stood uncertainly in the doorway, wondering what they should do.

'We must look for him,' said Grissel. 'He may yet be alive.'

But the words sounded hollow and hopeless, and Spindra replied, 'No. Lumst has gone. 'Tis no use to go after him. We should end up the same way.'

'Then we must wait for the others, as we planned,' said Grissel. There seemed little else they could do, and so, having quickly glanced about the farmyard, they ran across the cobbles to the plough once more and crawled beneath it. Here, to their surprise, they found Tod and Pank already hiding amongst the weeds. The Wisp and the Tinkler had waited in the farmhouse kitchen until they judged the hound to be asleep once more – which hadn't taken all that long – and then exited by the little door as quickly and quietly as they could, their nerves in tatters. To add to their troubles, Pank had then twisted his ankle as he dropped from the balustrade wall onto the cobbles. A loose stone had shifted treacherously as he landed upon it, and though fear had propelled him onwards to the relative safety of their hiding place, it became clear that he would not be able go much further – this night at least.

Now he sat nursing the rapidly swelling joint, rocking gently back and forth, and biting his lip with pain.

'Where's Lumst?' he whispered shakily, almost before Grissel and Spindra had manoeuvred themselves into the space beneath the plough. Grissel and Spindra, still wide eyed with the horror of what they had seen, shook their heads in silence.

'What's befallen him?' said Tod. 'Did you see?'

'We did,' said Spindra, quietly. 'And I hopes *never* to see such a thing again. 'Twas . . . dretful. Dretful. Some gurt thing – I don't know what 'twas . . .' He took a deep breath. 'Some . . . bcast . . . with eyes like . . . aach.' He groaned and covered his face with his hands, unable to go on.

' 'Twas a felix, wasn't it?' said Tod. 'What the Gorji calls a cat. I knew it – guessed it right enough – though I never saw one close to, before. I've heard 'em spoken of.'

'A felix?' breathed Pank, still clasping his ankle. 'Be there such things, then?' He had some distant memory of the mention of these mythical creatures, for that was what they were to the Tinklers – ancient myths, tales handed down from their ancestors, stories from the almanacs. Tales of beasts who lived in strange dwellings – pirrymids? – who could see in the dark, and had teeth and claws like huge tinsy-knives . . . a felix. He had not heard the word since childhood. And now they had left their pirrymids, apparently, to live among the Gorji, who called them . . . cat. What other terrible things might not the Gorji harbour among them? And Lumst, his poor friend Lumst, was *dead?* Killed by a felix?

'No!' he shouted, distraught, 'No! No!'

Tod grasped Pank firmly by the shoulders. 'Shh!' he hissed. 'Do you mean to bring the thing upon us all?'

'No,' said Pank, more quietly, and then dropped his head in desolation. The pain of his injury, and the shock of the night's events were making him feel sick. 'No. But my friend. My friend . . .' He raised his face, now streaming with tears, and turned on Grissel. 'Where were *you*,' he hissed, 'when this happened? Where were *you?*'

'We were in the near barns,' said Spindra. 'Grissel and me. Lumst had gone to the further barns, alone. We thought 'twould be quicker to divide. When we heard the noise, we ran to see – Grissel were ready to follow, but then the Gorji came running too, and we had to hide again. 'Twere too late by then, anyhow,' he said sadly. ' 'Twere all over in a few moments. But,' he added, quietly, ' 'twere our blame right enough. We should never have divided.'

'*My* blame,' said Grissel. 'For though 'twere Lumst who made suggestion that we separate, I should never have agreed to it. I should *never* have agreed.' He grasped the well-worn centre grip of his bow, and continued, his voice rising in anger. 'And I be willing to hunt down this *felix* even now. Precious little good it would do our companion, but I s'd dearly love to put an arrow through that evil eye, and bring him to agony. Just let me find him, and give him pain for pain – and 'twould be worth the risking.'

'No,' said Tod. ' 'Twould not. For you'd risk us all – and discovery by the Gorji to boot.' He thought for a few moments, then said, 'We stuck our heads up for this task, and we all knew 'twere likely to be a dangerous one. 'Tis no one's fault that Lumst is gone. But gone he is, and now here's Pank with a crock foot. Aye, that's right,' he said, seeing that Grissel and Spindra had not even noticed this latest complication, 'sprung his ankle. So what do us do now? Do us try to carry on across the wetlands to the Far Woods, or do us go back to the Royal Forest?' He looked up at the sky. ' 'Tis moon-wax, and we've lost ground. I don't believe we could reach the Gorji woods by sunrise, even if Pank were walking straight, and after sunrise it'd be too late. We don't want to be caught on open land by day. I reckon we must bide in these byres till tomorrow night, and then go on, or go back. Thass if the felix don't get us all first.' This last thought brought a listening silence upon the little group, but all they could hear was the tick of a lone bat, high above them, as it wheeled and patrolled the moonlit yard, hunting for insects.

Chapter Ten

Midge had found it difficult to get back to sleep after the excitement was over. She wondered what Tojo had caught. The cat was just horrible, and she half wished that Uncle Brian had found the wretched thing and bounced a brick off its head, as he had threatened to do.

Then more important considerations entered her mind. The Royal Forest, and what was about to happen there, seemed more urgent than Tojo's antics. She felt sure that the winged horse was connected to the forest somehow. And now the woods were to be cut down! Tomorrow she must speak to Pegs, and learn more.

Something else niggled at her. So much was happening that it was hard to keep track of her own thoughts. The sink – yes, *that* was a strange thing. She had meant to go back there and look again, but had forgotten about it. Her hand had touched something when she was searching for the torch. A bundle of rags, or dusters maybe – but it had felt . . . odd. And the strange thing was that she had been looking under there earlier that morning, when she was deciding what to use to clean Pegs up – that was how she remembered the whereabouts of the torch. There were no rags or cloths there then. So what *was* that beneath the sink? She shivered slightly. Maybe it was best not to know. No, that was silly. The more she thought about it, the more she felt she *had* to know. It was no good. There would be no sleep until she had put her mind at rest.

Midge put on her dressing gown once more and tip-toed from her room. Now that she was out of bed she wasn't so sure that this was a good idea. The dim landing light had been left on, and that was a comfort, but standing at the top of the stairs and peering down into the dark hallway made her feel a bit nervous. It looked creepy down there. Don't be silly, she thought, Phoebe would be snoring away at the foot of the stairs and everything was as it should be. She remembered her mum telling her something when she was little: 'There's nothing there in the darkness that isn't there in the daylight.' And Mum would briefly switch on her bedside lamp and say, 'See? There are your books, there are your toys, here's Bobs, and I'm just next door.' Bobs was her toy rabbit. She still had him – most of him anyway, for he had been loved to bits.

She gingerly put a bare foot onto the first stair, and instantly jumped. There had been a slight noise down in there in the darkness – a faint double click. Not the sort of noise that Phoebe would make, it was more metallic, or mechanical. Right by the front door. Maybe it *was* the front door. No, that wasn't it. She suddenly realized what it was – the cat flap. Definitely the cat flap. And that was *very* strange because no cat ever used the cat flap. She knew this was so because she had tried to help the Favoured One through it one day, and Uncle Brian had said, 'Sorry, Midge. No cats in the house. The flap was put there when Katie was younger, against my better judgement. She wanted to keep one of the kittens as a house pet but Phoebe just wouldn't have it, I'm afraid. Can't say I blame her. It was never used in the end, and I'm not going to upset the old girl now. Play with the kitten outside if you like, but don't encourage her to come in. I keep meaning to unscrew the thing – spoils a good oak door.'

But now *something* had gone out through the cat flap – or come in. Maybe it was Tojo. At that thought, her nerve finally broke. She scuttled back to her room and shut herself in. Whatever it was, it could wait till morning.

She had slept in later than she had intended. Uncle Brian was already in the kitchen, talking to someone on the phone – or rather he was listening to someone talking at the other end while he munched a piece of toast and marmalade. He waved the toast cheerily at Midge as she entered, and rolled his eyes. Midge gathered that whoever was on the phone to him was a bit of a talker. 'Mm . . . fine,' said Uncle Brian. A long pause. 'Excellent . . . couldn't be better. No, no, it's no prob . . .'

Midge took a cereal bowl down from the dresser, and noticed the heavy red and black rubber torch standing on the main shelf.

'Absolutely . . .' said Uncle Brian. 'Really . . . it's . . .'

He bit off another piece of toast, and looked around to see where he had left his coffee.

Midge put down her cereal bowl and picked up the torch. Glancing surreptitiously at her uncle and seeing that he was preoccupied, she took the torch and casually walked over to the sink. She lifted the little curtain, and replaced the torch beneath the sink, pretending to tidy up a few of the things in order to make room for it. Her eyes scanned the clutter of objects quickly and thoroughly. There were no rags or bundles of cloths there – nothing but the same few bottles and boxes that had been there yesterday morning. Midge straightened up, the curtain still raised in her hand, and gazed thoughtfully at the confined space.

'Don't give it another thought,' said Uncle Brian. 'Four thirty. Yes . . . yes . . . OK. OK, Pat. I'll be there. Don't . . . don't worry. Yup. OK. Bye.' He put the phone down, and grasped the table as though for support. 'Ye Gods, can that woman talk. Sheesh! Gets it from her mother of course. Now *there* was a woman with a tongue. Miss Whiplash, I used to call her. Morning, Midge – all well? What are you looking for – cornflakes? We keep 'em in the cupboard, sweetheart, not under the sink.'

'Oh . . . no, it's OK,' murmured Midge, absently. 'Just putting the torch back.' She let the curtain fall and walked over to the food cupboard. 'Who was that?' she said, more to distract her uncle than anything else.

'Well, it was . . . actually, no, perhaps it can wait till later,' said Uncle Brian. 'Bit of a surprise.' He had intended to sound slightly mysterious, but Midge had hardly heard him. 'You all right?' he said, looking at her solemn little face. She forced a half smile, and brightened up a bit.

'Yes,' she said. 'Didn't sleep very well, that's all.'

'No surprises *there*,' said Uncle Brian. 'Which reminds me – I think I'll round up the bantams and count heads. And if there's so much as a *feather* out of place . . .' he gulped down the last of his coffee, '. . . I'll be reaching for the twelve-bore, swear to God I will. See you later.'

Pegs was looking much better. His head was already raised as Midge sidled in through the doorway of the pig-barn, and his eyes had lost much of their former pain.

'I've brought water,' said the girl, kneeling beside him on the sheet, 'and you really ought to try to eat something.' As an afterthought she added, 'What *do* you eat?'

What do Gorji horses eat? Again there was humour in the voice that moved, so strangely, through the colours she saw in her mind.

'Well, grass, I suppose,' Midge replied. 'Um . . . hay. Oats, I think. I live in a city. I . . . don't know very much about horses.'

And I know little of . . . cities. We may learn from each other. But yes, I thank you, some grass would be good.

Midge stepped back out into the sunshine and pulled up a few handfuls of fresh green grass. She returned and propped herself up beside the small white creature, so magical and mystical – and yet so real and alive. She loved the warm animal smell of his coat, still mixed faintly with the soap she had used to wash him down. She gently inspected the wounded wing, and was gratified to see that it seemed no worse – better, she thought, though she was no expert in such matters. The soft mouth ate the fresh greenstuff that she offered, a little at a time, and she could feel Pegs' breath, warm, on her pale hands. Her fingers were the same colour as the delicate shell pink around his nostrils. She gave him water, from a plastic bottle as before, wiping the clear droplets from his mouth with the chequered teacloth she had brought.

When he had taken enough, she said, 'Pegs, I have to talk to you.'

The deep eyes looked into hers, waiting.

'The Royal Forest . . .' she began, and noticed the immediate wariness, the slight stiffening of the muscles on the horse's neck. '. . . The wood, which I call the Royal Forest – and I think perhaps you do too, though I don't know why – well, it belongs to my uncle. The land is his. I'm not sure if you can under-stand that. But it means that he can do what he likes with it – the land, I mean, and the forest. Well, he told me last night that he means to sell it. The forest, I mean and . . . oh I'm not explaining this very well, but he's going to get rid of it. The forest will be cut down. It'll be gone, and then where will you . . . I mean if that's where you live, where will you . . . ?'

Hush, maid. Let me try to understand you. Your kinsman, as you said before, has charge of this land – and the forest too? Midge nodded. *And he would destroy it? Why?*

'Well . . .' Midge was about to say 'money', but didn't feel equal to trying to explain what money might be. She tried a different tack. 'The forest will be cut down so that new houses can be built,' she said.

Houses? Is this a word for . . . dwellings? For new Gorji dwellings?

'Yes,' said Midge.

So he would root up the forest in order that . . . But when? The voice became more urgent now. *When will this be?*

'Soon,' said Midge, earnestly. 'Just a few weeks from now, I think. What will you do?'

Weeks? What are weeks?

'Well, there are seven days in a week,' said Midge, 'so . . . I don't know . . . maybe in a month, um, thirty days? You know what days are?'

Thirty days? One moon?

'That's right,' said Midge. 'One moon. Perhaps.'

Are you sure of this, child? Pegs was attempting to struggle to his feet.

'Well, that's what he *said.* I'm as sure as I can be. What are you doing?'

Help me maid. Help me to rise. I can lie here no more. I must leave.

'But you can't! You're not strong enough.' Midge nevertheless tried to assist the animal in his struggles. Finally he stood, very shakily, on the polythene sheet. He looked so fragile and helpless on the unstable surface of the polythene, the thin legs barely able to support the weight of his body, the wings half extended in a vain attempt to gain balance, that

Midge could see that she had been right. Pegs was unable to go anywhere of his own accord. She put her arms beneath the animal's chest in support as he sank on to the sheet again, exhausted. Pegs lay down with a sigh, and looked at Midge. The dark eyes were filled with pain once more. There was a long moment of thought.

Maid, have you the strength to carry me?

'Pegs,' said Midge, 'I don't know if I can carry you. I'll try, of course I will. But you'll have to tell me where you want to go – and why. And who you are, and what you're doing here. You have to trust me. A little more than you do.'

Yes. It is so. You have shown kindness, and faith, and you have earned my faith in return. But all that I know, I cannot tell you. I have not the power – it is not in my gift. There are others to . . . protect.

'Others like you? Other horses?'

No. There are none like me. But what do you know of the . . . little people?

'Little people? You mean . . . leprechauns, and pixies and things? Fairies?'

The same.

'Well, not much.'

Then you may learn much, before this day is out. But more I cannot say, until I have returned to the forest. Trust me, Midge, and forbear my silence a while longer – for I shall indeed put my trust in you. I must.

'Is that where you want to go then? To the forest?'

Aye. Back to the forest – the Royal Forest.

She found that once she was upright, she was able to carry the horse, slung around her shoulders, without too much difficulty. She was small for her age, but she was no weakling and she had a determined nature. Pegs, moreover, was light – so slenderly built and so fine boned, that he was no heavier than a tiny deer. Under Pegs' direction they had made their way diagonally up the slope from the pig-barn, working round the hill towards a point, a few hundred yards distant, where there was a small gully in the hillside. Along this gully, from a spring in the forest, water flowed – a stream in winter, although at this time of year it was merely a damp trickle.

Follow the gwylie up to the edge of the forest.

Midge carefully walked sideways down into the hollow of the gully, and then said, 'I'm going to have to stop for a moment.' She was getting tired and thirsty, and her shoulders were aching. She leaned forward and bent her knees, slowly lowering Pegs to the ground. Pegs found that he was able to stand, now that he was on a firmer footing than the polythene sheet had provided, and was even able to walk a few paces. He shook his head, to loosen the stiff muscles in his neck, and glanced about him nervously, his silvery mane and tail shining in the sunlight. They had been very exposed on the open hillside, and he felt slightly safer in the hollow of the gully. He stared up towards the forest, anxiously scanning the high branches of the beech trees. Midge sat down for a moment. She had brought water with her in a plastic bottle. The bottle dug uncomfortably into her hip, but to retrieve it would mean standing up again. She looked up the path of the gully. It became narrower, and deeper towards the forest's edge, and she could see that the soil had been washed away to reveal the bluish local stone. Most of the houses around were built of this material. Mill Farm, unusually, was built of the honey coloured stone quarried from Ham Hill, some fifteen miles south. The gully ran right up to the edge of the forest, where its source was buried beneath a thick over-hanging curtain of dense brambles.

'Is that where we're going?' she said to Pegs.

It is where I am going. Carry me just a little further, if you are able, good friend, and then I shall ask you to rest awhile and wait for me.

So Midge crouched down once more, tucked her head beneath the horse's body, and stood up straight – holding on to the slim legs. She walked up the long grassy gully, picking her way carefully as it grew more stony and wet. The sun was higher now and she was hot. She glanced at her watch, shifting her grip on the horse's fetlocks in order to do so. Ten-fifteen. It felt later. As they drew closer to the forest, she noticed that Pegs kept raising his head and looking intensely up at the trees – as if searching for something.

At the head of the gully, Midge once again lowered Pegs to the ground. The little horse slipped un-certainly on the wet stones and Midge grasped the base of one of his wings to help steady him. She looked doubtfully at the seemingly impenetrable mass of brambles, from which the stream trickled.

161

'How will you get through there?' she said.

Midge, you have done much for me. Now it seems I must . . . insult you. The voice, quiet at first, became louder and firmer, *Please . . . I have to ask you to look away. Face the way we have come for a short while. Do not turn again, for the space of – a long cooling drink. Then wait here till I return – I shall make what haste I can. Please, I must ask.*

Midge reluctantly turned away. As she did so, the voice echoed in her head, loud and clear – *Briefly parted, soon united.* Midge felt slightly huffy, nevertheless. She was so curious, and she had worked so hard, that it did seem a bit mean to be parted like this – no matter how soon they might be reunited. She pulled the plastic bottle of water from the pocket of her dungarees, and stared down the path of the gully, aware of a slight movement behind her – the faintest rustle of foliage.

'I still don't think you're strong enough to do this without some more help,' she said. 'Are you sure you can manage? Pegs?' She unscrewed the cap of the water bottle and paused, listening. There was no sound. 'Pegs?' She turned round. The winged horse had gone.

Glim had watched the Gorji maid, in astonishment, as she struggled up the path of the gully, carrying Pegs on her shoulders. The archer had hardly been able to believe his eyes, and his first instinct had been to try and shoot the child, for he assumed that Pegs was a captive. He doubted, though, whether even he was skilled enough to bring down one so large with a single small arrow at this distance. He looked

162

frantically around him to see if Aken or any of the other East Wood hunters were close by, but the woods were silent. He was alone.

Peering down through the leaves of the tall beech tree, he observed the girl closely as she picked her way slowly up through the gully. The horse was conscious, and by the way it lifted its head occasionally and brought it close to that of the Gorji maid, Glim judged that it was perhaps communicating with her. How could that be? Was he pleading with her? Yet Pegs seemed undistressed – injured maybe, but not necessarily a prisoner. The horse lifted its head again – and now Glim could see that it was looking up at the trees, as though searching for something, or someone . . . him? Was Pegs hoping that there would be someone waiting for him? The maid was looking down, watching where she put her feet. Glim waited until the horse's head was raised once more, and then, taking a huge risk, he stepped into view and waved an arm briefly. He hoped that Pegs had seen him, because, by Elysse, he would not do it a second time. It made him feel too nervous. He watched the strange pair for a few seconds more. It was apparent that they would eventually reach the top of the gully – and the hidden exit of East Wood. What would happen then? This was an urgent matter.

The hunter soared quickly from branch to branch, descending in the direction of the forest spring that flowed out through the East Wood tunnel. He would get there first, follow the spring into the tunnel, then watch and wait. What could Pegs be thinking of, to allow the giant to come so close?

As he reached the low branches of the trees that overhung the source of the little freshwater spring, he spotted Raim, his fellow archer, perched in a young sycamore on the opposite bank. Glim softly clicked his fingers three times in quick succession, to catch Raim's attention, then flapped his arms and pointed to the ground, signalling that he should descend from the tree. Raim glanced over at him, frowning slightly. He had been watching a small wagtail hopping among the wet stones at the mouth of the forest spring, willing the bird to be still for a moment, and now here was Glim, waving his arms around like a hemmed fool. What could be the matter? He sighed as the wagtail flew away, and, sheathing his arrow, he jumped lightly to the ground. He waited by the spring for Glim to join him.

'Well, I hope you've meat to spare, Glim – for now I find myself shorter'n I'd reckoned to be,' he said, 'thanks to thee. Half a squirrel should see us square, I judge.'

But Glim had no time for idle talk. He grasped Raim by the arm. ' 'Tis Pegs!' he whispered urgently. 'Pegs is coming!' He pointed down the wooded gully to where the spring flowed under the thick wall of brambles, which bounded the forest and shielded it from the wide world beyond. 'He's wrapped about the shoulders of a Gorji maid! They're coming up the gwylie, t'other side o' the briars!'

'What?' said Raim, his face blank, uncomprehending. '*What?*'

If the situation hadn't been so urgent, Glim would

have laughed – Raim looked so stupefied. Glim kept a grip on his friend's arm and hurried him along the bank of the thin stream. They ducked beneath the undergrowth and around the bushes that grew beside the water until they came to where the trickle disappeared beneath the wild brambles.

Running through the middle of this tangled mass of thorns was a closely woven wicker tunnel, arched over the path of the little stream. As the hedge of briars had grown over the decades, so the wicker tunnel had been extended, until it was now over twenty feet long – the thickness of the hedge. There were four such emergency exits through the wall of brambles which enclosed the forest, one for each of the North, South, East, and West Woods, maintained and repaired by the woodlanders against the day when they might be needed – although the West Wood tunnel was in more or less constant use by the Wisp for their fishing expeditions.

Glim and Raim crept quietly along the East Wood tunnel, until they came to the doors at the far end. These opened inwards and were also made of wicker, culled from the Gorji withy beds. Woven into the out-side face of the basketwork doors were lengths of old bramble foliage, dry grass, and bits of creeper. With a dense curtain of living brambles hanging over the front of the camouflaged doors, it became impossible to see them – they were part of the thick undergrowth.

The Ickri hunters stood behind the doors, in the semi-darkness of the tunnel, waiting and listening – Raim still struggling to understand exactly what was going on. Pinpricks of light penetrated the wicker-work here and there, catching the dark ripples of the trickling water at their feet. The gentle flow seemed loud in the dim seclusion of the woven tunnel. After a minute or two, Glim thought he heard the click of small hooves on wet rocks outside. He nudged Raim and put his fingers to his lips. Then came the loud, clear voice of the Gorji chi', sounding very close – 'How will you get through there?' Pegs was heard to mutter some reply, but neither hunter could catch what was said. This was a dangerous business. Where was the signal? And what of the maid? Pegs spoke again, clearly this time – asking the maid to turn away. Glim glanced quickly at Raim and raised his hand, waiting for the signal.

Briefly parted, soon united.

Immediately the two Ickri pulled gently on the wicker doors. Light flooded in to the basketwork tunnel, through the curtain of brambles on the out-side. Glim and Raim moved rapidly forward, helping to silently part the brambles as Pegs stepped between them. The little animal ducked as it entered the tunnel, treading quietly and carefully along the slippery path of the stream. The hunters quickly closed the wicker doors once more – having caught a brief glimpse of the girl, standing in the bright sun-shine with her back towards them, no more than a cricket's jump away.

The winged horse emerged from the wicker tunnel and, with help from the two Ickri archers, stumbled

166

onto the grassy bank beside the little stream. Pegs raised his head and sniffed the air. It felt good to be back among the familiar surroundings of the forest.

Glim and Raim were full of concern – and wonder. 'Pegs – what's happened to 'ee?' said Raim. 'And what bist doing wi' a Gorji maid? Bist hurt? Did the giants do 'ee harm?'

Pegs lowered himself onto the grass, the effort of doing so making him catch his breath. *I am indeed injured – but I improve, thanks to the Gorji chi'. She has tended me, and I owe her my life. But listen – for I have but little strength for talk. Raim – you must go to Maglin and tell him to summon the Elders and the Queen. The forest is in great peril. The maid will explain. Glim – go back to the tunnel and open the gates once more. Then keep from sight. I am bringing the maid into the forest – aye, this very hour. I shall lead her to the Counsel – and then you shall see why. Follow us and watch, Glim, till we reach the Counsel Clearing.*

The Ickri archers stared at Pegs in amazement and disbelief. Bring the Gorji maid into the forest? What madness was this? No Gorji had entered the forest for nigh on a hundred years. The last giant to walk these woods had been Celandine, and the story of Celandine had passed so far into legend that nobody really knew the truth of it any more.

'Pegs,' said Glim, gently. 'You ain't well. You'm badly. Let us take 'ee home and we'll hear more when you'm strong again.'

No, Glim. Do as I say. Open the gates once more and then keep a distance. Go, Raim, and summon the Queen and

Counsel – warn all others to stay hidden till the maid has spoken. Have no fear. I will answer to Maglin.

As members of the Ickri tribe, Glim and Raim were under the immediate command of their captain, Aken, but Maglin was their General. Ba-betts, herself an Ickri, was Queen of all the Various – yet it was Maglin who held the real power. All members of all tribes were ultimately answerable to Maglin. Pegs had no command over the Ickri archers, yet they both recognized that the horse was somehow beyond the command of all others. Not Maglin, nor the Queen, nor even Spindra, from whose herd Pegs had been bred, could be said to have control over this creature. The animal was young, yet born of another time – truly magical, in ways that were beyond their understanding. Even as a foal he had the mystifying ability to speak in soundless words – in an accent that was unfamiliar to the woodlanders, though the language was similar to their own. Like mad Maven, the horse could not be fathomed or placed. Maven-the-Green was old, old beyond all memory – ancient when the Counsel Elders were childer, so it was said – and a law unto herself. Pegs was not old, yet still seemed to belong to that same other-world. He had been born before, and had walked the earth before. Pegs was witchi.

So Glim and Raim, hesitant at first to do as Pegs bade them – decided after all to follow his instructions. Raim took a few quick steps across the mossy grass, then flapped his wings and rose up into the branches of the trees. He disappeared into the greenery, making his way from tree to tree like a flying squirrel.

Glim helped Pegs down to the stream once more, and together they crept back along the wicker tunnel. Glim quietly opened the camouflaged doors and squinted through the overhanging brambles. He could see the Gorji giant sitting on the grass just a few yards away, and he shook his head as he turned to Pegs.

'This don't feel right,' he whispered. 'Shouldn't us wait till we've had word from Maglin? Bist sure?'

Pegs looked at the girl as she sat in the sunshine, winding a long piece of grass around her finger. He sighed. *I am sure.*

Glim paused, still uncertain, then turned to go. 'I shan't be far away, mind,' he said. 'And I shan't take my eyes off 'ee, neither.'

Pegs waited until Glim had gone, and then slowly moved forward, silently nosing his way through the curtain of brambles. The Gorji child sat dreamily on the sunny bank of the gully, her grey-blue eyes staring placidly into the distance. Pegs stood still and watched her for a few moments. Everything was about to change.

Midge. The girl was startled, and she jumped, breaking the strand of grass that she had wrapped around her forefinger. *Follow me.*

She had to crouch very low in order to enter the tunnel. The sharp ends of the interwoven withies scratched her shoulder blades as she followed the white horse along the path of the stream. There wasn't much light, and her feet kept slipping on the wet stones. She felt the cold water soaking through her trainers, and realized, suddenly, that she was afraid. More than at any other time since she had met Pegs, she sensed that she had stumbled upon, and was stumbling towards, a strange secret – something hidden and dark, and perhaps dangerous. She didn't like it, and if there had been room to turn around and go back she would have done so. Her notion that Pegs was perhaps man-made, an experiment, some zoo-bred cross between a horse and a bird, finally disappeared for good. She was in a strange wicker-work tunnel, cramped, wet and uncomfortable – and she was following a horse with a damaged wing, a horse that could speak in strange colours, a magical creature such as the world had never seen. She wished, suddenly, that she was in London – sitting on the low wall in front of Teck Mansions, swinging her legs and watching the traffic. Or in the flat, helping her mum make fairy cakes. This was scary, and she didn't like it. The basketwork roof snagged at her clothing, and her feet were soaked and muddy. The cut end of a withy scraped the back of her head and got caught up in her hair. What was she doing in this horrible place? She ducked lower and saw that Pegs had reached the end of the tunnel. He turned to face her, framed for a moment against the light, stretching his wings as he awaited her. He looked beautiful, like a picture from the Bible, or a book of legends. Midge felt less panicky. She splashed through the last few yards of darkness and emerged into the sunlit forest.

Chapter Eleven

They stood on the bank of the stream, the girl and the horse, bathed in the hot sunshine that fell upon the quiet woodland. And it *was* quiet. No bird sang, and no creature stirred. Only the faint trickle of spring-water broke the silence. Midge rubbed the grazed skin on her neck and shoulder blades, as she looked about her. How tangled and confused everything was.

The trees looked ancient, twisted and overgrown. Many were dead, and huge moss-covered limbs lay on the ground, or were propped up at crazy angles against trunks overgrown with ivy and creepers. The thick wall of brambles and briars extended far into the woods, surrounding the bases of the trees, and sprouting in great clumps along the banks of the spring. A strong smell of wild garlic and leaf-mould hung on the still air.

Away from the spring, the ground rose, rocky and quite steep, and through the distant cedar trees, Midge could see the beginnings of open ground. She turned to Pegs, who had been watching her as he rested his aching limbs.

'Why have you brought me here?' she said. 'What are we doing?'

Come. We will walk together, and I will talk as we go. The horse moved off in the direction of the high ground and began to pick his way, slowly and painfully, between the bushes and clumps of briars. Midge followed, walking beside Pegs when space allowed, and falling behind when the path grew narrow.

Do not be afraid, Midge, for I bring you here as a friend, and no harm will come to you. I quizzed you before as to whether you knew aught of the little people – known to your kind as 'fairies'. Today you shall meet with the forest dwellers, those who live in this protected place. Five tribes there are, and they may be all that remain of the little people – the Various Impish Tribes who dwelt in this land long before the Gorji came to claim it. You are of the Gorji, Midge, the giants and ogres who now rule the earth. The Impish tribes – that you call fairies – are known to themselves as the Various, and are descended from the great travelling tribes of Elysse. They have become trapped here, who once travelled where the wind took them, and they may soon be no more. This wood, that they call the Royal Forest, is their last home. By chance and good fortune it has been spared – for the Gorji do not enter here. Now your tribe would destroy the forest, so you say. And therefore the Various will be destroyed also.

I am taking you to speak with the Queen and her Counsel, that you may explain to them their likely fate, and they will see for themselves, and believe, what is to be. In doing so, I take great risk – for you may bring your kind down upon us – yet so shall they come if I do nothing. And it may be that you can help us. If not, it will make matters no worse.

Midge listened to this in amazement, completely dumbfounded. And when Pegs stopped to rest for a moment, she still found no words to say. Little people – what did Pegs call them – the *Various*? Living in her uncle's woods? It wasn't possible! Yet when she looked at Pegs – a miniature horse with wings – she knew that all things were possible. She thought of the TV programme she had watched with Uncle Brian, and the closing words – 'there are other worlds, worlds within this world ... it is an absolute fact that there are creatures on this planet that have never been seen by man ...' And so it was true – though she suspected that the author of those words was thinking of deep-sea life rather than flying horses. She knew so little, understood so little. She didn't even know how he had come to be trapped in a barn, behind a closed door.

The horse was looking at her expectantly – waiting for some sort of reaction. 'Sorry,' she said, lamely. 'I was just thinking.'

The urgent thrum of a woodpecker sounded in the distance, and it seemed to catch the horse's attention. At any rate, he spoke no more for a while.

In silence, they climbed up into the rocky area. Here grew a few stunted hawthorn trees and buddleia bushes, but for the most part the soil was dusty and the ground stony. There were caves, Midge realized, four or five entrances of which were visible among the bushes and the boulders. She then saw, with a little shock of excitement, the first few signs of habitation. A couple of small pots stood by the mouth of one of the caves – they seemed to be made of some kind of dull metal, like the pewter mugs she had seen on the dresser at Mill Farm – and a third lay on its side in a stain of dark liquid, that trickled among the flaky bits of grey shale and collected in a small pool. It was apparent that the vessel had only just been knocked over. She noticed, also, a few damp scraps of coloured cloth, orange and mustard yellow, draped on one of the hawthorn bushes, as though lately hung out to dry. Staring into the mouth of one of the caves, she thought she saw some spark of movement in the darkness, a brief glint of light on metal – or an eye perhaps? – but nothing more. The humid air hung still about them, quiet and tense.

Pegs paused again for breath and followed Midge's gaze. *Here dwell the Troggles and the Tinklers – the underground tribes – though I doubt you will see aught of them, this day. They are timid folk and seldom come out till moonrise. Cave-dwellers they are now, though once they were of the water-tribes, Naiad and Wisp. They broke from the water-*

174

tribes, and came to these woods long before the others. Troggles and Tinklers they became, by their own naming. The Gorji were few on the levels then, but when their number increased, the last of the water-folk – the tribes called Naiad and Wisp – were forced to find refuge in the forest also. Lastly came the Ickri, the wandering hunters, tree-dwellers, returning to these lands after many generations absence. The Troggles and the Tinklers then dug tunnels, like coneys, and withdrew to themselves, living nobody knows how – for no other tribes-people enter their domain. They fashion strange devices, gewgaws and baubles, and are altogether a most curious folk.

Midge stared in amazement at the little cluster of caves, and was desperate to hear more of the lives being lived in such an unlikely place. Her head was filled with questions, and her tongue was loosened at last.

'But how – how do they make things? And what things? And what do they dig with? Do they have tools? Shovels?' She was reminded of Snow White, and wondered whether the cave-dwellers were like the seven dwarves. She imagined little bearded men running around with pickaxes, digging, and singing 'Hi Ho!' Ridiculous! But what *were* they like, then? She wanted to see.

The horse was already moving on, however, climbing up towards the plateau beyond the thinning tree line. *Come. There is much to do.*

Pegs stood in the long dry grass at the edge of the Great Clearing, catching his breath, and waiting for Midge to draw level. The girl had become distracted by one of the Ickri dwellings, a wicker pod hanging among the sycamores, and had stopped to stare at it – calling out to him for explanations. 'What's this? Pegs? What's this thing for?' How loud the child was. Her voice rang through the silent, watchful trees and echoed around the deserted clearing. Pegs waited as the girl came swishing through the grass, twigs snapping beneath her feet. She sounded like a forest fire.

'Pegs,' she said, breathless and excited, 'There's a big basket thing back there, hanging in the trees. What is it?'

Benzo's dwelling.

'What?'

It is a pod – a dwelling. The home of an Ickri hunter.

'You mean someone lives in there?'

The sound of the woodpecker, insistent, commanding, rattled once more across the clearing and Pegs looked up. Good. The Queen and Counsel were gathering.

Yes. Someone lives in there – and has likely gone deaf from your asking. Maid, you must temper your voice. We are unused to such clatter. Remember where you are, move and speak gently, and all will be well. Many eyes are watching you, and many ears are listening. Many hearts are fearful of your presence. Be calm, and soft and easy. All your questions will presently be answered.

Midge looked around apprehensively. The thought that she was being watched had not occurred to her, and she immediately felt self-conscious.

'Sorry,' she whispered. 'But where are we now?' She

176

gazed along the green expanse of the clearing and suddenly realized that it was cultivated. How unobservant she was! At first glance she had not registered the fact that the clearing was, in reality, like a big plantation. All manner of greenery – potato plants, carrot tops, lettuces, and onions stretched out before her, and in the distance she could see pea sticks and the wigwam rows of runner beans.

'Who does all this?' she gasped. 'It's like – I don't know, like an allotment or something.' That sounded silly. 'I mean, I can't believe that all this is going on in the middle of Uncle Brian's old woods.'

They were standing at the southern end of the Great Clearing. In the distance, Pegs could just see the hazel bushes that marked the entrance to Counsel Clearing. He wondered what was happening there. Much confusion, no doubt. Perhaps he should allow the Queen and Counsel a little more time to prepare themselves.

He turned his attention to the Gorji maid once more: *This is the Great Clearing – tended by the Naiad tribe for the most part. Here are grown the crops that the Various depend upon for their existence. The summer has been kind, but the recent winters have been hard, and the soil grows thin . . .*

Raim had found it relatively easy to convince Maglin of the truth of the news he bore and of the need for swift action, but Maglin was finding it much harder to convince the Queen of the same. The Ickri General swept down from the Royal Pod in exasperation and stamped over to Aken, who was waiting by the Rowdy-

Dow tree. Little-Marten was already at his post, seated high upon the Perch.

'Sound general alarum,' shouted Maglin to the Woodpecker, 'and be quickly at it. A Gorji has entered the forest. All to conceal themselves. Then sound Queen and Counsel – summoned to Counsel Clearing. Once you are done, get out of it and hide yourself. Jump to it, fellow!' Little-Marten jumped. 'We'll see if *that* will shift the old wosbird from her bed,' added Maglin, sourly.

He spoke to his captain amid the sharp rattle of the clavensticks. 'Aken. The Naiad horse has returned, and has brought a Gorji maid for company, if you please. What can the hemmed animal be about? We must prepare ourselves as best we may. Find what company of archers you can and get to the trees, as close to the Queen as you be able. Tell Scurl to leave the West Wood and come over to the East. No action till you hear it from me. Go.'

Maglin ran back to the Royal Oak where Raim stood next to the Queen's guards, awaiting further in- struction. 'Raim, make swift return to South Wood and watch for Pegs and the Gorji. Be Glim there also? Well and good. Bring further warning to Counsel Clearing when they draw near. No attack, mind. If the chi' is unprotected, as you say, then we may deal with her when we learn more of Pegs' intention.'

Maglin finally addressed the Ickri guards. 'Stay at your post, bows ready, arrows notched. The Queen may descend, or,' the General muttered something beneath his breath, 'she may not.' He turned and

178

made his way towards the Counsel Pods where Ardel was the first of the Elders to begin a shaky descent of the willow ladder.

'Maglin!' It was the imperious voice of Ba-betts, calling him from the entrance of the Royal Pod. She had apparently decided to sit up and take notice after all. The General muttered a few more things beneath his breath and began to retrace his footsteps.

Having given the Gorji maid as much information regarding the forest and its inhabitants as time allowed, Pegs now attempted to prepare her for their arrival at Counsel Clearing. He had already spoken of the separate tribes, explained that the Ickri were hunters, winged, and able to fly after a fashion, that the Naiad were farmers, for the most part; and that the Wisp were fishers. Now he needed to tell of the Queen and her Counsel.

It is certain that you will meet with the Counsel Elders, and likely that you will meet with the Queen. The Elders are the eldest members of the Ickri, Naiad and Wisp tribes. They are named Crozer, Ardel and Damsk. The Queen is named . . .

'What about the Troggles and the . . . Tim . . . Tinklers?' said Midge. 'Don't they have Elders too? Will they be there as well?'

The Elders are of the upper tribes. There are no cave-dwellers on the Counsel.

'Why not? That doesn't seem very fair.'

It is not for me to judge such matters. The Queen is named . . .

179

'It sounds to me as though the cave-dwellers are treated rather badly,' Midge persisted. 'First they have to put up with other tribes invading their forest, then they have to go and dig holes and live underground, and then they don't even have anybody on the Counsel. And if the ones who live above ground are called the *upper* tribes, does that mean that the ones who live below are called the *lower* tribes?'

Yes, they are known as the lower tribes. However . . .

'Aha! And are they called lower tribes *just* because they live below ground, or because they're lower in, um . . . value, or something? Lower, as if they're not as good? Lesser – that's the word. Lesser tribes? It sounds like prejudice to me,' she added, loftily. It was nervousness, she knew, which made her act like this. She did it at school sometimes – arguing in class with Miss Clifton over some point of history to disguise the fact that she had forgotten her homework or PE kit, or something. Now she was apprehensive, afraid of what she was about to see. She felt that she was being watched, judged, and that she was all alone, and perhaps unwelcome, in a strange, strange land. And here she was, upsetting Pegs – her friend.

But Pegs was wiser than she knew. He had already told her that the Counsel Clearing lay directly beyond the bushes at the end of the Great Clearing, and he had noticed the girl's increasing agitation as they approached the path that wound through the bushes. Naturally the child would be uneasy. A towering giant she may be, but a child nevertheless.

Let us rest for a moment, for I am weary. I little thought this day that I would make such a journey, who could barely stand at sunrise. Carry me again, gentle maid, as you did before. Bring me before the Counsel upon your shoulders and let all see how I am in your debt, and how I should never have returned to the forest were it not for you.

The idea was appealing, if a little theatrical – Pegs being probably capable of walking the last fifty yards or so unaided – but it had the desired effect, which was to make Midge feel that her presence was justified and deserving of tolerance, if not gratitude and honour. Gratitude, and honour, of a sort, were amongst her own feelings as she knelt once again to lift the snow-white creature onto her slim shoulders.

It was a dramatic picture the pair made, therefore, as they emerged from the pathway through the hazel bushes and entered Counsel Clearing – a Gorji child, fair-haired, clad in green dungarees and a pale yellow T-shirt, with a white horse draped about her shoulders.

Midge stepped self consciously into the clearing, feeling the comforting warmth and weight of the horse's body around her neck, gripping the delicate fetlocks tightly with her clammy fingers. She couldn't seem to catch her breath, and her heart was beating painfully. It was impossible for her to imagine what she was about to see, and she needed to get it over with, to find the reality of it immediately. Her eyes darted around the arena. The centre point, some kind of small stone post with a pyramid top, registered quickly with her: a large white tree, dead, over on the other side, more of the strange hanging baskets – pods; something in the bare branches of the dead tree – a bird? Colours. Or rather, black and white. A speckly patch of black, white and grey to the far left of the clearing. There! She saw them. A group of figures, huddled in the dappled shadows beneath the sycamores. They were real! Ten, maybe a dozen little people, standing very erect, like ... meercats. Yes, they reminded her of meercats, the way they stood stiffly upright, motionless, wary and alert, all looking in the same direction ... winged, like Pegs, and magically ... real ... alive. Mostly dressed in black and white – just a few colours here and there. A strange and breathtaking sight.

Walk slowly. Approach the Counsel and kneel. Lay me down, and remain kneeling.

Midge felt dizzy. She breathed in deeply, trying to be calm, and began to follow Pegs' instructions, walking very slowly across the clearing, her eyes fixed wonderingly on the little group. Their skin was quite dark, and their faces were broad-featured – from a distance they looked gypsy-like, or aboriginal perhaps. The dumpy little figure in the chair, though, (the Queen?) was paler. Or maybe her face was powdered. They had weapons – bows and arrows. And spears.

Midge drew closer, and began to get a better perspective – the figures were bigger than she would have imagined. Maybe two feet tall? Not quite, perhaps, but certainly not the tiny creatures riding on the backs of swallows that she had seen in picture books. About knee height, they would be.

182

They looked so *funny*! She would have to watch herself. She had a terrible habit of giggling when she was
nervous. Most of the men (should they be called
men?) were bearded, and some of them were quite
grey – in fact the three who stood apart, wearing long
cloaks and leaning on sticks, looked positively ancient.
They must be the Counsel Elders. How they stared at
her! Their eyes – dark, dark eyes – never blinked.
Something was odd about the clothing.

A slight commotion in the dead white tree made
her jump and look upwards. A little winged figure sat
astride a high broken stump. He had dropped something – a stick – and the scowling eyes of the group
flashed briefly in his direction, as the piece of wood
clattered among the dead branches and fell to the
ground with a slight thump. The stick was dark, and
polished.

(Poor Little-Marten. He had deliberately disobeyed
Maglin by staying on his Perch – for he wouldn't have
missed this for the world – and now he had disgraced
himself further by dropping one of the clavensticks.
Later, no doubt, there would be trouble.)

Midge continued to gaze in wonder at the small
figure in the stark leafless tree, but then felt a pang of
sympathy for him. She could see that he had done
wrong, made a mistake of some sort. He was a little
brown creature – brown bare feet, brown leggings,
some sort of brown leather jerkin and thick brown
curly hair. He had another polished stick, like the one
that had fallen to the ground, tucked beneath his arm.
In his hands he held a brown hat of some description,

which he twisted in an agony of embarrassment. Only his face was red – bright red with humiliation. It would be a kindness to look away, Midge realized, and she turned her attention to the group once more.

She focused on the Queen – an extraordinary being, who sat very properly, majestically, in a faded blue wicker chair, her grey hair scraped back into an untidy bun. The chair had handles at each end, and looked a bit like an open carriage without wheels. The near side had a very low middle section – so that its occupant could step in and out, presumably. The Queen held aloft a large black fan – far too big for her – and in her other hand, resting in her lap, she held a tangerine. No, Midge realized, not a tangerine, but an orangey-red ball – it looked like polished stone. Her stiff regal pose was made ridiculous by the details of her appearance – her heavy make-up had been applied very approximately, so that her face looked like a child's painting that had gone badly wrong, and her off-white dress was purple-stained with what might have been Ribena – though that seemed unlikely. Some sort of fruit juice at any rate. Midge could not meet the imperious stare of the puffy little eyes, and the smudgy eyebrows, raised in query, without desperately wanting to laugh. This was all so . . . impossible. She could feel the beginnings of a kind of hysteria rising inside her. It became worse as she imagined the squat little occupant of the wicker chair trying to fly. She bit the inside of her cheeks, hard enough for it to hurt. Sometimes this worked.

She stood uncertainly before the assembled

company, having momentarily forgotten Pegs' instructions – in fact she had ceased to be aware of Pegs altogether, so enthralled was she by what was happening. What was she supposed to do? She tried to stay calm. The suspicious eyes of the archers continued to gaze into hers. It was the warrior figures, she realized, who were dressed in black and white, or shades of grey. Their spears and arrows were not pointing at her directly, but they were obviously at the ready, and it occurred to her that she might actually be in some danger. Yet this made her want to laugh even more, the whole thing was just so fantastic. The tense silence was becoming unbearable.

Then a stray sycamore seed caught her attention, as it twirled gently down from the trees, to land, unnoticed, upon the Queen's head. It stayed there, perfectly positioned, a neat decoration for her grey bun. And that did it. The laughter that had been building up inside her spluttered forth, and she had a helpless attack – giggling and snorting so much that it startled the very pigeons in the trees. The bows of the archers were raised slightly as the company continued to stare at her, in silent outrage.

Cease this laughter, maid. Lower me to the ground. Do not speak until you are addressed.

Pegs sounded quite cross, and Midge did as she was told. She half-apologized, took a deep breath and knelt, rather awkwardly, on the warm grass in front of the group. Leaning forward, she gently allowed Pegs to slide from her shoulders to the ground, breathing out again as she did so. The horse lay, like an offering, or sacrifice, before the Queen in her blue wicker chair. Sitting back on her heels, Midge was now only a little taller than the gathered company.

The Queen half turned and beckoned to a figure standing behind her, a drab and careworn little thing in a beige smock – a maid possibly – who drew closer and inclined her head.

'Doolie, is this the missing animal?' the Queen inquired. Her voice was high, and went up and down in a funny way, almost as though she were singing the words. Doolie glanced at Pegs.

'I believe 'tis, my Lady,' she replied.

The Queen gave the winged horse a dubious look. 'That's not a goat,' she said – to the astonishment and delight of Midge, who had to drop her eyes in an attempt to hide her amusement. She found herself staring at the feet of the royal personage, but then had to fight even harder to control herself. Her upper lip began to quiver once more.

A warrior figure, armed with a spear, stepped forward decisively – taking control of the situation. He addressed the Queen – although he never took his dark eyes off Midge.

'If I may speak, my Lady,' he said. His voice had a harsh rasp to it, and his fierce gaze immediately dispelled any further attacks of giggling. He looked tough – close-cropped hair, iron grey, a silver leather waistcoat over an otherwise bare torso, and knee-length britches of a black and grey striped material. Pin-striped? Yes – but how weird. And yet that was *it*, thought Midge, their clothing was *familiar*. Or rather, many of the materials from which they were made were familiar. She glanced quickly around. Here and there were odd bits of evidence to confirm her growing realization that the Ickri were dressed in clothing which must have originated in the outside world. A pair of britches in what looked like old deckchair canvas, a frayed jerkin that might once have been the leg of a pair of faded black jeans, a belt from a towelling bath-robe, a knitted pixie-hat in a shiny acrylic grey wool that had probably been worn by a baby long before it had come into the possession of its current owner – a pixie for all she knew.

Certainly there was evidence of the homemade – jerkins of silvery-grey fur, squirrel perhaps, rabbit-skin boots, and some curious black-and-white caps made from magpie feathers, these last being worn by the three stooping Elders – but there was no doubt that odds and ends of human clothing had also found their way into the forest, somehow, and had been cut up and adapted to the purpose of this astonishing little tribe. And there was no mistaking the origin of the tiny pink rubber boots worn by the Queen, for Midge had once possessed just such a pair herself when she was at playschool, and remembered how proud she had been of their shiny newness. These were even smaller than hers had been, though they were still too big for the Queen. They looked old and very worn – but the Little Pony logo was still just visible. Midge tried not to look at them.

The tough-looking fellow in the silver waistcoat (what had *that* been originally?) glanced upwards into the trees that encircled the clearing – a deliberate and purposeful look, as though he were issuing a silent command. His spear was decorated with feathers, again black and white, tied in bunches along its length. It may have been ceremonial, although the metal tip – fashioned from an old carving knife perhaps – looked dangerous enough.

Pegs had now raised himself up on to his chest and was lying directly in front of where Midge knelt, his head turned towards the assembled company. The warrior approached to within three or four feet of where the horse lay. The sun glinted momentarily on the tip of his spear – a warning flash, a reminder of its purpose. He continued to hold Midge in his steady gaze, but his words were for Pegs.

'A welcome return,' he said, allowing the butt of his spear to rest on the ground, 'though in a manner so unforeseen that I might be dreaming. I, and all those about me. What be *you* dreaming of, Pegs, to bring the Gorji within our midst? You are ailing, so we learn. Did you lose your wits along with your wings?'

I am ailing, Maglin, it is true. And without the kindness of this maid, there would have been no return, welcome or otherwise, for me. The news that she bears would not then have reached you until it was too late. As to my wits, you shall judge. And all here shall judge. Help me to my feet, maid, then remain as you are.

Midge shuffled forward and put her hands under the horse's belly, helping to support the weakened animal as it struggled to a standing position. She stayed kneeling, hunched over a little, her shoulder now being about level with the horse's back. Her hand strayed, comfortingly, to the base of Pegs' damaged wing, and she allowed it to gently rest there as he continued.

When I flew from this place, five nights ago, I made way across the dark wetlands as was intended. I saw the lighted Gorji settlement far below me, and beat on till at last I gained the Far Woods beyond – much exhausted, for I have never flown a distance greater than the length of the clearings of the Royal Forest. I was in great need of rest, but I dare not lay me down for fear of what might befall me in the darkness. Pegs paused for a moment, as if gathering the strength to continue. *I can scarce recount the loneliness of that night – nor the terrors of the following day. If we had hoped that the Far Woods might provide us with the means of our further existence, then we must abandon such hopes forthwith.* Pegs paused again and Midge felt the creature's body shudder slightly beneath her touch.

At sunrise, or soon after, the woods were filled with such a noise that I scarce held on to my wits. Such a beating and hammering there was – seemingly all around me – and such a din of Gorji voices that I believed the world to be gone mad. I thought to hide myself amongst the thickets and brambles – yet from these very thickets came great quantities of birds, I never saw their like, flapping and running, in terror also of the fearful noise. I fled likewise, not knowing what else I should do, even to the very edges of the woods, and all the while the Gorji came crashing on. But now, from beyond the confine of the trees, came loud cracks and explosions, so that all was an even greater confusion. The birds left the woods, and took to their wings, but I durst not. I durst not stay and

I durst not break for open ground – or sky – though the very hordes of giants were nigh upon me. I was certain then that my death was near.

The clearing was silent as Pegs rested yet again. His breathing was fast and shallow, and it was clear that the memory of his experience was a torture to him. Midge looked at the little assembly before her, as they stared wide-eyed – at Pegs now, not at her – and noticed that the Queen had begun to fan herself. Her mouth was open and her whitened face was shiny with perspiration. The warrior in the silver waistcoat – Maglin? – scratched his grey stubble and shifted his stance slightly, but said nothing.

In dark despair, continued Pegs, *I found a desperate refuge – a great tunnel, surrounded by fresh earth near the edge of the wood. I reckoned it to be the lair of some beast from its stink, but cared little, nor gave a thought to what might await me there. I crawled within and hid me from the raving world above – hearing the boots and sticks and hounds of the Gorji as they passed over my head. On they came, and more – crashing and thrashing as though they would beat the trees to flinders. None here can know, and I hope will never know, that terror. And yet they may – for it is of such things, and worse, that this chi' would tell.*

'Was she among them then, that day?' said the grey-headed warrior, looking at Midge. 'And did she find you there?'

No, Maglin. My tale is not over. When at last the woods grew quiet again, I thought to rest a little and recover my senses – but then I was aware that deep in the tunnel some beast was astir. Scrapings and shuffling I heard, and knew

190

that I was not alone in that noisome place. I had no wish to escape the Gorji only to face the jaws of a brock, and so I crept from the ground once more and hid me in the woods till sunwane. A worse day I never spent – in great fear and with little rest. There is no relief from our plight to be found in the Far Woods. I speak plainly, and as one who has seen it to be so.

When it grew dark once more, at moon-wax, I stood at the edge of the trees and looked out across the wetlands. I knew not whether I had the strength to return to the Royal Forest, yet I would not stay a moment longer. I launched from the hillside therefore, and made way as best I might towards the dark shape of our own horizon – yet was greatly wearied, even as I passed over the Gorji settlement. With all my effort I beat onward, but found that I could not gain the forest without pause. I fell from the sky and came down upon a byre that stood on the near hillside, making a great clatter on the ridges of rot-metal with which it was clad. This landing proved treacherous and I slipped headlong, falling through it as a stone through ice, and down into I knew not what – a thicket of spears it seemed, which pierced and smote me till I was entangled and broken. I felt great pain, and thought I did revolve upon a wheel that rolled red among the havens of Elysse. Then blackness came upon me, and upon the world entire.

Midge felt a lump in her throat, and the group of little figures before her became blurred as her eyes welled up with tears. The memory of her struggle with the barn door came back to her. It had occurred to her on several occasions to ask how Pegs came to be trapped behind a locked door, but the opportunity seemed not to have arisen. So he had fallen through the roof. One of the galvanized sheets must have partially given way and then sprung back more or less into place. He would have landed on one of those spiky wheels, which had obviously turned beneath his weight and so pinned him to the ground. It was a wonder she had found him alive after all he had been through. How brave he had been.

She sniffed and rubbed her forearm across her eyes, bringing the world back into focus once more. Pegs turned to look at her, and spoke now as if to her alone.

Days and nights I lay in a swoon, pinned down by some cruel device and ever in pain, bleeding – dying, I knew. Then came this maid, a Gorji chi', and in my despair I called out, reckless, hoping that it might be Spindra. Great kindness she has shown me – and much cunning, for I was held to the ground by an immense Gorji contraption which I judge would take many giants to lift, yet this she achieved alone, with a child's hand. And by that hand did I live, and did mend, and was returned to my home. She is my saviour, and I name her as such, though she call herself . . . Midge. She has all my gratitude and trust – yet not for this reason did I bring her to the forest this day. Maid, rise now and tell, if you will, what is to befall this place, and let all hear of their coming fate.

This caught Midge by surprise and it took a few seconds for her to gather her wits. She rose uncertainly to her feet, wiping her hands on her dungarees – but then reached out once more for Pegs, seeking reassurance, and buried her fingers in the long silvery mane at the nape of his neck. They stood closely together, facing the Counsel, as she searched for the right words.

'This place,' she began, 'the forest, belongs to my uncle.'

The little people flinched at the unaccustomed loudness of her voice, and the broad faces stared up at her, wary, unsettled. The warrior with the spear had taken a step backwards – not through fear or intimidation, but simply to lessen the angle required to look up at her. The silence grew. She tried again.

'The Royal Forest is in the charge of one of my . . . tribe. A man. A . . . Gorji? It belongs to him, and he can do what he likes with it.' Her voice was too loud. Everything about her was too big, and too loud. She spoke again, softly and gently.

'All land belongs to someone. This forest, your home, belongs to him. He's my mother's brother. He doesn't want it anymore. So he's going to let someone else have it. Those people will get rid of it. They will chop down all the trees, and they will build houses – dwellings – here instead. And roads. You won't be able to live here anymore.' Midge looked down at Pegs. 'I don't know how to say it, Pegs. I don't know how to explain.'

'Your meaning is plain enough. You are here – the Gorji are here – at last. We knew this day would have to come.' It was Ardel, the Naiad Elder, who spoke – and his voice was bitter. The aged and stooped little figure drew his brown cloak around him as he raised his willow staff and pointed it angrily at Midge. 'You are here. No more need be said.'

'Well, it's not *me*,' Midge began indignantly. '*I'm* not the one who's doing this to you . . .' But Pegs nudged his shoulder against her knee and she stopped talking.

'How long?' said Maglin. 'What time do we have?'

Perhaps one moon, Pegs spoke again. *The maid cannot name the time of their coming. But it will not be long, Maglin. Come they will. And if she is mistaken, or if the hand of her kinsman may be stayed awhile – what of it? Ardel is right – though his anger be misdirected – the day will surely come. All lands are Gorji lands. They are here, and so this is no place for us. Our time here is nearly over.*

'That may be so,' said Ardel. 'Yet I will not say that you have acted wisely in this, Pegs. You could have brought us this news yourself. And yet you brought her. There was no need for the Gorji maid to enter the forest, but you have thrust her upon us without warning.'

Do you not yet see? Were it not for the maid, if she had not healed me – aye and carried me back here – then I could not have returned. And all the Gorji would have been upon us without warning. The forest would be crushed, and we along with it. Now we have had warning, thanks to this chi', and she may help us further – for whatever plans are laid it is clear we shall need assistance and knowledge from the outside world. Let this maid be our ally then, if she will, for I believe that it was meant to be so and that she was sent to us not by chance entire.

Ardel spoke again. 'Is *this* your advice? That this – *Gorji* – should act as go-between? That she should petition her kinsmen in our cause? Or be privy to our own strategies – and be so entrusted? It is by no means clear to the Counsel, or indeed to the Queen . . .'

194

here Ardel bowed briefly towards Ba-Betts, who looked vaguely startled at the mention of her name, '. . . whether we should even permit this intruder to *leave* the forest, let alone act as emissary . . .'

'Oh, but I can't stay very much longer,' Midge blurted out loudly, without thinking. 'My uncle will start to wonder where I am . . .'

The little people flinched once more at the sound of her voice, and Maglin glared at her, furious that he should have been seen to take another step backwards – this time in an involuntary and undignified fashion. He resumed his former position and thrust his spear towards her.

'Speak when you are spoken to,' he growled.

Midge, not wishing to be stabbed in the shins, kept quiet.

'It is clear to me,' said Crozer, the Elder Ickri, moving away from his fellow Counsellors and advancing towards the blue wicker chair, 'that no purpose can be served by detaining this maid longer. To attempt to keep her a prisoner would be foolishness. My Lady,' he addressed the Queen, 'my advice would be to dismiss this person immediately. There is much to discuss. Much. And let us not forget that there are others to consider – those who were sent to seek, and have not yet returned . . . Whether or not the Gorji maid can be of assistance to us is in itself a matter for discourse. She should not be privy to any further knowledge regarding our thoughts and decisions, until we have mooted the same. I would beg that you command her to leave.'

The Queen ignored Crozer and stared up at Midge. Her vacant expression gradually seemed to focus, and she ceased waving her fan. 'What *are* you?' she said.

'A . . . girl,' said Midge, quietly.

'A girl. Girrrl. A strange word. I have heard it before. A girl.' Ba-Betts turned to Doolie, who hovered nervously at the Queen's shoulder. 'Have we *seen* this . . . *girrl* . . . before?'

'No, m'm.'

'No? No. Yet, she seems . . . she seems . . . are you sure?'

'Yes, m'm. Very sure.'

Ba-Betts sighed. 'The Queen is not a well Queen. Not well . . . not well . . . and all is not well.' She began to fan herself once more. 'Girl,' she said, 'there are no girls here. We have no girls here, and there will be no girls. Go. Leave. The Queen commands. Guards! To the Royal Pod! I would rest.'

Maglin nodded to the four winged guards who stood waiting at the foot of the Royal Oak. They hurried over and lifted the Queen in her wicker chair, transporting her away from the little group. The sycamore seed was still perched on her head, Midge noticed. Doolie, the Queen's maid, left the group also, joining the procession towards the Royal Oak. Midge looked up and saw the wicker pod hanging in the branches, for all the world like some big beehive or wasp's nest, dark among the green shadows. She watched with amazement as the guards began to hoist the wicker chair up into the tree. Doolie sat in the chair also, opposite the Queen, and the two little figures rocked gently to and fro like children in a swingboat. The Queen was helped out onto a sort of platform and the whole company watched in silence as Doolie held aside the colourful entrance cloth to the Royal Pod. Midge wondered what it was like in there. The Queen crossed the threshold, stumbling slightly in her oversized children's boots, and vanished into the dim interior.

Some slight tension seemed to disappear along with the Queen. Maglin, now in complete control, turned to the Counsellors. 'The Queen commands that the chi' should leave. And so it shall be.' He raised his hand to stay any objection that might be raised. 'We will decide upon our actions once she has gone. Pegs, you brought this . . . girl . . . here, and I would give you the task of taking her back to the tunnel she came in by. However, you be ailing. The Ickri Captains shall escort her instead. Aken! Scurl! Notch your bows.'

Maglin, the maid is here as a friend, and at my plea – not as an unwelcome intruder. She is but young, and means us no harm. It shames me to see her treated thus. Perhaps it is best that she departs for the moment, but I would not see her leave at arrow-point. I will gladly take her to the tunnel once more.

'No, Pegs,' said Midge. 'You should rest. And don't worry, I'll be fine. I can find my own way back. It's easy.'

Then wait for word from me before you come again. And there surely will be word – for you are needed here, if all here did but know it.

Maglin grunted. 'Even so, she must have escort. I'll take her myself – no, I have a better idea. Woodpecker!' He called up to Little-Marten, who was still sitting high up on his perch. 'Come down.'

Little-Marten, caught off guard, scrambled about, then half-flew and half-fell from the broken stump of the Perch to land, inelegantly, a few feet away. He was still holding his single clavenstick.

'Lay your stick alongside its fallen brother and come here,' said Maglin. 'And now, Woodpecker,' he continued, 'since you be unable to keep away when commanded – I shall command the opposite. Come closer. Closer . . .'

The youthful figure shuffled forward, keeping one wary eye on Maglin, the other on Midge. He tilted his head back, to look up in open-mouthed wonder at the giant who had entered the forest – such a sight as he had never expected to witness – and almost over-balanced as Maglin's hand snaked out to catch him by the ear. 'Ow!' he said, and dropped his cap.

Midge instinctively bent down to pick up the cap, and Maglin shot her a glance of surprise and irritation as he continued to address his underling. 'Since I *have* your ear, at last, perhaps you'll heed me when I speak. Walk with this Gorji maid, and lead her back to the East Wood tunnel. See that she don't miss her way. Then, when she has departed, report directly back to Aken or me – unless she decides to carry thee off on her shoulder to roast on a Gorji spit. Aye, and a spit-roast Woodpecker might seem pretty eating to such as they, for aught I know. Go. And mind me better, if you would keep your Perch.'

The Ickri General released the errant Woodpecker from his grasp, and the youth quickly took a couple of steps sideways, rubbing his ear – which had turned bright scarlet. He looked up uncertainly at Midge.

'Go!' roared Maglin. Little-Marten ran a few yards out into the clearing, and turned, waiting for Midge to follow. He was like a little brown dog.

Midge put out a hand to touch Pegs. 'How will I know . . . when . . . what to do?' she said, utterly confused.

I will bring word. Have no fear. But, friend – if true friend you be – say naught to anyone of what you have seen here today, for we are all at your mercy.

'No, of course I won't.'

All speed, then, till we meet once more.

'Briefly parted, soon united?'

I hope it may be so. And remember those words, maid, should you enter this place again – they will open the gates to you.

Midge walked out into the clearing, to where Little-Marten stood waiting for her, his dark eyes narrowed against the glare of the sun.

Maglin looked up into the dense foliage of the sycamores, and he nodded imperceptibly to the hunters who were hidden there. Child or no child, the Gorji were the enemy, and had to be watched. He would take no more chances – had taken too many already, it would seem. For what had become of the five who had been sent to seek for this wayward beast? Once the Gorji had gone, there would be time for more questions.

* * *

199

Midge followed the Woodpecker closely along the well-worn track that ran through the hazel bushes. His hair was a deep reddish brown, cola-coloured, and she loved the way the loose curls fell upon the nape of his boyish and rather grubby-looking neck. His wings, protruding from roughly hemmed slits in the back of his leather jerkin, were similar to Pegs' – in that they were like a soft parchment membrane over bone – but proportionately smaller than that of the horse. They were partly extended, and he seemed to use them to help him keep balance as he jumped lightly along the uneven surface of the well-worn dirt path. She noticed that there was a small design painted on one of his wings – a dark blue motif of some sort, like a tattoo.

They came to the Great Clearing, and Midge stopped to marvel once more at the rows of pea sticks and the patchwork greenery of the vegetable beds. A motley collection of colours among the currant bushes on the other side of the clearing caught her attention, and she realized that another group of the little people stood watching her from a safe distance. Their appearance was dissimilar to that of the warlike Ickri, dressed as they were in broad-brimmed hats of straw, or dried grass perhaps, smocks and leggings in various dull hues of green, yellow and brown. She gazed at them in fresh disbelief, and the little group stared back at her, leaning towards one another, curious, whispering. These were the Naiad, presumably – the farmers and vegetable growers.

Little-Marten stood beside her and waited, happy to be at the centre of so much attention. He ran his fingers casually through his dark curls, as though being in charge of a giant was all in a day's work to him.

'What's your name?' said Midge, and the Ickri youth jumped sideways. He looked up at her and quickly recovered himself.

'Little-Marten,' he said, almost inaudibly. He swallowed, and then said boldly, 'I knows thine.'

'Do you?' said Midge.

'Aye. 'Tis *Girl.* I heard them say.'

'No,' said Midge, turning away from the strange sight of the distant Naiad to look at him. 'I *am* a girl. Like you're a . . .' But what was he? A boy? Or would that be like a foreign word to him? 'Girl is the same as . . . maid,' she said. 'So I'm a girl, a maid, but my *name* is Midge.'

The small brown face looked up at her gravely for a moment, and was then suddenly split apart into a huge grin of delight. 'Midge? Like this . . . ?' He made a pantomime of scratching his head furiously, as though being bitten by insects.

Midge laughed. 'Well, sort of. But it also means small, in a way. I *am* small, you see. For my age.' Little-Marten looked her up and down. 'Small?' he said, doubtfully.

'For my age. For a Gorji, I'm not very big.'

'Comprend. I am also small, for my years. But I improve, I think.'

'Yes,' said Midge. 'I think I do, too.'

They began to walk slowly along the grassy track that bordered the vegetable plantation. Midge put her hands in her pockets, and suddenly realized that she was still carrying Little-Marten's cap. She must have put it in her pocket as she was saying goodbye to Pegs.

'Here,' she said, stooping slightly and handing him the rather battered and greasy piece of brown felt. It looked as though it may have been cut from the crown of an old trilby. Little-Marten reached up and took the object, but he didn't put it on.

'Thank 'ee,' he said shyly, and rolled it up. Midge was curious.

'Where did you get it?' she asked. ' 'Tis Woodpecker's cap,' replied Little-Marten, and there was a note of pride in his voice. ' 'Pecker-Petan gave it me when I took the Perch.' He looked up at her and smiled. 'I be Woodpecker, now. And I shall be but six-teen fourseasons, next moon.'

He might have been speaking a foreign tongue for all Midge could make of this, but she gathered that her strange companion had been honoured in some way. 'Gosh,' she said, 'that's very good . . . is it?'

' 'Tis,' said Little-Marten, firmly. He had a quick and lively air about him that Midge found friendly and comforting. There was none of the mysteriousness that surrounded Pegs, who, though also young in years, still seemed older than the universe somehow. Pegs was deep, and distant and wise. Little-Marten was as cheerful as a cricket, and about as capable of keep-ing still.

'Looksee!' he said, and half-hopped, half-flew along the grassy verge in front of her. He had spotted some-thing, a splash of colour – bright yellow – on the path ahead. He crouched down and picked up a bunch of flowers that had been laid on the verge. His quick eyes scanned the plantation, as he waited for Midge to catch up.

'Thine,' he said simply, and handed her the little bouquet. Midge took the flowers. The stalks had been neatly bound with dry grass.

'Mine?' she said. 'Are you sure they're for me? Who are they from?' No one had ever given her flowers before. Little-Marten looked about him again and shrugged. Midge sniffed the bouquet and said, 'Well, if you really think that they were left there for me, then thank you – whoever. I love buttercups.'

'Not buttercups,' said Little-Marten, combing his brown fingers through his curls. 'Celandines.' He glanced up at her as he spoke, and his fingers paused as he caught a glimpse, over the giant's shoulder, of a grey and white figure moving through the trees. He didn't see who it was. So. The archers had been sent to follow them after all. Little-Marten frowned, irritated that Maglin had apparently not seen fit to trust him.

'Come,' he said to Midge. 'Away.' He spat, unself-consciously, into a clump of cow parsley, and continued along the verge. Midge followed, and couldn't help looking at the little fleck of white spittle on the plant as she passed.

They made their way through the tall rough grass that marked the end of the Great Clearing, and walked among the cedar trees on the downward slope of the East Wood. Once again the heady scent of wild garlic rose up from below as they clambered sideways down the slippery shale path towards where the caves were cut into the side of the hill. Little-Marten, nimbler on his feet than Midge, paused for a few moments to wait for her, watching the clumsy giant as she gingerly negotiated the steep descent. He instinctively looked across the banks of shale towards the mouth of the large cave where he had first encountered Henty, the Tinkler maid – and was absolutely astonished to see her appear once again . . .

From the darkness she came, as before, not dancing this time, but in a sudden movement nonetheless – as though someone had been trying to hold her back and had then let her go. She threw her hair back, glanced behind her, defiantly it seemed, and stood framed in the dark mouth of the cave. Her eyes became huge as they fixed upon the Gorji giant, who came skittering and sliding down the stony path. Little-Marten caught the dull glint of some metallic object, which Henty clutched in one of her hands. He couldn't see what it was.

'Whoo!' said Midge, arriving in a scatter of stones and dust. 'It was easier getting up there than it is coming back down again.' She locked her right foot firmly against a hawthorn root and leaned forward, one hand upon her knee, the other still clutching her bouquet of yellow flowers. 'Phew!'

A couple of seconds passed in silence and Midge glanced at Little-Marten, wondering at his sudden stillness. She followed his gaze and saw the object of his attention standing in the mouth of the cave. It took her by surprise. The bright eyes of the Tinkler maid were staring straight at her, and Midge let out a little gasp. She was just so beautiful. Perfect she was, a perfect, perfect thing, utterly amazing, and wonderful.

'Who's this?' she murmured to her escort. Little-Marten hesitated. He had never spoken the name aloud before – though he had whispered it to himself, aye, and many a time.

' 'Tis . . . Henty,' he said, at last, reverently. And – now that he had a legitimate excuse – he said it again: 'Henty.'

The little figure in the mouth of the cave turned once more to look behind her, as though distracted momentarily, then shook her head and stepped further forward into the sunlight. She stood, barefoot, on the rough grey shale that sloped away from the entrance to the cave, her small pale hands cupping some object to her. A single brief glance at Little-Marten, and the dark eyes, wide with wonderment, turned to gaze at Midge once more. Then she spoke. Her voice seemed distant, tiny, yet very clear – and filled with excitement.

'Be you Celandine?' she said.

'What?' said Midge.

A sharp memory came rushing back to her, apparently unconnected to this moment, yet so powerful, so strong, that she could almost taste it. She was sitting on her father's shoulders, and they were standing by a gate looking at a big grey horse in a field. Her mum was there. Her mum said, 'Oh, look – violets! Aren't they sweet?' And she stooped to pluck something from the grass beside the gate. Her mum had then reached up to Midge, high as she was, higher than the world on her father's shoulders, and handed her a small flower. 'Look, Margaret, a violet.' It was blue, and she could see it now, the small blue flower, coming up towards her and the sun shining on her mother's upturned face. She had held the flower, and sniffed at it as the big grey horse began to amble slowly, heavily, towards the gate. Tall as she was, on her father's shoulders, the horse, shaking its massive head alarmingly, was taller still. It was huge and alive, and it made funny whiffly noises as it came up to them. She began to be frightened. 'Don't worry, sweetheart.' Her father's voice. 'She won't hurt you. It's only old Violet, come to say hello. Hello, Violet. Hello, old thing.' Her father's hand reaching out to pat the massive head. Violet. Midge had dropped her flower and begun to cry. She hadn't understood how the tiny blue flower and the huge grey horse could be the same thing.

'What?' she said.

'Be you Celandine?'

Midge raised her bunch of yellow flowers to her nose and sniffed at them. Celandines. That was where that long-forgotten memory had sprung from: the name of a flower being the name of something else also. The fairy girl thought that she was *called* Celandine. But why would she think that?

'No,' she said. 'My name is Midge. Well, it's Margaret, really, but nearly everyone calls me Midge. Henty's a nice name. That's what you're called isn't it

– Henty?' She looked at the beautiful little creature – how pale her skin was, strange, and so unlike the nut-brown complexion of her now silent guide.

But the Tinkler maid didn't answer. She seemed disappointed somehow, and uncertain. She looked down at her hands and made as if to move closer, then paused and began to back away again. Finally she ran forward, her bare feet making a light tip-tap sound on the grey shale, and reached up to Midge with both hands. She was holding up a small cup or bowl. For a moment, Midge had the startled idea that it was a begging bowl and that she was required to put something in it. Then she realized that the object was being offered to her. She stooped to take it with her free hand, her fingers making brief contact with the cool delicate hands of the woodland girl. Henty immediately turned and ran back towards the safety of the cave, her long black hair streaming behind her.

'Henty!' Little-Marten's voice sounded almost desperate. 'Don't go . . .'

But Henty, glancing once behind her – at Midge, not at Little-Marten – ran into the darkness and was gone.

Midge looked down at Little-Marten and saw the anguish on his small brown face. 'Is she your . . . ?' she began to say, and then thought better of it. 'She's *very* pretty,' she said instead.

Little-Marten muttered, 'She'm a Tinkler,' and turned away. 'Come,' he said. He began to make his way down the slope once more, and Midge followed. The back of his neck had gone quite red, she noticed.

Chapter Twelve

They approached the bank of the stream, and here, on easier ground, Midge was able to take a closer look at the thing Henty had given her. It was a small metal bowl, perhaps the size of a tennis ball cut in half. She held it slightly away from her, and turned it in her hand. The surface was dull grey, quite tarnished, and there was a design, like a frieze, all around the outside. Tiny engraved images she could see, groups of people, but it wasn't very clear what they were doing. It looked quite old. She would clean it up when she got home and then perhaps she would be able see more. She put it in her pocket, and accidentally bumped into Little-Marten as she did so. He had stopped abruptly, just ahead of her.

'Whoops – sorry!' she said, and stooped automatically to grab his shoulder as they both stumbled forward. Her hand brushed against his wing, velvety and bony at the same time. Little-Marten made no reply, but steadied himself, and then continued to look across the stream – to where a half a dozen figures sat on the ancient mossy trunk of a fallen tree.

They were Ickri archers, a casual, lounging group, who occupied the dead tree trunk with an air of lazy arrogance. They watched the Woodpecker and the Gorji giant dispassionately, as the strange pair came, warily now, towards the trickling spring. No move was made until Midge stepped out onto the stony bed of the shallow stream, intending to follow its path into the wicker tunnel that would lead her from the forest. Then, one of the archers slipped down from his perch and landed softly among the coarse dry grass that grew up around the fallen tree. The grass came up well above his waist. He glanced quickly round at his fellows before wading through the dry vegetation, wings slightly raised, and emerging onto the mossy ground that bordered the spring. One by one the others descended from the tree trunk also.

Midge stopped, mid-stream, and looked at the leader. He wore a sleeveless open tunic – it looked like washed-out black denim – and charcoal-grey britches, or pantaloons, which were tied around the knee, and made of a loose fitting silky material. He was barefoot, and his wiry arms and torso were dark brown from continual exposure to the elements. He carried a bow and arrow, casually, unthreateningly, and his eyes, dark and glittering beneath thick black eyebrows and a greying crop of hair, were mocking and fearless.

'Now then, Woodpecker,' he said softly, nodding slightly at Little-Marten, and showing his sharp white teeth in a dog-like grin. 'Now then, maid.' He looked up at her with the same half-nod, and fixed grin. It was Scurl, captain of the West Wood hunters.

Little-Marten remained on the bank of the stream and said nothing. Scurl and his crew were no friends of his. Midge, uneasy, but prepared to be amiable, said, 'Hullo. I'm, er, just leaving.'

'So?' said Scurl, his wolfish expression changing to one of mild regret. 'Stay awhile.' He raised his bow and arrow slightly – still not openly threatening, but with enough purpose to be noticeable. One of his followers gave a low chuckle. Midge was not so easily intimidated, however. She said, 'No, I have to go. Besides, your Queen has said I must.' She turned away from the Ickri hunters and started to move down-stream. Something whizzed past her ear – so close that the sound of it was like a coin being zipped smartly along a comb. An arrow! Midge's hand flew up to her head, and she gave a little squeal – her nerve broken. She turned fearfully around. Scurl was calmly notch-ing another arrow to his bow.

'What did you do that for?' said Midge, her voice beginning to shake. 'And who are you, anyway? You could have hurt me.'

'I could have killed 'ee,' said Scurl, simply. His eyes had lost their mocking look, and had become calm, detached, almost glazed – the eyes of a hunter whose prey is cornered. 'And so I may, even yet. For I ain't so certain that 'tis but folly to let 'ee go. I ain't so certain that come sun-wax tomorrow these woods won't be trampled down by a hundred more like 'ee perhaps – for I never knew a female yet that could keep a still tongue in her head, be her Gorji or Various. And though the day of the Gorji may be close upon us, if

210

what you say is true, to let 'ee go would surely bring that day closer still. Aye, and to this *very* day itself, for aught I may reckon. No, maid, I ain't such a fool as some.' He chewed the bottom corner of his lip thoughtfully, looking unhurriedly from the giant to the Woodpecker, considering the risks involved in disposing of the pair of them, and muttered again, 'No, I ain't such a fool as some.'

Little-Marten would have been shaking in his boots – had he boots to wear. He had no doubts as to what Scurl was capable of, and the others – Benzo, Flitch, Dregg, Tulgi and Snerk – would back him to the knife, he was sure of that. They were hunters and killers, born to the task. It wouldn't matter a whit to them whether their victims ran on four legs or two. Whatever Scurl decided upon would be done.

Little-Marten felt that he had naught to lose by speaking out, and so, amazed at his own audacity, said, 'Is Maglin such a fool then? 'Twas he who gave the command.'

Benzo spat and raised his bow, but Scurl merely glanced at the youth in mild surprise. 'What's this, you young snip? Does the Woodpecker speak?'

'The Woodpecker squawks,' said Benzo. 'And'll squawk no more.' He drew back his bow a little and looked at Scurl. 'Come, Scurl, let's finish this while us may.' But Scurl pursed his lips and rubbed the palm of his hand against the back of his neck. He was still thinking, and was in no particular hurry.

Midge, beginning to understand the real danger they were in, tried frantically to think of arguments that might help. 'But listen,' she said. 'My unc . . . my kinsmen are expecting me. They know where I am. They'll come looking for me straight away if I'm not home soon.'

Scurl looked at her impassively, considered her words, and then dismissed them. 'You may be looked for,' he said, 'but none, I reckon, would look for 'ee here. For none would think it possible for 'ee to enter. You'm but a chi'. And a maid, at that. How would such as you make passage through such briars as do surround this place? Even if your words were true, we should be no worse off . . .' He sounded as though he were talking to himself, rather than to her.

Midge tried another tack. 'Yes, that's right,' she said. 'I'm just a child! A girl. I'm twelve years old! Would you really kil . . .' she started to choke on the words, really frightened now as she saw the Ickri captain scanning the treetops, looking around to make sure that there were no other eyes watching. He wasn't listening to her, had not the slightest interest in what she was saying. He'd made up his mind.

And Benzo could read that mind. 'There's none to see,' he said. ''Tis best done, captain. Maglin will reckon the giant to have carried off Woodpecker, and we shall sleep the more easy for it. None shall know.' The group of archers looked at Scurl, and waited. The silence grew.

'Save one.' A harsh voice rang out from the tangled undergrowth near the fallen tree trunk. 'One shall know.'

Benzo and the rest of Scurl's crew whipped around,

their bows raised in confusion – but Scurl, tensing his body, continued to face the giant. He lowered his head, calmly it seemed at first, but when he raised it again his teeth were bared in fury.

'That meddling hag . . .' he roared, '*shoot her!*' He turned, black in the face with rage, and drew back his bow. There was nothing to shoot at.

The archers stood, bows drawn, their eyes seeking a target – but found only the quiet profusion of tangled tree limbs, dry grass and briars around them.

Little-Marten, seeing that all backs were now turned towards them, nudged Midge's leg and silently gestured to her to move away. They began to retreat downstream a little.

'Bide there,' said Scurl, without even bothering to turning round. 'Where's that hemmed witch?' he growled.

'I have her,' whispered Tulgi, with a quiet note of triumph. 'By the fallen oak.' He drew his bow back a little more, steadied his aim, and breathed out softly as he let fly. Seconds later, he lay motionless on the banks of the spring.

Nobody saw how it happened. Almost in the instant his arrow left the bowstring, it seemed, the Ickri archer had crumpled to the ground, his fingers making a little splash at the edge of the stony stream.

The hunters gaped uncomprehendingly at their fallen companion, then instinctively stumbled away from him, looking frantically about them in wild confusion. Only Scurl remained steady. He stared in the direction that Tulgi had fired his arrow, but could see no movement. He dropped warily onto one knee next to Tulgi's body, and turned it over, so that the torso was exposed. Nothing. No arrow, nor any wound that he could see. Yet the archer was dead – that much was plain. He began to rise again, cursing now, and then noticed a little mark on Tulgi's neck. Stooping once more, he touched it with his finger. Something was protruding – it looked like a dandelion spore or a piece of thistledown. What witchery was this? Poison?

'Maven!' he yelled, in a fury. 'Come out, you hag! Out with you, you witch!' His hunters were scattering away from the stream, flapping their wings and rising into trees of the South Wood. He was deserted, and alone with the body of Tulgi. He saw that the Woodpecker, and the now snivelling Gorji maid, had shuffled a few paces further downstream, but they stood still as he turned his gaze upon them. 'Bide *there*!' he shouted at them. They looked terrified enough to obey him for a little longer, and he turned once more in the direction of the fallen tree trunk.

'This be no business o' yourn, Maven!' he roared. 'Keep away from this!'

'Let the child go.' The voice came from another direction entirely, and Scurl swung his bow around. There was still nothing to be seen. 'What's it to thee, damn 'ee? Tis no concern o' yourn!' He was beginning to lose heart, realizing that he could easily end up lying next to Tulgi. 'The Gorji be no friend to thee, so what do 'ee care?' One clear shot, that's all he needed. Where was the hemmed old witch hiding?

'Let the child go.' Again the direction of the voice

had changed. He could risk this no longer. His shoulders slumped, and the tension went out of his body.

'Agreed then. I'll give 'ee best.' He lowered his bow and muttered inaudibly beneath his breath, 'but next time I catch 'ee, I'll stretch thy scrawny old neck – see if I don't.'

'The Woodpecker also. Let him be.'

Scurl turned to look at Little-Marten, his mouth set in a hard sour line. The Ickri captain breathed in deeply. With a horrible rattling sound of thick mucus, he hawked noisily, and spat into the stream. A long malevolent look at Midge, and a last quiet warning: 'We'd best not meet again, Gorji child. Stay out o' here. And hark 'ee, Woodpecker,' he added, with a nod, 'I'll sithee dead.' And then he was gone, stalking away into the undergrowth, leaving both Midge and Little-Marten in no doubt that they had made a deadly enemy – who would hunt them down if ever he could.

Midge wanted to get out. She stumbled along the stony path of the stream, half sobbing, and careless of her soaking wet feet. She was now running ahead of Little-Marten who, after looking round in vain for some sign of Maven, could do no more but follow with a miserable heart, determined at least to see out the final part of his errand and report back to Maglin. Always provided, of course, that he wasn't waylaid on the return journey. He would not think of that.

They came to the end of the wicker tunnel, and Midge, scratched and sore across her back and shoulders, wrenched open the withy doors. The welcome light of the outside world filtered through the curtain of brambles, and she pushed her way backwards between the trailing thorns, panic-stricken, mindless of her skin and clothing. She caught a last glimpse of Little-Marten in the gloom of the tunnel. His small worried face seemed to hang there in the darkness – like a sad little mask, abandoned in a closet – as the doors slowly closed. They had not spoken. They had not even said goodbye. She ran along the gully for fifty yards or so, then climbed out of it and up onto the rising bank, throwing herself down into the sweet meadow-grass to sob with fear and relief.

Somewhere along the way, she realized dimly, she had lost her bunch of celandines.

She sat up after a while, her arms hugged about her shins, rocking to and fro and wiping her eyes occasionally on her knees, feeling the comforting warmth of the material on her cheek. There was a small rip just below her right knee, and some of the stitching had been pulled apart along the seam. She thought of the day she had bought the dungarees, shopping in the mall with her mum, and wished that her mum were with her now. Her clothes were torn and her arms were all scratched. Her mum would know what to do. She started to cry again, but then stopped, suddenly, and looked at her watch. Ten past five. Was that all? It seemed as though days had passed since she had climbed up the gully this morning, with Pegs on her shoulders. Days. She sniffed and stood up. What was she supposed to do about it all? Nothing, she decided. She was only twelve. What *could* she do?

She looked back at the thick tangle of brambles and trees. It was hateful in there. Nobody had wanted her there in the first place. They had tried to kill her! Pegs had said that she would come to no harm and they had tried to kill her! He had lied to her. It was no thanks to *him* that she was still alive. She had only tried to help – and look what had happened to her. Nearly. Well, they could help themselves from now on. She was done with the lot of them. She would never go there again.

She turned her back on the forest and kicked her way down the sunny slopes of Howard's Hill, looking out across the wetlands, the soft friendly countryside seeming to welcome her back from her ordeal.

By the time she had crossed the Field of Thistles, the whole experience felt so unreal as to make her doubt it could have actually happened. Had she really been threatened, at arrow-point, with her life? She stopped at the rusty metal gate by the corner of the old stables. But, seriously, she wondered – *was* it true? Maybe she was mad. Her favourite kitten – the Favoured One – suddenly sprang around the corner of the old stable block in a sideways leap, landing on the cobbles in front of her and giving her such a comical look of surprise that she laughed out loud.

'Hallo, you darling!' she said. 'You are soooo cute! Did you know that?'

The kitten gave a tiny *meep* and came a little closer, allowing itself to be picked up and cuddled for a few moments, before wriggling free again. It gave another *meep* and wandered into the open-sided barn, sniffing at the dusty earth floor beneath the disused machinery, its tail upright and twitching.

Uncle Brian's battered estate car was parked in the cobbled yard. The tailgate had been left open and an interior light was on. The three red hens – her Deputation from Rhode Island – scratched fussily around the front door, and the Wellington boot still lay on the flagstone path, as it had done all week. These things were a comfort. Midge felt as though she had returned from a long journey. Now she was very tired, she realized, very hungry, and *very* glad to be back. She would have something to eat – perhaps Uncle Brian would have cooked something, or bought something nice – then she would have a long luxurious shower, watch a bit of telly if she could stay awake, and go to bed. She would worry no more. Eat, shower, bed – that's all she would think about. Nothing else.

Walking up the front path, she was suddenly tempted to kick the rubber boot, just to see if it *would* move, but stepped over it instead, because it seemed like bad luck somehow. She stopped to wipe her feet on the tatty doormat – force of habit really, you could probably bring more dust *out* of the house than you could take in – and paused as she heard voices from the kitchen. Well, she could hear Uncle Brian's voice anyway. He was laughing. There was a murmur, and then she heard him say, 'Well yes – but darling, you have to admit that I'm a whizz with the mixing bowl. My rock cakes are a triumph, you know. Somebody once said that to me. No, it's true, they did. A triumph!'

Did he have a woman in there with him? Midge's heart sank. Was she now to be introduced to some old broad who was mad for Uncle Brian's baking? (It wasn't *that* good. She'd had some.) She sighed, combed her fingers quickly through her hair, and crossed the threshold. Well, with any luck she could be out of there and into the shower in five minutes, ten at the most. She mustered up the best smile that she could, and put her head cautiously around the kitchen door.

'Aha!' said Uncle Brian. 'Here she is! Just in time, sweetheart – tea's all ready! We've already started. Midge, come and say hello to George and Katie!'

Chapter Thirteen

Midge felt her carefully prepared smile crumpling, her mouth falling open in shock. She hadn't expected this. She stepped hesitantly around the door and her expression of horrified surprise was reflected back at her, mirrored in the faces of Uncle Brian and her newly arrived cousins as they saw her in full view.

The girl, Katie, fresh and summery in a pink top and cream trousers, her wavy golden hair neatly clipped back, sat staring at her with wide blue eyes – a piece of half chewed rock cake visible in her open mouth. George, who had swept back his long blond fringe with a practised flick as Midge had entered, paused with one hand hovering over a plate of sandwiches, raised his eyebrows and said, 'Crikey.'

Uncle Brian had been leaning casually against the towel rail on the Rayburn, but at the sight of Midge he jerked upright and slopped tea onto his brown shoes. The little splatter was audible in the suddenly quiet kitchen.

'Good God, Midge!' he said. 'What on earth's

happened to you? You look like you've been dragged through a hedge backwards!'

For once, the observation was accurate. In her flight from the forest, Midge had become covered in scratches and cuts, her arms and face were streaked with blood and dirt, her clothes were torn and stained – and, yes, she had indeed dragged herself through a hedge backwards. She looked ruefully at her sore hands, put them in her pockets – realized that it was futile to attempt to cover them up, and took them out again. She stood awkwardly by the door and could find nothing to say. George allowed his outstretched fingers to pick up the sandwich he had been reaching for. He bit into it mechanically, and continued to regard his cousin with astonishment – impressed, apparently, to see what an interesting person she had become in the years since he had last seen her. Katie closed her mouth and swallowed her piece of cake, her expression now cool and slightly disdainful. She glanced at Uncle Brian.

Midge was still speechless and Uncle Brian said, 'Dear oh dear oh *dear*. What *have* you been up to now? Come here – let's have a look at you.' But his voice was kind and full of concern, not anger. He had a little blob of cream on his chin. Midge suddenly wanted to cry again. This was all too much. On top of everything else, this was all just too much.

'I . . . I . . .' she began, wanting to blurt out the whole story, to tell everything, to be free of the burden she felt she was carrying. But she couldn't do it. It was impossible. There seemed to be no place to begin. She sought frantically for some reasonable explanation for the state she was in – and somehow the words began to spill out, words which were as close to the truth as she dared tell.

'I tried to get into the Roy . . . the wood,' she said. 'The old wood. I wanted to see . . . like you did, Uncle Brian, with Mum, when you were . . . I just wanted to see, that's all. I got stuck. In the brambles. It was horrible. I got stuck, and I couldn't get out . . . I . . . it was horrible.' She could allow the tears to fall, she realized. It was all right to cry. Even in her misery she dimly realized that the words sounded true – *were* true – and that it was all right to be upset. 'I got all scratched trying to get out again . . .' Her nose had started to run, and she could feel the tears, hot, on her cheeks. Uncle Brian moved towards her, uncertain as to what he should do – and found a practical solution in grabbing the roll of paper towel that stood near the sink. He tore off a great hank of the stuff and Midge took it gratefully, burying her streaming wet face in the clean soft texture, wiping her eyes and blowing her nose.

'It's OK,' said Uncle Brian, putting his arm around her sore shoulders and leading her to the big old carver chair that stood at the head of the table. 'Sweetheart, it's OK. Come and sit down. This isn't your fault – it's mine. I should have been here, and then perhaps this wouldn't have happened – whatever *has* happened. Anyway, you're safe, and that's the main thing. Are you sure it's nothing serious? No broken bones or anything? George, be a good chap and find me a damp flannel or something will you? Let's get this adventurer cleaned up a bit. All explanations can wait.' He took the balled-up handful of paper towel from Midge and pulled some more from the roll, as George ran upstairs to get a flannel.

Midge sniffed and said, 'I'm starving – could I have a sandwich?' Uncle Brian looked at Katie, who, without getting up, pushed the plate of sandwiches down the table. Uncle Brian stretched forward and brought the plate towards Midge.

'You tuck in, old thing,' he said. 'Eat something first, and get cleaned up later.' He winced as he saw the torn material on the back of the child's shoulders – the cuts and grazes around her neck – and was reminded of that other time, so many years ago, when he had arrived home with Midge's mother in more or less the same state. And had been whacked for it.

Midge, truly hungry, grabbed the biggest sandwich she could see and took the biggest bite she could manage. She didn't know what was in the sandwich, and she didn't care. It was half gone before the content had even registered. Ham and pickle. Nothing had ever tasted so good.

'That's right,' said Uncle Brian. 'We'll soon have you back on your feet.' Katie remained silent.

George came back with a cool damp flannel, and Midge wiped her grubby hands and face with it. 'Sorry,' she mumbled, her mouth full of food, 'I'm such a mess.' She wiped the flannel around the back of her neck, and held it there for a few seconds. It felt so good.

George pulled a chair up to the corner of the table and sat looking at her, taking the flannel back from her when she had finished with it and absently folding it into a neat square. He flicked his hair back again. I bet he does that a hundred times a day, thought Midge, biting into another sandwich. He had a nice face, though, open and curious – old-fashioned somehow, with his floppy haircut and plain grey open-necked shirt. There was a small white scar on the bridge of his nose. Katie sat further down the table, detached, crumbling her unfinished rock cake and rolling a sultana between her fingers, squeezing it, looking at the sultana, not at her.

'Did you actually get *in* there?' said George, now that the crisis seemed to have passed and a decent interval had been observed. Katie stopped playing with the sultana, but continued to look at it, waiting.

'I . . . don't really feel like talking about it right now,' said Midge, her voice sounding oddly prim. 'Sorry – I'm just so . . . Uncle Brian, is there any tea?' Funny. She never used to drink tea. She'd grown to like it.

'I'll make a fresh pot,' said Uncle Brian, glad, again, to be dealing in practicalities. Tea he was good at. Cleaning up wounds he was good at. Coping with emotional crises he was . . . less good at. 'And after that you must have a shower and get into some clean clothes. Your mother will have a fit when she sees what's happened to the stuff you've got on. Was it new?'

'Cost enough,' muttered Katie, speaking for the

first time since Midge had arrived. 'I think if *I* had a pair of Ozarks,' she said, referring to Midge's green dungarees, 'then I'd stay well clear of brambles in them.'

Hullo, thought Midge – what's *your* problem? But she said, 'I know. It was stupid.' She glanced at George who rolled his eyes slightly and pulled down the corners of his mouth.

Later, when she had showered and changed – and rubbed Germolene into as many of her scratches as she could reach – Midge sat on the corner of her bed and wondered what to do next. She didn't feel much like going back downstairs again, but supposed that she ought to. It was too early to sleep, and she could hardly just sit here until it was dark. She felt cross that Katie and George had been sprung upon her so suddenly. They were a week early. Why hadn't Uncle Brian told her that they were coming today? Wanted it to be a surprise, probably. Well, she could have done without it – Katie especially. What was the matter with *her*? At least George had been a bit friendly. And helpful.

She looked out of her window and saw the fields, still warm and golden in the early evening sunshine – but tried to avoid looking towards the long dark shadow of the Royal Forest perched on top of the hill over to the left. She would think no more about that today – she had promised herself not to. It was all a dream, just a dream. Better, then, to find some other distraction. She turned her attention to her dirty clothes, which lay in a heap on the floor. They were a reminder in themselves, however, of what she had been through, and the act of picking them up inevitably made her think back to the events that had led to their ruin. All a dream, all a dream. She could wash them, at any rate, and maybe they wouldn't look so bad then.

Then she remembered something else. She searched through her dungarees and drew out the little metal bowl – Henty's gift – from a side pocket, carrying the object over to the window where the light was better. It was delicately made, finely turned, and the weight of it surprised her. Once again she studied the tiny engravings, the small figures that surrounded the outer rim, trying to make out what they represented, but it was unclear – the surface of the metal was so blackened and tarnished. She would have to polish it up. And that would have to wait – besides, she didn't want to think any more about the forest. Not today. She put the little bowl on her window-sill, determined to concentrate on normal things, like washing.

Gathering up her battered little bundle of clothes once more, she went downstairs, quietly entering the kitchen to find that Uncle Brian was sitting there alone, reading a magazine. He put it down rather hastily as she entered and she realized that it was a girl's magazine – Katie's presumably – with pictures of popstars and makeover tips plastered all over it. She giggled. 'Uncle *Brian*! You're such a fashion victim!'

'Oh dear,' he laughed, blushing slightly, 'caught

red-handed. I'll never live it down with the darts team. How're you feeling, old thing? Any better?'

'Much. I'm just going to put these things in the washing machine. My trainers had better go in as well. Where's George,' she said, looking around, 'and Katie?'

'Oh, just having a wander round I think. Um, Midge, are you sure you're OK? You're looking rather pale, you know. I'm a bit worried about you, to tell you the truth. You've been really shaken up. Should we get someone to have a look at those scratches, and maybe give you a bit of a check up . . .wouldn't do any harm, I mean . . .'

'Really, I'm fine. I just got . . . frightened, that's all. Don't worry. I shouldn't have gone there. It was stupid.'

'Well, if you're sure. Midge, another thing, whilst the others aren't here – I should perhaps tell you to take no notice of Katie, if she's a bit, ah, stroppy. She can be a moody old thing sometimes – but it's just her way. She's fine once you get to know her. But the fact is that they've had their holiday with their mum cut short. They were supposed to be going to some resort, some park place, and now they can't – so they're here instead. Don't think George minds too much, but Katie's a bit jarred off about it, so if she seems grumpy with you, don't take it personally.'

'Oh, I hadn't noticed,' Midge lied, politely. 'But thanks.' She carried her bundle into the washroom, and stuck her tongue out at no one in particular.

* * *

227

She found George and Katie leaning over the gate that led into the Field of Thistles. George turned round as he heard her footsteps on the cobbles and gave her a smile.

'Hi,' he said. 'What do you get when you cross an elephant with a jar of peanut butter?'

'An elephant that sticks to the roof of your mouth,' said Katie in a very bored voice, continuing to gaze out across the fields, her back still turned. 'That is sooo *old*, George.' She punched his shoulder and he lost his balance, slithering down from the metal bars of the gate. But he was laughing all the same.

'I saw your mum on the telly at Christmas,' he said. 'I *think* it was her. With an orchestra on BBC2. Our mum said it was her, anyway.'

'Yes,' said Midge, cautiously, slightly awkward. 'Probably.' It wasn't something she cared to talk about much. Once or twice a year there would be a televized concert in aid of something or other, and she had seen her mum on a number of occasions, doing that other thing that her mum did – playing, or perhaps waiting to play, concentrating, watching and reading the music until it was time, raising the instrument gracefully to her chin, poised for a second – and then dipping forward, launching herself, drawing the bow across the strings in confident purposeful strokes, neat, precise, in perfect unison with all the others. Doing what she loved, being what she was. And not thinking about Midge.

She changed the subject. 'I'm sorry about your holiday,' she said. 'What happened?' A sore point, she

228

realized instantly – though she didn't much care, it was just something to say.

Katie grunted and turned to face her, acknowledging her presence at last. 'Yes, *we're* pretty sorry about it too,' she said, bitterly. 'Stuck in this dump, instead of Center Parc.' She looked at the little blue surfer top that Midge was wearing, unbuttoned, over a clean white T shirt. 'Hey, get you,' she said. 'Nice top. Off to Newquay, are we, *dude?*'

'What?' said Midge. But Katie had already turned around again, hunching her shoulders against the world. 'What a dump,' she muttered. 'You'd think he'd at least *pretend* to make an effort.'

Midge was getting cross, but said, as calmly as she could, 'I really like it here. I like it how it is. It's friendly.' Which is more than *you* are, she wanted to add. She looked at George, hoping for an ally, and George responded by flicking his hair back and saying, '*I* don't mind it.'

'Yeah, but *you* don't mind rock cakes. *You* don't mind disgusting rice pudding with skin on it. *You* don't mind rusty old cars. *You* don't mind *stupid* music, like jazz. You'd live in a shed full of sheep manure, and not *mind* it. Hick.'

George looked at Midge, and gave her an exaggeratedly loopy grin. 'It's true,' he said, with a mad cackle, 'I don't mind *anything.*' He jumped about, suddenly full of boy-energy, pretending to tap dance. He couldn't tap dance. Boys never can. 'How old are you?' he said, pirouetting gracelessly and coming to a standstill.

Midge laughed at his antics. What a twerp. 'Twelve,' she said.

'So am I,' said George, and then added 'nearly,' realizing that if he didn't correct his statement then Katie soon would. 'Do you remember when we went to Exmouth?'

'I remember the seaside,' said Midge – and suddenly she really did. There had been swingboats on the beach. And men with trumpets, playing on a balcony – a hotel? – and George . . . crying. That's right.

'I remember you crying!' she said, marvelling at how clear the picture was. She could see his little-boy face, screwed up in anguish. 'You had an ice cream – we all did – and you dropped yours. It was pink. The ice cream fell out of the cone and landed plop in the sand. I can see it! And then someone bought you another one, and the ice cream fell out of the cone *again*! The exact same thing happened twice!'

'Typical,' muttered Katie.

'And you had to give me some of yours,' said George, glancing at Midge with a faintly puzzled look on his face, trying to remember. 'And yours was . . .'

'Banana!' They both said the word at the same time.

'I'm going to have a shower,' said Katie, jumping down from the gate. 'And I really, *really*, hope the video's working.' She walked away across the yard, immaculate, with all the self-conscious grace of a pretty thirteen-and-a-half-year-old who believes herself to be the object of all attention.

'She's mad because you've got her room,' said George, once Katie was out of earshot.

'Oh,' said Midge.

'Though I don't know why it would bother her,' continued George, leaning back against the warm bars of the metal gate. 'She always says she hates it, and wishes Dad would make her up a bed in the little end room – which is where she is this time.'

'Well, *I* don't mind,' said Midge. 'I mean, I'll swap if she likes.'

'Shouldn't bother. That'd be wrong too.'

'Which is your room?'

'The one next to Dad's. I shall sleep there *tonight*,' George glanced surreptitiously at Midge, 'but most of the time I shall probably sleep in my tree house.' He watched her reaction to this.

'You've got a *tree* house?'

'Yes,' said George, airily, pleased that Midge had obviously not discovered his hideaway. He flicked his hair back. 'I'll show it to you tomorrow. You can help me set it up, if you like.' He looked at his hands shyly, putting his knuckles together and waggling his thumbs. 'That time with the ice cream,' he said quietly, 'you didn't *have* to give me some of yours. Nobody told you to. You just did.'

A few yards away, behind the half open door of the first of the disused stables, the four woodlanders listened to the muffled rise and fall of the children's voices outside. The sound entered the stable through the gaps between the loose pan tiles and the whitewashed end wall. Half-buried beneath the frowsty old hay, Tod, Pank, Spindra, and Grissel had spent the last

231

eighteen hours or so waiting for nightfall to come round once again. It had been a dismal time. Pank's injury had hardly seemed any better after a restless and wakeful night, and it was clear that he would be quite incapable of walking all the way to the Far Woods and back again in the search for Pegs. In fact it was doubtful whether he would even be able to return to the Royal Forest unaided. The four had discussed the possibility of dividing – two to go on with the search and one to return with Pank – but this idea seemed unworkable. Spindra had been willing, desperate even, to press on regardless, but neither Tod nor Grissel would return without the others. Tod felt that if Grissel and Spindra were allowed to continue alone, then their lack of knowledge regarding the ways of the Gorji would almost certainly bring them to grief. Grissel, for his part, felt that if Tod and Spindra were to continue alone then it would seem as though he were deserting his post – running away from danger whilst leaving others to brave it. He had no wish to try and justify such an action to Maglin – or to face the inevitable jeers of his fellow archers. In the end they had decided that they must all return – and this made the fate of poor Lumst seem doubly pointless, for what had been gained by this expedition? Nothing, it would seem. And yet what else they could do? Again, nothing. Spindra was heartbroken at having to give up the search, and Pank, of course, felt thoroughly miserable at having been the cause of all their problems.

And so they had passed the long hours, without

food or water, in more or less perpetual fear, some-times arguing, sometimes comforting one another. Every tiny sound ravelled their fragile nerves. The *vruma-vruma* that came and went, the big red birds that scratched and clucked or, worse, appeared silently and unexpectedly in the doorway before passing by; the voices, clumping boots, unexpected bangs and clatters – all served to keep their senses at an almost constant snapping point. There had been a period of respite. The heavy heat of the mid-afternoon had finally brought a long humid silence upon the yard, and the woodlanders had talked some more, examin-ing their situation in reckless whispers, going over the same ground again and again, trying to find another solution, another plan. They had no choice, in truth. There was no plan. From the outset their mission had been dependent upon good luck, and they had found only bad. Lumst was dead. Pank was injured. They had failed on all but one count: they at least knew where Pegs was *not*.

And now the Gorji were hovering nearby, talking of things that were incomprehensible to them. Seasides. Ice creams. What were these? Eventually the sound of the voices faded away as the giants walked back across the cobbles to the house, and a sleepy quiet fell once more upon the yard outside.

Spindra, tired almost beyond caring, lay back amongst the hay and gazed dully at the walls of their prison. Here were hung strange objects, unfamiliar to him for the most part – ancient metal hoops from long gone cartwheels, gin traps, horseshoes, a wheel brace, a small bow-saw (which he *did* know the purpose of, and which, moreover, he considered to be well worth stealing) and various straps and bits of chain, hanging from the rusty nails that were hammered into the rough-rendered walls. One particular object – a horse's bridle – was so familiar to him that he barely glanced at it, being more interested in guessing the possible uses of the other things. However, the bridle finally claimed his attention as he began to realize what a good one it was. The leather, although old and mildewed, was intricately tooled and embossed, and there were three little bells, green with age, mounted on the headpiece. A fine piece of work. And yet there was something odd about it, something wrong. The answer came to him, suddenly, and he sat up. The bridle was only familiar to him because it was of *Naiad* design and construction. It was not Gorji. To Gorji eyes it would be a tiny thing – far too small even for one of their hounds, let alone one of their horses. What was an old Naiad bridle doing in a Gorji byre?

He stood up and walked over to the wall to take a closer look, brushing the hay from his tunic, and squinting up at the long neglected little object, shading his eyes against the dusty sunbeams that fell through odd chinks in the sagging roof of the stable. The others watched him, mildly curious as to what he had seen.

'What be looking at, Spindra?' said Tod.

Spindra didn't reply. A strange feeling was slowly creeping over him – a feeling of revelation, and certainty. He turned to face the others, a puzzled look on his brown lined face.

'Pegs is back,' he said. 'Back home, in the forest. He'm there, I knows it.' A few moments of silence, then a general rustling of hay as his three companions sat up.

'How do 'ee know that?' Tod said, moving his head to one side in order to get a better view of the thing that Spindra had been looking at. It was a bridle. What did that mean?

'I just knows it,' said Spindra, puzzled himself as to how this should be. 'I knows he ain't *here* – knew that all along. But now I knows he ain't nowhere else, neither. Not in the Far Woods, not lost between here and there. Not nowhere 'cept where he should be. He's back.' And the little horse breeder scratched his balding head, perplexed at his own words, yet sure of his feelings.

Pegs had been born into Spindra's small herd some four years previously – an object of wonder and great pride to the Naiad, and as precious as a child to the herdsman. Pegs had been cared for as no other horse had ever been cared for, and none knew the magical creature better than Spindra. The animal was witchi, moreover, and could communicate in ways that were beyond their fathoming – perhaps even at this distance, for all they could tell. The other three were inclined to believe Spindra, then, when he said that Pegs was come home. If he knew, then he knew – as a father might know. Such things were possible. In the end they believed it to be so because they wanted it to be so.

Their decision was clear to them, then – for it had been Spindra who had been the most anxious to continue the search, and it was Spindra who was now satisfied that there was no need. All ideas of pressing on to the Far Woods were finally abandoned. They would return to the forest at nightfall – but they would not return completely empty-handed. They would take the opportunity to profit a little from their ordeal, and justify an otherwise fruitless expedition. A bundle of bean sticks was propped up in one corner of the stable, and, as the light grew dim, they used the longest to reach up and quietly unhook some of the objects that hung on the wall. The small bow-saw they took – for this was real treasure – along with the horse-shoes, four of them, which were useful lumps of metal – and although none could guess their original purpose, they might be fashioned by the Tinkler smiths into usable implements. The bridle Spindra lifted down and slung over his shoulder, sniffing curiously at the stiff fusty leather, and shaking the tarnished bells very gently. He would clean it up and it would be a fine adornment for one of his herd.

If Pegs were truly home then they would be glad, and if Spindra were wrong then at least another expedition could be planned. This thought comforted them somewhat, yet the sum total of their gain seemed a poor exchange for the life of Lumst, and it was a sombre little foursome who later peered out of the stable doorway to watch the moon rise over the hill. Their efforts, their fear, suffering, and ultimate loss, had largely been pointless.

One quick glance around the dark yard reassured them that the dreaded felix was nowhere to be seen, and they silently made their way round the corner of the stables, Pank supported between Tod and Spindra. They slipped through the bars of the gate into the Field of Thistles, and in a little less than an hour they were home.

Grissel's respect for his fellow woodlanders had grown, and though he smiled at the sly remarks of Benzo and Flitch upon his return – who were quick to suggest that he had fallen beneath his station by acting as guard to the likes of Troggles and Tinklers – he declared his travelling companions to be 'braver 'n most, and better company too' – an act of bravery on *his* part which was equal to any amount of renard-fighting.

Pank felt that he had had the adventure of a lifetime, notwithstanding the loss of poor Lumst and his own injury, and that he was unlikely to scale such heights again. His fellow cave dwellers never tired of hearing about the terrible encounters with the renard and the felix, and thought little Pank an awesome being in consequence. Many a timid soul wondered how they might have coped themselves under similar circumstance, and were glad enough to remain ignorant of the answer.

Tod simply added the experience to his growing knowledge of the Gorji and their ways: the more he learned, the better protected he felt in his regular excursions onto Gorji territory. Spindra was also left, ultimately, with few regrets. He had gone because he saw that he must, and his own strange insight – joyously justified upon his return and subsequent reunion with his beloved Pegs – had saved his fellow searchers from any further danger or needless deprivation.

The little bridle he kept to himself, and carefully restored to original condition – finding it to be a deep red, beneath the mildew of years, with tinsy-metal bells, and as clever a piece of work as you could wish for. Whoever had originally fashioned the thing had known what he was about – though what it was doing in a Gorji byre would remain a mystery for the time being. Spindra didn't use it on his own horses after all, but, in another moment of insight, decided that he must keep it safe for some future purpose, as yet un-defined, ready and waiting upon the day.

Chapter Fourteen

It sounded as though someone was dragging a coffin along the landing – a heavy scrape of wood on wood – and Midge, who had been lying half-awake, gingerly exploring the scratches on the back of her neck, opened her eyes at last and gave up all hopes of a long and peaceful lie-in. The sun was already streaming through the gap in her curtains, and she narrowed her eyes against the glare in order to look at her wristwatch. Five past nine. *Thump scrape thump.* What *was* all that racket? She heard George's voice – 'Give us a hand, Kate,' and Katie's muffled reply – 'Can't. I'm doing my hair.' More puffing and heavy scraping.

Midge sat up with a sigh and pulled back the duvet, swinging her legs out over the side of the bed – but quickly realized that she was going to have to stay where she was for a moment or two. She didn't feel good. Her whole body ached and her skin prickled in a hundred places from the cuts and scratches of yesterday's thorn bushes. It all came back to her in a rush – the fear, the pain and the shock of it – and she just wanted to lie back down on the bed, curled up in a ball, to sleep forever. She missed her mum.

'Ow!' She could hear George, cursing now beneath his breath, as he walked quickly up and down on the landing outside. Her curiosity and natural resilience overcame her desire to sink back down into the pillows, and she pushed herself up from the bed. She moved stiffly over to the door, turned the loose brass handle and peered out into the corridor. George was walking in a tight circle, red-faced, both hands tucked beneath his armpits

'Sugar!' he hissed under his breath. 'Sugarsugar-sugar . . .' He caught sight of Midge, still in her pyjamas, and realized that she must have heard him. 'Oh. Hullo. Er . . . sorry. Dropped it on my fingers.' He pulled his hands from beneath his armpits and blew vigorously on his fingertips. Midge rubbed her eyes and looked at the long wooden box that blocked the landing. It wasn't much smaller than a coffin after all.

'What is it?' she said.

'Ammo box,' said George. 'Found it last Easter.' His face was returning to something like its normal colour, and he had stopped walking in circles. 'Weighs a ton.' He sucked his fingers and blew on them again, his thick curtain of hair falling forward over his knuckles.

'What's in it?' said Midge. The box was made of rough planking, and painted army green. There was a broken bit of rope attached to one end – the remains of a carrying handle.

'Oh, everything,' said George, with a flick of his head. 'All my tree house stuff.'

'Well, can't you unpack some of it?'

'S'pose I'll have to,' said George gloomily. 'I thought that if I got it to the top of the stairs, it could make its own way down, more or less.' An exciting idea, but Midge didn't think it a very sensible one. And Phoebe, sound asleep as usual at the foot of the stairs, would doubtless have agreed with her.

'Hang on a tick,' she said. 'I'll get dressed.' She went back into her room and quickly put on the relatively clean clothes she had been wearing the night before, wincing as she raised her arms to wriggle into her T-shirt – *everything* seemed to hurt.

Outside in the corridor, George was already unpacking the long wooden crate. Midge found him kneeling amongst piles of tins and books, as well as other objects that were barely recognizable to her – a stack of old gramophone records, a folded up metal contraption that may or may not have been a cooking stove, an oil lantern, something that looked like a bomb or a rocket (but turned out to be a metal Thermos flask) and an oblong box finished in dusty black leatherette that said 'The Academy Nippy' on its lid. There were also various tools, a collection of battered old pipe-tobacco tins and a huge plastic water cannon – a brightly coloured and fearsome looking object with 'WaterBlaster' emblazoned along the side, that seemed very modern and out of place somehow. Midge knelt at one end of the crate and happily helped George to unpack his strange possessions, starting with the tobacco tins. Eventually the landing resembled a car boot sale.

Katie floated along the corridor at one point, dressed for cocktails apparently, in a little black outfit and sparkly tights, her blonde hair done up in an immaculate French plait. She picked her way disdainfully through the jumble, muttering 'Oh *God*, not all *this* rubbish again,' and began to descend the creaky stairs, her graceful appearance slightly at odds with the high pitched squeaks of the bare planking beneath her clunky heels.

'Hey!' said George, 'Where are *you* going?'

'Hollywood Bowl,' said Katie, over her shoulder. 'Dad's dropping me off.'

'You don't *bowl*,' said George.

'Who said anything about *bowling*? Sho long shuckers!'

'She's probably off to chat up the shoe-spray boys,' muttered George. 'How desperate is that?'

Uncle Brian's voice came up from below. 'Everything all right, you two? I'm off to Asda. Katie's going to come with me. I'll pick her up on the way back – shouldn't be more than a couple of hours. And George – I want to see all that rubbish gone by the time I get back. Place looks like a damn rubbish tip.' He didn't sound as though he was in a very good mood.

' 'Kay, Dad. See you later.'

George carried 'The Academy Nippy' and Midge struggled with an armful of tobacco tins on the first of

242

several journeys to the tree house. This turned out to be built in the crook of a curious cedar that dominated a small copse at the end of the back garden. Midge had spent very little time around this side of the house and had barely noticed the copse, let alone thought to explore it. The trunk of the cedar divided – in fact it was actually two trees, growing so close together that the stems had combined at ground level – and the platform base of the tree house was fixed among the strong jutting lower branches of the twin trunks, perhaps ten or twelve feet up. It looked more like an open-sided shed than a tree house, there being but three walls and a roof above the platform. There were no windows, and Midge could see that the walls, dark brown with creosote, were probably garden fencing panels. It looked good, though.

'What do you think?' said George.

'I love it!' said Midge. She allowed the heavy tobacco tins to slip gently to the ground, and then stepped back a little in order to get a better view. 'You are *lucky*. Wish I had a tree house. Or even a tree. Do you really sleep up there? Doesn't it get cold?'

'Gets a bit cold sometimes, but I only use it in the summer so it's usually OK. Dad wouldn't put a fourth side on it. Says I'd probably get locked in and burn it down with me still inside it. But *I* reckon he just couldn't be bothered to make a door.'

'Uncle Brian built it? Gosh. How do you get up there?'

'Rope ladder – look.' George walked round to the other side of the tree. 'Mind your head,' he said, and

243

pulled on a knotted length of yellow washing line. A rope ladder tumbled down from the branches above, suddenly and rather alarmingly, bouncing and swinging in all directions. It looked as though it had once belonged on a child's climbing frame. The rope was blue and made of nylon.

'This is great!' said Midge. 'Can we go up and have a look?'

'OK. You go first. I'll hold the ladder – it swings around a bit.'

Midge clambered up the ladder as George tried to hold it steady – it did indeed swing around a bit – and hesitated as she got to the top.

'Put your hand on that branch there,' said George. 'No not that one, the other one. That's right. Now if you put your foot – that's it – you've got it. OK?'

Midge had managed the slightly tricky manoeuvre of getting from the ladder to the platform without, she hoped, showing how nervous she felt, and was now walking around inside the three-sided house, stamping on the firm planking of the base. 'This is *great!*' she said again, as George swung himself up to join her.

Together they sat on the edge of the platform, their hands tucked beneath their knees, and looked out over the view. Through the blue-green foliage of the cedar, they could see beyond the garden and over the end of the old stable block that jutted out past the corner of the farmhouse. Here lay the lagoon – the abandoned muck pit – now an oddly discoloured area of greenish earth from which sprouted clumps of dark reeds. To their left they could see the flat patchwork of the wetlands, stretching for miles in the heat haze, to the faint hills beyond. A few jackdaws circled the cedar tree, cawing noisily, disgusted at having been so rudely invaded.

'Can you do this?' said George. He put both hands to his mouth – two fingers in each corner – and whistled, really loudly. His face looked funny, pulled apart.

'No,' said Midge. 'I can *whistle* all right, tunes and that. But not that sort of whistle.'

'I'll teach you, if you like.'

'OK,' said Midge, not particularly interested. 'Thanks. What do you sleep on?' The sharp edge of the platform was hurting her hands a bit, and she drew her knees up to her chin with her arms clasped about her shins.

'Folding camp bed,' said George. 'It's an army one. Come on, let's get the rest of the stuff, and I'll show you.' He stood up, hands thrust into the worn pockets of his khaki combat trousers.

Midge sighed. 'You *are* lucky,' she said again. George hesitated.

'Well . . . *you* could stay out here too. I mean if you wanted to.' He paused. 'Don't *think* Dad would mind.'

It was a slightly awkward moment. 'What about you?' said Midge, looking up at him. 'I mean it's your tree house and everything . . . would *you* mind?'

'No,' said George, sounding faintly surprised at having his feelings considered. '*I* don't mind.' He took his hands from his pockets and the stump of a blue birthday cake candle fell onto the planking. It bounced and rolled over the edge of the platform. 'Damn, I needed that. Anyway,' he continued, ' I bet there's an airbed or some cushions or something. Or you could have the camp bed. I don't mind.' He stood at the edge of the platform, wondering what had become of the candle stump, and said, 'See that big root down there? I broke my wrists on that. Both of them.'

'How?'

'Bungee jumping.'

'You *bungee* jumped? From here?'

'Well, I *thought* it'd be OK. There was some elastic rope stuff I found, and when I asked Dad what it was, he said 'bungee cord', so I thought I'd have a go at it. I mean, I assumed that was what it was for – bungee jumping. Pretty stupid calling something bungee cord if you can't use it for bungee jumping. I had it double thickness and everything – it *should*'ve been all right. I was in plaster for about a month.'

He started to climb down the rope ladder once more.

'We can cook and everything up here. I always do. Beans and stuff. It'll be more fun with two. Hullo, Phoebs. Did you hear me whistling? Sorry.' The old spaniel had wandered across the lawn to greet them. She snuffled vaguely at George's knee, as he reached the ground, but got no response from him. Disappointed at having been falsely summoned, she turned away, and gradually began to track another scent.

What *was* it with boys, thought Midge as she got to

the foot of the ladder safely and dusted her hands together. They were all crazy, one way or another. She wondered whether George was what her mother would consider a Liability, and a Bad Influence. Probably. But he was nice, too, she decided – saying that she could share the tree house, and being friendly to her in general. Not all boys would be like that. Glancing back at the tree house as they crossed the lawn, she was suddenly reminded of the pods – the wicker tree dwellings of the Ickri. The memory took her by surprise; it seemed so long ago. And yet it was only yesterday. She longed then to tell – to try to explain to someone, to George, all the strange things, incredible things, that had happened. But what could she say? She'd made a promise, and anyway, who would believe her? She could hardly believe her own memory. Once again she tried to put it all behind her, busying her mind instead with thoughts of camping out and cooking spaghetti hoops, and playing records by lantern light, the pleasures of which George was happily promoting as they returned to the farmhouse.

It took them the best part of an hour to ferry all the bits and pieces from the house to the cedar tree, and up onto the platform. They took everything but the outrageously garish water-cannon, which they left temporarily propped against the banister. ('It's no fun if you haven't both got one,' said George.) The whole exercise might have taken even longer had Midge not remembered seeing a sack truck in the cider barn, which, once loaded, they were able to pull between them, thus transporting a good deal of their cargo in one journey. It came in especially useful for carting the large wooden ammunition box to its destination, although getting the box up into the tree house itself was more of a problem. George was insistent that they should try, however, as he intended to use it for the permanent storage of his goods. Then, as he put it, he 'wouldn't keep having to go through *this* malarkey' every time he came to stay. He also felt that the box would serve as a useful table, or even a bench. Midge was not familiar with the word 'malarkey'. She said it to herself a couple of times and wondered if it was rude. George wasn't above a bit of cursing here and there, she'd noticed.

In the end, they managed to raise the empty box up into the tree by using the bungee cord that had once, literally, been George's downfall. The box bounced and swayed about in a barely controllable manner on its ascent, but between them they eventually hauled it safely over the lip of the platform and slid it into a corner. They both sat down on it simultaneously and wiped the perspiration from their foreheads. It *was* hot. 'I'm *starving*,' said Midge. They had brought a saucepan, various tins of food and half a loaf of sliced bread, and Midge felt about ready for anything that was going.

'Let's have some breakfast, then,' said George. 'You open some beans and I'll get things ready.' He jumped up again and cleared a space among all the bits and pieces that lay strewn around the platform. The little collapsible object that Midge had guessed to be a stove turned out to be just that, an old primus, and George soon had it standing on its legs, near the edge of the platform, ready to be lit. He hunted among his tobacco tins until he found the one in which he kept the Zippo lighter that he used for camping. The stove was primed and lit by the time Midge had found the can opener.

They sat once more on the edge of the platform, on either side of the primus stove, and dipped bits of bread into the saucepan of beans, taking it in turns to scoop up what they could, and licking their fingers with each mouthful. It was a sociable way to eat, and it tasted wonderful. Neither of them said much until the saucepan was wiped clean, by which time Midge was deep into a fierce reverie that involved living in a tree house with George forever, high above a flooded world, with nobody else in it. They would have a little boat tied to the tree and go fishing in it and look down through the cool waters at the cars and lorries and schools and clarinet lessons all drowned forever.

'How about a sardine?' said George, delving into his shirt pocket and producing a tin of them, like a conjuror. Midge giggled and gave a little burp. 'Whoops, sorry. No, I'm full up now.'

'Well, let's sort all this stuff out then. Tell you what – I *usually* put the camp bed along the back wall here, but if you're going to stay as well, then we could have one of these side walls each, put the beds along there, like that, and then have the box in between us. Like a table.' This seemed a good idea, and, although Midge's bed was imaginary as yet, they arranged the space according to George's plan. The stove they left at the front of the platform, and put the lantern next to that. The big box went end-on against the centre of the back wall, and they re-packed it with anything not immediately required and some of the tins of food. The heavy old-fashioned records, in their strange paper sleeves, were left out and stacked neatly on top of the green crate. And pride of place went to 'The Academy Nippy', which was revealed by George to be a wind-up gramophone. Midge had never seen such a thing. George placed it on top of the ammo box, undid the chrome clasps and opened the lid. Inside there was a turntable, covered in brown felt, and a complicated piece of chrome work, a swinging arm of some sort, which looked like a bit of fancy plumbing. There was a little winding handle, with a black plastic knob on the end of it, and a shiny lever that moved backwards and forwards in an arc. The whole thing appealed to Midge's fascination with things mechanical, and she loved it instantly, without completely understanding how it worked.

'Make it go,' she said. 'Play a record.'

'Well, pass one over then, whilst I wind it up.'

Midge took a record from the top of the pile and looked at it. The yellowing paper sleeve was mottled with age. She drew out the shiny black disc – how heavy it was! – and examined the label. It was red, and there was a picture of a dog listening to a gramophone – His Master's Voice. She'd seen that before. The song title was 'The Road To Mandalay' and under that it said 'Tommy Atkins'. Beneath that, in smaller letters, it said – Pianoforte: Mr Forbes Eaton.

George wound the handle a few more times, then took the disc from her and gently put it on the turntable. He moved the little lever, which started the disc turning, lifted the chrome arm and brought it towards the turntable, carefully lowering it onto the spinning disc.

Immediately there was a crackling noise, and a piano began to play. It was surprisingly loud, and yet somehow the deep rumbling piano chords seemed far away as though the sound had had to travel many years before it could reach them. A man's voice began to sing – 'By the old Moulmein Pagoda, looking east-ward to the sea, there's a Burma girl a-sittin', and I know she thinks of me . . .'

Midge looked at George who had turned away slightly, and now sat cross-legged on the bare planks, hunched forward, gazing out across the hazy wetlands, lost in the sound. Midge tried to listen, but the words were strange, and she had been instantly struck by how George seemed to be just like the Burma girl, looking eastward to the sea. How funny he was. 'On the road to Mandalay, where the flying fishes play . . .' the voice sang. How weird was that? Why would flying fishes be playing in the road? She couldn't figure that one out at all, yet she liked the sound of it. She watched the gramophone arm rising and falling slightly as the disc went round. It must have been a bit warped. The man sang how the girl was smoking a cheroot, 'and wasting Christian kisses on an 'eathen idol's foot.' What an odd song. But she liked the bit with the flying fishes, and recognized it when it came round again. The man's voice went up very high on the last line – 'And the sun comes up like thunder out of China crrooorst the bay!' The chrome arm reached the middle of the record and remained there, crackling, as the disc kept on going round and round.

George continued to sit staring at nothing in particular for a few moments, then turned and gently lifted the arm from the record. With his other hand he moved the chrome lever and the black disc came to a halt. He glanced across at her. The little white patch of skin on his scarred nose was shiny in the sunlight.

'Good, eh?' He sounded just like his dad. Midge wondered if she ever sounded like her mum. She hoped not – and then felt slightly ashamed of herself.

She wasn't too sure what to say. 'I love it – well I love the gramophone. Where did you get it?'

'It was already here – so were the records, most of 'em. I've collected a few since. There was tons of junk piled up in the little end room, before Dad cleared it out. He threw lots of it away, but he let me have a look at it all first, and I kept this.'

'It's a funny song,' said Midge. 'Is it what Katie said – jazz?'

'No,' said George. 'I don't know what it is. Don't know what it means either. I like it though. It's different, and – well, I just like music anyway.'

'What do you play?'

'What – like an instrument? I don't play anything.'

'Oh. Do you sing then, in a choir or something?'

'No. I can't sing. I'm terrible. I just listen. I just . . . well, I just like listening.'

'I play the clarinet,' said Midge. 'But only 'cause they make me.' Her feelings about music were mixed. She liked it – some of it – but music was what took her mum away. And she didn't much enjoy her clarinet lessons. She could do it, but it was boring. Practice, practice, practice, her mum said. Why? She didn't want to play in some old orchestra and be on BBC2.

'I like clarinet,' said George. 'And saxophone. I *really* like that. I've got a good one here – with clarinet, I mean.' He began to rummage through the stack of records.

'George! Are you up there?' It was Katie's voice. She was standing in the middle of the lawn, wearing jeans and a white blouse (how many times a day could a girl get dressed, Midge wondered?) and peering up through the branches. 'Oh, there you are. Lunch is ready.'

* * *

Lunch was a slightly uncomfortable meal. None of the children were hungry – Midge and George were still full of bread and beans, and Katie had bought herself a sandwich in Taunton – so Uncle Brian, who had gone to the effort of making a cauliflower cheese, was not best pleased. He'd been in a bad mood all morning, and, to make matters worse, he burnt his mouth on the hot cheese sauce and that made him crosser still – especially as everyone was watching him eat, whilst leaving their own food more or less untouched. So George's announcement that you couldn't beat good old baked beans straight from the pan could have been better timed – likewise his casual request that Midge be allowed to come and stay in the tree house with him.

'*Don't* think that's a very good idea,' said Uncle Brian, who had left the table to get a glass of water. He stood with one hand on the tap, and sipped at the glass, letting the water cool his tongue before swallowing.

'Why not?' said George. 'It's not as though she's going to . . . *molest* me, or anything.'

'*George . . . !*' spluttered Uncle Brian, 'Your being *molested*, as you put it, is not what concerns me. What concerns me is that in *your* company – and I'm going on past experience here – Midge has an excellent chance of ending up with her hair on fire and a couple of limbs broken. I'd *like* to be able to hand her back to her mother pretty well intact, and the way things stand at present it's already touch and go. And that's on her *own* account. Stick the pair of you up a tree with a box of matches for company, and I can see myself presenting Christine with the remains of her daughter *in* the matchbox. Like I said, not a very good idea.'

George let it rest for the time being, but remained hopeful. He gave Midge the thumbs up sign, whilst his father's back was turned, and nodded reassuringly.

Then Katie said, unhelpfully, 'Don't know why anyone'd build a stupid tree house in the first place. *Asking* for trouble, to build a tree house for a nimrod like George.'

'Who are you calling a nimrod, pig-nose?' said George, and Uncle Brian said that that would *do*. He put the glass down heavily on the draining board and took a deep breath, but said no more.

Midge felt embarrassed and tried to think of some way of changing the subject. She looked at the big black-and-white photograph that hung on the kitchen wall.

'Who's that girl,' she asked, 'in the photograph?' Nobody said anything for a few moments.

Then Uncle Brian turned round and leaned back against the sink, his arms folded. He still looked a bit cross. 'It's my . . . let's get this right . . . it's my grand-father's sister. So that makes her my great-aunt. She'd have been your great-great-aunt.'

'What, she's Midge's great-great-aunt too?' said George.

'Well, yes, you see, Midge's mum is my sister, Christine. So *my* grandad was Christine's grandad too.

So my grandad's sister, my great-aunt, was Christine's great-aunt too. Which makes her Midge's great-great aunt as well as yours.'

'It *is* confusing though,' said Midge. 'I never knew that I had a great-great-aunt.'

'Well, I could probably explain it better on a piece of paper,' said Uncle Brian, 'but, yes, she's one of your relatives, ancestors, whatever.'

They sat in silence and looked at the picture. The girl seemed to stare back at them, and past them, the dark eyes far away, looking beyond the camera at something else. The pale round face was echoed by the blurred clock face in the background. Twenty-five past ten. Unusual, those dark eyes seemed, in combination with such fair hair – a flossy cloud that must have been the despair of whoever had charge of it. The girl's dress had many buttons and the high collar was drawn up tight about her slim neck. Her boots, Midge thought, must have taken all morning to put on – so long and complicated were the lacings, criss-crossed from instep to shin. She could imagine what it must have been like to put them on . . .

'What's that in her lap?' said George. He had asked this question before – had had this conversation before – but was secretly intent on improving his father's temper, till such time as he could safely re-introduce the topic of the tree house.

'Don't know,' said Uncle Brian. 'Looks like a rattle or something. Although she'd have been a bit old for that. They might be bells, those little round things. She lived here, you know – in this house – grew up here.'

'And went nuts,' said Katie, bluntly.

'Yes, *thank* you, Katie – always useful to hear the informed opinion of a medical expert. Certainly she had . . . problems.'

'But she's so beautiful,' said Midge. 'I love her hair. She doesn't *look*, you know . . . mad . . . or ill or anything. What was her name?'

'Oh, lovely name,' said Uncle Brian, cheering up a bit. 'Celandine. Unusual, I think, for the time. They were quite a well-to-do family, so to be named after anything less exotic than a rose or a lily would have been a little out of the ordinary. A celandine isn't even a garden flower, really – more of a woodland thing. I like it, though. Celandine. Has a ring to it.'

'What was the matter with her?' said George, encouraging his father more, letting him talk his way out of his bad mood.

'Oh, voices, I think – hallucinations. Seeing and hearing things that weren't really there.'

'Like what?' Midge started to say – although her tongue seemed to have gone all funny. She swallowed and tried again. 'Like *what* things that weren't really there?'

'Well . . . like . . . fairies, I suppose, for a kick off. And for want of a better word.'

Chapter Fifteen

The drone of the Counsellors' voices below mingled with the surrounding hum of summer insects, and Little-Marten's aching head began to droop. High among the bleached and leafless branches of the Rowdy-Dow tree, there was nowhere to hide from the glaring sun, and no escape from the dull drubbing beat that thumped at his temples. Sick with apprehension, and dizzy with long hours of waiting in the heat, he clung miserably to his Perch and cradled the polished clavensticks – almost too hot to hold – against the soft leather of his jerkin.

After closing the wicker gates of the East Wood tunnel upon the Gorji maid, Little-Marten had fearfully made his way back through the humid forest, keeping well away from the main paths – and expecting at every minute to be waylaid by Scurl. He was alone and frightened among the silent looming trees, from any one of which a sudden arrow might come, and so by the time he had reached the relative safety of Counsel Clearing his clothes were sticking to him with the perspiration of terror. He thought in desperation to fling himself before Maglin, to tell all and beg protection – but why would the fearsome General take the part of the lowly Woodpecker against his own captain? And Scurl's cronies would back their leader's word, for certain sure. Snivelling would do no good – t'would make things worse, if worse they could be.

In the end he had sought out Aken and simply reported that the giant had gone. His other troubles he had kept to himself – he said nothing of what had happened at the spring. Aken, preoccupied, had merely glanced at him and sent him home. Little-Marten had then spent a fearful night, sleepless in dread anticipation of the wrath of Scurl, who would surely come and strangle him if he once closed his eyes.

And now, today, he had been forgotten. He had sat upon his Perch, hour after hour, awaiting orders with his head bowed, and slowly roasting in the unforgiving sun. The voices of the Elders and the tribe leaders rose and fell, endlessly. It was supposed to be a closed Counsel, yet few could keep away, and around noon more of the Various arrived in the clearing below, to listen, respectfully at first, to the long arguments of their leaders – but gradually, as the impossibility of their predicament became clearer, to disrupt and argue. The farmers and fishers, their wives and children, came in from the plantation, until soon all but the Tinklers and Troggles were gathered beneath the Rowdy-Dow tree – summoned, not by the clavensticks, but by rumours of disaster. The Gorji were coming. The Gorji were coming – nobody knew when, but soon. The noise grew louder. Little-Marten could hear Maglin's voice, calling for order.

He rested his head on his forearm and looked down at the crowd. He saw Tod and Spindra, returned in the night from the Gorji settlement, and whose opinions on the ways of giants were now in great demand. The news of Lumst's death, slain by a Gorji felix, had caused many a mouth to fall open in horror – though few would have known who Lumst was. He saw his father arguing with 'Pecker-Petan – not violently, but red in the face nevertheless, tapping the finger of one hand against the palm of the other as he made his point. Then Little-Marten saw Scurl.

The Ickri captain had appeared, alone, at the edge of the clearing, and was now making his way through the crowd. He looked up and caught Little-Marten's eye, paused for a second, fixing on him, and then held him in his impassive gaze as he calmly continued to weave his way among the restless woodlanders. Little-Marten felt the back of his neck go cold, prickly cold, even in the searing heat, and was certain that Scurl was coming for him then and there. He was going to shoot him, put a feathered arrow straight through him, in front of the whole crowd – Maglin or no Maglin. He gasped and shrank back against the hot dry trunk of the dead tree.

Scurl had stopped. He was standing next to his father and Petan. The two old men were still arguing. Scurl looked at the ageing fletcher and then looked back at Little-Marten. He raised his thick black eyebrows and, with a horrible smile, drew a lazy finger across his throat. What did he mean? What was he going to do? Little-Marten wrapped an arm back around the tree trunk behind him, trying to steady himself, trying to focus. It was so hot. The sweat trickled into his eyes and he couldn't seem to see properly.

Scurl, standing behind old Marten, raised his hand and suddenly clapped it down on the fletcher's shoulder. Little-Marten saw his father turn, his expression startled, as Scurl quickly whispered something in his ear. Then Scurl pointed up at the Rowdy-Dow tree, sharp white teeth showing in a wolfish grin, and his father looked across. His father smiled up at him and began to laugh. Petan leaned over in query, one hand to his ear. Scurl muttered something to him and Petan also looked up into the Rowdy-Dow tree. Then he began to laugh as well. What – what was happening? Scurl had his arm around his father's shoulder, as though he were a friend. Like three old friends, the men were sharing a jest. They were waving at him. The laughing faces, three laughing faces, like wurzel lanterns, seemed to rise up strangely then, on the noise of the crowd, lifted high upon the noise of the darkening crowd, before spinning away into blackness. Hwa hwa hwa!

The Woodpecker's wings must have half-opened by instinct, for his limp body spiralled down into the noisy throng, to slump, more or less unharmed, at the feet of Glim, the archer. Glim's wife, Zelma, gave a little gasp of shock but then quickly moved towards the crumpled figure. ''Tis Little-Marten,' she said, kneeling on the dusty earth and looking up at Glim. The archer leaned forward. 'He's in a swound. 'Tis the heat, most likely. We'd best bring him to shade.'

The tribespeople in the immediate vicinity of the Rowdy-Dow tree had pulled back in surprise, momentarily silenced by the incident, but seeing that Little-Marten was already beginning to stir and groan as Glim lifted him up into a sitting position, they gradually returned to more urgent considerations. Fletcher Marten and Petan, who had seen the young Woodpecker fall, pushed their way anxiously through the crowd and helped Glim and Zelma to carry the invalid into the shade of the trees. He was still, miraculously, holding on to the clavensticks. They propped him against the cool trunk of a great sycamore, and Zelma sent her husband for water.

'He'll mend,' she said to old Marten, seeing the worried look on the fletcher's wrinkled face. 'He's been too long in the sun – and no cap for his curls neither. 'Tis no small thing to sit up in that tree from sun-wax till noon.'

'You'm right there,' said Petan, with feeling – he remembered such duties all too clearly. 'How be doin', young 'un?'

Little-Marten had turned a pale yellow colour and didn't look at all well, but he groaned and said, 'I improve.'

Glim returned with a stoup of water, and old Marten lowered himself stiffly on to one knee to offer his son a drink. The lad took a few sips, and the fletcher dipped his fingers into the plain wooden bowl, bathing the bruised forehead of his son in cooling drops of water.

'Don't 'ee try such frolics again,' he said softly. 'I were near frit to death.'

Little-Marten was properly conscious now, and beginning to remember what had happened. He looked over his father's shoulder, anxiously searching for Scurl – but the Ickri captain was nowhere near. 'Scurl...' he whispered, grasping urgently at his father's woollen sleeve, 'he means us harm ... he ... put his finger on his throat ... he wants to ... kill me ...'

'Scurl? No, no,' said old Marten, 'bide still. You'm all mazed. Scurl means 'ee no *harm* – he were makin' jest wi' I and old 'Pecker-Petan, thass all. 'Twere a bit o' chaff, nothing more.'

'But 'tis so, Father – he tried to shoot the giant ... then Mad Maven was there ... Tulgi's dead ...'

'Hush, boy ... nobody's dead but a Troggle. You'm mazy ...'

'Let him rest,' said Zelma, 'that's what he wants now. Close your eyes, Little-Marten, and take some ease. Come, Petan, Marten, leave the lad be. We'll return presently. He'll do better without us fretting round him. Rest now.'

Little-Marten closed his eyes obediently – he would have liked nothing more than to sleep peacefully beneath the trees – but he was still whispering 'no, 'tis so, 'tis so,' as the others drew quietly away.

*   *   *

Maglin was finding it warm work trying to maintain some sort of order in the crowd. All attempts at reasoned debate had come to naught, and once it became clear that the Elders and tribe leaders could offer no immediate plans or solutions regarding the imminent arrival of the Gorji destroyers, the task of keeping control became increasingly difficult. Ba-betts had remained in the Royal Pod all morn – not that Maglin wished her present. His own archers were scattered who knows where, and those who were distantly visible, Benzo and the like, were more intent upon having their own say than in quieting the rising hubbub. Scurl was nowhere to be seen.

Only faithful Aken was on hand to help. Together they moved among the confused woodlanders, separating those who were close to blows and ordering one and all to return to their homes. If there had been any likelihood of this happening, a fresh piece of startling news soon put paid to it. Another death – Tulgi had been killed!

The rumour flew from mouth to mouth – Tulgi was murdered! Killed yestere'en by the mad hag! She had slain him with curses – with evil looks – with poisoned darts! The noise grew to a crescendo. What was happening to their world? They didn't understand.

Maglin glanced over at the Rowdy-Dow tree. Where had that hemmed Woodpecker got to? He caught a glimpse of Petan's white head, bobbing among the crowd, and plunged in after it.

*   *   *

On hearing the news of Tulgi's death, old Marten and Petan immediately remembered what Little-Marten had said. Perhaps the youth's words were not all the result of his fall. Together they pushed their way back to the edge of the clearing and hurried over to the sycamore tree. Little-Marten had gone.

He had gone, and at the foot of the tree, carefully placed, were the clavensticks. On top of the clavensticks lay the brown Woodpecker's cap, neatly rolled. The two old Ickri tribesmen gazed in sad wonder at the mournful little display. The Woodpecker had apparently deserted his post.

Maglin caught up with them and glanced down at the sticks and the cap. 'Where is he?' he said harshly. No reply. He grasped Petan by the shoulder. 'Can you still beat?' Petan looked startled, but nodded dumbly. 'Then get your old backside *up* on to that Perch, and beat for *silence*, and *you*' – he turned to old Marten – 'bring that youth of yourn back here. I don't care how, move. *Move*, before I use your witless old *heads* for clavensticks.' Maglin was just getting into his second wind. He'd thrash that mob into order, if he had to take them on one at a time – and he rather hoped it might come to that, for he was in that kind of temper.

The Ickri General stormed back to the Whipping Stone at the centre of Counsel Clearing, furiously grabbing such of his archers as were within grabbing distance along the way. He stood by the stone and waited, breathing heavily.

Old Petan gained the lower branch of the Rowdy-Dow tree at the fourth attempt, spurred on by the hoots of those who were near enough to witness his efforts, and by thoughts of what Maglin might do to him if he failed. He climbed up to the Perch, pulled on the cap, and took the clavensticks – heavier now, they felt, than he had remembered. He began to beat for silence. The dry rattle sounded high and sharp across the clearing, and the crowd, reacting by force of habit, was momentarily hushed. Their emotions were high, and no doubt the power of the sticks alone would have had no more than a fleeting effect – but that brief pause was all the opportunity that Maglin required. He opened his mouth and roared.

'*Silence!* SILENCE, YOU WITLESS FOOLS!'

The startled heads of the crowd turned dumbly in the direction of the Whipping Stone. Open-mouthed they gazed at Maglin – Maglin who was known to raise his voice when in a temper, but who had never raised it to anything like this volume before. It was a primary law of the forest that all business should be conducted as quietly as possible – shouting and yelling being dangerous pastimes – and so even extreme anger was usually conveyed in relatively muted tones. But now Maglin's voice rang through the high treetops, and was likely audible in the valley below.

Having gripped their attention at last, Maglin tore into one and all. 'Do I have your *ear*?' he cried. 'You? And *you*?' He jabbed his thick forefinger this way and that. 'And *you*? Do you *hear* me at last? Ha? Or must I nail each and all of 'ee up by the heels before you take notice? Ha? Speak up! Though, by *Elysse*, I'll have the tongue of the first that dares!'

266

And, as if to demonstrate his meaning, Maglin left the Whipping Stone and strode towards the crowd, grasping his spear in both hands. 'Hold your *ground*!' he roared as the crowd began to back away from his storming advance. 'Hold your ground till I give you leave to do otherwise! Aye, and let this be your watchword at all times – hold your *ground*. Hold till *I* say move. And when I *say* move, then move you will!' Face to face with the terrified mob, Maglin now paced up and down the straggly line, alternately thrusting his razor-sharp spear and his snarling countenance towards all within reach. '*When* I say – and *if* I say – *then* you'll do *as* I say! And not before.' He paused when he came to the three Elders. 'And *you*,' he addressed them collectively, 'who shall have the *final* say, think you?'

Ardel cleared his throat and began, tentatively, 'Well, of course, Ba-betts, as queen . . . although our laws are above all . . . and er, naturally, we as Counsel . . .'

'*Fool!*' roared Maglin. 'Be you *deaf*? I shall have the final say, from now on. *I*, Maglin! For 'tis clear to me that you've not a thing *worth* saying, nor listening to. *I* shall be the judge of all arguments, *I* shall decide what to do about the Gorji, *I* shall lead us away from here or command that we stay, as *I* see fit. Why? I'll tell 'ee. 'Tis clear to me that there's none other that *can*, that's why. None other *can*. And if there's a one of you who'll say me nay – then step up now and we'll have it out.' No one seemed inclined to take up this challenge, and Maglin continued, 'Very well, then. *I* say go back to

267

your homes – all of you, and wait *there*. And wait there until *I* say otherwise. *Go!'*

The assembled woodlanders needed no further bidding. They went. For this was testament – this was fire. This was what it meant to hold power and sway – and if any had been in the slightest doubt as to whom they were answerable to, and why, Maglin had put them right. Maglin had put them right, and having been put right, they were very glad to depart, in a quiet and humbled manner, to their respective homes – there to begin piecing together the remains of their shattered wits. Maglin was the law, and whilst Maglin could still stand and see, that law would be obeyed. This, at least, they understood.

Little-Marten hesitated in his stumbling flight through the trees as he heard the rattle of the clavensticks – his clavensticks, the hard-won emblems of his position, now returned to the hands of his old master. He had relinquished his post, lately the source of all his pleasure and pride, and was now but a fugitive, running he knew not where, fleeing he knew not what.

He stopped for a moment to press his hands to his pounding temples and to try and think. He had done no wrong. Maglin had given an order – to lead the Gorji child to the tunnel – and he had obeyed. But Scurl would have killed the girl, caring nothing for Maglin's wishes it seemed, and would now see him dead, as a witness to his actions. Scurl was beyond the law – that was what it came to. He could not remain in the forest and hope to live. 'I'll sithee dead.' It was a promise, simply made, quietly spoken. There was no reasoning against it.

Panic clutched at his heart once more and he lurched forward, his head bursting with the effects of the sun and his fall from the Perch. He would . . . he would . . . Wild ideas of leaving the forest came to him as he slithered down the shaly banks of the lower East Wood. He would run – run like a deer through the Gorji wetlands and go and live in the Far Woods – better to take his chances among the renards and the brocks than to face Scurl again. He would give himself up to the giants and be roast upon a spit – rather that, than to wake in fright with a cold hand at his throat. He would find a haven. Somewhere.

Panting and sobbing he leaned against the trunk of a sapling as the fierce blue sky seemed to whirl above him. There was nowhere, nowhere for him to go. He wound his arms about the young tree and pressed his burning cheek against the cool green bark. Through half-closed eyes he looked across the steep slopes of shale to the mouth of a Tinkler cave. The Tinkler cave where he had first seen Henty . . .

Henty . . . He pushed himself away from the tree and staggered up the bank of loose shale, stumbling forward, his fingertips touching the hot smooth stones. Henty . . . His feet crashed and floundered on the treacherous slope, and it seemed that he lost a yard for every foot of progress that he made. Salty drops of perspiration ran down his temples and stung his eyes as he dragged himself, at last, out of the burning sun and into the dim mouth of the cave. He paused for breath. Henty . . . The pitted walls were cool and the air smelt faintly of . . . lavender. He began to crawl, hearing his own breathing, loud and echoing in the sheltered quiet of the dim cave. A little further, further into the darkness, just a little further – away from the forest he would crawl. He licked the salt from his lips. Just a little further, into the cool darkness, to Henty, and safety, and the sweet smell of . . . lavender.

Chapter Sixteen

Maglin's violent tirade had exhausted him. He felt old and spent, though none would have guessed it to look at him. He stood by the Whipping Stone, gaunt, upright and formidable, facing every last tribesperson down till all had left Counsel Clearing and gone to their homes as he had ordered. Only then did he allow himself to lay a weary forearm on the stone and bow his grizzled head. Ah, but he was too long in the tooth for this game. A few more seasons and he would begin to look a fool.

Maglin.

It was the white horse. Appearing like a ghost from nowhere. Was there to be no respite?

'Go back to your pastures, Pegs. Leave me.'

We must talk.

'Talk? You've said enough of late to keep me in talk till the leaves fall. Go.'

We must talk.

Maglin took a deep breath. Were his words not clear? Must he begin *again*? He drew himself up angrily and turned to look at the winged creature. The dark brown eyes gazed steadily into his, and something in that wise expression checked the flow of curses rising within him. He breathed out again in exasperation.

'Come then. I shall walk the bounds. Talk if you must.' He strode away from the Whipping Stone at a furious rate, knowing that the injured animal would be hard put to keep up with him. But after a dozen paces he stopped and turned round. The horse hadn't moved. Maglin sighed, and walked slowly back to the stone, beaten. He reached out and roughly tousled the horse's mane, still half angry. 'Ah, Pegs. Pegs-pegs-pegs. Hemmed if I know what this day shall come to. What are we to do?'

What would you? They moved away from the centre of the clearing, and made their way across the rough turf towards the West Wood.

'What would I? Set all the Gorji to a blaze and bide here content. Or find new lands. But all lands are Gorji lands.'

No. Not all *lands.*

'So?' Maglin's voice was bitter. 'Do 'ee know of another?'

We are travellers, Maglin. And ever were. Travellers through the ages, our forefathers were, and so may we be again, though now we may seem to have lost our way. What do you know of the Touchstone?

Maglin was thrown. 'The Queen's bauble?' he said guardedly. ' 'Tis but a . . . a lump of red rock. I know naught of it.'

And yet, I believe you do. I believe you to have seen a little of its art.

Maglin was now deeply suspicious of this conversation. 'What have I seen?' he said. 'And what is it to you? What do you know?'

I know many things. And the time has come for you to know a little more than you do. Know this, Maglin – I am here to a purpose. I was born to a purpose, which you may understand in time. But tell me – would you not save your people if it were in your gift? I say you would – for you have a true heart, and are a believer if you could but see it. I will be your guide – but you must follow me.

Maglin was dumbfounded, and his voice rose once again. '*I*? Follow *you*? You will be *my* guide – a Naiad horse?'

I am Ickri.

'Ickri! You were born into Spindra's herd.'

Yet I am Ickri. No matter – all tribes are one. The Various are one. Travellers we are, Maglin, and we shall travel from here – far from here – when the Touchstone is restored. For this is my purpose, Maglin – to restore that which is broken, the strength of the Touchstone, and to see it in the hands of its rightful inheritor.

Maglin snorted. 'What fey riddles are these? You talk like the mad hag. I am trapped by the Gorji – beset by troubles within and without the forest – and you, *horse*, come to me with ravings of witchi stones and strange travels? These be *myths*, Pegs, tales told by old fools to gulled childer. What *strength*, what magic *art*, does the bauble have? And who be the rightful owner? 'Tis the Queen's.'

Not so. It is meant for one younger and fairer than she. As to its power – it is the lodestar of the Various, and in the

273

hands of its inheritor it will take us where we would go. These are matters of truth, Maglin, not myth. Yet they are also matters of faith, and your faith in this I would crave. You have seen something of that power, a little – I know it to be so. Believe a little more, and be my ally now – I am bidden to beg you.

'You are *bidden?* What would 'ee have me do?'

Listen to my words.

They had reached the edge of the clearing, and stood looking through the gaps in the foliage at the low flat expanses of the wetlands far below. Maglin felt out of his depth. He was ruler of the Various in all but name, and had laid about him with a strong hand as he saw fit. His way had served its purpose, and that the woodlanders still survived was due in part to his own strength. Now the Gorji were coming. If ever a strong hand and a clear mind were needed it was surely in this moment. Yet today he felt that he could offer neither. He had held the throng for the time being – bluffed them into submission – but doubted that he could do so for much longer. Panic and lawlessness would soon rise, and he feared that he would be help-less to prevent it. There had been two deaths since yesterday – how many more might there be come the morrow? And now here was the winged horse, come out of another age it would seem, with fey words and gimcrack notions, that he was bidden to put his faith in.

Yet the world turned, and he must turn with it – though it turn widdershins. He grunted, in annoyance. 'Say on, then. But I've little enough time for witchi-pocus, horse. I've little time for't, and little patience neither. I put my faith in what I can see, and let the rest go hang.'

Do you not see me?

'Plain enough.'

And what am I, think you? Am I but one of Spindra's herd – a horse? Tell me what you see.

'See? I see a meddlesome creature. Aye, a horse.' Maglin looked at Pegs, and then gave a long sigh, hooking his thumbs over his belt and letting the last of his anger evaporate. 'I give 'ee best, then. I see a wondrous thing. I see a thing I never saw the like of before – and I see where you be driving to. Talk, Pegs, and I shall listen.'

A good beginning. Understand, then, that we are not as the Gorji, rooted in the clay beneath our feet. And we do not belong here. We are not of this world, Maglin. We are descended from the great travelling tribes of Elysse, and are rooted in the wind. And like the wind we may go where we will, even to spanning the ages. We may take many forms – we may be Ickri or Naiad, but so may we be hares or jackdaws – we may even be horses, aye and winged if it suit our purpose, and if we have faith. We are not Gorji. We are Various. Yet we have forgotten much that we once knew, so long have we remained here. We have lost our faith, and we have lost our way. And so we have forgotten what we are. Now we must needs have faith again – and the Touchstone is the very article of that faith. Without the Touchstone, we are lost.

It was too big a mouthful for Maglin to swallow in one go, but he walked quietly beside the white horse, down through the mossy paths beneath the trees of the West Wood, and he listened . . . and learned.

There is much to know – and much that must remain hidden. For now, you need understand only this: with the Touchstone restored, and returned to its true inheritor, will come faith once more. Then the Various may journey far from this place, unhindered, untrammelled by the bonds of world or welkin, even to the very fields of Elysse. Faith is all.

'But the Queen already holds the Touchstone. How should it be restored?'

Ba-betts is not its true inheritor. And the Touchstone is incomplete.

'Incomplete? How?'

Part of it was taken, many years ago – by a Gorji giant. That which you have seen is but the stone. The stone is pierced through and once was fixed within an orbis – a silver cage wherein it might revolve upon an axis. It is this part, this metal device, that the giant took – and which must be found if the Various are to be saved. For without it we are doomed to languish here until the Gorji come at last. It is my task, our *task, Maglin, to recover the orbis, and thus restore the Touchstone, assembled and complete, to its power.*

Maglin laughed with sour disbelief. 'Then languish we must. What waste of words is this? Are we to now go chasing *giants*? A pretty pastime! We'll spend our days a-hunting – eh, Pegs? – and lead a merry life.' Maglin laughed again. 'And if we should ever find the giant as stole this . . . *thing* – would he give it back, think you? Or might he reckon to keep it after all?'

Mock me if you wish, Maglin, but you'll hear me out first. The giant was Celandine.

'*Celandine?*' Maglin looked more incredulous than ever. 'That old ogre-tale? 'Twere half forgotten when I was a snip! Celandine? Was there ever such a being then?'

There was – though I suppose her to be now dead, for it was indeed long before you were born that she came to these woods. A child she was then, a Gorji maid, and the last giant to enter this place – until yesternoon, when another like her did tread the same path; the girl, Midge.

'Brought hither by you.'

Aye, brought by me. And for the reason that I believe our history may turn in a circle, and that the device taken by Celandine may be returned by her kin.

'Her kin?'

Her kin – for the maid you saw is of the same tribe as she who took from us. I cannot pretend to see clearly into the realms of what may be – but I am certain that the girl Midge has a part to play. Remember that I myself am born to a purpose, and yet I would be already dead were it not for her. I owe her my life. She is bound up in my task, and in all of this. I know it.

'That's as it may be. But this missing thing, this stolen part of the bauble – do 'ee think it to be in her possession?'

I think it unlikely. But she is our nearest stepping stone on the path towards it – our only stepping stone. With her we must begin.

Maglin, who had been momentarily intrigued by the story, now began to lose interest once more. ' 'Tis but a tale, Pegs. There be nothing here to grasp a hold of. And even if we should ever find this thing – no. I cannot hang our existence on such a flimsy branch. We need action this day, and plans, not dreams.'

And what plans do you make? What actions do you command? The horse had stopped walking, pausing to look at Maglin directly.

Maglin felt uncomfortable and could find no reply. He avoided Pegs' eye by glancing upwards into the trees. He caught a glimpse of a squirrel, disappearing in alarm among the thick foliage.

Heed my words, Maglin. The Touchstone has great power – more than Ba-betts could know, or any in this forest could know. The orbis – that missing part of the Touchstone that was stolen by the Gorji maid – shall bring us all we desire, and more, when it is restored. Then you, Maglin, who have known what it is to bend others to your will and to command hunters and fishers, shall witness what it is to bend the very elements and to command the wind. Power beyond your imagining.

Maglin was still unconvinced. 'The elements are not so biddable as hunters and fishers, Pegs, and I doubt the wind is to be commanded by red stones and metal adornments – however prettily fashioned.'

Yet in the right hands, and with faith, they may.

'And in whose hands, friend, shall the restored Touchstone hold such powers? You have not said.'

Nor may I. But grant me this; let me go to the girl once more, with your leave and assistance, and speak with her, for I know that what we seek is dependent upon her.

Maglin gave a short, bitter laugh. 'With my *leave*? My leave was not sought when you brought her here. When have you asked my leave in anything?'

I ask for it now – and for your trust, and your assistance, and your faith.

The Ickri General had grown impatient once more. 'Do what you will. Talk to her if you must, and find out what you can – though I doubt the child has the thing. You have my leave, and what aid I may be able to give. As for trust, and as for faith – these be less easily given. Interesting words, Pegs – yet they are but words. Let me be, now, and I shall think on. Do *nothing* until the morrow at least. We shall talk again.' And Maglin, quickening his pace, walked on alone.

Pegs stood for a few moments more, undecided as to whether he should follow and attempt to press the General further. The matter was of sufficient urgency. No, he had said enough. He turned and slowly walked back the way they had come.

From his position high above, hidden among the thick foliage of an ancient lime tree, Benzo looked silently down and watched the horse and the General as they departed in opposite directions.

His purpose had been innocent enough – he was squirrel hunting. The Gorji hordes might be at the tunnel gates, yet the daily business of hunting for food must continue, and so, having been dismissed from Counsel Clearing by Maglin, Benzo had taken to the trees of the West Wood.

Benzo's method of hunting was simple: sit tight and wait. Sooner or later the innocent and the unwary would cross his path. It was a lazy strategy, but productive enough to get him by – certainly during the summer months, when both leaf cover and prey were plentiful. He had heard the murmur of voices approaching, and spied the General and the white horse coming along the path. Strict adherence to Maglin's command meant that he should have gone home – and he had no particular wish to be caught in breach of that command. He drew back among the high foliage and waited for the unlikely pair to pass by.

Maglin and Pegs had stopped, however, close to the tree in which Benzo was hiding, and he had caught the tail end of their conversation.

Heed my words, Maglin, the Touchstone has great power . . . more than . . . any in this forest could know. The orbis – that missing part of the Touchstone that was stolen by the Gorji maid – shall bring us all we desire, and more, when it is restored . . . (What was this?) *You, Maglin . . . shall witness what it is to bend the very elements and to command the wind . . . power beyond your imagining.*

Some slight rustle among the leaves nearby at one point had caught Maglin's attention and he had looked up. A squirrel. Benzo held his breath, and the moment passed. But what was this of the Touchstone and the Gorji maid, and power . . . to bend the wind? Benzo had continued to listen, and went carefully over what he had heard, still trying to divine the meaning of it long after Pegs and Maglin had gone their separate ways. Strange words. Strange – and valuable perhaps? Yet Maglin had seemed unimpressed . . .

Scurl's reaction on hearing the tale, however, was very different to Maglin's. He grasped Benzo by the shoulder of his ragged waistcoat and made him repeat what he had overheard, quizzing him closely over each remembered detail, listening intently, his dark eyes narrowed in concentration.

When at last it became clear that Benzo had told all that he knew, Scurl relaxed his grip and stood for a long time in silence, his back turned, gazing at the red evening sky through the darkening trees at the edge of the West Wood. Benzo looked at Grissel and Flitch, also present, who raised their eyebrows and shrugged. They waited for Scurl to say something, and speculatively watched the rooks that drifted lazily above the distant cedars, silhouetted against the pink and purple clouds. A chilly whisper of air blew across the clearing, a sly hint – even in high summer – that autumn would surely come again. Flitch twisted the knotted laces of his leather jerkin together.

'Maglin's a fool.' Scurl finally spoke, turning to face his archers once more. 'And the horse speaks true, I be sure of it. What reason would he have to speak otherwise, unless he be upsides in the head? The creature be unlike arn o' we, nor his own kind neither. He'm witchi. And whatever it was the Gorji maid have stole, 'twould be worth the finding of, aye, for more have been forgotten of the old ways than have been remembered, that I *do* believe. The Ickri be standing proof of that – there ain't many of the Gorji as has wings, that I know of. They ain't like we – nor we like they. Aye, this thing would be worth the finding of. And I reckon that *we* should be the ones to find it.' Scurl spoke decisively and looked closely at his companions. 'Come – who'll gainsay us? Maglin don't care, so says Benzo, and the old wosbird don't see no further than the end of his nose anyhow. Why not we? If we'm to be driven out o' here, like mice from the corn, straight into the arms of the Gorji, then a witchi-stone might be summat as we'd be glad of – if only to barter for safe passage.' Scurl tugged thoughtfully at one of his hairy ears. 'What I casn't see is why we've not heard of this thing afore – and why it haven't been *used* afore, if 'tis so full o' magic and here all this time. I've never seed no metal gewgaws on that stone the Queen do dandle wi'. Maybe 'twere hid – but then how did the giant come to get her hands on it? Bist *certain*, Benzo, that 'twas the *maid* who took it? Tell me once more.'

'Aye, 'twas she,' said Benzo. ''Cording to the horse. A metal zummat-or-t'other, *that missing part of the Touchstone as was stolen by the Gorji maid* ... Plain enough, he spoke – *stolen by the Gorji maid* – and plain enough I heard 'un.'

Flitch suddenly recalled something, and spoke up. 'I reckon I saw her tuck it in her roundabout!' he said, wonderingly. 'When she were comin' down to the spring wi' the Woodpecker. Some metal thing – I saw it right enough.'

'You'm *right!*' cried Benzo, also remembering. 'I seed it too – a bit o' metal! She has it for certain, captain – aye, for certain sure. Maglin don't believe it, though. I heard 'un say so.'

'Then we know more than he do,' said Scurl. 'And so we'm further along the path. Now then, Grissel –

tell us again what you know of the Gorji settlement. Who's there, besides the maid?'

Grissel hesitated. He wasn't sure he liked the way this was going. 'But one man,' he said, and added softly, 'and one hemmed gurt felix.'

'Never mind about the felix,' said Scurl angrily. 'You'm with your company now – not raggle-tags and hobbledehoys. I ain't worried 'bout a felix – nor aught else that goes on four legs neither. There's but one man, you say? One man and a Gorji chi'. *Six* of us there be – with Dregg and Snerk. Six of us against but one man and a snip. What do 'ee say, now? Are we like to best 'em?'

Grissel's face was expressionless, but Flitch and Benzo grinned from ear to ear.

Chapter Seventeen

It was the lamp-lighter who found Little-Marten, slumped in a heap on the bare floor of the main passageway, just a few yards in from the cave entrance. As the old Troggle-dame passed along the end tunnel, she happened to glance towards the entrance and saw the motionless form, a dark huddle against the harsh light that entered the cave from the outside world. She peered into the glare, drawing her little bundle of tinder and tapers closer towards her. Something there. What was it? Something from the outside. Massie didn't like the look of it.

She drew closer, and a little closer still, until she was sure – yes, she could see now, the crumpled shape of the wings. It was a heathen. She went to seek help.

They had laid him on a low pallet in a little ante-chamber, bare but for the guttering tallow candle with its scent of lavender. He had been dimly aware of the strong hands that lifted him, aware of the rough woollen coverlet they had draped over him, the low voices and the soft departing footsteps. And he had slept.

Now he was awake, feeling much better, if astonished at his surroundings. He was conscious of general movement a little distance away – murmured conversations amid the shuffling of many feet – as of a line of people moving along a passageway. Closer still, somebody stirred and yawned. 'Be you awake, Woodpecker?'

Little-Marten jumped, and sat up, shading his hand against the flickering light of the candle. A small figure was sitting by the open entrance to the stone chamber, leaning against the wall with legs outstretched and arms folded. Beside him, propped against the wall, was a hobble-stick. A little light entered the room from the corridor outside and one or two shadowy faces peeped curiously in, then quickly withdrew – whispering – to rejoin their fellows in the nearby moving line.

'Aye,' said Little-Marten at last, combing his fingers through his curls in bewilderment. 'Awake. But still upsides in the head, I reckon. Who brought me here?'

'Lamp-lighter found thee,' said the Tinkler, taking hold of the hobble-stick and rising to his feet with a grunt. 'And she ran to Tadgemole. Tadgemole would've slung thee straight back outside again, I reckon – but his daughter said she knew thee. Said you were Woodpecker, and pled to let thee bide till you'd had chance to speak.'

'Tadgemole's daughter?' whispered Little-Marten, looking more bewildered than ever.

'Do you *not* know her?' said his companion. 'Well I hope you ain't going to make her out a liar. 'Twould not please her father to find her out in an untruth. Terrible fearsome he would be if . . .'

'Enough, Pank.'

Tadgemole, the cave-dwellers' leader, had appeared in the entranceway. The stocky figure stepped into the little chamber and, after glancing severely at Pank, stood with his hands on his hips, looking down at Little-Marten. His unsmiling face was colourless, ghostly in the flickering candle-light, and deeply lined.

'Why did you come here?' The low tones echoed in the confined space – a strange voice, the accent unlike that of the upper tribes.

'I . . . was running away,' said the Woodpecker. He struggled to his feet, feeling uncomfortable to be talking to Tadgemole from his position on the floor. Tadgemole waited, in cold silence, for further explanation.

Little-Marten hung his head. 'I was running away from Scurl. He reckons to kill me – and has said as much. I . . . I led the giant, the Gorji maid, to the tunnels, as Maglin told me – and Scurl was waiting there. He was like to shoot us both, for he reckoned the maid would bring other Gorji down upon us. Then the old crone . . . Mad Maven . . . she up and killed Tulgi, and she made Scurl to let the maid and I go. And the maid *did* go. But I . . . don't have nowhere *to* go. Scurl says he'll kill me – and he will if he finds me. I *would* go too, leave the forest even, if I could – but I don't have nowhere. And then I run – and I came here. I didn't mean to. I just . . . came here.'

'And you thought to – what? Stay here? With Troggles and Tinklers – those your kind despise?'

'I didn't think . . .wasn't thinking . . .'

'Think on this, then. You of the Ickri bring your troubles upon yourselves – and upon the innocent heads of all about you. I'll have naught to do with you. Were I to give sanctuary to the longest line of black-guards from all the heathen tribes that ever were, then the last in that line would be an Ickri. These woods were ours long before your kind came, and now we live here perforce, upon your charity, or so you imagine in your ignorance. And you think to crawl in here begging for aid? Who are you?'

'Little-Marten, the Woodpecker – least I was. Now I be nobody.'

'Nobody. Well, Master Nobody, I think you must pick up your troubles and take them back to where they came from – for there's no home for the heathen to be found here. Shameless you are – and all your tribe. And shame you may someday feel.'

'I do – and did, long afore this day.'

'What? What do you mean? How?'

'I came here many a time – to be close . . . to listen . . .'

'To listen? To spy, was it?'

'No! The singing . . . I like . . . the singing.' Little-Marten sought for the words to explain how he felt. 'They said 'twere but the squawling of throstles, but I come here many and many a time. I hid by the thorn bushes, though 'twere the turn of winter and terrible cold, just to hear . . . and I never did hear such . . . could never hear enough. Then I felt shame. Then I wished that I could be – that I were not Ickri – that I were . . .' – he said it at last – 'Tinkler.'

Tadgemole took a step back at this, and regarded Little-Marten for a long time, deeply suspicious at first – was he being mocked? But then came the growing conviction that the youth was sincere, had been genuinely moved by whatever he had heard. He turned to look at Pank.

'Are you listening to this?' he said.

'Yes,' said Pank, his eyebrows raised in puzzlement.

'And what do you hear?'

'A song I never heard before.'

'Hm. Yes. A good answer. 'Tis a song I've never heard before, either. Bring him to Midnight Almanac. We're soon to start. Let him hear some songs *he's* never heard before, and then we shall see about this . . . winged Tinkler. Stay with him, Pank, and mind that he falls into no mischief.' Tadgemole turned to go, but suddenly remembered something else. 'My daughter, Henty,' he said. 'She knows of you. When have you spoken?'

Little-Marten, whose shoulders had begun to relax slightly, became tense again and said, as truthfully as he could, 'She . . . found me listening one night. By the caves – here. But she've never . . . spoken. Leastways not to I.'

Tadgemole regarded him for a few moments longer, then nodded and left, saying no more.

* * *

288

'Come, then,' said Pank when Tadgemole had gone, 'or we shall be late.'

The two small figures left the chamber and stepped out into the dim corridor. This was but a short spur, leading off to the right where it joined a larger and wider passageway. Pank led the way, shuffling along on his injured ankle with the aid of his stick, down the dark length of the main passageway. Little-Marten followed, frequently missing his footing on the rough stone floor. Small recesses were set into the tunnel walls at occasional intervals, each containing a tiny oil lamp. These were of clay – little more than a dish with a pinched spout to hold the wick. The burning oil gave off the sweet smell of lavender but not much light, and the distorted shadows thrown across the tunnel made the going seem more confusing than ever to Little-Marten. He was unused to dark cramped spaces, and felt nervous and uncomfortable.

A dim red glow became visible from a side-shoot a little further ahead and there was a sudden *tink tink* of metal upon metal. The sound echoed and bounced around the stone walls for a few moments and the high ring of it seemed to linger in Little-Marten's ears, even after it had ceased.

'What's that?' he said.

'Only old Bibber,' replied Pank, half-turning, and glancing over his shoulder, 'we'll give him how-do, shall we? Be sure and speak sweetly now, for he's 'mazin crotchety – and 'ud fling his hammer at thee for a bad word.'

They approached the entranceway, Little-Marten

289

following Pank's cautious lead, and peered around the corner. A warm radiance fell upon their faces and the smell of burning charcoal was in their nostrils. In the centre of a high round cavern was a glowing furnace, built of metal and stone, and standing over it, was the red-faced and burly figure of Bibber, the Tinkler heavy-smith. He was holding a curved length of dull red metal in a long pair of tongs, and stood examining it, his perspiring brow furrowed into a deep frown. Around the walls hung great metal objects – curious and unfathomable things they seemed to Little-Marten – and on the floor stood a long stone trough, black with soot and half-filled with water. Into this water Bibber suddenly plunged the tongs, and there was a deep bubbling hiss and a cloud of vapour. The billowing cloud seemed to fill the cavern, then rose and disappeared into the high darkness above. Little-Marten had never seen such a sight, and was both awe-struck and frightened by it. He drew back into the passageway, but Pank suddenly collared him and pulled him forward into the light.

'Ho there, Bibber!' shouted Pank. 'I've brought a young heathen for thee. He's been calling thee a fat old wosbird, and says he means to set about thee. He reckons to teach thee a thing or two about smithyin' too, for a blind toad couldn't do worse than thee, 'cordin' to him. What do 'ee say to that?'

Little-Marten's mouth fell open in horror at this, and he quailed as the great scowling face of Bibber turned towards him, tongs raised in his soot-blackened fist.

'Eh?' growled the heavy-smith.

' 'Tis a young heathen, Bibber! Come to march thee up and down and give thee a good duckin' in that trough of yours!'

'No!' gasped Little-Marten. 'I didn't . . . I never . . .'

'Never fear,' said Pank. 'He's deaf as an adder.' He grabbed Little-Marten and dragged him out of the forge as unceremoniously as he had dragged him in, pausing only to bow briefly in the direction of the old heavy-smith before leaving. 'We're away to Almanac!' he shouted.

'Eh?' said Bibber.

Pank hobbled on ahead until he reached the end of the corridor, and then looked back, beckoning to Little-Marten. 'Come!' he hissed, and turned the corner.

Little-Marten followed, deeply wary now, rounding the corner with great caution when he reached it for fear of further japes from Master Pank, but found his guide to be quietly standing a little way on, at yet another side entranceway. Here were mounted heavy wooden doors, dry and cracked with age, opening inwards. Bright candlelight spilled out from the portal, throwing a warm yellow glow across the grey stone of the tunnel, and illuminating the little figure of Pank, who stood waiting for him.

Little-Marten approached, and, although he heard no definite sound, he could suddenly and instinctively feel the presence of a hushed crowd beyond the door-way – a crowd who had seen Pank, and who were now anticipating the arrival of a stranger. He was aware of the slight *pad-pad* of his own footsteps in the passageway, and the bare stone, cool, beneath his toes. The scent of burning wax and lavender was very strong.

He reached the open doors and stood for a moment in the light, dipping his head in confusion at the daunting sight of so many faces, all turned in his direction. Pank put a hand on his shoulder and ushered him into a large crowded chamber, steering him towards a long wooden board, mercifully just a short distance from the door, where it was apparent that he was expected to sit – everyone else in the room being already seated in rows upon similar boards. He shuffled along and lowered himself awkwardly onto the unfamiliar object, gripping the rounded edge of the dark polished wood.

Furniture of any kind was a rarity among the upper tribes, the tree-dwelling Ickri in particular having no use for it. The Queen had her Gondla, and some of the more elderly had upturned wicker baskets to sit on, but little more. Yet here, in the large candle-lit cavern, side by side and in neat rows, sat the Tinklers and the Troggles on wooden seats built for the purpose. Little-Marten could hardly have been more surprised if he had found them hanging from the roof like bats.

Abashed at being the object of such open curiosity, the youth hung his head and put his hands between his knees, but gradually the staring faces turned to the front once more – amid much whispering – and Little-Marten was able to look up. Pank, sitting next to him, put his finger to his lips – an unnecessary warning – as Little-Marten glanced surreptitiously about him. How could it be that those who lived above ground had so little knowledge of those who lived below?

To his left sat an old Troggle-dame, who had moved as far away from him as possible yet continued to gawp at him, grinning toothlessly and nodding, half-frightened by him, half-fascinated, it would seem. Around the cavern walls were fixed devices of metal, each of which held several brightly burning candles. Candles, again, were a rarity among the upper tribes – not because they were so very difficult to make – but because any visible light at night was a dangerous thing. Hollowed-out wurzel lanterns were sometimes used, sparingly, but open flames were forbidden. Certainly there could be no open fires – willow charcoal and earth ovens were used for cooking and for hardening the arrow-tips of the Ickri archers. The bright glow of Bibber's forge and the flaring candles on the walls undoubtedly amounted to more naked fire than Little-Marten had seen in his lifetime.

At the front of the room, patiently waiting for the crowd to settle, stood Tadgemole. His hand rested upon another wooden construction – somewhat akin to the seats, but larger. The Naiad carpenters, Little-Marten knew, deployed a similar object – a work-board they called it – kneeling at it as they carved. This board had longer legs, and upon it stood several solid looking blocks of some strange stuff, wood perhaps – but hued in blue and green and scarlet.

'Now we are assembled,' Tadgemole spoke, 'and

you see that we have a wayfarer as a guest. I will say no more of him, save that – rare among his kith – he has a liking for a song. We must encourage this heresy where we find it,' Tadgemole allowed himself a wintry smile, 'and hope it may spread like a very plague above ground. Welcome then, Master Ickri – and all – to Midnight Almanac. Not quite all, I see, as Bibber is once again absent – no matter, we shall manage. Now then, who'll take up almanacs and instruct us this night?'

Half a dozen hands were raised and Tadgemole, glancing quickly around, said, 'Tingel, we've not heard from you in a moon or two. Come, give us a passage.'

There were one or two murmurs of approval as Tingel rose from his seat, and shuffled, with the aid of a curved hobble-stick, to the front of the room. Tingel was a powerful speaker, despite his years, and was known to have some lively notions beneath his straggly crown of white hair. He hooked his stick over the edge of the high board and rested his swollen knuckles on the polished top, staring at the coloured blocks laid out before him.

'Now, friend,' said Tadgemole, 'what will you give us?'

Tingel reached out and chose the green block. He dragged it towards him and picked it up with both hands – it was obviously heavy – and then, to Little-Marten's astonishment, seemed to split it asunder. The thing simply fell apart within his grasp – first into two, then into many sections as he turned it back and forth, flicking it this way and that. It was marvellous to watch. Finally he made the wayward object whole again, and replaced it on the board. Little-Marten glanced at Pank, ready to huzzah this clever display if prompted, but the room remained silent. Once more, Tingel reached out and this time chose the scarlet block. He held this aloft briefly, having come to a decision.

'Pears' Cyclopaedia,' he said, and there was another murmur of approval and anticipation from the audience. Pears' Cyclopaedia was one of their favourites.

Chapter Eighteen

Uncle Brian had finally relented, as George had known that he would, and said that it was OK for Midge to stay in the tree house, *provided* . . . and there had followed such a long list of conditions that George eventually became bored and started to wander off.

'Hoy!' said Uncle Brian, sharply, 'I haven't finished yet.'

'*Dad*,' sighed George, in exasperation, 'don't *fuss*. I promise, OK?'

'Promise what?'

'Everything. Everything you said. We're only at the end of the lawn, not . . . *Jamaica*.' He didn't know why he said Jamaica.

'*Jamaica?*' Uncle Brian laughed. 'What's Jamaica got to do with anything?'

'Wish *I* was in Jamaica,' said Katie. 'Wish I was any-where but here.' She sat with her legs over the arms of the old sitting room sofa, flicking gloomily through the TV guide. Uncle Brian glanced at her, but refused to be drawn on that one. He returned his attention to George.

'Well, just ... watch it, that's all,' he finished, lamely, and let it go. 'Anything good on?' he said to Katie, but she didn't reply.

'Yesss!' said George, galloping up the stairs in search of Midge. The door to her room was open, and he saw her standing at the window, gazing out towards the horizon. 'Dad says yes,' he said, slightly breathless from the stairs. Midge was silent, so George had a go at that thing where you put your heels firmly against the wall and try to touch your toes. He slowly toppled forward and reached out for the corner of the bed at the last minute to break his fall. The bed moved, and he bumped his knee on the floor.

'Are you OK?' he said, picking himself up, and rubbing his knee.

'Yeah, sorry,' said Midge, turning away from the window. 'Just thinking, that's all.'

They found an airbed and an old foot pump in the linen cupboard next to the end bathroom. The rubber foot pump looked perished, and had faded from its original red to a dusty pink colour, but it still seemed to work. They put these, together with Midge's bedding, into a couple of black bin-liners and lugged them up onto the tree house platform.

'Forgot my toothbrush, and my jimmies,' said Midge, struggling to untie one of the sacks. 'I'll go back later.'

'Your *jimmies*?' George laughed.

'Sorry,' said Midge, slightly embarrassed. 'Pyjamas. That's my mum for you. Anyway,' she said, rallying, 'I bet your mum has some stupid names for things too. They all do.'

'Yeah, well, she *does* still . . .' George hesitated, unwilling to come right out and say that on chilly nights his mother was still liable to offer him a 'hottie-bottie'. He winced, and changed the subject. 'You're probably right. Shall I put a record on?'

'Maybe later.' Midge gave up trying to undo the black sack, and ripped it open instead. She sat back on her heels, looking at the swirly colours of her duvet cover as it emerged from the split black plastic. 'This looks like a butterfly, coming out of its . . .' She couldn't remember the word. 'George, what do you think about all that stuff about Celandine? Great-aunt Celandine, I mean?'

'Great-*great*-aunt Celandine,' corrected George. 'Well, like what?'

'Well, do you think . . . she might have been telling the truth?'

'What – about seeing fairies? Come on.' George snorted disparagingly as he scuttled after the airbed stopper which had made a sudden bid for freedom. 'Mad as a hatstand, if you ask me.' He caught the stopper before it fell over the edge of the platform, and sat trying to thread it back onto the bit of string that was attached to the airbed. He sucked the frayed end of the string and frowned in concentration, his hair flopping forward over his face.

Midge watched him, and was suddenly desperate to tell. It had been bad enough before, but the conversation at lunchtime – the talk of Celandine –

had really shaken her up. Under different circumstances, the news that someone else had apparently encountered the Various years ago could almost have been a comfort – but then to learn that that person was generally regarded as being crazy . . . well, what did that make *her*? For what if people were right? What if Celandine *had* been 'seeing things that weren't there'? Hallucinations, that's what Uncle Brian had said. People must have them sometimes, or the word wouldn't exist. And, what was really strange, and frightening, was that, almost from the moment she had left the forest, everything that had happened there had begun to seem unreal, as if she'd imagined it. Even before the business with Celandine had come up, she had been trying to tell herself that it was all a dream, and that she must try to just forget it. Maybe she had whatever Celandine had – some sort of illness. Maybe it ran in the family, whatever it was. This thought really frightened her. But then, she reasoned, it would hardly be likely that she and her ancestor would have the *same* hallucinations – would it? So maybe she hadn't imagined it after all. Maybe it had actually happened. And this thought calmed her, until it occurred to her to wonder which was worse: *imagining* that little people were shooting at you with bows and arrows, or for little people to be *actually* shooting at you with bows and arrows, for real. It was too weird. She so wanted to tell. Up until now she had managed to keep her secret simply because she had made a promise – but now there was another reason for not telling: she didn't want people to think she was nuts. Like Celandine. She remembered Henty, standing on the grey shale outside the cave, and saying, 'Are you Celandine?' And at that point she hadn't known the name of the girl in the picture. So it must be true. It *must* be. But that didn't make it any easier to bear.

She pulled her duvet and her pillow out of the plastic sack. Chrysalis – that was the word.

They made up their beds, one each side of the ammo box, as they had planned, and it was fun in a way – but Midge couldn't find much to say, and she felt that George must be wondering why he had bothered to work so hard on his father for the pleasure of her company. He kept asking her if she was OK, and that annoyed her, so that by the time they had finished setting everything up they were a bit grumpy with each other. They sat at the edge of the platform, swinging their legs, and wondering what to do next. It was too early for tea, and they seemed to have run out of things to talk about. George had a thought, and he cheered up.

'Let's go and throw stones into the lagoon,' he said.

'What?' said Midge. Throw stones into the *lagoon?* What kind of a dumb idea was *that?* A dumb boy-idea. She nearly said that she'd rather just sit and read for a while – which would have been true – but it seemed a bit unfriendly. Also, she felt that she owed George something. He *had* been nice to her and it wasn't his fault that she was worried and thinking of other things.

'It's *great!*' said George, enthusiastically, 'It's like *quicksand.* Well, it is sometimes – when it's been raining a lot.'

'It hasn't been raining at all since I've been here,' Midge pointed out. 'But come on,' she added, determined to try and brighten up a bit, 'Show me what to do.'

It was a funny word, 'lagoon'. One of those words that you could say over and over until it made no sense. Like 'pillow'. The patch of scrubby ground at the back of the old stables didn't seem to fit the word, no matter how many times you said it. *Goonlagoonlagoonlagoon.* The remains of a wooden fence – just a few rotten posts and broken rails – indicated the original boundary of the slurry pit, now a flat piece of greenish earth, more or less circular, out of which grew odd tufts of reedy grass. It was perhaps forty feet across, slightly lower than the surrounding ground level, and looked as though it was covered in a yellowy green mould.

George and Midge searched among the shadows behind the stables for suitable things to throw. Bits of old roof tiles, they found, together with odd lumps of hamstone and broken masonry. They kicked around in the nettles and thistles to see what else there might be.

'Your dad said I should stay away from here,' said Midge, feeling that she ought to make that clear, in case of trouble. 'Oh, he stresses too much,' said George, dismissively. 'Tell him I made you do it.'

'Hmph,' said Midge, unwilling that Uncle Brian, or anyone else for that matter, should think her so easily led. Azzie, her friend at school, had sometimes got her

301

into hot water – but just as often it had been the other way round. They both got bored during the same lessons, that was part of the problem.

'Come on, then,' said George. 'Let's have a bung.'

They carted their booty over to the broken fence, and George had first go, shot-putting a big lump of hamstone out on to the surface of the lagoon. The rock didn't travel very far, and the result was disappointing. It landed just a few feet in from the edge, breaking the surface crust slightly like a spoon cracking the shell of a hard-boiled egg, but showed no sign of sinking to its doom. It just sat there, in a dull and somewhat reproachful manner.

'No good,' said George. 'Got to get further out towards the middle.' He picked up another lump of stone and stepped down the shallow bank, cautiously standing at the edge of the lagoon. He gingerly tried his weight on the outer rim of the mouldy green earth, and, finding it safe, moved forward another pace or two. Midge looked on with a kind of delicious terror – it was like watching a tightrope walker – as George ventured out just a little further and then heaved the second stone towards the middle of the lagoon. The effort of doing this caused the crust beneath George's feet to begin to break up, and he immediately had to dance back to safety, lifting his knees high, but still looking towards the centre of the lagoon to see how his stone was doing. And this time the result was much better. The second stone landed a lot further out than the first, with a soft and quivering squelch. It didn't sink, but sat for a while, half-buried in the ooze, giving

George ample time to examine his trainers and to wipe them on the grass.

They watched for a while, quite a long while, and were eventually rewarded with the eerie sight of the stone disappearing slowly, slowly, beneath the surface. Gone, forever.

'Isn't it *great?*' said George, and actually it *was* pretty great.

'Let me have a go,' said Midge. She picked up a large triangular piece of orange-coloured roof tile and took it down to where George had been standing – although she didn't venture out onto the surface. She swung her arm back and forth a couple of times, and let go. The broken tile landed on the edge and stayed upright, held by the thick consistency of the ancient slurry. It sank in a very slow and satisfying manner, reminding them both of the stern of the *Titanic*, disappearing beneath the icy waves, with the loss of many lives.

It was a very good game, and when they had exhausted their supplies of missiles they hunted around for more. This time it took longer to find anything worthwhile, and they drifted apart as they searched the ground at the back of the stables. Midge had managed to retrieve a whole red brick – a real treasure – after much kicking down of thistles, and held it aloft to catch George's eye. She saw him stoop to pick something up, something far too small to be of any use, and then saw him drop it – simultaneously hearing his voice, 'Ugh! Ughhh! *Ughhhhh!*' as he backed away in horror, wiping his hands frantically on his khaki combat trousers.

Midge put down the brick. 'What is it?' she called.

'Ughhhh!' George had half-turned away, his hands up to his face now – he looked like he was going to be sick or something. What had he found? She half-walked, half-ran, through the scrubby dock leaves and dandelions to where he was.

'What is it?' she said again. His face was white, really white, and he was shuddering. He pointed, and Midge crept fearfully towards the spot, moving sideways, ready to run, and almost as terrified now as her cousin. A small brown thing was lying on the ground where George had dropped it. A sparrow, or a dead toad or something? What? She couldn't make it out – then suddenly she could, and jumped back in gasping horror, as George had done. 'Ughhh!'

It was a hand. A tiny severed hand, swollen and a purply-brown, the fingers curled and puffy, the thumb bent inwards. It lay on a patch of bright green grass like a small creature on its back, locked in a last hopeless struggle, clutching desperately at nothing at all.

George was backing quickly away, his eyes still wide with horror. He glanced briefly at Midge, not really seeing her, and turned, undecided as to which way to run. The quickest route back to the house was by the metal gate at the end of the stable block, and he began to stumble uncertainly in this direction.

Midge, after staring in horror at the thing on the grass for a few moments longer, suddenly seemed to come back to life, and became aware of George's departure.

'Wait!' she called, realizing instinctively what he was about to do. 'George, wait!' George stopped running, but continued to move away – walking backwards, arms straight by his side, fists clenched, and staring once more towards the spot where the hand was.

'Wait a minute!' said Midge, 'Stop!' She caught up with him and grabbed the olive-green sleeve of his T-shirt.

'George – I . . . I know what it is,' she hissed. 'Please, listen, I know what it is.'

George stared through her, wild-eyed, and panicky. 'So do I,' he croaked. 'It's a . . . baby's . . . I'm gonna get my dad. Tell my dad . . .'

'No!' said Midge urgently. 'It's not that. It's not what you think. You don't understand, George, but I do. You've got to stop and listen to me for a minute.'

George looked at her, seeming to focus on her at last. He grabbed her wrist. 'Don't worry,' he said, 'my dad'll know what to do . . . get the police . . . they'll know. It's not our fault. We didn't do anything.'

'George, *please*,' begged Midge. 'Please listen. You don't understand. It's not what you think it is. Come back to the tree house – I've got something to tell you. I *promise* you it's got nothing to do with the police . . . I mean, it's . . . well there hasn't been any crime . . . but it's just really *really* important that I talk to you for a minute. Don't tell your dad, George, not for a bit – just let me *explain* something first.'

She had got through to him, she could tell. George frowned slightly – his face now puzzled – but his eyes had lost that wild panicky look. He flicked his hair back.

305

'What?' he said, his voice sounding a little more normal. 'Tell me what?'

It took quite a long time. They sat on the tree house platform, and Midge talked – letting it all spill out at last, the whole confused impossible story, from the moment she had found the winged horse to the moment she had entered the kitchen to find George and Katie staring at her dishevelled state in amazement. She recalled the night that Tojo had woken them; the presence of something inexplicable beneath the kitchen sink, and her guess that the hand was the remains of whatever it was that Tojo had caught. She held back, though, from saying that the winged horse could communicate – could talk in strange colours, could make words appear like soft explosions inside her head. There just didn't seem to be a way of getting this across – it sounded *so* impossible.

George listened to all that she had to say. He didn't interrupt, but gazed out over the moorlands, shimmering gold in the evening sunshine, occasionally giving her a sideways glance, and taking deep, slightly shaky, breaths.

Midge came to a halt at last, and waited for George to say something. He remained silent, picking at a small hole in the knee of his trousers. A terrible realization stole over the girl.

'You don't believe me, do you?' she said. George didn't speak, and Midge felt a rising pain in her chest.

* * *

He didn't know what to say. He just didn't know what to say. How *could* it be true? And yet the hand was there, and perhaps it *hadn't* looked much like a baby's . . . apart from its size. He remembered the clutching fingers, but then didn't want to remember. There was nothing he could think of to say – yet some words finally came out.

'Let's . . . go back, then . . . have another look.' He didn't know why he'd said that – it was the last thing he wanted to do – but without waiting for a reply he got up and began to descend the rope ladder once more.

Midge followed, feeling as though there was a tennis ball stuck in her throat. She could hardly breathe. After all that had happened to her, all that she had carried by herself, the weight of her secret and her promise not to tell – it was just unbearable. And now, to have broken that promise, to have told, only find that she was disbelieved . . . she trailed across the lawn behind George, speechless with misery. A robber band of jackdaws flew across the lawn, squabbling noisily, and flapped up to the roof of the old farmhouse. The children glanced towards the chimney-stack, watching the clamorous birds beating their wings at each other.

'I keep asking Dad for an air-rifle,' said George, 'but he won't get me one.'

Good, thought Midge – inwardly punishing her faithless cousin.

They climbed back over the gate that led into the Field of Thistles, and walked down the long shadow behind the rear wall of the stable-block, tense and nervous. It was worse, in a way, knowing what they were about to see, than it had been the first time. George was trying to catch his breath – but Midge was lifted slightly by the thought that here, at least, was some proof that her tale was true. And yet there wasn't – for it became apparent, even from a distance, that the hand had gone. The patch of grass was bare.

They stood and stared hopelessly at the place where the thing had been, then kicked around half-heartedly amongst the already trampled thistles and dock leaves.

'Where exactly did you find it?' asked Midge, just for something to say.

'Just there, where you are now,' said George. 'It was hidden in all the thistles and stuff. I thought maybe it was a bit of tree root or, I dunno, a toadstool or something. Couldn't tell *what* it was, till I picked it up. Then when I saw . . .'

'Well, it's gone, anyhow. Something's taken it. No point in telling your dad about it now.'

'S'pose not . . .'

'He wouldn't believe you,' said Midge. 'Even though you were telling the *truth*,' she added, pressing the point home.

'I didn't *say* I didn't believe you,' said George. 'It's just, well you have to admit . . .'

'Yeah, I know. It's mad. Do you think *I* might be mad? Like Celandine?'

George – to whom the thought had most definitely occurred – shook his head. 'Nooo . . . but, well . . .' Another thought occurred to him. 'I mean, take that

. . . that hand. Say it *wasn't* a hand at all. Say it was a *paw*. Like maybe a monkey's paw. It *could've* been.'

'It wasn't a monkey's paw, George.'

'But it *could've* been. It *looked* like a hand, but it could've been something else.'

'Oh, I see. Right. So you're saying that I *thought* I saw a horse, but it *could've* been a . . . a . . .' Midge sought for a word, ' a hatstand.' George laughed at that. He thought that was quite funny. Midge didn't know whether to laugh or cry.

They walked slowly back to the tree house and George asked Midge if she knew how to cook scrambled eggs. The jackdaws were quieter now. Perched upon the TV aerial, they surveyed the farm-yard with eyes that seldom blinked.

Chapter Nineteen

'Flying fish,' spoke Tingel, pausing to look at the expectant faces before him, 'are frequently to be seen in southern waters, and are capable of flying considerable distances – a quarter of a mole or more' – he hesitated – 'no, that cannot be . . . ah, comprend, a quarter of a *mile* or more, without touching the water. They can be caught in nets, while in flight.' He kept his finger on the place in the Cyclopaedia, and allowed the full effect of his words to sink in. A buzz of excitement ran round the candlelit room. Flying fish! So it was true – there *were* such things!

'Is this not news of some import, my friends? Once again we turn to the almanacs, and so we come to truth. If only we will seek hard enough, and long enough, then all is delivered to us. Flying fish – I have them here beneath my finger! Flying fishes! Now, did not she who gave us voices sing to us of such creatures? And did not she who taught us our letters give us the power to discover the knowledge of all such things for ourselves?'

Tingel closed the Cyclopaedia, lowered it gently

to the table and placed his hand upon it.

'These gifts,' he said, indicating the almanacs, 'were bestowed upon us long ago, not by chance, but by providence, I believe.' The old Tinkler's eyes were shining with delight and enthusiasm. Little-Marten leaned forward, holding on to the rim of the long bench.

'Do you see how we learn?' continued Tingel. 'Hardly a day goes by without some fresh revelation to astonish us. What may we not know, come tomorrow? And all of it from here – from the almanacs.' He spread his arms and beamed at his audience. 'Of Bread, To Make, we learned, from the Cyclopaedia. And of Jam, Blackberry, we learned – from the Cyclopaedia – and how precious this knowledge has been to us, these last few winters. Of The Dove-Tail, and all the cunning secrets of Joinery, we learned from The Home Workshop, aye, and much of Metalcraft also. Of songs, and verses, and fables we learned – and what comfort they bring. Are we not the most fortunate of forest-dwellers, to have been given so much?

And there are more boons to come, of that I am certain. The Campfire Songs we all know by heart – yet only understand in part. We have learned what a boat is, but as yet we have no clear notion of what a *sky*-boat is, or whether it may truly speed, like a bird, over the sea to sky. And we have no notion at all of what Matilda may be, or how it may be Waltzed – *but we may learn.*

'Flying fish were, but yesterday, seeming words of

311

fancy. Today, we learn that such things are *truly so.* Is that not wonderful? If fish may fly, then, surely, *all* things are possible. And all things *are* possible, through knowledge and belief. For knowledge and belief are the steps upon which we climb – away from fancy, towards truth.

'So we *shall* climb, my friends, even up to Elysse – itself no mere word of fancy – upon those steps of knowledge and belief. I marvel at how much we learn. What may we not discover? What may we not do?'

Tingel stepped back from the high board, and Little-Marten nearly jumped out of his skin as all about him made a sudden and loud clattering noise by smacking their hands together. He'd never seen or heard such a thing. Should he do the same? He clapped his palms, experimentally, one upon the other. A good sound it made – a bit like the claven-sticks. He applied himself with enthusiasm and fell into a pattern – part of Queen's Herald – but then faltered, in confusion, when he realized that everyone else had ceased. He sat on his offending hands, mortified.

Tingel had hobbled back to his seat, and Tadgemole stepped forward once more.

'Yes,' he said, 'a worthy discovery, Tingel, and a credit to the long hours of labour which I know you devote to your letters. Flying fishes. Remarkable. Now, who will come and sing? One of you youngsters, per-haps? Come, our guest has arrived on his very hands and knees for the privilege of listening.'

None seemed inclined to lead the way – an Ickri in

their midst was enough to bring on a general attack of bashfulness, certainly among the younger element who regarded the Woodpecker as being a personage of some reckoning – a fact that would have astonished Little-Marten had he realized it.

'Very well,' said Tadgemole, with a slight show of impatience. 'I shall exercise a father's right, if there be such a thing, and call upon Henty to begin. A reasonable request, as she holds *some* responsibility for the heathen's presence. Henty, come.'

From a knot of other youngsters on the farthest side of the cavern, towards the front, rose Henty – unnoticed until now by Little-Marten. So transfixed had he been by all that was happening, that he had not given the possibility of her presence a thought until Tadgemole had mentioned her name. She walked quickly to the front and turned to face the crowd, flashing her father a dark look as she passed him. She was furious with him. He had embarrassed her – not so much by making her sing, as by alluding to the fact that she had begged him to allow Little-Marten to stay.

'Take the Songbook, Henty,' said Tadgemole, his voice echoing slightly in the hushed room.

'I've no need of it,' said Henty. Tight-lipped, and looking even paler than usual, she ignored her father and the almanacs, standing to one side of the table rather than behind it, her hands clasped in front of her. ' "Early One Morning",' she announced, and began immediately.

Early one morning,
Just as the sun was rising,
I heard a maiden sing in the valley below –
O never leave me,
O don't deceive me,
How could you use a poor maiden so?

Her anger could not disguise her beautiful voice. There was no whisper of sound in the crowded cavern as Henty moved into the song, weaving her way through its simple tapestry, the clear high notes reverberating softly against the bare stone walls, gently echoing, and threading their way into the very hair roots at the back of Little-Marten's neck. Then, all around him, there was a slow intake of breath and the crowd began the second verse, as Henty stood silent:

Remember the vows,
That you made in the garden,
Remember the vows,
That you made to be true

And then Henty, singing all alone once more:

O never leave me
O don't deceive me –

And finally the whole room joining her, for the last line:

How could you use a poor maiden so?

The voices lingered over the last few words, slowly filling the cavern with a huge warm harmony that seemed to melt the very walls. Little-Marten, awestruck, would have given his wings to have been able to join in. And, as the sound died away, he made a small vow of his own: he would learn this – how to do this. Singing.

Henty walked back to her seat, bearing Little-Marten's heart and soul with her, and Tadgemole, slightly humbled as he always was whenever he heard his daughter sing, said, 'Thank you, my dear. Prettily done,' and secretly thought there was none to touch her for carrying a tune. The child *could* sing. He lifted his head and looked towards the back of the cavern. 'Come, Massie,' he said. 'Choose a partner and give us "No John".'

The old Troggle-dame next to Little-Marten made a brief show of protest, but was on her feet far too quickly for this to be convincing, and began shuffling along the row of benches toward the centre aisle. She put her hand upon Little-Marten's shoulder as she passed and gave him her toothy grin. 'Do 'ee sing, master?'

Little-Marten looked up at her, horrified. 'Nn . . . no', he stammered .

'Oh, no John, no John no?' she queried. There was laughter at this and Little-Marten hung his head.

'Well then, Gudge,' called out Massie. ' 'Tis thee and me again. I thought as I might find a younger John, and a prettier one, but 'tweren't to be.' A bald Troggle with amazingly bushy eyebrows stood up from the next row, grumbling good-humouredly, and the pair made their way to the front, he ceremoniously lending her his arm.

They took up one of the almanacs, a blue one, and once again Little-Marten watched curiously as Gudge split this in two, thumbed it back and forth a few times, then, apparently satisfied, offered it to Massie to share as they held it between them. Pank gave Little-Marten a nudge and whispered, 'You can sing too on this. We all do – just watch your place.'

Little-Marten looked startled at this, and nervously rubbed his palms upon his knees.

'Ready?' said Gudge, his eyebrows rising high up his forehead.

'Always ready for you, my dear,' said Massie, and there was a general chuckle.

' "No John",' announced Gudge, and began to sing.

> *On yonder hill there lives a lady,*
> *But her name I do not know,*
> *I will court her for her beauty,*
> *Will she answer yes or no?*

Then everyone joined Massie in singing:

> *Ohhh, no John, no John, no John no!*

'See?' said Pank. 'Nothing simpler.'

Two more verses and Little-Marten had caught on to it, singing out '*Ohhh, no John,*' with the best of them, as though he'd been doing it all his life, and thinking himself no small potatoes for his efforts.

316

Gudge then stood alone, leading the company with 'Drink To Me Only With Thine Eyes', which Little-Marten found impossible to follow, and so became rather crestfallen – but he cheered up at the sight of the jugs of hawthorn-beer which were thoughtfully provided as an accompaniment to the song, for singing was proving to be thirsty work, and took a draught and passed it on – and laughed with the rest as Bibber the heavy-smith arrived at last, just in time, as always, to prove that his throat was as dry as any present, though he sang not a note.

They worked their way through 'The Skye Boat Song', 'The Road To Mandalay' and 'Waltzing Matilda', with Little-Marten having but the faintest idea of what any of them could be about – though the chorus of the latter was repeated enough times that he was soon able to grasp it and join in, and then, finally, Tadgemole said it was time for the vesper, or the night would be over and no work done.

There was some protest at this, with cries of 'No, no! One more song, one more song!' and Little-Marten turned to Pank and said, 'Work? Do 'ee go out now and work?'

''Course,' Pank replied. 'Forage nights, sleep days – that's us. But never fear, we'll have one more yet.' And he broke off to add his voice to the cries for more.

Tadgemole raised his hands in defeat, amid cheers, and said, 'Very well, we'll have "Celandine", before we go. And I think that, this being something of an occasion, and it being many years since we had a visitor in our midst, we might bring out Celandine's

317

Cup. You will be too young, many of you, to know aught of this – but Celandine's Cup was fashioned and engraved by our forefathers, long ago, for that dear maid. Alas, she left us before it was finished, and she never received it – but we keep it still, awaiting her return, though return she never will. Our gift to her, it would have been – and a precious gift at that, much skill having gone into the making of it. Now, I think, it could be used as a cup of kindness – raised as a toast to *all* strangers who come here in faith, as she did. We shall raise it tonight as a toast to *this* young stranger – that perhaps he and his kind may think the better of us and we of them. Where one may lead, others may follow – and we shall not be the ones to refuse to meet respect with respect. Henty, my dear, fetch it to me, as a favour – you know where it is kept. "Sweet Celandine" it shall be, then. Who'll lead us?'

Little-Marten watched Henty as she rose and walked down the side aisle towards the door where he had entered. Her head was low, but as she turned to pass through the doorway he caught the briefest of glimpses from her as their eyes met. Recognition he saw there – but also deep confusion and fear. What ever could be the matter? She left the room, and it was as if all the candles had been blown out.

'Sweet Celandine', the song that had first drawn Little-Marten towards the caves, rose and fell in soft harmonies about him, but his mind was on Henty, and that troubled little glance. Why would she look at him in such a way? The song came to an end, and all about him rose to their feet.

Henty had not returned, and Tadgemole looked impatiently towards the doors. The crowd stood in silence for a few moments longer, and Tadgemole nodded at Pank, who left his place and hopped out into the corridor, to see if the maid was on her way. He came back into the cavern and shook his head.

'Hmph,' said Tadgemole, obviously annoyed at the delay. 'Well, we'll wait no longer. I'll say the vesper. Remember, those who would have been pestling tonight, please join the trufflers on this occasion – there's a good early crop in North Wood, I'm told, and I should like to see them gathered in by sun-wax. Remember, also, that at Almanac tomorrow night we shall be keeping memoriam for poor Lumst. And now, "No Busy Tongue" – he waited a few moments for silence, then spoke:

> *No busy tongue, nor idle hand*
> *Shall ever enter that dear land,*
> *Nor faithless pass beyond the gate,*
> *Where all our fathers stand in wait.*
>
> *So must we hammer, hard and true,*
> *The soul each day to forge anew,*
> *Our better selves may yet evolve,*
> *Upon the anvils of resolve.*
>
> *And when, at last, we grasp the key*
> *To virtue's kingdom – we are free,*
> *And thus shall find our sweet release,*
> *Upon the borders of Elysse.*

The crowd softly murmured, 'So,' and began to break up. Tadgemole caught Pank's eye once again and beckoned him and Little-Marten to the front.

'My regrets, Master Ickri,' he said to Little-Marten, 'my daughter seems to have lost herself. Our cup of kindness will have to wait on another occasion. What would you do now?'

'I . . . don't know,' Little-Marten hesitated. 'Could I stay, awhile longer? I'll . . . work, or do anything . . .'

'*Work?*' said Tadgemole, incredulously. 'Well now, that might be an interesting sight to view, an Ickri who . . .' – he broke off and sighed. 'I must learn to be more charitable. Old habits die very hard, I'm afraid, and treating an Ickri as a person of faith and good intention, let alone industry, may take some getting used to. But I shall do so from now on, until shown to be wrong. Stay, then, and welcome – and yes, you shall work, as we all must. I must also do you the respect of remembering your name – what was it again?'

'Little-Marten.'

'Of course. I think I know of your father – a crafts-man, at least. And you, too, have a talent, I recall. The Woodpecker. Yes. Well, then, Pank, take Little-Marten into your care and put him to truffling – this night at any rate – and we'll see what the morrow brings. Now I must find what has become of Henty.'

By the time the foraging parties left the caves, the moon was sailing very high, bathing the forest floor in a silvery grey light, criss-crossed with the deep blue shadows thrown by the ancient trees. The Troggles and Tinklers moved silently among the oaks and horn-beams, stooping low, occasionally probing the ground, kneeling to dig or moving on, depending on their findings.

Little-Marten, girt about with a forage bag and carrying a rough metal trowel, followed Pank and tried to emulate the actions of his companion – with the least possible success. Not a single truffle had he found so far – indeed he hardly knew what he was looking for, the tuberous fungi having no place in the diet of the upper tribes. Pank had shown him some of his own trove, but the small dark objects may as well have been clods of earth for all Little-Marten could see.

'How do 'ee know,' he asked, talking in a whisper, 'where to look?'

Pank was rather at a loss as to how to explain what was very largely instinct. 'Sort of smell 'em,' he murmured, casting about beneath a mid-grown oak. 'And, see? Look at the ring, see, about these roots – how 'tis cracked a bit, and how the ground raises up. That's a good sign.' He knelt and dibbled around with his trowel, eventually revealing more of these strange fruits of the earth.

'And I always thought 'ee only lived on what came from the baskets,' said Little-Marten. Pank snorted with contempt. 'Precious few of us there'd be if that were the case,' he said. 'The only reason we take it is that Tadgemole says 'tis sin to see even scraps go to waste.' He dusted the loose earth from the truffles and added them to his growing store.

Little-Marten despaired of ever finding one, and scratched about hopelessly, until Pank eventually took pity on him and said, 'Do 'ee know a mushroom from a toadstool?'

'Yees,' said Little-Marten, perhaps not as confidently as he might have, had the same question been asked in daylight.

'Then take yourself yonder – see down between the coppices – there's a place there, good as any for mushrooms, I know.'

So Little-Marten wandered off among the trees, feeling that he had been demoted, but he cheered up within a short while on discovering three fat puffballs, pale and strange in the moonlight, taut-skinned, damp from the night air, and as fresh and sweet smelling as you could wish for. These filled his bag to bursting, and so, feeling that he might deservedly rest for just a few moments after what had suddenly seemed an endless day, he flapped up to a low over-hanging beech branch, shimmied along it, and climbed a little higher till he found a comfortable crook to sit in. He would just stay a short while, till he judged that Pank might have found a few more truffles, and then perhaps they could go home. Home. He yawned – where was that? He let his tired shoulders drop, and tried to empty his crowded mind. Scurl and Tadgemole, his father, Petan, Pank and Henty – all were there, jumbled about and claiming his attention in one way or another. The peaceful night air stole about him, and gradually washed away all his thoughts, save one.

* * *

The light had changed. In truth he had not slept for very long, but now the moon had given up and gone elsewhere, and the night hung upon that chilly hour when the first hint of dawn starts to break through. The leaves about him were more green than grey, and the shadows less deep. He could see through the trees now, down to the silent wetlands far below, where strips of morning mist rippled the dark fields and slowly threaded among the leaning willows that stood, forever regarding their sombre reflections in the watery ditches. The sun would be up soon, but, for the moment, it was cold – and Little-Marten shivered. He put his hands under his armpits, yawning, and rubbed his bare feet together. Pank and the others must have gone long since. He began to be angry with himself. This was not a good beginning, falling asleep when he should have been working. He looked in his forage bag. The puffballs were still safe, and would show that he had not been entirely idle. He would go soon. He *must* go soon, or there was a danger that Scurl and his cronies would be up and doing – though surely not at this hour. Some sort of bird caught his eye, moving through the misty fields below, greyish-white – a heron? *Not* a bird though . . . something else. Little-Marten sat up and moved his head, to get a better view. A figure. Yes, a figure – and his heart jumped, for there was suddenly no mistaking that dark mane of hair. Henty! It was Henty – out there, alone, far from the forest and crossing Gorji territory! What could she be about?

He struggled to his feet, stiff from sleep, and scrambled clumsily through the branches, trying to track the movements of the tiny patch of grey, among all else that was grey in that silent dawn landscape. He kept losing sight of her as he climbed to a higher vantage point, working his way closer to the edge of the wood. Now he could see the dark shapes of the Gorji settlement, a huddled group of dwellings, rising from the shifting ribbons of mist, partially obscured by a copse of cedars and cypress trees. Henty was crossing an open field – heading, it seemed, straight for the settlement. Had she turned upsides in the head? She was all alone, and walking straight into the arms of the Gorji – into their very settlement! What *could* she be about?

A panicky muddle of thoughts raced round his head – and one of them suddenly began to make sense. He remembered the frightened look Henty had given him when her father had sent her to fetch Celandine's Cup. And then something made him think of the exchange between Henty and Midge at the mouth of the cave. Henty had given the Gorji maid a metal object – some tinsy thing, a stoup or a cup as it had appeared to him. *Celandine*'s Cup, perhaps? Could *that* have been the thing she had given to the giant – Celandine's Cup? A gift that had not been hers to give? And was she now frightened that her father – and all her tribe – would be angry to find it gone? Was she about to try to get it back? He could think of no other reason that would explain the madness of her present behaviour.

He watched, helpless, as the tiny distant figure reached the very gates of the settlement, hesitated, it seemed, for a few moments – and then disappeared from view. Frantic now, he scrabbled about from branch to branch, trying to catch another glimpse of her, but it was no good. She had gone. Who knew what might become of her in there? Her fellow cave-dweller, Lumst, had met a dreadful fate behind those walls, so 'twas said. Slain by a felix! The first shafts of sunlight rose above the early morning cloud, and the world was suddenly awake.

He should run for help – but to whom? Tadgemole? Maglin? But as he stood, gnawing his knuckles in desperate indecision, a further astonishing thing happened. Three, four – *six* winged figures came into view, ghostly as owls, soaring down from the trees to his left, launching out over the steep incline of the hillside, silently gliding across the empty landscape, wheeling, spiralling, and finally descending into the thin vapours below. Ickri archers they were, and for a wild miraculous moment, Little-Marten thought that Maglin had already been summoned and was leading a rescue party – but it wasn't Maglin at all. It was the West Wood hunters. He recognized them well enough: Benzo, Flitch, Dregg, Snerk, Grissel – and Scurl. What *their* purpose was Little-Marten couldn't begin to imagine, but he doubted if it had anything to do with bringing Henty safely back again. Were they after her? What could be happening?

Maglin. He must find Maglin. He jumped, swooped, fell down through the trees – flinging aside the cumbersome forage bag on the way and scratching his cheek as he did so – swung from a branch that was too big for him to grasp, and landed with an undignified thump among the hard protruding roots of the tree he had slept in, banging the side of his head in the process. Part of one of the roots came away in his hand as he struggled to sit up, and he found himself looking at a truffle.

I see you are up betimes, Woodpecker. Or are you still at your revels?

From the nearby coppices stepped the winged horse, his coat dappled grey and white in the hesitant sunbeams of early dawn.

'Pegs!' Little-Marten dropped the truffle and got back onto his feet. 'Pegs, I be so glad you're here! I've seen a terrible thing – you must help – 'tis Henty, Pegs, she's gone to the Gorji! And Scurl – he's gone after her!'

Henty? Is that the . . . Tinkler's daughter? And Scurl? Tell me your story – what is it that you have seen?

Little-Marten explained as best he could while Pegs listened gravely – puzzled as to the meaning of it all. For the Tinkler maid's actions there seemed to be some possible explanation – but none for Scurl's. What did he hope to gain? What did he seek?

This gift of Henty's to the Gorji maid – Celandine's Cup, by your guess – did Scurl know aught of it?

'I don't reckon. Though he might have *seen* it when he . . . aye, he *might* have seen it, for she carried it down to the stream . . . but he wouldn't know what 'twas. Some little tinsy thing – wouldn't be nothing to him – and I don't reckon he knows aught of Henty at all. Can't see that he would.'

Carried it to the stream? When was this?

Little-Marten told of his encounter with Scurl, and how he and Midge had been threatened with their lives. The horse seemed unsurprised at this – as though it confirmed that which he already knew – yet his manner now became more agitated, and his speech more urgent.

Scurl may be visiting the Gorji settlement for reasons more connected with the Gorji maid than with Henty, I believe – though both their lives may be in danger. We must act quickly. Pegs glanced over his shoulder, seemingly towards the bushes from where he had appeared, then began to move away. *Come, we will find Maglin and speak with him.*

Little-Marten came to a decision. 'You find him, Pegs – and as quick as you like – but I be going down there. Maglin'll have none o' me, as I suppose. Scurl would kill that Gorji maid if he sees her – and has vowed so. And I reckon that's why he's there – couldn't find me, so he'll do for her instead. But Henty's in amongst it – and I don't care about nothing else. And if she's stood between Scurl and a felix, well, she won't be stood there alone, and me standing here listening to Maglin. So you go and tell him what you like, and maybe he'll do something about it, and maybe he won't. But I'm away.' And Little-Marten took a couple of steps backwards, hopped up into the tree he had lately tumbled out of, and began to climb.

Woodpecker . . .

The youth glanced briefly down at the white horse.

I shall come. Tell the maid that, for me, if you see her.
Whatever Maglin decides, I shall come.

Little-Marten grunted, and continued to climb. It was a fair distance to the settlement, and his wings were small. He would need as much height as he could get. The sun shook itself free from the purple horizon – and the long hot day began.

It took Pegs a little more time to find Maglin than he had anticipated – the Ickri leader had sat up deep into the night talking with Aken, and then, finding himself unable to sleep, had decided upon a thorough tour of the boundaries to include a personal check on all the exit tunnels.

The weary General was not in the most receptive of moods when Pegs finally discovered him and told him the news of the various expeditions to the Gorji settlement. Henty had gone, then the West Wood archers, and now Little-Marten. Maglin was at first disbelieving, then furious – but when Pegs declared his own intention of adding to their number, the Ickri General fairly boiled over.

'Has the world turned witless overnight?' he roared. 'Do we deliver ourselves to the Gorji holus bolus, now? I wonder, Pegs, that you let the Woodpecker go – that was foolishness enough – but to now reckon on taking the same path . . .! And the archers – *my* company! Do 'ee all think that I count for naught? Do 'ee? Well, maybe 'tis so – maybe I toil in vain – in which case, why come to me? Why tell me your mazy tales? If I no longer hold sway in the affairs of this place, then what would you of me?'

Maglin, we agreed yesterday, you and I, that I would go to speak with the Gorji maid – but that I would do naught until today. Now, it seems, I may be too late – for I doubt that Scurl has any honourable reason to visit the settlement. He has vowed harm to the child. Her life is in danger – the life of one who has saved mine. And in seeking you out I may have already delayed too long. What would I of you? Come with me. Now. You are needed there. We go together.

Maglin's eyes opened even wider with astonishment. He looked as though he might explode.

Chapter Twenty

The creeping dawn had fallen, clammy and chill, upon the slight shoulders of Henty as she stood among the thistles and dew-soaked camomiles. She shivered as she looked through the rusty bars of the gate and saw the abandoned plough – the Gorji contraption that she had heard Pank speak of when recounting his ventures. That was where the woodlanders had hidden. Companions there had been for Pank – stout-hearted Tod, Spindra, an Ickri archer, and poor Lumst, of course. For her there was nobody. She was alone – all alone – and with no idea of how she was to achieve her purpose. Somehow she must retrieve the tinsy stoup, Celandine's Cup, which she had so foolishly given to the Gorji giant. *Why* had she done such a thing? Reason had told her at the time that the maid who had visited the forest with Pegs could not have been Celandine – that story was old when her father was a boy. Yet she had half-believed – wanted to believe – that the good spirit of the woods had somehow magically returned once again, and that all would be well. She had wanted to be the one to give the gift so long overdue, although even as she had put it into the giant's hands she had known it was wrong. Well, now she was paying the price for her impetuous gesture. The cup, unused and long neglected, was wanted once more. Her father, and all her tribe, would be furious to learn that she had given it away to the Gorji. She *must* find it.

Henty recalled details of Pank's astonishing and terrifying tale – of his entry into the very dwelling of the giants through a small door within a big door, of the byres where he and his company had hidden, and how one of those byres had contained the monster, the felix, and of this rot-metal contraption before her, from where the whole settlement could be surveyed. Giving herself no time to think – lest thinking should diminish her fragile store of courage – she scrambled through the bars of the gate and ran across the cobbles to the grassy verge where the plough stood. To enter the dwelling, find the giant, and either steal or beg the tinsy cup – this was the extent of her plan. She was well aware of how feeble it was, and so acted in haste before she had time to tell herself that she was heaping foolishness upon foolishness.

A quick glance about the empty yard, then, and she left the plough almost as soon as she had hidden herself beneath it – running along the foot of the balustrade wall and peering round the end pillar to look along the flagstone path leading to the front door. She had to stand on tiptoe to see over the two deep steps that dropped from the path down to the level of the yard. Yes, she could see the little door and knew that it had to be but pushed in order to open it.

Something lay on the grey flags – a huge Gorji boot – and, as Henty made ready to risk that long exposed dash to the dwelling, the boot suddenly seemed to stir, and some creature began to emerge from its depths. Henty stood, horrified, as the head of a felix appeared. She hadn't been prepared for this. The ways of the Gorji were strange, it was known, but never would she have imagined that they kept felixes in their very footwear. The dreaded beast had not yet seen her, but peered, blinking, in the early light, showing its sharp fangs in a gaping yawn. It was perhaps not quite as big as Pank had claimed – being more the size of a young coney than the giant brock of his description – but it was big enough for her liking.

Henty looked across the yard, beginning to feel the panic rising inside her. Where could she hide? The line of byres, she knew, had provided a haven for the woodlanders but they also housed the felix – when it wasn't lurking elsewhere. At the end of the yard stood a larger byre, and she could see that one of the great doors was slightly ajar. Ducking low, beneath the level of the steps, she braved the gap at the end of the path and then sprinted down the full length of the yard, her bare feet soundless on the mossy cobblestones.

She reached the great rust-coloured doors of the cider barn, and glanced, terrified, over her shoulder in case she was pursued, then, finding that she had apparently been unobserved, looked cautiously around the open door. Great metal stanchions loomed in the darkness at the far end of the barn, with a massive cross beam and various crates and wooden constructions, broken barrels, planks, stone jars as tall as she, and all the paraphernalia of an industry long abandoned. Stepping into the gloom, her nose wrinkled at the unfamiliar smell of cats and the ghosts of countless fermentations. A high ladder, she could see, fixed to a great upper platform that spanned the width of the barn and projected forward to perhaps a third of its length. This was the old apple store and to Henty it seemed as though it might provide a safe haven, although she doubted that she could scale the ladder – the rungs would be almost waist high to her. However, she wasn't here to hide, but to find what she had come for and then return with all speed to the forest. She ran back to the door once more and looked down the yard. What she saw then made her gasp with fright.

Emerging from beneath the broken door of one of the near byres, was the felix. *The* felix. Then she understood. Then she knew the terror of that recent night, when Lumst had lost his life. It was the biggest animal she had ever seen.

Tojo stretched and yawned, extending his sabre claws to the full and displaying the fearsome capacity of his gaping jaws. He looked towards the barn. The door was open. With his great brush of a tail almost touching the ground, and his flat broad head held low, he began to make his way purposefully across the yard.

Henty found that she was able to scale that ladder after all, and quickly. Throwing herself down on to the boards of the apple loft, she peered in terror over the edge, just in time to see the shadow of Tojo appearing in the doorway below. The monster slowly entered the barn, sniffing the ground, his baleful yellow eyes scanning the gloom. His wives and children were apparently absent. No matter. They would return. He sat in the doorway, a grim sentinel, occasionally squeezing his eyelids shut, tail ceaselessly twitching.

Henty could feel her heart pounding against the dusty boards, her breathing painful and shaky. She was trapped.

Chapter Twenty-one

George woke before Midge, rolled over a couple of times, and finally sat up, resting his head and shoulders against the back wall of the tree house. He looked at his watch. Not even six o'clock, but already he could feel the heat of the sun, warm on his shoulders, through the rough wooden panelling.

It was like sitting in a cinema. In the dim interior of the three-sided wooden house, the open end became a bright oblong screen, with all the early morning world showing in brilliant technicolour – a slow moving nature film, in real time. A bird or an insect would appear in the frame, play out its part, and then disappear off-screen once more. From his low position on the army camp bed, it was the upper branches of the cedar that were visible – foreign, they looked somehow, exotic, in searingly bright colours against the pale morning sky, the sun shining on the dewy branches and defining every powder-blue needle, every glistening cone.

Midge was still asleep on the other side of the ammo box. He looked at the little metal bowl she had placed on the box the night before. When he had asked her what it was, she said that she would tell him some other time, he could have a look at it some other time – like it was some sort of mystery. She was tired, she said, and anyway it was too dark by the light of the tilly lamp to see it properly. Well, now was some other time, so, in that case, she wouldn't mind if he had a look. He reached across and gently picked up the bowl, feeling the strange weight of it. It was engraved in some way, and he held it up to the light, frowning slightly as he tried to make out what it could be. He licked his fingers and rubbed them on the grubby metal surface. A crowd of tiny figures he could see – encircling the outside rim, like something from an old painting, mediaeval perhaps – in what seemed to be belted smocks, hoods, and tight leggings, or maybe just bare legs, and bare feet. All wore the same open-mouthed expression. George smiled. It looked as though the whole lot of them had just seen a ghost. He turned the bowl some more, made it wet again, and found a much larger figure, twice the height of the little ones. It was a girl – and she was different, not just bigger, but different in some other way. Strangely dressed, yet still more . . . modern. She too had her mouth open. Weird.

A disturbing and unhappy thought suddenly came to him. This was like Midge. This was like her story, about seeing little people. *This* was where the idea had come from. She had found this thing, picked it up from somewhere, and had invented a story about her-self. It must have taken her ages to think it all up. That was even more weird.

George looked inside the bowl. There was something else engraved around the inner rim – but his tongue tasted funny now, and he couldn't be bothered with it any more. He felt sad, and worried – it just wasn't . . . *normal* to make all that stuff up, was it? That was, like . . . what did people say . . . *disturbed*, wasn't it? He quietly reached over to replace the bowl, pausing for a moment to look wonderingly at the sleeping form of his cousin as he leaned across the ammo box. She was huddled up in her quilt, her back to him, just the top of her head visible. Poor Midge. He'd never really thought about what it must be like to be someone else – what it must be like to be . . .

There was a dry flapping sound, brief and startling, and a sudden rustle of foliage as something alighted in the cedar tree outside. George looked up, and felt his neck lock solid. His mouth fell open as if he might scream, yet his breath so failed him that he couldn't even gasp. Some fantastic creature – like a winged monkey, an impossible thing – was clinging to the slim upper branches of the tree. The spiky blue cedar fronds swayed up and down in the framed oblong of brilliant colour, as the creature

gained its balance and folded its wings. It had its back to the open end of the tree house – but there was no doubting what it was, and it was just as Midge had described. George was quite unable to breathe, or even to move, and remained frozen in the act of replacing the metal cup. He heard the thing sniff, and his amazement turning to creeping horror as the figure slowly turned, still swaying slightly on the cedar branch, to peer directly into the tree house.

Its jaw was long and its mouth hung open slightly. The eyes, screwed up tight against the dazzling sunlight, were set low and deep, beneath a heavily jutting brow and a bedraggled crop of wispy hair. It lifted a skinny brown hand as a shade against the bright glare, ducked slightly, and stared straight at him The dark eyes were open now, glints of light visible beneath the shadow of the small weather-beaten hand. George shrank back against the end wall, certain that his presence would now be obvious – yet the expression on the thing's face remained dull, inanimate, the jaw still hanging slightly open. It turned away, and gazed in the direction of the farmhouse. George was astounded that the creature had apparently not seen him – but still he dared not, could not, move. The glare from the sun, shining above the roof of the tree house, must have made the dark interior invisible.

Yet, from his perspective, every tiny detail was lit with amazing clarity. He could see the rough stitching on the greasy leather quiver that was slung over the miniature monster's back – the bat-like wings, folding and unfolding, flexing like a man might flex his shoulder blades, and the curious designs, coloured tattoos, that covered the semi transparent membranes. He saw the tiny orange hairs among the grey squirrel-tail cuffs that adorned the wrists and ankles, the small but sturdy looking longbow, hung with a tuft of magpie feathers at one end, the incongruous knee-length britches made of black corduroy, worn threadbare across the seat – which were held up, even more surprisingly, by a grubby elastic belt, black-and-white striped.

At last George let out his breath, in as quiet and controlled a way as possible, and gently, *gently* replaced the bowl on the ammo box. This was *something*. This was . . . *the* most amazing something . . . He looked across at Midge and wondered how to wake her. Her fair hair was still visible above her duvet cover, and she slept on, peacefully. George saw in an instant all that she must have been through, and his heart went out to her. He hadn't believed her. Thought she was crazy. Well, he believed her now – and would make up for his doubting her, if ever he could. Because this was *something* . . .

The creature in the tree had stiffened, was now suddenly alert. It was staring intently into the distance – had obviously spotted some approaching danger. The body sank into a crouch, and the skinny brown fingers rested lightly on the branch, a pause, a slight raising of the head, quickly ducking down again, and then the wings opened out to full stretch.

Dregg was not the brightest of the West Wood archers, but he recognized danger – when he could see it. He launched himself silently from the branches and was gone.

George gaped in open-mouthed wonder at the now empty vista at the end of the tree house. The cedar tree ceased to sway, and stood, snapshot still, against the cloudless sky. He heard the slight crack and tick of the timber wall panel behind him as it expanded in the heat.

'Midge!' he whispered, urgently, elatedly, 'Midge! Wake up! I've seen one!'

Midge turned her head slightly. 'Wha? Hnn?'

'Wake up, Midge! I'm so – I can't *believe* this . . .'

'George?' It was his father's voice, slightly muffled, coming up from ground level. 'Midge? Are you awake?'

'Dad?'

What was going on? Why was his dad here? There was a heavy creak and a slight movement of the tree house as his father began to ascend the rope ladder. Midge sat up as Uncle Brian clambered up the ladder and appeared over the edge of the wooden platform. 'Phew!' he said, staggering slightly as he stood up, 'Getting too old for this malarkey. Are you awake, you two? Probably weren't – I *am* sorry. Really – I'm sorry – but I've left it as late as I dare. Midge – well, both of you, I've had some bad news. Well, sort of bad news – nothing too alarming, but, um, not too good either.' He sat on the end of the ammo box, facing Midge – who was still barely awake. 'I'm sorry, sweetheart, you're still half asleep. Listen, Midge, it's your mum, I'm afraid. Don't – no, it's OK, don't worry, she hasn't come to any harm.

Look, let's go into the house – have a cup of tea or something – and I'll tell you all about it.'

'No!' said Midge, her eyes now open, and wild with alarm. 'What's happened to Mum? What's going on? Tell me now!'

'Well, all right. But I don't want you to *worry*. She's had to pull out of her tour.'

'What? Why?'

'She's not . . . feeling too good. She's not . . .'

'What do you mean? Is she ill?' Horrible thoughts were racing through Midge's head. Horrible things . . .

'No, not exactly. She's not feeling up to it. She just can't . . . do it any more. It's like her nerve has gone. It's all just become too much for her. She phoned late last night, long, long after you'd gone to bed. I didn't want to wake you then. She's *OK*, Midge, really, she's OK – you mustn't go imagining the worst, but for the moment anyway, she's out of the tour. She wants to – well, I persuaded her – to come down here, take it easy for a few days. It's just pressure, I think. It can happen in any job. Anyway, she didn't want to travel by herself, so I said I'd go and pick her up. And that's why I've come to wake you. I'm going up to London to meet her, and then I'll come back down with her.'

'What today? Now? Can I come with you?'

'Well, come and give her a ring. She wants to talk to you.'

Her mum didn't sound like her mum. Her voice was different, very calm – super-calm and dreamy almost.

341

'You sound . . . different,' said Midge.

'Do I?' her mum laughed. 'To be honest, it's probably the pills, darling. The doctor said I should take them – but I really don't think I shall bother anymore. I'm not *that* bad. It's just the playing. I'm OK till it comes to the playing. Now that I've made the decision not to do it – for the time being anyway – I feel a lot better. Really, lots better. It's like having a phobia – fear of flying or something. There's nothing wrong with you, as long as someone doesn't make you get on a plane. I've decided to get off the plane, that's all. I'll tell you all about it darling, and don't *worry*, I'm not frothing at the mouth or anything. And I'm so looking forward to seeing you. Really looking forward to it. I can't tell you what a relief it is to just . . . stop. Can you understand that?'

'Yes. Can I come up with Uncle Brian?'

'You could – but there's something I want to talk to him about. Nothing drastic – well nothing to be concerned about – but, Midge, it's a long journey, and I'll be with you by teatime anyway. Can you bear that?'

'OK. If you're sure you're going to be all right.'

'I'm fine. But how have *you* been? What have you been up to?'

'Oh, well . . . I'll tell you when you get here.' It was the first time she could remember her mum calling her Midge.

They hovered about the hallway while Uncle Brian got ready to go. He went through his list: 'Car keys, glasses, credit card . . . um . . .'

342

'Timetable?' said George.

'Don't really need one,' said Uncle Brian. 'I shall just leave the car at the station and catch the first available train. They're pretty regular at this time in the morning. Now listen, Katie's in charge, though I doubt you'll see her before midday, and I'll be back – *we'll* be back – tea-timeish I should think. Has your mum got a mobile, Midge? Yes, of course she would have. So you can contact us if you need to. Well, I'm off. Keep safe, now. I *mean* it, George – remember all those promises you made.'

'OK. Dad. Don't worry.'

'Well, just be careful. Oh, and I'm expecting a phone call from a land agent – Dunmow's. Tell them – oh I don't know – tell them I'll ring them tomorrow. Makes no difference now anyway – the sale's fallen through.'

'What do you mean?' said Midge.

'The sale of the land – it's fallen through – for the time being anyway. Had a letter yesterday. There's trouble with the planning permission. Looks like we may not get it after all.' Uncle Brian patted his pockets and began to hurry down the front path, stepping automatically over the wellington boot. Midge and George followed him to the car. Midge, absolutely bewildered now, said, 'Does that mean that the . . . woods . . . aren't going to be cut down?'

'Looks like it,' said Uncle Brian, grimly. 'At least, not by me. Some future owner may have better luck.'

'Future owner of what?' said George.

Uncle Brian yanked open the door of the old estate

car. 'Future owner of Mill Farm, old son. If I can't get planning permission, then that bit of land's not worth much. And that means no money – so I might just have to sell the lot for whatever it'll fetch.' He glanced guiltily at George's confused expression. 'Fact of life, George. Fact of life.' He started the engine and put the car into reverse, the gears making a high whining sound as he backed the vehicle round the yard. George and Midge watched in silence as the battered red estate bumped over the pot-holes in the gateway and disappeared down the lane. The exhaust fumes hung, blue and acrid, on the still morning air.

George was desperate to tell his news – not-withstanding the bombshell that his father had dropped on departing – and he could be silent no longer. He grabbed the cotton sleeve of Midge's shirt.

'I've *seen* one!' he said excitedly.

Midge was still gazing at the empty lane. Her mum wasn't well, and now the forest had been saved, only to be . . . *not* saved, again. Maybe. Everything was turning upside down and round and round. She couldn't take it all in.

She became aware of George, tugging at her sleeve. His eyes peered wildly at her, through the tumbling fringe of thick hair. Why didn't he just get it cut?

'What?' she said.

Chapter Twenty-two

It had taken some courage for Little-Marten to launch himself from the high trees of the North Wood. He had scarcely flown further than from the Perch to the ground before today – seldom having had the need – so now the steep falling-away of the hillside and the sight of the distant Gorji settlement amid the hazy wetlands below, made him wonder whether he had the strength and control to attempt such a distance. But he thought again of Henty and laid aside his fear. She may be facing worse things than this. He leaned forward and sprang from the topmost branches of the sycamore, immediately wheeling to the right, in an attempt to set himself on the most direct line that he could. The manoeuvre lost him more height than he had anticipated, and he flapped hard, in order to try and regain a little. It didn't seem to help much – he felt that he was dropping at an alarming speed, and would never reach the far-off copse that he had set as his goal. The Ickri hunters, bigger, stronger, and longer in the wing than he, had made a much better show of it. Well, so be it. Provided that he could only land on soft ground, then he would be able to walk the rest of the way – as Henty had done.

He came to earth, in the event, not so very far from the belt of trees, and was pleased to find himself unhurt. Pushing his way through the reedy under-growth, he made progress as quickly as he could towards the copse. The sun had risen over the hill, and the dry crackle of last year's vegetation seemed frighteningly loud in the misty silence of the early morning. Exposed and easily visible on the open ground, he was glad when he reached the copse, and was able to creep beneath the sheltering comfort of trees once more. He dodged among the bushes and in between the ivy-covered trunks, pausing frequently to look and to listen. It was the first time he had ever left the Royal Forest, and he felt very vulnerable. Everything smelt different. The damp grass under-foot, the woodland plants – the very trees smelt different. They smelt of the Gorji and of danger.

The sudden jabber of loud voices made him drop into a crouching position, beneath a rhododendron bush. He could hear the deep boom of a full-grown giant, and then the lighter sound of childer. The voices apparently came from above, and squinting up through the leaves of the rhododendron he was able to see three figures descending from some sort of dwelling in the trees. This surprised him. He had not thought that the Gorji were tree-dwellers. Perhaps this was a different tribe to the land dwellers. But then he recognized Midge as being one of the three, and was even more puzzled. The Gorji departed, talking loudly, and made their way towards the big stone dwelling – just visible beyond the deep shadows of the copse.

He reasoned that perhaps the safest place to begin his search for Henty might be where he was certain that these giants were *not*, so he approached the tall cedar from which the Gorji had just descended. Perhaps they had Henty already captured, and she was up there in their strange pod? He would see.

Ignoring the rope ladder – though he could divine its purpose well enough – he flapped up into the lower branches of the cedar and climbed to the platform.

It was a good place to be. Crouching low on the strange smelling wooden floor, he could view the stone dwelling through the trees, and much of the surrounding area. If danger should suddenly present itself, he had a fair chance of escaping it. He sniffed the air, and listened. All was quiet. Emboldened, he turned to glance at the interior of the three-sided dwelling. The sun was still very low, and Little-Marten had to move into the shadow in order to see. It was immediately apparent that Henty was not there, but his curious nature could not resist a brief exploration. The little time he had spent with the cave-dwellers had taught him, at least, to recognize what were likely sleeping arrangements, and he guessed the purpose of Midge's air mattress and George's similarly shaped camp bed. The wind-up record player that stood, with its lid open, on the ammunition box was a mystery however. He touched the shiny chrome arm. It looked like tinsy, before it became aged and blackened. The arm swung gently outwards, and Little-Marten hesitated, then touched it again, gingerly, making it swivel back and forth. He found that part of the swinging arm moved in another direction, up and down, and he experimented with that for a while too, fascinated. After a while he couldn't remember exactly how it had been when he had found it – whether the arm had been positioned up or down, in or out – but in any case, there were more important considerations, and he felt guilty for having momentarily forgotten them. He took a final glance round, and crouched once more at the front of the platform, thinking now that he could hear voices again. Vague sounds drifted up through the trees from the other side of the dwelling. Eventually he heard the noise of a Gorji contraption – one of their *vruma-vrumas* – as it began its terrible racket, and then gradually faded into the distance.

He continued to watch and wait, patiently listening for some indication of what the Gorji were doing. There was no more noise. Perhaps they had all gone and it would be safe to continue his search? But there was something else niggling in his head. Something . . . half-remembered . . . something that he had seen before the shiny metal thing had attracted his magpie attention. Turning around once more, he scanned the dim interior of the dwelling. He hopped over to the ammo box, remaining in a crouching position. Then he saw it. The tinsy cup. He picked it up, realizing – certain – that *this* was what Henty had given to the Gorji maid, *this* was what she now sought, and that he

348

had found it! He was elated. All he had to do now was find Henty, and bring her safely home.

Thrusting the cup up towards the sky in glee, he overbalanced slightly and put out a hand to steady himself. His fingers brushed the shiny metal thing, and something began to move. A slow roaring sound came bursting from the contraption, speeding up and blaring at him: '. . . Onnn tthhhe rroad to Mandalay-ay, where the flying fishes play . . .' Little-Marten leapt off the platform in terror, and swooped down into the bushes.

Midge leaned against the warm towel rail, torn in confusion between the things she wanted to think about, and the things George wanted to tell her. She gathered that he must have seen an Ickri archer, but she wanted to think about her mum . . . and all that business about the land sale having fallen through. And now there were still more – and worse – possibilities ahead, if the house had to go . . . She tried to concentrate on George.

'I just couldn't *believe* it,' he was saying. 'And all that time I thought you were making it up – especially when I saw what was on the bowl . . .'

Midge was even more puzzled. 'The bowl? Did you look at it, then? What *was* on it?'

'Well, it's like . . . it's like *you*,' said George. 'Haven't you seen it? There's all these little people, a whole crowd of them, with their mouths open – and then there's a picture of a girl, a big person. Standing in the middle of them. It's just like *you*. I mean, it doesn't *look* like you, exactly – sort of more old-fashioned. But *I* thought that's where you got the idea from; saw this picture and then made up the whole story about yourself.'

'Thanks,' said Midge, huffily.

'Yeah, I know. I'm really sorry, Midge. Really, I am. I thought you were . . .'

'Nuts. You can say it. Having hallucinations . . . like . . . her.'

They both looked at the picture on the wall. The dark eyes of Celandine gazed past them, through them, seeing something, maybe, that nobody else could.

'That's what the bowl is all about, isn't it?' said George. 'It's a picture of her, isn't it?'

'Yes,' said Midge, quietly. 'It must be. I haven't seen it properly – couldn't make out what it was. But the . . . girl . . . who gave it to me, said, "Are you Celandine?" She thought that I was her. And so Celandine must have been there, in the forest, years ago. She must have seen them too. But now they're *here*? On the farm? I wonder who it was you saw, and what they want . . .' There was a long silence as they both thought about it.

'What are you two *talking* about?' Katie stepped quietly around the doorway, her head swathed in a pink towel. She was wearing bright red jeans and a blouse that might have featured in a soap-powder advert. There had been no sound of her approach, and it was obvious that she must have been listening. George looked at Midge, ready to take his cue from her. Midge could see no point in trying to conceal things further. 'There are these . . . people, living in the forest,' she said. 'Little people.'

'There *are*, Katie,' said George, eagerly. 'I've seen them! Well, one of them. He had a bow and arrow, and,' he added, incongruously, 'an elastic belt.'

'Oh, that's OK, then,' said Katie, taking the kettle over to the tap. 'As long as he had something to keep his pants up with.' She glanced at her watch. 'What is it, April Fool's? Oh, no. Bit late for that. Must be sunstroke in that case.' She filled the kettle noisily, letting it clatter against the already chipped ceramic sink. 'You're both headbangers, the pair of you. What was all that stuff about Celandine? Got you at it as well, has she?'

'Well, it's *true*,' said George, emphatically. 'She *did* see . . . what she said she saw. I know – we know – because we've seen them too. Haven't we, Midge?'

Midge grunted. She couldn't be bothered to answer. Katie would find out for herself – or she wouldn't. Either way it didn't seem to matter much. There were other things to think about – like why would an Ickri archer come to Mill Farm? If it had been Pegs, or even Little-Marten, she would have been less surprised, but an Ickri?

'Where's the bowl?' she said to George. 'Didn't bring it with you, did you?'

'No,' said George. 'I put it back on the ammo box. Tell you what, I'll go and get it now – perhaps Miss Know-All might like to see it.' He scraped back his chair and dashed out of the kitchen. The front door slammed shut, and a few flakes of whitewash fell from the kitchen ceiling.

George's departure was observed by Scurl and his crew – as had been Uncle Brian's. The six hunters were huddled among the weeds and long grass that grew beneath the plough. Grissel's prior knowledge of how the land lay was proving very useful.

'Who be that one?' whispered Scurl, watching the boy as he ran round the outside of the farmhouse.

'Never seen him afore,' muttered Grissel. He was feeling even more uncomfortable about the nature of this second visit to the Gorji settlement than he had about the first one.

'Benzo – get arter 'un,' growled Scurl. 'Take Flitch and Dregg here and see what he be about. Don't let 'un leave – not on no account. Grab a hold on 'un, and bring 'un back here, to me. But, Benzo – no harm to 'un, mind. Not yet. Not till we has what we come for. Go on, then! What bist waiting for?'

Benzo scuttled away, keeping low, followed by Flitch and Dregg. They slipped between the balustrade pillars at the far end of the garden wall, and made their way around the corner of the farmhouse, heading in the direction of the back lawn.

Scurl looked at Snerk and Grissel. 'Well then,' he leered. 'I reckon our maid be all alone in there. Now, that don't seem too much to chew on, do it? We shall have this witchi gewgaw directly – and be home afore breakfast. Then we shall see what to make o'it, and whether 'tis all Pegs has it cracked up to be. And if 'tis

352

so – then who's to say what the morrow may bring us? And if 'tis but some mazy tale, then no matter – for we shall have some sport, I can promise 'ee that. I've a score to settle here. I ain't forgotten Tulgi, and what that maid brought down upon 'un.'

He peered out from between the weeds and rusting machinery to glance quickly round the farmyard, rubbing his nose briefly on the back of his hand. 'Now then, Grissel,' he said, 'you'd best lead on, and show us the way in. Ready? Away, then – and mark 'ee now – leave that maid to me.'

Chapter Twenty-three

'Why are you putting all these stupid ideas into his head?' said Katie, when George had gone. 'He's bad enough as it is, without your help. Why don't you just act *normal*?'

'Why are *you* so *horrible*, all the time?' retorted Midge, angrily. 'I mean what's your problem? All you do is watch telly and read dumb magazines all day – you haven't got a *clue* what's going on, or what's happening to anyone else round here. Not that you'd care about anyone else. And as for stupid ideas – well, you wouldn't know an idea if it jumped up and bit you on the bum. Never having had one.' And she stormed out of the kitchen, banging the door behind her.

'Oooh, get *you*,' said Katie, to the empty room. And then, as an even less effective afterthought, added, 'Get back in the knife drawer, Miss Sharp.' She'd read that in a magazine somewhere.

She stared crossly out of the grubby kitchen window as she waited for the kettle to boil, and wondered whether there might be such a thing as an egg in the house. Probably not. Stupid house. Then she noticed, between the gaps in the balustrade pillars of the front garden wall, some sort of movement . . . something . . . odd . . . moving quickly across the yard. She leaned closer to the windowpane, peering apprehensively through the dusty glass. Three small figures – shocking, inconceivable things – suddenly appeared at the end of the path, hurdled the steps in flying leaps, their brightly painted wings outstretched, and scuttled, crouching, towards the house. They were barefoot – and they were armed with bows and arrows.

Katie fell back against the towel rail, gripping it for support, feeling the warm metal, slippery on her wet palms. She heard the snick and clack of the cat flap, and a whimpering panic began to rise within her. There was a pause, the sound of hurried whispers in the hallway, and then something pushed against the kitchen door. Katie shrieked. Another push on the door – committed now, determined. Gibbering and quaking with terror, Katie looked frantically about her for some sort of weapon – but then escape, rather than defence, became her uppermost instinct, and she remembered the scullery. She dashed into the washroom, slammed that door behind her, and opened the door to the scullery. Here there was a small high window. She dragged the Ali Baba basket from the washroom, positioned it beneath the window and clambered up on to it, frantically struggling with the stiff metal catch until at last it opened. Squeezing herself painfully through the narrow frame, she was grateful to see the makeshift compost heap below her

– the grass clippings, rotten cabbage leaves and potato peelings would help break her fall.

George hurried across the back lawn, thinking, 'I'll show *you*, Miss Smartypants – just wait till you see *this*,' but then stopped, and looked about him, listening. He could hear music. The sound of the wind-up record player came drifting through the trees. It was playing 'On The Road To Mandalay'. He looked vacantly at Phoebe, lying, bored, beneath the apple tree. She twitched her stump of a tail, hoping that he might whistle her up for a walk, but he ignored her and continued towards the copse, his puzzled face squinting up into the sunlight. Phoebe stood up, panting slightly, and took a few hesitant steps in the same direction as George – but then changed her mind and ambled back towards the yard, stopping every so often to sniff the grass.

The song had ended by the time George had clambered up the rope ladder, but the record needle was still turning in its groove, *kurtick-kurtick* – an eerie sound when all around was quiet and still. He stood for a few moments longer, looking at the shiny black disc with its red revolving label, and then, lost in thought, moved the lever back to the 'stop' position. The sudden feeling that he was being watched came over him, a creepy tingle across his shoulders. He looked back over the lawn but could only see poor old Phoebs, padding slowly and aimlessly across the uncut grass.

The sun had risen above the roof of the tree house

now, and George was conscious that the heat would do his record no good. He gently lifted the disc from the turntable and found the paper sleeve to put it in – glancing down at the ammo box as he did so, reminding himself of what he'd actually come for. The record remained half in and half out of its sleeve, as George stared in bewilderment at the empty space at the other end of the box. Where was the little bowl?

There was something weird going on. George put down the record and knelt by the box, peered under his bed, lifted his pillow, then Midge's, pulled back both duvets – and finally sat back on his heels to try and think for a minute. 'Right,' he muttered, flicking his fringe out of his eyes, 'where was the *last* place you saw it?'

'Did 'ee *lose* summat then, young'un?'

George spun round in fright, then overbalanced – toppling sideways and banging his elbow on the corner of the ammo box. Three of them there were – three of them, looking down upon him from the branches of the cedar tree, all dressed in raggedy greys and blacks, bits of fur, white feathers here and there, bows and arrows – and their arrows were pointing at him. The dull eyes of the one he'd seen earlier gazed at him incuriously, the long jaw still hanging half open, but it was another who had spoken – and now spoke again.

'What do 'ee seek, then? Perhaps we could help 'ee.' This one looked sharper – with quick dark eyes that seemed to look everywhere at once. He wore a tatty little waistcoat, once black and silver striped but now stained, green with age and tree sap. 'Come, now,' he said – the creaky little voice had grown harder, 'Don't be back'ard. Zpeak up.'

'I've lost my . . . glasses,' George said, astonished to hear the words actually come out. It was as though someone else was speaking for him. His tongue felt as though it had fallen down his throat, and he had to keep swallowing. This couldn't be happening, it *couldn't* be. 'I . . . I put them here somewhere.' He was trying to control the terrible panic that he felt, trying to appear calm, glancing around as though looking for the non-existent pair of glasses, wondering whether he could jump from the platform and make a run for it – but realizing that his legs would never allow him to stand, let alone run. He could feel himself beginning to quake from the shock of what was happening to him.

'Put . . . *them*, somewhere?' said Waistcoat. '*Them?* Now I don't know as I've met *glaaarsses* afore, but I reckons I heard 'ee say "where'd I last see . . . *it?*" Now *them's* seldom *it* – not to my way of thinking. Tell 'ee what. Why not come along o' we – and us'll zee 'bout *glaaarsses* presently.' And with a nod to the other two, the archer jumped lightly from the cedar tree to the platform, standing squarely and firmly on the creosoted boards, his bare feet slightly apart, an arrow notched to his bow. He looked at his companions and said, 'Now then, Flitch, do you and Master Dregg go on down to bottom of this yer tree and make zertain our good friend here don't hurt 'unself coming down.' The little figure stood more or less eye to eye with George, who was still on his knees, helpless, and added, 'For 'tis surprising how easy 'tis to get hurt, if thee don't watch thee step.'

George was beginning to crack. 'Wh—what do you want?' he said, unable now to keep the tremor from his voice. 'Why are you here? I—I've got nothing for you.'

'P'raps not,' said Waistcoat. 'But I reckons that a friend o' yourn might. And we means to find that out.'

'Are you – Scurl?' Again his words seemed to appear of their own accord, as though somebody else was in charge of his voice.

The archer seemed slightly taken aback. 'Someone been talking, have 'em? No, I bain't he. If I were Scurl you'd unlikely still be gabbing. Nor be able to. But you'll meet 'un soon enough.' He nodded towards the edge of the platform. 'Goo on then.'

George managed to get to his feet, feeling slightly sick, and clambered shakily from the platform onto the branch of the cedar tree where the rope ladder hung. The archer leaned over to watch him descend, and one of the two below said, 'All right, Benzo, we've got 'un.'

It was the noise of the cat flap, rather than Katie's muffled scream, that got Midge up from the corner of her bed and brought her out into the landing corridor once more. Katie was probably the sort of person who'd scream at some wimpsy little spider – in which case she could scream away, as far as Midge was concerned. But the cat flap . . . that reminded her of the night that Tojo's terrible yowling had got them up, and of the presence of something odd beneath the sink . . .

There was a commotion of sorts going on down in the hallway – grunts and repeated thuds. Midge, still furious, and less cautious than she might have been, walked out on to the landing and leaned over the banister to see what was happening. She couldn't help but give a little squeal of shock at the unexpected sight of the intruders below – and though she immediately put her hand over her mouth, the involuntary sound had been enough to catch the attention of one of them. He quickly glanced over his shoulder, tilted his cropped grey head in her direction, and she found herself staring down at the ugly little face of Scurl. Surprised he looked, just for a second, mouth open, dark eyebrows slightly raised – but then his expression hardened as he fixed his gaze upon her, holding her to the spot. Never taking his eyes off her, he placed his hand firmly upon the shoulder of one of his companions – who was apparently trying to break down the kitchen door – and muttered, 'Hold hard there, Snerk. We'm chasing the wrong bird I reckon. Now then, maidy,' he called up, 'how bist? We'm come to see thee. No, don't fly off' – Midge had begun to draw back from the banister in fright – 'for thee s'll come to no harm, if 'ee give us what we'm here for.' The Ickri hunter adopted a friendly expression, a horrible smile that, if anything, was even more sinister than his habitual scowl.

'What . . . what's that, then?' said Midge, recovering

her senses a little, and realizing that if she ran she would be immediately pursued. She kept her hand on the banister, and desperately tried to appear calm. Play for time and think. *Think.* Hide, or escape – those were her options. *Where* could she hide, though? *How* could she escape?

'Zummat that ain't yourn,' said Scurl. 'Zummat you took from the forest. 'Twas no blame to thee, we knows that.' He wiped the back of his hand across his nose and sniffed.

'I haven't taken anything,' said Midge. Could she get out of a window? Yes, she could get *out* all right – but was unlikely to survive the drop unhurt. She could lock herself in the bathroom, but then she really *would* be trapped. Think of something else.

'Honestly, I didn't take anything.'

The three hunters looked tense and uncertain, completely at odds with their surroundings. Their small glittering eyes shone up at her, wild and strange and foreign in the homely familiarity of the hallway. There was a faint smell about them, the odour of hunting animals in a confined space – carthy, nervous, and dangerous. She could hear their breathing.

Scurl edged towards the stairs, placing one dusty brown foot on Phoebe's old mat. There wasn't much time. Midge mentally ran around the upstairs rooms, searching in her mind for a hiding place. In her wardrobe? Linen cupboard? No – anywhere that was *in* something was ultimately a prison, a trap.

More time. She needed more time.

'Tell me what it is you're looking for,' she said. 'Just

tell me. I don't understand what you mean.' The expression on Scurl's face had changed. The smile had gone and something like a snarl had taken its place. He wasn't a talker, a negotiator. He was used to getting his own way, without parley. He was about to make a move.

'Listen,' said Midge (height, she needed height. Not *in* something, nor *under* something, but *on* something. High up, where they couldn't see her), 'I think I know what you mean. Yes, *now* I know what it is you want. It isn't up here, though, it's . . . down there. But I'm scared to come down.' The wardrobe in the middle room. It was huge. Maybe she could get up there and hide on top of it. Then at least if she was discovered, there may still be a chance of jumping down and escaping. But *how* could she get up there?

Scurl had backed off a little. The ingratiating expression, sickening to her, had returned to his ugly little face. 'Ah,' he said, 'now we'm more like to strike a bargain, now that you knows what we wants. And I knows what *you* wants, maidy. You wants to forget all these troubles o' yourn, and go decent and peaceful 'bout your . . . whatever 'tis you do. Just like we. Now that's easy done. Just you come down yurr, and I do make a proper vow that there's none shall harm 'ee. Then you may lead us to where 'tis to.'

There was a card table, a little octagonal thing with thin legs – not tall enough by itself, though perhaps if she put a chair on top of it . . . but then they would see. Maybe she could drag the chair up after her . . .

'All right. But . . . but you've got to . . . you've got to

362

. . . close your eyes first . . .' Her reasoning had started to go. What a *stupid* thing to say. She'd blown it.

She saw the shadow of puzzlement as it crossed Scurl's face – and then the look of decision. He'd had enough. He glanced at the other two and flicked his head in her direction. Midge fled.

There wasn't enough time – there would never be enough time. She ran straight along the corridor to the bedroom next to Uncle Brian's and grabbed the cane chair next to the bed. She lifted it up and managed, with a struggle, to place it on top of the card table next to the huge walnut wardrobe, wedging it right back into the corner between the wardrobe and the wall. Shouts and curses echoed up from the stair-well, and she felt as though she wanted to scream with panic. But they hadn't reached the landing yet. It was a miracle that the table didn't topple over as she clambered up onto it, yet somehow the wobbly con-struction stayed upright. She knelt on the chair, gripped the top of the wardrobe, straightened her legs, and heaved herself up over the raised lip. There wasn't room to pull the chair onto the wardrobe as well. In desperation, she leaned over the edge, caught hold of the back of the chair and lifted the thing up. Swinging it with all her might, she managed to clumsily throw it onto the unmade bed. The chair hung over the edge of the mattress, almost balanced, and then slid gently down until the back legs rested on the floor. It seemed obvious, to her, what she'd done and where she was. But she could do no more. The voices had almost reached the top of the stairs now.

She curled up into the smallest space she could – and waited.

She was lucky. The Ickri hunters, so adept at moving from branch to branch, gliding, floating and swooping through the airy foliage of the forest, were not so good with narrow staircases. Vertical take-off – in fact any sort of take-off – was not their strong point. They needed space, and a good long run up, in order to get airborne. Their hunting strategy was to climb, and then swoop. So whereas Midge had imagined that they would fly up the stairs in a trice, the reality was far from that. The stairs were high obstacles to them, and their wings only an encumbrance. That, coupled with the fact that the three of them were trying to negotiate these obstacles simultaneously, had given Midge more than enough time to reach her goal. It got to the point where she wondered what was keeping them.

But now they were coming. Unfamiliar with the interiors of Gorji dwellings, the footsteps and actions of the hunters were hesitant. Midge could hear their confusion as they ran up and down the corridor and in and out of the end rooms, bare feet slapping on the lino like those of small children. She heard them struggling with various doors – kicking and pushing at those that opened outwards, tugging at those that opened inwards. But they were making progress, and they were beginning to think.

'Snerk!' The voice of Scurl: 'You bide there – and make sure she don't come back down that gurt ladder again. Grissel – you make a beginning up that end, and I'll make a beginning up yurr. Best we start again.'

Snerk was thinking too. 'I reckon she've gone,' he said. 'Looksee how this be open.' Midge gathered that he must be talking about the corridor window, for she heard Scurl hurry back down from the bathroom end and scrabble up onto the window seat. His voice became muffled as he leant out, and then louder as he drew back inside.

'She ain't got no wings,' he said. 'And she wouldn't have no legs, either, if she'd gone out o' there. No, I reckon she'm still yurr. Back to it.'

Eventually the bumps and scuffles of doors being opened and furniture being moved, or overturned, drew closer, and Midge was aware that someone had entered the room she was in – someone breathing heavily from exertion. She squeezed her eyes tight shut and prayed and prayed for her safe delivery from all this. Don't let them find me, please don't let them find me, don't don't don't.

Immediately she heard, and felt, the tremor of small strong fingers, prying at the wardrobe door. Too short to reach the handles, whoever it was had got hold of the beaded wooden edge and was tugging on it. There was a slight ping, as the catch gave way, and the door opened with a shudder and a squeak. Midge could hear the faint musical clang of wire coat hangers beneath her. Once again, the harsh dry voice of Scurl. 'Not there, Grissel? Well, she ain't up t'other end neither. So she must be in yurr. Come out maidy!' he shouted. ' 'Twill only make it hotter for 'ee when we do grab a hold on 'ee.'

Midge stifled a whimper, and pushed her fists against

her mouth. They would see the chair, and the table – and surely they would figure it out. It seemed so obvious.

'I reckon Snerk was right,' came the voice of Grissel. 'She's long gone.'

'No!' snapped Scurl. 'She'm still yurr. I knows it. And when I finds her—' there was a horrible guttural sound, as of a throat being slit.

But then came a long silence. This was even harder for Midge to bear than the rummaging and blundering about that had preceded it. Now she could hear nothing.

After a while, Scurl said, more calmly, 'Ah, p'raps thee'm right, Grissel. Maybe she've gone arter all.' The hunters moved out into the corridor, and Scurl shouted, 'Snerk! Come on out o' it. Reckon she've gone, like 'ee said. We'll jump out o' here, and take a looksee round the byres.'

Snerk's footsteps came padding along the corridor. The three of them seemed to be by the open window once more. 'Out you go then, Grissel,' said Scurl, loudly. 'And we'll follow 'ee. 'Tis quicker'n climbing back down that gurt old ladder.'

Midge could hear scuffling, and then a quick flap of wings. One of them, at least, appeared to have jumped out of the window. Then more scuffling, Scurl's voice shouting, 'We'm right behind 'ee, Grissel!' and a faint muffled reply. Then silence.

It was a very amateur piece, and Midge wasn't fooled for a second. Scurl, at least, was still up here – and maybe the other one, Snerk, as well.

So it was to be a waiting game. It gave her time to

think, if nothing else. Why were they here? What did they want? She'd taken nothing from the forest, apart from the curious bowl – which she still hadn't looked at properly – and which was a gift from Henty. Could *that* be what they were after? Why?

The minutes ticked by, and the silence grew. Maybe they had gone, after all. Or maybe, worse, they were up to something else – like setting the place on fire. They *could* be. What would she do then?

She risked a quick look, raising her head very gently, and peering over the top of the wardrobe. There was nobody in the room, and she ducked down again. Then the tiniest of sounds caught her ear. A brief *pfft*. It came from the bathroom, and she recognized it as being an aerosol – a can of deodorant or something – accidentally touched. They were up at the bathroom end, so the route to the top of the stairs was clear. If she went *now*, before they moved, she may have a chance of getting out. But clambering down from the wardrobe would make too much noise, and would take too much time. Could she jump? Could she jump down onto the bed – and then run? Do it. Don't think about it, just *do* it.

She sat up and swung her legs over the front of the wardrobe – the old piece of furniture creaking horribly – lifted herself up onto the lip of the frame, and launched herself into space, realizing even as she did so that she had made a terrible mistake. The sound from the bathroom had only meant that *one* of the hunters was there for sure. The other might be anywhere. She bounced off the bed, stumbled, righted herself, and dashed out of the room. Swinging round the door frame, she catapulted herself along the corridor – reaching the top of the stairs just as Snerk appeared from the little room at the far end of the landing. An arrow clattered off the banister post as she leaped down the stairs, two at a time, squealing now in terror. The arrow must have been fired by Scurl, because Snerk was still struggling with his bow, unable to shoot over the top of the banister, and so trying to aim between the rails instead. Down she went, as another arrow hit the plastered wall of the stairwell with a sharp crack, like a cap pistol going off. A bit of plaster grit stung her eyelid, as she jumped the last three steps and flung herself at the front door. She yanked the thing open – wrenching her shoulder muscles, and feeling instant pain. Then more pain – something tearing the hair from her scalp – as she turned to heave the door closed behind her. A glimpse she caught, in that fraction of a second, of Scurl, mid-flight as he jumped from the landing with painted wings outstretched – bow and arrow in his grasp. He reminded Midge of a cupid, a terrible, evil kind of cupid.

Down the front path she fled, aware, suddenly, of a dreadful howling sound coming from the direction of the cider barn – the same screeching siren wail that had given her nightmares ever since she'd first heard it. Tojo.

She ran towards the awful noise – and could never later explain why she had done so. The flustered rattle of the cat flap sounded somewhere behind her – she knew that Scurl and Snerk were in close pursuit of her – and all instinct should have told her to run away from further danger, rather than towards it; yet towards the sound of Tojo she ran. Something may have told her that the great tom cat might act as a deterrent, or at least a distraction, to her pursuers, but it was certainly not a conscious piece of reasoning. It was simply what she did.

Flying down the length of the yard, feeling as though her heart would burst, she was enveloped in the jagged screeching sounds which grew louder as she came hurtling towards the barn doors, but which then ceased, abruptly, cut to strangulated silence the instant her reaching fingers made contact with the peeling wood. It was as if, in touching the door, she had pressed a switch.

Chapter Twenty-four

Whatever lay at the end of the line for George, he was in no hurry to discover. Certainly he had no wish to meet Scurl. Like Midge he decided to play for time – but unlike her, he had no idea of what he would try to do, no plan, beyond waiting for some opportunity to arise. Halfway down the rope ladder, he bumped his nose on one of the wooden rungs, and as the tears sprang to his eyes his fear began to turn to anger. Who did these little mutants think they were, pushing him around? The idea of pretending that he couldn't see very well occurred to him – it might serve to slow up progress until he came up with a better plan. He deliberately missed his footing, and clung to the swinging ladder.

'Goo on!' shouted Benzo, from above.

'Sorry,' said George, as he reached the ground. 'It's my glasses.' He pointed to his watery eyes, and peered dimly about him. 'I'm almost blind, without my glasses.' His voice was still shaky, and whatever it was that he was saying sounded guileless, at least, to his captors.

Flitch and Dregg looked at him, and Flitch said,

'Ah. Comprend. He be like a mole, Benzo. Casn't see too good.'

Benzo only grunted, and then swooped down from the platform. 'We'd best get 'un to the dwelling – see what Scurl wants to do with 'un.' Benzo looked about him, uncertain, getting his bearing, and George immediately led off through the copse – hands slightly outstretched, as though he were guarding against collisions.

'Here!' Benzo skipped in front of him, drawing back his bow. 'Where be off to, do 'ee reckon?'

'Sorry,' said George, coming to a halt. 'I though you wanted to go to the house – where Scurl is. This is the quickest way – down through the copse.'

'Zo it may be,' said Benzo (it wasn't), 'but you just bide, and not move till we tell 'ee to move. Now then, Flitch, I shall lead on, then our friend here, then you and Dregg keep to hindermost. And you,' he said to George, 'better step careful, 'less 'ee want wood where wood never grew.'

'OK,' said George. 'It's straight down there, through the trees.' He hadn't misled them entirely – part of the house could be glimpsed beyond the edge of the copse – but it would have been quicker to go back across the lawn. Benzo now led the way, turning round frequently, and George followed, hands spread out slightly, apparently protecting himself from danger.

The dense copse grew parallel to the lane that led up to the house, and there was an overgrown stile, a little further on, that opened on to the lane. George

371

wondered if he could simply make a break for it. He bumped into a sapling, accidentally on purpose, and Dregg snickered in a dim-witted sort of way. Benzo glanced round, but said nothing.

The stile was coming up on the left, not really visible through the trees and undergrowth, but there nevertheless. If he got away, and made it over the stile, what then? Run down the lane? Then at last a plan, of sorts, came to him. The mudslide. He bumped into another tree, and pretended to hurt his head. Dregg thought this hilarious, and it bought another few seconds.

They'd already passed the mudslide – a sloping channel, originally a badger run, that ran from the bank of the copse down into the lane. It was simply a narrow gap in the hedge, but George had opened it out a bit, and used to slither down it on a plastic fertilizer bag – till his dad had put a stop to his fun. 'Messy *and* dangerous,' he'd said. '*Well* up to your usual standard. Really, George, I wonder if you've the brains you were born with sometimes. What would you do if there was a car coming?'

'Hear it,' George had replied, not unreasonably, he felt. But anyway, that was the end of the mudslide game.

They had drawn almost level with the stile, and it was now or never. Pointing to the right, George suddenly yelled, '*Look out!*' and immediately broke away to the left, ducking and weaving through the saplings, going like a rabbit. He was over the stile and pelting down the lane before the hunters had recovered from their surprise. Twenty yards along the lane, he scrabbled up the bank, where the mudslide was, and was creeping back into the copse by the time the furious hunters were peering over the stile. Benzo jumped down into the lane and looked from left to right. There was no sign of George. On the other side of the lane was another stile, leading into an open field. Benzo ran across, beckoning to the others. The boy must have gone that way.

They stood in the field and gazed at the empty grassland. 'Hang it!' shouted Benzo. 'We've lost 'un! Us'll be baked in charcoal for this, if'n Scurl learns of it.'

'We'd best not show our faces till we've found 'un again,' said Flitch.

Benzo looked back at the copse on the other side of the road. 'We'll get back up into they trees,' he muttered. ' 'Twill keep us out o' Scurl's way – and give us a chance to look out for that young snip.'

They returned to the copse once more and climbed the cedar tree. It afforded a good view of much of the settlement, and Benzo felt confident that they had not seen the last of Master Mole – nor he of them.

' 'Ee weren't much a mole as we did reckon,' said Dregg, slowly. 'More like a eel.' Benzo gave him a kick.

Freedom is a wonderful thing – if only you know what to do with it. Having escaped Benzo and Co., George's initial elation soon evaporated, and he felt at a bit of a loss as to where he could safely go. They had been taking him to the house, on Scurl's orders apparently, so going there was out. They would almost certainly return to the copse any minute, so staying put was out, too. He decided to make his way round to the back of the stables and hide there, among the thistles, until he could think of some better course of action.

The untended shrub borders of the rear lawn gave ample cover for his purpose, and he crept through the laurels and rhododendrons, keeping as low as possible – a necessary precaution as it turned out, for another archer suddenly floated down from an upstairs window at the rear of the farmhouse, shouted something up, and then scurried off round the corner. Some other strange thing he thought he saw – a green shadow, that disappeared among the laurels – it may have been another archer, or it may just have been a moving beam of sunlight through a passing cloud. He pressed on, regardless, and reached the rear corner of the cider house without having been seen, as far as he could tell.

As George picked his way through the junk behind the cider house, he heard a brief scream – distant it seemed, too tiny to be human, like the noise a baby rabbit might make when being attacked by a stoat. He paused for a few seconds to listen, but heard no more and kept going. He had problems enough of his own.

There was a gap between the cider barn and the end of the stable block – a gap that was visible from the entire length of the yard. He listened again, but still heard nothing. The yard seemed quiet. He braced himself for the dash across the open gap. One, two, three: he was away, and was spurred on, suddenly, by a terrible noise – an awful wailing sound – as though some creature from hell was at his heels. He vaulted the rickety fence that continued the line of the field beyond the end of the stables, ran between the lagoon and the rear wall of the block, and crouched, panting with fear, very close to the spot where he and Midge had found the hand. The dreadful sound continued, and George realized what it was: Tojo. It seemed to be coming from the cider barn. On and on it went, yowling and screeching – then there were shouts and yells, running feet, confusion. Then silence. It all just stopped. What was happening? He thought of Midge. She was out there, somewhere, amongst all that mayhem. And he was skulking here. It was no good, he would have to go and see if she was OK . . .

'Ah, *there* 'ee be. Lost thee *glaaarsses* again? They do get about, don't 'em?'

George jumped, and backed away from the wall in alarm. They sat on the ridge of the stable roof like three wise monkeys, Benzo, Snerk, and Dregg, the sun shining on their painted wings and grinning faces, their nasty little arrows pointing at him – relaxed now, able to pick him off at will, had they so desired. No, it hadn't taken them very long to find him again.

George continued to back away, stumbling across the firm edge of the lagoon without thinking, keeping an eye all the time on those sharp little arrows.

'Thass far enough!' shouted Benzo, warningly. 'You bide there, now.' He slithered down the slope of the roof tiles and remained perched just above the guttering. The other two followed suit.

George moved sideways a little, shuffling round the outer crust of the lagoon until the entire span of it lay between him and the stables. He had no plan. There *was* no plan – but there was such a thing as luck, such a thing as being in the right place at the right time. He backed away a little further.

Benzo stood up, balancing on the loose tiles. George moved back another foot, stepping off the outer crust of the lagoon, and onto normal pasture – though the line where one began and the other ended was not obvious. Flitch drew back his bow, but Benzo shook his head.

'No harm to 'un,' he muttered. 'Scurl's orders. Wait till he runs – then we s'll know which way to jump.' Benzo glanced down at the strange expanse of bare earth, interspersed with just a few clumps of grass. Fair going, by the look of it. The snip would be easy enough to catch.

George took another step backwards, and looked over his shoulder, tensing – as if deciding to make a break straight over to the far side of the field. He turned, and seemed to commit himself.

'Come on,' hissed Benzo, and launched himself from the guttering.

He landed just beyond the centre of the lagoon, and may well have escaped trouble – had not Flitch and Dregg landed right beside him. The thin sun-dried crust gave way beneath their combined weight, and they fell against one another, staggering and floundering, knee-deep – and then chest-deep – in ancient slurry. A pleasant sound their beleaguered screams were, to George's unsympathetic ears – the more so when it became apparent that the trio were unlikely to sink much further. Their wings, it seemed, would probably save them from disappearing entirely. He wouldn't have wanted to witness their deaths, but, for the moment, he was happy enough to witness their discomfort.

He put his fingers in his mouth and gave a loud whistle. Phoebe might enjoy this, he thought.

Chapter Twenty-five

The great felix had been calm for a while, half dozing in the welcome rays of early sunshine that splashed through the partly open doorway of the cider barn, but now he began to grow restless. Tojo was hungry, and tired of waiting.

Henty could see that Pank's description of the beast had not been an exaggeration. She watched, quaking with fright, as the immense animal paced up and down the beam of light that fell along the floor of the cider house. Tiny specks of golden dust glinted in the sunbeams, surrounding the felix and making it look as though slow-burning sparks were drifting from its shock-haired pelt. Wisps of vapour rose from the threshold, where the warm sunlight fell on ground still damp with morning dew, and as Tojo walked it seemed as though the very earth burned beneath his feet. As a child looking down from a sea wall is drawn to the waves, so Henty felt the terrible pull of Tojo's magnetic power. Could such a creature really exist?

She dragged her attention away, and looked once more around the confines of her high prison. There was a door – but she had silently examined this earlier, and there was no release for her there. She knew nothing of the mechanisms the Gorji employed, but she did know that she could never open this thing unaided. Worse was the fact that there was a small gap beneath the door – a broken corner – but it was just too small even for her slight frame to squeeze through. The outside world was tantalizingly close, but unreachable.

One or two dusty bottles and a big stone jar stood in one corner of the loft, and there was a large wooden rake, odd bits of rot-metal – but nothing that would aid either her defence or escape. She was alone – none knew that she had come here – and now she was but a few steps away from the terrible thing that had murdered her kinsman. She lowered her chin on her tiny fists once more, and continued to watch the beast below as it paced the golden shaft of light, occasionally leaving the barn for a few moments and then re-entering, waiting – like her – and waiting . . .

The grey rat that dropped lightly onto her motionless back from the high wooden cross-beam was no less horrified at the event than she. It scurried away with a squeak of alarm. Henty jumped up and screamed – backing away along the edge of the platform as she watched the horrible creature desperately wriggle beneath the corner of the door, its long pink tail whipping in the dust. The felix lifted its head.

Tojo moved out of the sun and into the shadow, the better to see, and the Tinkler maid looked down. Down she looked, at last, into the volcano, the fires that would swallow her up, the amber eyes of Tojo. It had happened – as she knew it must. Folly upon folly she had committed, foolishness upon foolishness. She had walked into the lands of the Gorji – what greater folly could there be? – and now she would never walk back. As if to confirm this, her legs ceased to function and her heart stopped beating. She stood, immobile, as Tojo began to wind the siren of her doom.

The felix backed slowly into a crouch, flexing its front claws in a strange mesmerizing shuffle, gaining purchase on the pitted texture of the flagstones, judging the effort required. Here was another invasion of his territory. Here was another lesson to be taught.

As his shoulder muscles rippled and the pitch of that terrifying wail began to rise, a shadow briefly flickered across the doorway. Then flickered again. Tojo turned round, distracted, delaying his spring for a few moments – then hissed, a thick steam-valve sound, as another invader came running into the barn, flapped its wings, and rose over his head to land high up on the ladder. In a few seconds the newcomer

had reached the loft and there were now two of them up there.

Little-Marten, creeping round the stables, had heard Henty's scream and run to the door of the cider house. Hearing Tojo, and seeing how things lay, he had skipped a few paces back into the yard, taken a good run up and very nearly reached the top of the ladder in one go. Now he stood at the edge of the apple-loft, staring down at Tojo. Henty, still in a trance almost, looked wildly at Little-Marten – open-mouthed, speechless.

Tojo, momentarily wrong-footed, had recovered and now began his ritual again, the eerie guttural sound from his throat, low at first, rising to that chainsaw-howl as his muscles tensed for the spring.

Little-Marten cast frantically round for likely weapons. There wasn't much to choose from, but instead of waiting for Tojo to dictate proceedings, he picked up the big stone jar and heaved it down onto the floor below. The jar landed with a great crash, and Tojo leapt sideways, dodging the flying pieces of stoneware and screeching with surprise. It didn't stop him, though. Dispensing with any further rituals or formalities, Tojo sprang at the ladder and began to scale it, his great limbs easily spanning the fixed wooden rungs and his open jaws spitting with fury. Little-Marten was ready with a glass bottle which he flung at the beast, but which missed – to his horror, for now the thing would surely be upon them. But then a second bottle, appearing from nowhere, caught the animal a solid blow across the neck, and the cat was unbalanced – clinging for a moment to one of the uprights and dropping to the floor again.

Henty stood waiting with a third – and last – bottle, her face alive now with concentration and her eyes bright and fiery. The Woodpecker and the Tinkler maid glanced at each other and knew that they were in this – and perhaps all else that might follow – together.

'You be a better marksman than I,' said Little-Marten, and grabbed the heavy wooden rake.

The great felix paced the floor below, lashing its tail, eyes fixed on the pair, moaning low its utter hatred, prophesying – vowing – that vengeance would come. Boiling oil might have held him back but empty bottles never would. There came another yowling attack, and this time, Little-Marten, kneeling at the edge of the platform, managed to manoeuvre the big apple rake down the ladder so that the broad head blocked the animal's progress. He jabbed at Tojo as the huge creature attempted to slash his way past the wooden teeth that blocked his ascent. Once more, Henty managed to strike her target, the third bottle catching Tojo in the ribs before smashing on the floor below – but this time the cat clung on, sensing, as one laying siege to a castle might, that the defenders had flung all they had to fling – and that it would not be enough.

Little-Marten could not hold the monster back much longer, and he knew it. The cat had grown wily, even in the blind heat of its rage, and was beginning to wriggle under the rake, rather than try to get around it or over it.

'Jump!' he yelled to Henty. 'Go on! Hang to the edge and drop down – 'tain't that far! Run!'

But Henty ignored him, gathering up whatever bits of rubbish she could find and continuing to hurl them at the struggling felix.

'I ain't *going*,' she shouted at him. 'Not without you, I ain't.'

It was almost over. The mighty Tojo had managed to get his head and one foreleg beneath the rake and was now pushing his broad shoulders upwards. Little-Marten could feel the rake being lifted, raised against his straining muscles by a power far beyond him to control. He felt also, suddenly, Henty's arm through his as she knelt beside him – and was glad that he had not been too late. The jaws of Tojo came spitting closer, unstoppable, merciless, howling triumph—

– and then froze, with a slight choking shudder, into a ghastly and silent mask. Everything – the whole world – seemed to have come to a halt. The death mask of Tojo glared at them, the great orange eyes filled with one driving, hell-bent purpose, to rend them apart. All the fury was there, captured forever, but – unbelievably – there was no longer any sound.

Henty and Little-Marten stared in wonder at the arrow, deeply buried in the dark fur, the slim pale shaft that had brought so mighty a beast to so sudden an end. The Woodpecker saw the black-and-white flights – neatly trimmed magpie feathers – tied, un-mistakably, by his father's hand . . .

And Grissel, stepping out from the shadows, watched the felix slide from the ladder to slump lifeless among the broken glass that littered the ground, and felt that he had done right, and was on the side of what was right for the first time in a long time. He rested the end of his bow on the ground and turned, calmly, to look at the Gorji child who stood, gasping for breath, in the doorway.

There was no escape – there never had been – and even as Midge stumbled, panting, into the strange apple-scented gloom of the cider barn, she could hear the dry flapping of her pursuers' wings and their skittering footsteps as they landed just outside. She just had time to catch a glimpse of Tojo, silent now and lying dead upon the floor, and the small shocked faces of Henty and Little-Marten at the top of the ladder as Scurl and Snerk blocked the doorway behind her.

There was no escape, but she felt more angry than frightened – now that the chase was over – angry and utterly confused. *How* could this be happening to her, and what was it that everyone *wanted*? What were Little-Marten and Henty doing here? Why were *any* of them here?

Midge stood and faced Scurl, standing in the doorway, with his silly bow and arrow. She felt like walking over to him and giving him a kick.

'What is it you *want*, you ... you little *twerp*? Why don't you just go away and leave me alone? I've never done anything to you.'

Scurl didn't reply. He was looking around the barn, sizing up the situation. He wondered at the presence of the Woodpecker and the Tinkler maid, but they posed no threat to him. The great felix most certainly would have been a threat – except that it now lay dead, killed, apparently, by an archer. It was only then that he saw Grissel, standing by the wall, in the shadow of a cider barrel. Scurl nodded, understanding now, and believed himself to be in as strong a position as he could wish for. There would be no more mistakes – or escapes.

'Zummat that ain't yourn, as I told 'ee before,' he replied at last, returning his attention to Midge. 'Zummat as you took from the forest, that's what I do *want*. And I be about done wi' you and your slippery ways, maidy.' He drew back his bow. 'Either you knows, and you'll tell I, or you don't and you won't, in which case 'tis all up with 'ee. Now – do 'ee want to run about on thy hind legs a little longer, or do 'ee want a good long rest, like that gurt felix over there? 'Tis all one to I.'

The reference to Tojo struck home. If a fearsome creature, a life force as powerful as Tojo could be brought down by one small arrow, then anything – anyone – could. Midge blanched at this realization, and her bravado disappeared. She was a helpless child once more, completely at the mercy of these murderous beings.

'I'll have no part o' this.' It was Grissel who quietly spoke, from his position by the wall. Midge and Scurl both turned to look at him in surprise – Midge at the presence of yet another woodlander, and Scurl at the heresy of his words.

'What's this?' said Scurl, in disbelief. 'Bist soft in the head, Grissel? You'll have no *part* o' this? Well then, thee s'll have it *all*. 'Twas thee as shot the felix, and 'twill be thee as shoots this giant.' And he turned his arrow in the direction of Grissel.

'I'll not do it,' said Grissel, his bow still resting on the ground. 'And I'll not stand by and see it done, neither. For giant or no giant – Gorji or no Gorji – this be but a *maid*, Scurl. I were in the dwelling when 'ee quizzed her and I be here now – and I don't believe she have a notion of what thee be looking for. Not a notion. And what bist looking for anyhow? A bit o' tinsy metal. Some part o' the Touchstone. Some witchi thing as Benzo heard Pegs talking of. Well who's to say that the Touchstone is aught but a bit o' red rock? 'Tis but a tale. And now 'ee would see murder done, just for that?'

'Not just for that!' roared Scurl, his temper beginning to boil. ''Ave 'ee forgotten about Tulgi? And how the mad hag killed 'un for the sake of this *Gorji*? Aye, and for the sake o' that fletcher's ratling!' And Scurl pointed up at Little-Marten, still standing with Henty on the edge of the apple loft.

'Tulgi!' snorted Grissel. 'You cared no more for Tulgi than if he were a squirrel – less, I reckon, for a squirrel would make prettier eating.'

'I cared more for Tulgi than if he were a *Gorji*, that I do know,' said Scurl, 'And you may make your own choices, master. Do it or no – 'tis all one to I.' He spoke coldly and calmly now, glancing briefly at Snerk to assure himself that there was no danger of revolt from that direction as he drew his bow back to the full. Scurl's arrow pointed directly at Grissel, and his eyes became distant and glazed, as was his habit when moving in for the kill.

He was the last to notice that something was happening up in the apple loft.

There was a loud scraping and a shudder of rotting timber as the ancient door to the loft was dragged open, and light – the blinding sunshine of early morning – flooded in to the upper reaches of the dusty barn, bathing the grey cobwebbed roof timbers in golden fire.

A tall figure dressed in gleaming white, and carrying some great low-slung object, moved into the dazzling shaft of sunlight, an awesome being – a very angel of vengeance it seemed to those who witnessed it.

Henty and Little-Marten fell back on to the boards in terror, pushing themselves away on their hands and heels, as the shining figure stepped majestically to the front of the high loft, to gaze down upon those beneath. Scurl had barely recovered his senses enough to redirect his aim towards this new peril before a powerful jet of water caught him square in the chest, sending him spinning in confusion to the floor. Another deluge hit the open-mouthed face of Snerk, leaving him, in an instant, half drowned and gasping for his very life. He dropped to his knees, racked with fits of coughing and spluttering. The vision in white turned towards the stunned figure of Grissel, but Midge stepped forward and waved her hands. 'Not that one, Katie! Not that one!'

The awesome being then looked uncertainly at the cowering bodies of Little-Marten and Henty, but once again Midge shouted up, 'No, not them either! They're OK.' Katie lowered the huge plastic water cannon, George's WaterBlaster, but continued to keep a wary eye on Scurl and Snerk.

'Get their stupid bows and arrows,' she said to Midge. 'I'm coming down.'

A pitiful enough sight the would-be giant killers made, drenched to the bone and under threat of more of the same as they crouched in the corner by the front door of the cider house. Katie stood guard over the pair as Midge tried to untangle a mess of binder twine, and the elder girl couldn't resist giving the occasional warning squirt from the powerful cannon – splattering the wall to either side of Scurl and Snerk, as a warning to stay put, working the pump action in a practised and professional manner, and generally cutting a thoroughly imposing figure in her snow white denim jeans and jacket. She was enjoying herself, and appeared surprisingly unfazed – given the unreal nature of her situation.

'Ugly little dorks, aren't they?' she said, and then added, 'This thing is *so* cool – better than mine ever was. No wonder George would never swap.'

Midge was less self-assured. She had managed to salvage a few lengths of binder twine, but now looked hesitantly at Scurl and Snerk, wondering how to go about the business of tying them up whilst maintaining a safe distance. Scurl sneered at her indecision.

'Bist afeard I might bite thee tongue off?' he said. 'Well, zo I might. Why don't 'ee come closer and find out?'

Katie gave him a short squirt with the gun, and

Scurl reeled sideways. 'I don't *think* so,' she said, and then added, to Midge, 'Don't *you* tie them up. Get *him* to do it.' She looked at Grissel. 'Hoy, you. Let's see whose side you're on, then. Tie their hands behind their backs.'

Midge offered the strands of orange binder twine to Grissel, who waited for a moment, looking at Katie. He didn't trust her – wasn't at all sure that he might not end up pinned to the wall with the other two – but then took a length of the loosely twisted nylon rope and knelt on the wet ground beside his former companions.

'I'll sithee suffer for this,' growled Scurl, baring his teeth in a snarl as Grissel – committed now – roughly pulled the Ickri captain's dripping wet hands behind his back and bound them. 'I'll bring 'ee to sorrow, Grissel, I can promise 'ee that.' And Scurl spat into the dirty puddle he was sitting in.

George ran past the doorway, checked himself, and skipped back a few paces. He looked in wonderingly. 'What's going on – hey! – who said you could borrow my WaterBlaster, Katie?'

Katie rolled her eyes. 'Well, under the *circumstances* . . .' she said, witheringly. George looked around and said, 'Oh. Yeah. OK.' He began to get a clearer idea of the situation and said, 'Blimey! How many have you *got* in here? And what's . . . is that Tojo? Who're those two up there? And look at all this glass and stuff. It's like there's been a *war* in here or something.'

'There has,' said Katie. 'We won.'

Chapter Twenty-six

Phoebe, having been left to guard the struggling occupants of the lagoon, was becoming increasingly disenchanted with the whole business. She didn't like the lagoon, for a start. It was obviously unsafe out there. She had crept cautiously around the outer rim, alternately barking at the strange intruders, and then looking worried as she felt the tremors of the less than solid surface beneath her paws.

She had vague memories of other times – times when she had leapt into the rhynes to retrieve water-fowl, splashed and paddled across the flooded fields for whatever it was that needed fetching. ('Fetch, Phoebe! Fetch! Good girl!') In recent years a quiet stroll on firmer ground – to the jolly place where they all made a fuss of her and fed her titbits – was more to her liking. Nowadays she might fetch a crisp, if it was thrown within reach, but little more. She certainly didn't fancy trying to retrieve whatever it was that was squelching and shrieking and floundering about in the middle of the lagoon.

There was a tree she knew of, a shady place,

peaceful and not far away, where she could be happy. She gave a final woof, and padded off, half guiltily, towards the gate at the far end of the stables.

Maglin's eyes were not what they were, perhaps, but from the forest, he could still see sharply enough to track the distant speck of the black Gorji hound as it disappeared within the settlement once more. He sighed. This was against his judgement – and his will. It was madness indeed. He looked down through the branches at Pegs, who stood waiting on the hillside at the edge of the wood.

'I be ready then, Pegs,' he called down, resignedly, 'though I never looked for this day, I'll tell 'ee that.' He spread his wings and dived out over the hillside, the bunch of feathers on his spear fluttering noisily as he picked up speed. The white horse took a few short steps, and then leapt forward, beating hard.

Pegs landed at the back of the stables, and waited for Maglin – who came to earth rather heavily, cursing as he dropped his spear. They quickly moved closer to the shelter of the stable wall, glanced around warily, and then stood regarding the commotion going on in the centre of the lagoon. Maglin took a few deep breaths through his flared nostrils. He wasn't used to such sustained exertion – moreover, he felt exposed and uncomfortable so far from his own territory, unconvinced, also, of the wisdom of this venture.

'Hemmed fools,' he muttered, looking at the struggling bodies in the lagoon – unrecognizable almost, so pitiable a state were they in. 'Though no more so than we, I reckon. There ain't a one of us has any business being here.'

Perhaps. Although we may do good, even yet.

'Well, we shan't do *they* much good. There'll be no easy way out o' that lot. And *I* shan't be going in after them, that I *do* know. Well, let 'em rot then – I care not – we'd be better to find what's become of t'others. If I can get my own hide back to the forest safe, along with Tadgemole's maid and the Woodpecker, then maybe 'twill have been worth the toil – though they may wish they'd drownded along with that band o' cut-throats by the time I've finished with 'em. And as for *Scurl* – well he might reckon 'twould be better to cut his *own* throat, than let me get a hold of it.'

They shrank back against the wall at that moment, for there was a sound of approaching voices.

'There they are!' A Gorji youth jumped over the fence at the barn end of the stables and walked over to the lagoon. He was followed by a strange procession of woodlanders and more of the Gorji.

Scurl and Snerk, dripping wet, their hands bound behind their backs, stumbled through the docks and thistles, apparently under the direction of a tall Gorji maid, who bore some desperate-looking weapon. Grissel also, astonishingly, seemed to be assisting the Gorji in keeping his fellow archers under guard. Maglin recognized the second maid to appear: it was the girl, Midge. She followed, carrying bows and quivers and a skein of twine – brightly hued stuff – slung over her arm. Finally, the Woodpecker and the

Tinkler maid – safe, it would seem, and unbound. This unlikely company gathered at the edge of the lagoon, their backs toward the stable wall – none had yet noticed Pegs and Maglin, all their attention being on the three dismal figures trapped in the stinking mire.

George said, 'Here, let me see if I can throw them a line.'

Midge put the bows and arrows down and handed the binder twine to George – feeling that while she would have been just as capable of throwing a line as he, she would rather not be attached by a bit of string to the likes of Benzo if she could avoid it.

It took a minute or two to unravel the twine and rewind it into a loose coil. Then George shouted, 'Hoy, see if you can grab hold of this!' and slung the coil out over the lagoon. It wasn't a bad throw, landing as it did within reach of the tangle of limbs that thrashed around in the ooze – and frantic hands instantly battled with each other to grasp the twine. Shouts and spluttered curses rang out on the still morning air, each of the archers prepared to trample the others into a horrible grave if only their own wretched skin could be saved.

'This is no good,' gasped George, unable to make headway, and he shouted, 'One at a time! Take it in turns!' He might as well have tried to get a pack of starving jackals to form an orderly queuing system. The struggle deepened, with more murderous curses, and it was apparent that none would give up whatever hold they had on the lifeline.

'Benzo! Leave go of it. And you, Flitch! Let it be, if you value your hides. Leave go, the pair of 'ee!' Maglin had walked quietly forward and appeared as if by magic among the group – standing next to Grissel (who jumped sideways in surprise) and giving orders in his familiar rough bark. He looked up at George, who was staring at him in amazement, and said, 'Now, young'un, haul away, and see what 'ee do fish out o' there.'

Katie had hesitantly turned the WaterBlaster in the direction of the newcomer, but Midge touched her on the arm and shook her head.

'It's their leader,' she said, quietly, 'Maglin. Don't know where *he's* come from though.' She glanced around, and her eyes widened as she saw Pegs, standing motionless, half-hidden among the tall thistles by the stable wall. He was obviously in no hurry to make himself known, so Midge just gave him a smile – pleased that he had come – and turned back to face the lagoon once more.

Maglin was indeed their leader, and it was evidence of his authority that Benzo and Flitch immediately let go of the binder twine, thus allowing Dregg to be first out of the mire. It proved heavy going, however, and Midge had to help George after all, wrapping the twine around her hands and heaving on a count of three. Bit by bit, and with many squelching and sucking noises, Dregg was hauled from the black ooze. On reaching firmer ground, the wretched little being struggled to his knees and tried to rise, but Maglin stepped forward and pushed against him with his foot,

394

growling, 'Stay down,' so Dregg slumped into a miserable and smelly heap at the edge of the lagoon.

Flitch and Benzo were dragged from the pit in a similar fashion, until at last the noisome trio were sprawling, covered from head to toe in ancient manure, on more or less dry land. Maglin looked at them in disgust, and then spoke to Midge, resting the butt of his spear on the ground and standing before her, square on.

'So then, maid, we'm face to face once more – and the sooner than I should have liked. What shall we say of this? Here's half my company near drownded in muck, others bound in thy power, and one,' he looked accusingly at Grissel, 'ready to do thy bidding, it seems. And what that hemmed Woodpecker and Tadgemole's maid be doing here's a puzzlement beyond my ravelling. Perhaps thee'd care to make a beginning, then – for I be all ears.'

'Oh!' Katie gasped. She had just seen the white horse. All eyes followed the direction of her astonished gaze, and Pegs, seeing himself to be discovered, stepped into the open, gracefully picking his way among the tall clumps of dock and thistle – a thing of shining and unutterable beauty against the ugly contrast of scrub and weed. He tossed his head as he approached, the sunlight catching on his long silver mane and the white velvety folds of his wings. Midge glanced at George and Katie, who stood open-mouthed in wonder, and she thought her heart would burst with pride as the magical creature walked slowly up to her and nuzzled her hand.

'Hallo, Pegs,' she whispered, 'how are you?'

She had expected that her friend might reply – that the word-colours might enter her consciousness and of those about her, so that her cousins might see how truly extraordinary the animal was – but Pegs just whinnied softly and looked about him. He doesn't want them to know, thought Midge, and somehow this pleased her too.

Maglin looked at Pegs, and also understood. He would be careful.

'Come, maid,' he said, gruffly, 'I be listening.'

'I don't *know* what's going on,' said Midge, turning away from Pegs towards Maglin once more. 'Honestly. They broke in,' she pointed at Scurl, '*him*, and all the rest of them. They *want* something, some metal thing, a . . . a touchstone? Something to do with a touchstone? *I* don't know what it is. *I* haven't got it. Henty gave me a little bowl, but that's all. And they've been trying to *kill* us – shooting at us . . .'

' 'Tis a lie!' broke in Scurl. 'Don't 'ee believe her, Maglin. She lies, as all the Gorji do lie. We were but hunting, trying our luck on Gorji land as do the Wisp. Trying to bring a bit o' good to our hungry tribespeople. 'Twas no more 'n that! Trapped and tricked, we've been, by these hemmed giants, till we'm near run to death. 'Tis right good to see thee, General, and now I hopes we can all return safe to our own.'

Maglin turned on Scurl and said, 'Don't speak to me, *captain*, for I ain't begun with *thee* yet. Nor thee, Benzo, nor any of 'ee. And when I do, thee s'll know it – for 'twill be look out all! Here's trouble this day as shall lay heavy on thy broken heads for many a moon to come – I can promise 'ee that.' The irate Ickri leader looked thoughtfully at Grissel. 'Now, what be your tale, I wonder, to turn you against your own? For that's as 'twould seem, that you be with the Gorji in this. Speak.'

'What the maid says is true,' said Grissel, quietly. 'We did come here – not to hunt, as Scurl claims – but to find some precious thing, some part o' the Touchstone that Benzo heard 'ee talking 'bout . . .'

'Lickspittle!' roared Scurl. 'Turncoat! What bist fooling at, Grissel?'

Maglin brandished his spear at Scurl. 'Be silent! If I find an open mouth on 'ee again, then *you'll* find *this* sticking out of it! The Touchstone,' he said to Grissel, 'What do 'ee know of it?'

'Only that there be some part o' it gone – stolen by the Gorji maid, 'cording to Benzo – and that if we was to get it back then it might have some witchi-pocus that could be used to our good.'

Maglin threw Pegs a puzzled glance as he continued to quiz Grissel. 'Stolen by the *Gorji* maid?' he said. '*This* Gorji maid, thought you?'

' 'Cording to Benzo – for he and Flitch saw her put some tinsy thing in her roundabout when she were leaving the forest.'

'But that was just a little bowl!' broke in Midge. 'Henty *gave* it to me. I haven't stolen anything.'

Maglin thought that he began to see daylight. It was obvious that Scurl had somehow got wind of his conversation with Pegs about the missing part of the

Touchstone – although he couldn't see how, as yet. No matter. They must have heard mention that a Gorji maid had taken it – and assumed that it was Midge, rather than Celandine. Then they had seen Midge with some trinket that the Tinkler chi' had given her . . .

'This thing, this . . . bowl,' he said to Midge. 'Where is it?'

Midge looked at George. 'Did you pick it up?' she said.

'No,' George looked puzzled, remembering. 'I went back, but it had gone.'

'I have it,' Little-Marten spoke for the first time. He drew the metal bowl from his tunic, and Henty put her hands up to her mouth with relief. 'I found it. I knew 'twere what Henty had come here for, so I took it – to give to her.'

Maglin was becoming exasperated. 'But if this Tinkler chi' gave it to the Gorji maid, then why does she come here to take it back?'

' 'Tweren't mine to give,' said Henty, timid now, as she spoke to the great Maglin – for the very first time in her life. She put a shy hand through Little-Marten's arm for support – which he was very glad to give. ' 'Twas wrong. The cup were made by the Tinklers, for Celandine.' She looked over at Midge. 'I thought . . . I thought that *she* . . . I don't know what I thought.'

'But you came back here to get it,' said Maglin. 'So we all stand here for the sake of some *trinket*, a tinsy *stoup* . . .' He snorted in annoyance, his anger growing again as he turned to Scurl. 'And you would have done *murder*? For *this*?'

'Never!' cried Scurl. 'There's none harmed. 'Tis all Grissel's lies! Turncoat!'

'Aye!' said Grissel. 'A turncoat. And I would ever turn my coat, and my back, and my arms against any as would slay childer – be 'em Gorji or no. And slay them 'ee *would* have done – *and tried to*. I told 'ee I'd have no part of it, and I won't.'

'It's true,' said Midge. 'Grissel tried to help us – he *has* helped us. But *that* one,' she pointed to Scurl, 'and all the others – they would have killed us all if they could. *And* this wasn't the first time. He tried once before – Scurl did – to kill me and Little-Marten, when I was leaving the forest. It was only because of that . . . what was her name . . . that old woman . . .?'

'Maven,' said Little-Marten. ' 'Twas Maven as did for Tulgi – that's how we got away. But Scurl vowed he'd kill us both – and have been like to ever since . . . that's why I ran away . . . left the clavensticks . . .'

'Enough,' said Maglin, raising an arm in exasperation. 'Enough! 'Tis plain enough, too. Scurl, if the Whipping Stone were here, I'd strap thy miserable carcass across it and keep 'ee there for a moon or more. But that stone be in the forest – and I can vow that you'll never come to it. For you'll never come to the forest no more, neither – not if 'ee wants to live. You'll go from here *now*, and take this ragtag o' yours with 'ee. That's thee, Benzo, and thee, Flitch, and Snerk, and Dregg. Get away from me before I raddle the lot of 'ee on a skewer. Grissel, you may choose which way to turn thy coat – though I reckon you've made a choice already. Stay if you will. As for the rest – be out of my sight. You may travel to the Far Woods, or to the bottom of this Gorji muck-pit, for aught I care. You may take your chances where you will. But if I *ever* see thee at the tunnels of the Royal Forest again, I'll shoot 'ee myself – and think it a good day's hunting. Get away from here, and from me – *now.*' And Maglin, white with quiet rage, watched as his former company, the West Wood archers, gathered up their bows and quivers and made to leave.

A wretched sight they made – the three who had fallen in the lagoon looked as though they had been fashioned from muck rather than merely dipped in it – and the other two, Scurl and Snerk, were little better, soaked and bound as they were.

Scurl, apparently humbled at last, said, 'You'll loose our bonds, Maglin, I hope.' Maglin said nothing, but stepped behind Snerk and slashed through the binder twine with the sharp blade of his spear. Snerk stood rubbing his wrists, and watched as Maglin cut through Scurl's bonds in a similar fashion.

Scurl stared coldly at Midge as Maglin sliced through the binder twine. His eyes seemed to glaze over for a moment, and Midge began to quail – she had seen that look before. The moment passed, however. Scurl had too strong a sense of self-preservation to try anything foolish.

Benzo had other, wilder, ideas. Seeing his leader stand free, he snatched an arrow from his quiver and drew back his bow, yelling, 'Arms! Scurl – we have them – to arms!' and in the same instant let fly directly at Midge. It all happened so quickly, and in such an unforeseen manner, that none were prepared for it; none save Pegs.

Pegs didn't see the arrow. He didn't even see Benzo draw back the bow – yet some wild intuition made him lurch towards the girl rather than Maglin, a wing beginning to extend in a sheltering, protective movement. He felt the sharp pain of the arrow penetrating the still folded membranes of his wing – and then gladness with that pain, conscious that the maid was unharmed by the attempt on her life. He turned to face the attacker, and was in time to see Benzo drop like a stone, crumpling in a heap beside the lagoon, his slurry-strewn limbs skewed awkwardly among the tufts of reedy vegetation, his bow lying beneath him.

Nobody had moved. Maglin's spear was still in his hand, Grissel's bow still pointed downwards, George and Katie had barely begun to react. All simply stared at the motionless body of Benzo.

To most of those present, the moment of realization was not long in dawning. This had happened before. This had been the fate of Tulgi. They turned their eyes in wonderment towards the stable block – the only possible cover in that open space – and knew. *She* was in there, somewhere, or had been. Now she might be anywhere, watching, waiting – unfathomable, vengeful, following some path known only to herself. Maven.

They muttered her name, those who first guessed –

401

and they spoke it as a physician might diagnose the cause of death. Maven. Only Katie was totally mystified – for even George had heard the name before. Katie stared at the body of Benzo, wanting to look away, but scarcely able to.

'Maven?' she whispered to George. 'What's Maven?'

Scurl wasted no words on this occasion. He was beaten – beaten and banished. He roared no threats, spat no curses, made no murderous vows. Resting the end of his bow on the ground for a moment, he bent it slightly against his knee and unstrung it. Then he began to walk away, across the open field, in the direction of the Far Woods. The dismal figures of Snerk, Flitch and Dregg watched him for a few seconds, and then they made as if to leave also – but Maglin hadn't quite finished with them yet. He said nothing, but simply caught their eye and pointed to the motionless body of Benzo. The merest flick of Maglin's finger indicated to the miserable threesome that they were to take their erstwhile companion with them, and this they did – with a struggle – half carrying, half hauling the body between them as they stumbled along in the wake of Scurl. A wretched and bedraggled group they made, living scarecrows on the bright summer landscape.

Midge hardly gave their departure a second glance. Her concern was all for Pegs, who had silently borne his pain for her, and whose instinctively protective reaction had saved her life. The arrow had done little real damage, having pierced a fold in the outer edge of the wing membrane, and then dropped away to the ground, its force spent. Pegs had survived much worse – his still-healing wounds from the raking machine had been far more serious. Midge stood beside him, crouching slightly as she gently unfolded the wing, feeling again the now familiar soft texture of the velvety skin between the quill-like bones. There was a double wound where the arrow had gone through the folded membrane – but there was very little blood.

'I think you'll live,' whispered Midge, 'which is more than I would have done, if you hadn't been so quick. Dear Pegs. It's OK – don't say anything, but listen to me for a minute. I have some news: I don't think anything is going to happen to the woods – not for a while, anyway. Certainly not for a few months – moons. I'll find out more about it, and then come and see you very soon, OK? Tomorrow – I'll come to the gully tomorrow. Soon as I know more. But in the meantime, don't worry. You're safe there for a while longer.'

Pegs nuzzled briefly against her, relief and under-standing in his dark eyes. Midge tenderly folded the wing again, and stood up. She looked towards the stable block once more, wondering about Maven, and why this mysterious person, whom she had never seen, was so concerned for her welfare . . . Twice, now, had vengeance been brought down on the heads of her would-be attackers. Why? Who *was* Maven?

Maglin was anxious to leave, now that the crisis was over. He was getting fidgety, and impatient. He glanced up at the sun, riding high in the morning sky.

'Come, my brave friend,' he said to Pegs. 'Can 'ee

walk? 'Tis best we were gone, then. We've gotten what we want – and left some of what we don't.' He looked up at the faces of the three children, his dark serious eyes resting finally on Midge.

'You're caught up here in things which never concerned 'ee, maid, as we be caught up in those which don't concern us. And a sorry business it is – for now we be at the mercy of the Gorji at long last. The Various must look to thee and thine to keep a still tongue, till we can find our path. 'Tain't over yet – and I doubt that this is the last time we shall meet. Though you'll not see me, or any one of us, on Gorji land again – I can promise 'ee that.'

The Ickri General then looked around at his diminished company and led off across the Field of Thistles towards the Royal Forest. Pegs and Grissel followed. The white horse turned once to look at Midge, the soft eyes holding hers for a moment. Henty and Little-Marten walked a few paces behind, and, when all backs were turned, they moved closer together and held hands.

Chapter Twenty-seven

They sat at the cream-painted kitchen table, and Katie slumped forward dramatically, putting her head down onto her arms.

'I'll never, ever, *ever* say that this place is boring again,' she murmured, her voice muffled by the crook of her elbow. She rested her chin on her arm and looked in wonderment at Midge. 'How long have you *known*?' she said.

'Since about . . . three days after I got here,' said Midge. 'I found the white horse, up in that old pig barn on the hill . . .' She told her story, briefly, once more – and felt glad that this time she didn't have to make it sound convincing. It was simply the truth.

They talked long past lunchtime and into the afternoon, Katie telling how she had come back into the house – once she had seen the Ickri leave in pursuit of Midge – and remembered the water cannon propped against the landing banister, filled it at the kitchen tap, carried it up the flight of hamstone steps on the outer wall of the cider barn – and very nearly dropped the thing as she yanked open the apple-loft door.

'You were *amazing*, Katie,' said Midge. 'I don't even like to *think* about what would have happened if you weren't there. It was like Joan of Arc arriving, or a tank division or something.'

'Yes, I *think* I prefer Joan of Arc,' said Katie, coolly. But then she confessed – 'Actually, I pretty much *wet* myself when I first saw them. I can't imagine what it must have been like for you, Midge, the first time . . . I mean at least I had a *bit* of warning. About two seconds worth.'

George recounted his strange experience with the wind-up gramophone, and how he had managed to give Benzo the slip, only to get caught again – and how he had lured the archers onto the lagoon.

'If I'd *tried* to make it happen, it probably wouldn't have worked,' he said.

Midge told of her terrifying game of hide-and-seek on top of the wardrobe – then thought of something else, and said to Katie, 'But why *did* you come back into the house? You hadn't long escaped – they might still have been in here, for all you knew.'

'No,' said Katie, 'I saw them go – chasing you, remember? Then I ran straight in.'

'To get the WaterBlaster?'

'Um . . . well, actually, I think I was sort of coming in to get changed. *Then* I thought of the WaterBlaster.'

'You came back in to get *changed*?'

'*Well*? I'd just fallen into a load of old potato peel-ings and slimy rotten cabbage leaves and compost and stuff. I was covered in . . . what are you looking at me like that for? *Somebody* has to keep up the standards around here.' She may have been joking. It was hard to tell with Katie, Midge decided.

Eventually it came round to a question of what they were to do next. Should they tell Uncle Brian – and Midge's mum? They thought about the body of Tojo, stretched out on the floor of the cider barn. What were they supposed to do about that?

'We're going to have to tell,' murmured George. 'We've got to.'

'Yes,' said Katie, looking at Midge. 'I s'pose so.'

Midge didn't know what to say. She so wanted to pass the responsibility to somebody else – to let someone else decide. It was such a relief that George, and now Katie, knew all about it – or nearly all. Such a relief not to have to bear the burden alone. Yet, if Uncle Brian knew – and her mum – there was no telling what they might do. They might get the police or something. What would happen to the Various then? To Pegs? Wouldn't that be a betrayal?

'I don't know what they'd do, that's the trouble – I mean your dad and my mum. They might tell the police. Or phone a zoo, or TV, or the government . . . I don't know. And what good would it do? It would be like we'd ruined everything, ruined their lives – the Various, I mean. We'd have . . . it'd be like throwing them all to the dogs, or the wolves, or whatever it is. I *promised*, you see, that I wouldn't tell.'

'Yes, but now *we* know,' said George. 'Katie and me.

And they know that. They've already given themselves away by coming here. It wasn't your fault.'

'No,' said Midge, doubtfully. 'I s'pose not. But my mum – that's another thing – she's not very well. I mean, I don't even know whether she could *cope* with all this right now.'

'Yes,' said Katie. 'Last thing you want to hear when you're having a breakdown – Oh hi, Mum. We've got fairies at the bottom of our garden. *Not* a very good idea, as Dad would say.'

'Ka-tie!' said George, horrified.

But Midge laughed. She couldn't help herself – Katie was such a scream.

Round and round they went, and whereas it had at first seemed obvious that the events of this astonishing day would be difficult to keep to themselves, it slowly became clear that it would be even more difficult to convince their respective parents of what had really happened. Maglin had vowed that the Various would not be showing themselves again, and so, short of entering the wood and hunting them down, their existence would be impossible to prove. Midge, who had so far contributed little to the argument, now returned to her original thought.

'What good would it do, if we did tell? It wouldn't help anyone – I mean, like Katie said, what's the point? And nobody *needs* to know. Maybe, if the land was going to be sold . . . maybe we should tell then . . . oh, *I* don't know. Maybe we should just say nothing. I think that's what we should do. Say nothing, just for a while anyway, and see what happens.'

They thought about this, and agreed in the end that it was the least complicated course of action to take, and the only one that made any sense. Midge pushed the general agreement a stage further by saying, 'We should all make a promise never to tell unless the others are there too. Just so we all know it's still a secret, OK? Promise?' The others understood, and muttered their assent, Katie adding, 'Catch *me* saying anything. I still don't believe it myself.' It was a relief to have made a decision, and each felt a trust in the others, bound as they were by their shared experience. There was still the question of Tojo to consider, however. If they *were* going to keep all this a secret, then Tojo would have to disappear completely.

'Bury him,' said Katie. 'He could have just gone missing. Cats do.'

'*Bury* him?' said George. 'Where? What if Phoebe found him – and started digging him up or something?' He had a mental picture of his dad being witness to such a gruesome discovery – and the trouble that would follow. 'Well, it would have to be somewhere pretty well hidden, that's all. If Dad ever found out . . .' He looked at the alarm clock on the dresser. 'They could be back in about an hour – two at the most – so we'd better come up with something good. *And* there's all that mess in the cider barn that'd need clearing up, or we'll have to explain that as well. Don't think Dad goes in there much, but still – this'd be the one time he did.'

Midge had a thought, but she was hesitant in voicing it – it seemed so . . . disrespectful.

'What about . . . the lagoon? Nobody would *ever* find him then.' It came out as almost a whisper.

The other two just stared at her, and she wondered if she'd said something really terrible. Tojo had not been a pet – far from it – but he had been more their cat than hers, after all. Katie scraped back her chair and jumped up.

'Brilliant!' she said. 'We'll bung him in there!'

It wasn't going to be that easy, disposing of the corpse, after all. They stood at the edge of the lagoon and con- sidered the problems – the first of which was how to get Tojo right out to the middle where the lagoon was at its most liquid.

'Well, wouldn't you be able to just . . . swing him by the leg, or something, and then let go?' said Katie. She was addressing George.

'What if he didn't land in the right place?' said George. 'Who's going to go out there and pick him up and try again – you? And anyway, who says it's *me* that's doing the throwing?'

'Oh, definitely man's work,' said Katie, who had absolutely *no* intention of picking up a dead cat.

'I'm not sure he'd sink, even if we *did* get him in the right place,' said Midge. 'We're probably going to have to weigh him down with something. It would be awful if he just lay there. Floating.'

She nearly had an attack of the giggles – the whole business was just so ghoulish that she felt semi-hysterical, and glancing at the faces of George and Katie, she could see that they too were trying not to laugh.

They felt sober enough, though, when they entered the humid silence of the cider barn. The body of Tojo lay among the shards of broken bottles and stoneware, eerily lit by the sunbeams that streamed in from the open door of the apple store above. Midge was reminded of the way that Pegs had looked, lying on the floor of the pig barn, like something on a stage. But this felt more like being in a morgue than in a theatre, and as they gathered around the body they spoke in whispers. The eyes had closed in death, which was a mercy, but the feathered shank of the arrow that had slain him was a horrible thing to behold, protruding as it did from the coarse fur of the rib cage, the black-and-white flights so neatly trimmed and precise.

'He's *huge*,' muttered George, and it was true that, close up, the body of Tojo seemed even bigger in death than it had in life – the probable reason being that you'd never get this close to Tojo when he was alive. And yet, thought Midge, he must have been a kitten once. Was Tojo ever cute and cuddly, like the Favoured One? Did anyone ever pet him, and love him, and tell him how pretty he was? It was hard to imagine.

George said, 'I can't see how . . . well, I don't think this is going to work.'

Midge turned away from the disturbing sight and began looking round for inspiration, vaguely wondering whether it might be possible to use a pole or something. There were a couple of builders' planks lying on their sides against one of the walls, and she began to imagine trying to use one of these to push the body out onto the lagoon. Would that work? Then she had a better idea.

Once again they stood beside the evil-smelling lagoon, and now they had a plan. They had put the body of Tojo in an old hessian sack (or rather George had – Midge having agreed with Katie that this was 'man's work') and had then picked up all the bits of glass and stoneware and put those in the sack also. This had served the double purpose of clearing up all the mess in the cider barn, whilst hopefully providing enough ballast for the sack to sink. Certainly it had seemed heavy enough on the journey between the cider barn and the lagoon. Another journey had then been made in order to fetch one of the builders' planks.

They walked out upon the firm surface of the lagoon as far as they dared and, in accordance with Midge's plan, managed to stand the builders' plank on end. This wasn't at all easy, and the long plank swayed about precariously as they tried to position it so that it would fall across the surface of the lagoon in as controlled a manner as possible.

'If you stand with your foot against the bottom of the plank, Katie, and George and I try to lower it . . .' grunted Midge – and so that's what they did, though the thick length of timber became too heavy for Midge and George to hang on to beyond a certain point and they had to let go. The plank dropped with a bump and the bottom end kicked back a bit, catching Katie on the ankle – but there it lay, extending out over the surface of the lagoon, probably reaching about halfway to the centre.

'Now then, if two of us stand on this end, and the other walks along the plank carrying the sack, then they ought to be able to get it pretty well out to where it's . . . you know . . . more runny.'

'I'm heavier than you two,' said Katie, who had been sizing up the situation and was quick to bag the role least likely to end in disaster, 'so it'll be best if I stay here and stand on the plank. Keep it steady.'

'Oh, *I* get it,' said George. 'This is going to be blimmin' *man*'s work again, isn't it? Well, I've already had to pick the . . . him up. I don't think it should be my turn for the worst job, *every* time.'

'I'll do it,' said Midge. 'I'm probably the lightest, in any case.'

''S alright. *I* don't mind,' George suddenly preferred the idea of taking the risk himself to standing there like a wimp and watching Midge go out there.

'No, I want to.' She didn't really know why she said it, or why she should suddenly feel sorry that Tojo was dead – she had always hated him – but now it seemed as though his death had somehow been her fault, and that she should at least take some responsibility for the burial. Such as it was.

About halfway along the plank, she wished that she'd let George go after all – and George, watching her with his heart in his mouth, was wishing the same.

'Come back,' he said, urgently. 'Let me do it.

413

Midge! Come on, let me do it.' But this made her more determined, and she shook her head.

The sack was so awkward, that was the trouble – that and the fact that the plank wobbled slightly, every time she moved. She stood sideways, shuffled along a few inches, and then dragged the sack towards her. Slowly, slowly, a bit at a time she progressed to the point where she was about two thirds of the way along. The plank still seemed to be resting firmly on the surface – no sign of it disappearing into the mire. That was good, but it also meant that she would have to go further before she reached a point where the sack would sink. She really didn't think that she would be able to swing it very far, and so she needed to be standing over an area where the lagoon was virtually liquid. It seemed as though this would mean travelling right to the very end – for it was here that the surface became discoloured, where Benzo and the other two Ickri had fallen in.

Every little shuffle took her further away from safety and deeper into danger, but she ignored George – and Katie too now – pleading for her to give up and come back, and she continued to take one step at a time, making each step exactly the same as the last; slow, safe, sure, drag-the-bag. Slow, safe, sure, drag-the-bag. She was walking the plank like a pirate – and yet it was Tojo who was the pirate. Tojo was the pirate, and it was Tojo who was going overboard, down, down, down to Davy Jones' locker . . . She stopped, suddenly feeling dizzy. This was a horrible thing to be doing. And it was really dangerous. It stank, the lagoon, now that she was approaching the area where the surface had been broken, and she felt sick and unsteady. There were masses of flies.

'Are you OK?' George's voice sounded anxious, and miserable – and far away. No, she wasn't OK. She wasn't a bit OK. She felt that her nerve was beginning to go – dizzy and shaky and frightened, she felt. It had to be done quickly. Just a few more steps. If she allowed herself any more time to think, it would be too late . . .

At the end of the plank now, she looked at the ghastly mess where the Ickri had been – so close it was, at her very feet the orangey-grey porridge, reeking and foul. She was standing alone in the middle of a lake of slurry and angry humming flies, and the lake was ready to swallow her up, pull her down, suck her under into the choking swampy darkness – no! – she would *not* think of that. Lift the sack, quick. Get rid of it!

The untried weight of it almost overbalanced her, and her mouth filled instantly with water at the sudden fright. She felt her knees go funny, and was terrified that she might faint and fall in. The flies buzzed louder. She breathed out, breathed in, gagged slightly at the stench – and tried again. Now she had the measure of it, the weight of the sack, the best way to grip it, the best way to stand. Very gingerly she began to swing, getting used to the pendulum effect. She would not let go, not till she was certain that her rhythm and balance were absolutely under control. Backwards, forwards, gently swinging, no sudden movement, just backwards, forwards, a little more, a little more, just one more swing, and then g-e-e-e-ntly let her fingers loosen. The sack rose and fell gracefully in a short but satisfying arc, landing perhaps six feet from the plank, more or less where she hoped it would go . . . but the *noise* . . . the *voices* . . . screaming her name.

'*Miiiidge! Miiiidge! You're sinking!*' George and Katie were frantically shrieking at her and she began to panic. What? What? She looked down and saw that the end of the plank was beginning to disappear into the oozing mire. It was already touching her trainers. All control suddenly deserted her, her nerve broke completely, and she ran – *ran* – back down the length of the plank, arms flailing, the board wobbling, feeling her balance beginning to go, her body teetering sideways, until she reached a point where she could stay on the thing no longer. She gave a final leap and landed on the surface of the lagoon. The crust cracked and gave way beneath her feet, and she screeched with fright, yet managed to plough onwards, reaching firm ground and the outstretched hands of George and Katie, falling onto the grassy rim of the lagoon to laugh and cry at the same time, soaked with perspiration, shaking with relief and shock. All three rolled around shrieking, with the sudden release of built-up tension, and it took a while before they remembered the purpose of it all and sat up to see what was happening in the middle of the lagoon.

Not much was happening, which was rather

disappointing – and worrying. The knotted sack seemed to be just sitting there. But after a while, like watching the minute hand on a clock, it seemed that there must have been some progress, for now, surely, there was slightly less sack visible than there had been. Another five minutes and they were certain. They couldn't *see* any movement, but the thing was definitely going under. George glanced sideways at Katie's watch.

'It had better hurry up,' he said.

Eventually they stood up and pulled the plank back from the lagoon. The far end was messy, and so they dragged it through the weeds and thistles for a while until it was relatively clean again. This took a bit of time, and when they returned to the edge of the lagoon the sack was three-quarters gone.

'I'm bored with this,' said Katie. 'Think I'll go back now.'

But George and Midge stayed to witness the passing of Tojo, hugging their knees in sombre silence until the dark hessian sack finally disappeared altogether beneath the surface of the lagoon. The last little corner looked disconcertingly like an ear, the tip of a cat's ear, pricked up, listening – though there was nothing to hear but the song of the flies, a humming choir, a final serenade to accompany Tojo into the underworld.

Chapter Twenty-eight

Katie went upstairs to have another shower ('I can *still* smell old cabbage leaves on me – ughh!') and Midge and George wandered into the sitting room. George put the TV on and flicked disinterestedly around the channels, whilst Midge leaned over the back of the battered sofa and looked out of the window.

'Fancy a game of Cluedo, or something?' said George, but Midge shook her head. 'Not really.'

'Think I might go and muck about in the tree house then.'

' 'Kay. I might come over later.'

George wandered off and Midge was left alone in the quiet room, hearing the distant rumble of the shower upstairs, and the faint dull thud of Katie's CD system. She leaned further over the sofa and opened a window, letting in the summer sounds of the birds and insects. It struck her again how very different it was here, compared to the flat in Streatham, and how – if only things weren't such a mess – she could love it. But things *were* a mess. The business at the lagoon had been just horrible. What would make things right, she

418

wondered? How could any of this ever come right? She smiled, remembering what Katie had said about fairies at the bottom of the garden. They weren't at the bottom of the garden though. And they weren't fairies. They were people. People. That was another funny word, like lagoon.

Lagoonlagoonlagoonlagoooonla. Goonla. Goon.

People. Peepull. Pee. Pullpee. Pullpeepullpeepull.

The sound of the car coming up the lane took her by surprise, she had been so lost in her thoughts. Now, suddenly, she felt nervous about seeing her mum. Really nervous. What would she be like? She imagined her mum in dark glasses and a headscarf. Her mum never wore a headscarf. Nobody did. Except the Queen.

She got off the creaky sofa, intending to go to the front door, but then remained where she was, standing, watching through the open window. The nose of the red estate appeared in the gateway, dipping over the bumps, and the car swung round, pulling noisily into the yard. The engine cut out, and again she could hear the bass thump of Katie's CD system from upstairs. The car doors didn't open straight away.

Uncle Brian wound down the car window, and looked out, pointing up at the roof of the house – craning his neck in order to see something – then withdrew and turned towards the shadowy figure in the passenger seat. He suddenly slumped forwards, and his head touched the steering wheel. The horn gave a little toot. Midge could hear him laughing. The passenger door opened and she saw her mum's head appear over the top of the car. She too was laughing, shading her eyes against the sun, and squinting up at the roof of the house. She wasn't wearing dark glasses or a headscarf.

Midge ran out of the room and into the hallway to open the heavy front door. The Deputation from Rhode Island scattered, as she leapt over the threshold and bounded down the flagstone path, narrowly avoiding the wellington boot. 'Mum!'

'Hey! Look at *you*, Miss Suntan!'

Her mum smelled of all the things she had missed – and she clung on tight, *tight*, burying her head against the clean soft linen, feeling the buttons pressing into her cheek, the cool fingers upon her neck. She squeezed hard and saw the golden glint, blurry through the tears, of the tiny buckles on her mum's unsuitable shoes.

'Are you OK?' she whispered. 'Are you OK, Mum?'

'I'm OK.' The calm hands stroked the top of her head. 'These crack-ups aren't all they're cracked up to be.'

It was a line – and one that had been rehearsed – but Midge could tell that her mum was still her mum. She hadn't gone anywhere.

'Missed you,' she said, and meant it so much that she said it again, 'Missed you, Mummy.'

The click and clack of her mother's heels sounded strange on the red brick floor of the farmhouse kitchen, and her perfume seemed oddly exotic in the atmosphere of cooking smells and wood ash that came from the old Rayburn. She walked around with the sleeves of her smart navy-blue jacket pushed up slightly, her arms half-folded, shaking her head in wonderment.

'How long has it been, Brian?' she said. 'I just can't believe how nothing – *nothing* – has changed. In twelve years. Nothing. Even that old alarm clock – I remember that.'

Uncle Brian made a pot of tea. Slow and comfortable he seemed, unhurried in his movements, slightly clumsy – banging the kettle noisily against the tap, struggling a little to get the lid back on. How unalike they were, thought Midge. Brother and sister – you wouldn't have guessed it.

'I've never seen you drink tea before,' her mum said, as Midge picked up her mug and took a sip.

'I know. I've sort of got used to it.'

'Do you know where George is?' said Uncle Brian, 'And Katie?'

'Um, Katie's in the shower, I think, and George said he was going over to the tree house.'

'Excuse me for a minute, then, whilst I round them up.'

When Uncle Brian had left the kitchen, her mum said, 'Listen, darling, now might be a good moment to explain what's been going on with me.' She pulled her chair a little closer to the table, and hunched forward slightly, tapping a neat fingernail against the handle of her cup. Her mum didn't look like other people's mums – she was prettier. She still looked young, alive.

Her hair was always nice. 'It helps,' she had sometimes said, 'with the job, I'm afraid – not having a face like the back of a bus. It sounds terrible, I know, and it shouldn't matter, but presentation is part of every-thing nowadays. Even stuffy old orchestral music.' And it was true. Midge had seen the Philharmonic on TV a few times – and had noticed how the camera seemed to come back to her mum's face more often than to any of the other players. She could see why it would.

'About eighteen months ago – actually it must be more like two years – this weird thing happened to me. I was playing in Berlin. Strauss. And I was up on the stand, not nervous, particularly – it wasn't our first night, or anything, and I'd played the piece tons of times. We were just about to start, and I looked at the dots – the music – and suddenly none of it *meant* any-thing. I knew what the notes were – it's difficult to explain – but it was just a pattern on the page. I'd lost the sense of it, somehow. All my concentration went. I saw the dots, but they were all just . . .'

'Like when you keep saying the same word? Over and over – like "lagoon".'

'Sorry?'

'If you keep saying "lagoon", then after a while it doesn't mean anything. It's just a funny sound. Lagoonlagoonlagoon.'

Her mum looked at her. 'Actually, that's very good. It *was* a bit like that. Yes, just patterns that didn't mean anything. Anyway, it didn't last long, and once we'd started I was all right. But it frightened the *life* out of me – and of course I was worried that it would happen

422

again. Which it did – *and* it got worse. I was fine by myself, practising, and in rehearsals, but as soon as there was the pressure of actual performances, I'd get this weird thing. And you just can't *be* that way. Not if you want to hold down a chair in a top-flight orchestra, you can't. So this last couple of years hasn't been easy. It's affected me, and so it affects us – you and me – because I'm on edge all the time, and now, two weeks into this tour, I've suddenly had enough. I'm just not going to do it any more. And it's not such an uncommon thing. I've talked to other players – had to in the end, because you can't easily disguise the fact that there's something wrong, not at that level – and everyone knows of someone that it's happened *to*. They take tablets, beta blockers, whatever, get counselling. But not me. I'm simply going to stop. Pack it all in, for the time being anyway. It's shaken me up, and I'm sad to walk away from it all – but so relieved at the same time.'

She reached out and held Midge's hand. 'And I'm so glad to be here,' she said, smiling, 'and with you. I can't tell you how happy that makes me. And I'm also *very* excited about something else – I have some news, but it can wait for a moment till Brian gets back. You look *fantastic*, by the way. Really healthy and well. Have you been OK? What's been happening with you?'

Here was the first test. She wanted to tell. She didn't like having secrets, she was discovering – and she really didn't like having secrets from her mum. Through all their ups and downs, the happy times and the angry times, she had always been able to unburden herself, to tell her mum what was on her mind. Secrets were like lies, weren't they? She didn't like telling lies, and she didn't like having to cover things up – but now she was going to have to.

'Oh, well,' she began, 'actually, it's been great here. Much more . . . interesting . . . than I thought it would be. Really, I just love it. Honestly, I do. George has got a tree house. And a wind-up gramophone. We've been sleeping in it – the tree house, I mean, not the . . .'

But then George wandered in, flicking his hair back and being George. Uncle Brian's voice was saying, 'Here we are, then. Come on, Katie.' And suddenly the kitchen was full of chatter.

'Hallo, *George*! Looking handsomer than ever, I see. Come and give your mad auntie a kiss!' George submitted to this indignity, blushing a little. 'And Katie! Wow! Just *look* at you! I bet she's breaking a few hearts around here, Brian.'

'Breaks mine, on a more or less daily basis,' said Uncle Brian. 'Kidding – just kidding!' he added, as Katie scowled at him from beneath her towel-turban.

'Hallo, Auntie Christine,' said Katie. 'How are you, er . . . feeling?'

'I'm absolutely fine, darling. Really. I've just been telling Midge about it. All that's happened is I've decided to stop playing for a while. It just got to be too much pressure. Tell you what – shall we drop the "Auntie" bit? I've never like being called "Auntie". It makes me feel so old – especially now that you're all getting to be so grown-up. I much prefer Christine, or Chris.'

424

'I quite like being called "Uncle",' said Uncle Brian.

'Well, you *look* like an uncle,' said Christine. 'But then you always did.'

'Thanks!' laughed Uncle Brian. There was a pause, a slightly uncomfortable silence, and so Christine took a deep breath and said, 'Shall we tell them? Straight away? I mean there's no point in delaying it, is there?'

'OK. You do it. You're better than me, at talking.'

'Don't know whether that's a compliment or not, but OK – here goes. Well, I had an idea – the beginnings of an idea, anyway – some little while ago. Just a daydream, really. I think maybe I was looking for ways of giving up the playing before all this happened – jumping before I was pushed, so to speak – and that I was already imagining how life might be without it. Anyway, I told Brian about it, coming down on the train, and we've been talking non-stop all the way. Now, it's just an *idea*, and by tomorrow it might seem like a very *bad* idea. Also, it depends – a lot – on what you three make of it all. So, nothing is *fixed* yet – OK? Don't imagine that this is what's *going* to happen. But it's what *could* happen if we all agree.'

Christine put her hands to her cheeks for a moment, then pushed her hair back behind her ears, as she stopped to think. Midge knew that something big was coming – and that it had already as good as happened, whatever it was. Her mum was not one to dither about. Once she'd made up her mind, that was it. It was to do with Mill Farm. Her mum was going to take over the sale – they were going to sell up and move to Cardiff, they were going to plough up the forest and grow carnations, they were going into the logging business, they were going to start a bicycle hire company in Norway . . . It was another of Uncle Brian's mad schemes, and now her mum was going that way too and everything was about to change . . .

There was a child's drawing in ballpoint pen, faint indentations in the chipped cream paintwork of the kitchen table top. It looked like it was supposed to be a cat. The ink had faded, but the marks remained. Underneath the drawing there were three letters – K, A, and T. Was that supposed to be 'cat' or 'Katie', Midge wondered? She let her middle finger trace the outline of the drawing, feeling the slight grooves and ridges in the discoloured paintwork. She suddenly felt sad, and exhausted. It had been such a long day. Some horrible things had happened, and now she was sure that there was worse to come.

'It's to do with Mill Farm,' continued Christine, slightly breathless, the way she spoke sometimes. 'And us. All of us. As things stand, the place would have to be sold – the lot. Brian can't afford to just . . . carry on, it's too big, too run down, too expensive . . .'

'No!' Midge was really upset. She knew it. Everything was going wrong. 'You *can't* just get rid of it . . .'

'Hang on a minute, darling – I haven't finished. *So* – the only way we can *keep* it is if it pays its way. It has to be turned into a business. It's *not* viable as a farm any more, and Brian was never really a farmer anyway. But it *could* be turned into something else – *if* a lot of money was invested in it, *if* the buildings were renovated and *if* it was run as a proper business. It could be a bed and breakfast, for instance. Or a restaurant. There are a lot of things that *could* be done with it, provided that money was pumped into it. Do you see what I'm getting at? It just takes money, and hard, hard work. And we could *do* that. What I'm saying is that we could live here – you and me, Midge – if we wanted to. Brian would still be here of course, and George and Katie would visit, just as they do now. So, forgetting about the money side of things for a minute – what do you think? How would it be, if, for example, the house was split into two – Midge and I would have our own apartment or whatever, and Brian another – the cider barn could perhaps be turned into a restaurant, the stables into self-catering accommodation, maybe. What do you think?'

There was absolute silence at this – nobody said a word.

'Well,' said Christine, 'I didn't get a lot of clapping for *that* . . .'

But of course it seemed like a wonderful idea – it was just that the children were taken so completely by surprise, and that there were so many questions to ask.

'What about school?' said Midge. 'And, well, *everything* . . . the flat, and . . . could we *really* just *move?* I mean I'd love to be here . . . but I don't see how . . .' She trailed off. Everything was happening so quickly – she couldn't take it all in. The Various, she thought – would that mean that they could stay where they were?

'What would happen to the land,' she said, 'and the

427

forest – would we keep all that too? It wouldn't have to be cut down or anything?'

'The *forest*?' said her mum. 'Oh, the old woods on Howard's Hill, you mean? Well, no, I suppose that we'd keep all that – continue to let out the land to the local farmers, or whatever. There's not much you could do with the woods anyway – it's all more or less protected around here, which is why Brian wasn't able to get planning permission. No, I suppose we'd just keep it all – but what a funny question! The important thing is that it would mean a complete change of lifestyle – and that's what you need to be thinking about. Probably it would affect you more than anyone, Midge. I've already decided to stop what I'm doing, whatever happens. For Katie and George, it would mean that *this* place would change – but for the better – and that whenever they came to see their dad, we'd be here too. Brian's all for it – but it's *you* who would be going through the biggest upheaval, Midge. Certainly you'd have to change schools – but your friends could always come and stay. Azzie could come down any time she liked. People *do* move. Why not think about it, sleep on it – all of us – and we'll talk about it some more, tomorrow?'

'Well, I don't need to think about it,' said Midge. 'I'd just love it. I love it here. I'd really . . . love it.' She was overwhelmed. To not have to leave, to stay here forever – to properly *live* here. It still seemed impossible.

'But it'd cost a fortune, wouldn't it?' said Katie. 'I mean, what you were saying about all that . . .

converting . . . and everything. Wouldn't it be really really expensive?'

'I'd sell up in London,' said Christine, 'and invest the money in this. There'd be enough, I think.'

'What – just from our flat?' said Midge.

'Ah – but it wouldn't be just *our* flat, remember,' said her mum. 'It would be the whole building – *all* the flats. They belong to me, as you know. The building was left to your dad, Midge – by his father. Then it came to me.'

'I keep forgetting ' said Midge. 'It never *feels* like we've got any money.'

'Well we never *do* have any *money*, as such. But, we do have a little bit of property – though I must admit that I tend to keep fairly quiet about it. I certainly wasn't going to advertise the fact to the other tenants. Could you imagine what Colin Bond would be like, for instance, if he knew that I was his landlady? No, Daddy and I lived there when the place was owned by his father – and we simply stayed on when the old man died. The flats were let through an agency. We never said anything to anyone in the building – didn't want the hassle of people knocking on our door every time there was a dripping tap or something. Anyway, after Daddy died it became mine. I was happy to stay in the flat – it was big enough for you and me. So that's how things went on. Now, if I were to sell the lot, then yes – it might just about raise enough money to do pretty much all the work that needs doing here. Just about. Although it wouldn't be an easy couple of years. There'd be an awful lot of work involved – I can't pretend that everything would be instantly perfect. And we certainly wouldn't be rich. What do you think, though? Would it be *exciting*?'

'It's *fantastic*! I just can't believe it. I mean I just can't . . . *believe* it . . .'

'You're very quiet, George,' said Uncle Brian. 'What do *you* think?'

'Would I be able to keep my tree house?' said George.

They talked and talked. There was suddenly so much to think about – how the house might be divided into two, where a second kitchen might go, how another staircase might be fitted in. The neglected old farm suddenly seemed full of possibilities. It was only when Christine suggested a tour of the outbuildings that the three children glanced at one another, each thinking of the cider barn, and wondering whether their hasty clean-up job would be noticed.

But the expedition went off without incident – Uncle Brian merely sniffing as they entered the cider barn, and saying 'Bit whiffy in here. Sort of drainy smell.' It was the builders' plank of course, lately dragged out of the lagoon – but as the children had hidden it behind another plank, there was no visible evidence, and the adults were soon far too pre-occupied with renovation plans to bother about anything else.

Midge had decided not to sleep in the tree house that night – glad to be in a proper bed after what had seemed an endless day. And it was so good to have her mum with her, to tuck her in again, like at home. And now *this* would be home, she thought. This funny room, where she had been born, where she had felt that she belonged, right from the very first day.

The world seemed to have speeded up. Her life had been altered at such a rate that it had been as much as she could do to cling on from one day to the next, coping as best as she had been able. And now here was another huge and unexpected surge forward. She was flying.

'Everything's going to change, Mum, isn't it? For us.'

'Yes, it is. And it's going to be a change for the good, darling. It feels right. This is where we should be – you were born here, by the way, did I ever tell you that?'

'I know. Uncle Brian told me the first day I was here. And it was really strange – but I felt like I was home, right from the first day. Like I *had* been here before. It seems like years ago. What *about* you and Uncle Brian, though? You've never had very nice things to say about him. *I* like him – but I never thought that *you* did, much.'

'Mm. I think that maybe I was always jealous – and a bit cross. This was my home too, you know, as a child, and I loved it. When he got the farm and I got nothing, I was upset. And then when everything he tried seemed to fail, and the place just went down and down – well, that made me crosser still. No, we'll probably have a few arguments – but we can get along all right. And we wouldn't be living in each other's pockets all the time – we'll be like neighbours. He's very good with people, you know, in a funny sort of way. Better than me at that side of things, I think. People like him. He'd be great as a front-of-house person, if we got this up and running. And there's very little *wrong* with the ideas he has – most of the things he's thought of for this place *could* have worked, with the right amount of capital, and a proper business plan. He's just not good with money that's all. I am, though, and that's why it'll be fine, I'm sure of it. I'll tell you something else – though you mustn't breathe a word – I reckon he and Pat will get back together again, someday. They still love each other, I'm certain. It's just that she couldn't stand it any longer – one scheme after another going down the pan. I wouldn't be at all surprised if making a success of this place helped bring them back together again. All she ever wanted was a bit of stability, I think.'

'He has girlfriends, you know. Well, I *think* he does.'

'Hmm. Frankie Seymour, you mean? I don't believe that *that's* a very serious option. Frankie's got far too much sense.'

'Would *you* ever get married again?'

'Oh, hullo. What's brought all this on? Well, I don't know. Anything's possible, I suppose. Would it bother you?'

'Depends.'

'Of course it does. Well . . . I *have* been seeing some-one, a bit. But I don't think you need worry about it too much. No wedding bells just around the corner, I think I can guarantee that much.'

'I bet he's a musician.'

'Well, yes, as it happens – but no one from the orchestra, if that's what you mean. Anyway, enough. I'm not going to say another word.'

'So it's a secret.'

'Well, it's not a *secret* as such. It's just that now doesn't feel like the right time to talk about it.'

'It's OK to have secrets though, isn't it?'

'Course it is. Why – have you got some?'

'Might have,' said Midge, coyly.

'Well then, you might tell me about them, when you feel like it. Or you might not, if you'd prefer. I shan't mind.'

'It was a secret about the flats, wasn't it? For a long time you kept that a secret. Years. But then you told about it in the end.'

'Yes – because the time was right. And as I said, if you've got something you want to tell *me* about . . .'

'Mum, you've started to call me Midge.'

'I know. Do you mind? It seems silly not to, when everyone else does. I've sort of got used to it. Like you drinking tea.'

It was still light when her mum kissed her and left the room. Midge could hear the distant cawing of the rooks as they began to settle down for the night, and the evening song of a blackbird, through her open window, clear liquid sounds, joyous on the peaceful summer air. She heard Uncle Brian cross the yard, open and shut the car boot – bringing her mum's bags in, probably – and the occasional creak of the beams up in the roof, the house cooling down as the long day came to a close. These would be *her* sounds, now, the sounds that she would hear for years to come. And it was all right to have secrets. Next week, next year, maybe in twenty years when she had babies of her own – someday when the time was right, she would tell. But not today. And not tomorrow. Tomorrow she would ... she yawned and closed her eyes. Whatever she would do tomorrow, could wait until then.

Chapter Twenty-nine

She was awake long before anyone else in the morning, and anxious, now, to break her news to Pegs. It was going to be all right, everything was going to be all right. The Various were safe – as safe as they had ever been – and she had to let them know.

The dew had soaked through her trainers by the time she had reached the top of the gully, and she could feel the damp between her toes. The wicker doors were already open, ready and waiting for her.

Once more she stepped into that other world, that world within a world, stood by the little spring, the heady scent of wild garlic in her nostrils, and met with Pegs – the amazing, mysterious, magical Pegs. She reached out her hand to touch the soft silvery mane, let the tips of her fingers brush the velvety texture of the folded wings, and once more she was overwhelmed by the strangeness of it all.

'This is like a dream,' she said. 'It just feels as though I'm dreaming all the time.'

Yes. Comprend. And perhaps there will come a time when

you will believe it to have been so. And I too. But for today let us imagine that we are here. Tell me what you have to say.

She had thought that the news she brought – the wonderful news of how the forest was to remain undisturbed, and its secrets undiscovered – would provoke more of a reaction from her friend than it seemed to. Pegs shook back his head, as though releasing a tension in his neck muscles, then turned to look at her. For a long moment he gazed into her eyes, searching, it appeared, puzzled almost.

I too have dreams, my friend. And through them I see ever more clearly. I am flying towards a great light, and as the light grows ever brighter, so does my understanding of what is, and was, and will be.

'But . . . *I* had a dream like that!' cried Midge, astonished. 'I was flying . . . towards a light . . . and *you* were there!'

Yes. I was there. Be accepting, maid, accepting of who you are and of what may happen to you. And know this – all that may happen has already happened. Aye, and all that has happened will happen again. Know that there is a circle, unjoined as yet, and that you are a part of it. Know also that you will come to no harm. Have no fear, and you will take no ill from this – I am certain of it.

Midge had expected a little more gratitude for the fact that she had brought a promise of safety for Pegs. She felt a bit peeved, suddenly, that he talked as though it was to be the other way about – that he was promising her own safety. Easy to say, now that all danger seemed to be past, she thought. And those other things he said . . . she simply didn't understand.

436

They just seemed to be riddles.

'Well, I very nearly *have* come to harm, once or twice,' she said. 'That time when Scurl tried to shoot me – and he would have done too if it hadn't been for . . . Maven. *And* that other time with Benzo. If you hadn't been there, then, well . . . I don't know what would have happened.'

Yet I was there. And am there. And will ever be there. As you were there, when I lay broken beneath a cruel wheel, and were ever there. Where else may we be, other than where we were, and are, and will be?

'What? How do you mean? Do you mean that it's all . . . I don't know the word . . . I can't think of it . . .' She knew there was a word somewhere, but it had gone. 'And what about Maven? Who *is* she, anyway?'

I cannot say. But I begin to see who you are, and what you are . . . and I say again – be accepting, and have no fear. Have no fear, Midge, no matter what may betide. And now, enough – for here are others, eager for your news.

Henty and Little-Marten were making their way

along the bank of the little stream. Shy with her at first, they were, tongue-tied, as she was with them. No amount of meetings could ever diminish the strangeness of it all. It would never feel comfortable, normal. She didn't belong here. But the couple seemed glad to see her, and glad of the excuse to be away for an hour – for they had said nothing to Tadgemole yet, nor to anyone, of their being together. A union between an Ickri and a Tinkler was unheard of – and it was doubtful that either of their fathers would have approved. Eventually, they hoped, it might be accepted – but for the moment it was a secret, and besides, the future of the forest and of all the Various was so uncertain that now was not the time to seek approval.

But here was Midge, the Gorji maid, with news to gladden their hearts, and give them hope. The crisis had passed, they learned. They could not comprehend the details, and nor were they interested – they understood only that the forest was not to be destroyed, and that their peace would remain undisturbed. For the time being, at least, they were safe – and this was news indeed.

'Nothing will change,' said Midge. 'I promise. And nobody will ever come here. Everything will be like it was – better, now that you don't have to worry any more.'

Little-Marten and Henty were very happy at this, and inwardly planned to launch the announcement of their union on the tide of good news that they would bring to their fathers. Pegs remained thoughtful, though.

I knew in my heart that your coming here was meant to be – and that with your coming the wheel of our story would begin to turn again. Yet, as I have said, the circle remains unjoined, and we are not yet free to come and go as we will. For this is the birthright of all travelling tribes – to travel – and we have stayed here too long. We are but visitors here, maid – we come, and we go. All of us are but visitors, aye, even the Gorji – though few of them know it. For today, and this news, I am glad – and those who wait now for word in Counsel Clearing will be glad also. This will still the unquiet hearts, and bring us peace where all has been upset. Yet the soil remains thin, and the woods are not as fruitful as they were. We have some respite, but cannot stay forever. We shall talk again, maid – you and I – a task remains concerning the Touchstone, and I believe that your part is not yet played entire. There are other times to come – aye, other times to come. Remember that. Briefly parted, then, maid. And soon united, I hope.

'Yes. Soon united, Pegs – I hope so too. Goodbye, Henty. Goodbye, Little-Marten – you know where I'll be from now on. Right here.'

The Tinkler maid stepped shyly forward, her beautiful dark eyes shining with pleasure, and she offered some bright object in her outstretched hand. It was the tinsy bowl. 'A gift,' she said. 'And now 'tis mine to give. A gift from my father – a cup of kindness to thee for my safe return.'

'Well, I'm not to thank for that,' said Midge. 'But I'd love to have it, and I shall keep it always, I promise. I never did get the chance to look at it properly.'

' 'Twas for Celandine,' said Henty. 'She that showed

us how to sing. See – 'tis rubbed up now.'

'Do you really think I should take it?' Midge was speaking to Henty, but she glanced at Pegs. The white horse bowed his graceful head slightly.

It is for you, as it ever was. You should take it.

Midge took the little bowl, polished and gleaming in the sunlight, and saw the finely engraved figures, tiny people, around the outer rim. And there was the picture of Celandine, standing in their midst. All their mouths were open. They were *singing*. Of course – now she could see it. And on the inside of the bowl, around the inner rim, was engraved the name Celandine. It was a beautiful, lovely thing.

'They're all *singing*,' said Midge. 'It's gorgeous. Thank you, Henty. You'll have to tell me the story of this – I shall come and see you, and we'll sit down together, and you can tell me all about it.'

'I can do singing,' said Little-Marten proudly. 'I be learning.'

The Naiad field workers straightened their backs and looked across the plantation as the white horse appeared among the cedar trees at the corner of the East Wood. They saw him pause there for a few moments with the Woodpecker and the Tinkler maid, then walk on, alone, towards Counsel Clearing. Maglin, they knew, would be waiting there, with the Elders and the tribe leaders – and Ba-Betts, perhaps, if she were up betimes. There had already been a reprieve, or so they had heard when Maglin and Pegs had returned the previous day – the forest might survive for a little longer. Another season, two seasons, maybe more. And now Pegs had met with the Gorji maid once again – she whose arrival would no doubt bring many changes, like the arrival of that other maid, so long ago. Whether those changes would be for good or ill they could not yet tell, but optimism and hope were in their nature – as it must be in the nature of all those whose lives are precarious. Perhaps there would be more news. They laid down their implements, and made their way to Counsel Clearing, to listen to whatever it was that the winged horse had to say.

But the Woodpecker and the Tinkler maid slipped away by themselves. They knew all there was to know, they felt, and more. Had they not faced the worst that the Gorji world could throw at them – certain death? And had they not clung to each other in that moment, prepared to face it together, rather than be separated? What else did they need to know? They would listen to no more speeches, or declarations or wordy arguments. There were other words, and better ways of using them.

Midge carefully parted the brambles at the gates of East Wood and slowly climbed the steep banks of the gully. She remembered the last occasion she had done this – her blind panic, her torn clothes, and her vow never to return. How differently she felt today.

Near the top of the gully she fumbled her footing slightly and put out a hand to steady herself. Her eye fell upon a small yellow flower, nestling in the rough grass, and her fingers seemed to reach out to it as she stumbled forward. It was a celandine, a single late bloom, and she crouched down on the bank to examine it. The moment seemed to have some sort of meaning, and she thought she would pick the flower and carry it home with her. But she didn't. Instead, she turned round for some reason and looked back towards the brambles at the head of the gully. Standing down below, motionless beside the little stream, was a stooping figure – a fantastic creature, wreathed in trailing strands of ivy, robed in tattered emerald, hair and hands and features daubed in viridian. Midge looked down in shock at the silent figure, feeling that of all the strange things these woods had revealed to her this was surely the strangest – this fey yet deadly woodland spirit, this wild apparition, her guardian angel. Maven-the-Green.

Still as stone at the water's edge, the crooked figure returned her wondering gaze, but made no sound and gave no sign – a woodland statue, expressionless, unfathomable. She reminded Midge of carvings seen in foreign shrines, there forever, decked in offerings, watching a changing world through changeless eyes.

If there had been a moment when she might have spoken, then that moment had passed. Midge felt calm, and content just to sit and stare – as one might stare at a deer or a fox in a rare and privileged encounter, each aware that the one does not belong in the other's world, each aware that the one means the other no harm, a mirrored glance of curiosity and acknowledgement, before travelling on.

She picked the celandine after all, held it up for Maven to see, and thought that she detected the ghost of a reaction – the slightest inclination of the head, perhaps, the faintest of smiles. Maybe she had been mistaken – at any rate she was reminded, as she held up the flower, of the bunch of celandines that had been laid beside the woodland path, and she thought that she knew whose hand had placed them there for her. She rose to her feet and turned to go. After a few paces it became impossible to resist a last quick glance over her shoulder – even though she knew in advance that the figure would no longer be there.

Back down Howard's Hill she walked, holding the cup of kindness, feeling the rounded lip of the rim between her fingers. A warm haze hung over the wetlands, softening the colours of the landscape and the rooflines of Mill Farm, down below. The air was alive with the sounds of insects and birds, everything busy doing what it was supposed to be doing. She had done what *she* was supposed to do, she felt – and soon would be as busy as they. But not today. There would be plans to make, and conversations to have, and a million things to think about. There would be architects and builders and decorators. There would be furniture and wallpaper to choose, schools to visit, clarinet lessons to be organized and everything, everything, everything. And there would be the Various, and other mysteries to unravel. But not today. Today she would lie in the sun.

*   *   *

443

She rested on her tummy on top of the low balustrade wall in front of the house, feeling the warmth on her back, and turning the little bowl round and round between her fingers as she gazed at the pictures. She thought, I live here. My name is Margaret Walters, and I live at Mill Farm, near Withney, Somerset.

Margaret Walters – nobody ever called her that, except when they had a supply teacher taking the register at school ... Thomas Vincent, Margaret Walters, Astral Weekes. Then everyone would laugh, because it was never Margaret and Astral, always Midge and Azzie. She would miss Azzie. But she could come down from London, like Mum had said, and visit. Azzie would love it here.

She scratched at the flaky grey lichen with her fingernail, and tried to think of other things she would miss: trips to the mall on a Saturday afternoon, she supposed, and looking at the clothes. Mr McColl, her English teacher – he was a laugh. But then she thought, oddly enough, of Tojo – and thought that she would miss *him* almost as much as she would miss anything in London. And that was odd, because she'd hated Tojo when he was alive. He was part of Mill Farm though, a powerful presence – terrible, yet awe-inspiring at the same time. Like having a tiger or a grizzly bear in the yard. And now he was gone forever.

She wondered about Celandine and all the questions that remained unanswered, about the Touchstone, and what Pegs had said about there being other times to come. What sort of times? And all that business about being visitors – all just visitors. What

444

had he meant by that? Was Tojo just a visitor? Was *she?*

Be accepting. That was another thing that Pegs had said. Don't be afraid – no matter what may happen. There didn't seem to be anything left to be afraid of. She stared dreamily at the little engraved figures, their mouths open, Celandine standing in their midst. Beautiful, they were, in their plain smocks and simple shifts. Beautiful, like Henty, and all with their mouths open, singing, singing . . . Then, as she looked at them, she *heard* them – a rush of sound, a brief snatch of song, quite audible, as though somebody had switched a radio on and off. She blinked, and half sat up. It had been so sudden, and clear, so real, that she had nearly dropped the bowl. *Where the flying fishes play* . . . She could still hear the words echoing in her head, the high harmony of many small voices, like a children's choir. The funny thing was that she knew what the next line would have been. She remembered it.

For quite a long while she sat staring apprehensively at the bowl, then eventually shrugged her shoulders and lay down again, gradually letting her eyelids droop once more. Be accepting, be accepting. *Don't be afraid.*

A tiny yellow butterfly tumbled into her hazy vision, and landed on the warm flagstones by the old Wellington boot. She watched it as it sunned itself – the delicate wings moving backwards and forwards like breathing. Then another twitch of movement caught her eye, as the boot began to stir. From its shadowy depths the tiny face of the Favoured One slowly emerged – all eyes and whiskers – watching, concentrating, intent upon the butterfly. The bright insect seemed oblivious to any danger and remained where it was, its wings continuing to rise and fall. Half out of the boot now, the kitten crouched low, her miniature front paws flexing in a curious shuffling movement. The pounce, when it came, was hesitant and clumsy – and the butterfly casually floated up from the flagstones, escaping unharmed into the warm summer air. But the Favoured One's cute little face had looked different in that moment – fiercely intense – the expression familiar somehow. She was her father's daughter, Midge realized, and in those pretty blue eyes there was a darker look, a reminder of her ancestry, and a glimpse of the powerful huntress she would someday become.

It was too hot to lie on the wall any longer, and Midge sat up again. The farmyard was quiet, the others having gone into Taunton on various shopping errands. She had been happy to stay behind, alone and peaceful.

Now she wandered into the silent kitchen to get a drink of water, carrying her bowl with her and laying it on the big cream table. She took a glass from the draining board and moved towards the tap, but then stopped for a moment, listening. Something was different. Something had happened – or was about to happen. A tingly feeling began to steal around her shoulders, not creepy exactly, but . . . odd. It was as though she was being watched. Or as though she was watching herself. She let her hand rest on the tap, and turned to look about the room. All seemed as it should be, so what was it? There was nothing, nobody there, no sound that she could determine, and so she filled her glass and drank the cool water.

She sat down on one of the big wooden chairs, picked up her bowl and held it in her lap, thoughtfully turning it in her hand, stroking the engraved surface with the ball of her thumb and listening to the silence. The unfamiliar silence. Of course. It was the clock, she realized – the little alarm clock that stood on the dresser. It had stopped ticking. Twenty-five past ten, it said. She looked at her watch – twenty-five past ten – and then glanced up at the photograph of Celandine, suddenly knowing, in that split second, what was about to happen. It had happened before.

The searing flare of white light seemed to burst in her head, blinding her completely, and the smell of burning magnesium filled her nostrils. She couldn't see a thing – but in that helpless moment knew only that her boots were too tightly laced and that her toes were pinched, and that her scalp was sore from where her impossibly frizzy hair had been scraped and scraped back in a futile attempt to make it behave. She was chilly, and her shoulders ached with having to pose upright and still for so very long. Between her fingers and the ball of her thumb, she could feel the leathery textures of the little red bridle – tooled and embossed and smooth on one side, slightly rougher and less finished on the other. The silver bells jingled briefly as her hands jumped in a late reaction to the photographer's flash.

*   *   *

447

Gradually her vision returned, though the smell of magnesium lingered, and the shrinking spot of white light – greenish around the edges – continued to dance about the room for quite a long time afterwards. Midge put the bowl back on the kitchen table, and waited as the friendly familiar atmosphere of Mill Farm descended upon her once more – the warm scent of apple-wood from the old Rayburn, the faint clucking of the hens around the front door, and the fast tick of the little alarm clock on the dresser. It was OK. Everything was OK. She knew who she was. She accepted it, and she wasn't afraid.